Carolina Heat

Carolina Heat

Reed Bunzel

coffeetownpress

Kenmore, WA

coffeetownpress

Epicenter Press
6524 NE 181st St.
Suite 2
Kenmore, WA 98028
www. Epicenterpress.com
www. Coffeetownpress.com
www. Camelpress.com

For more information go to: www.coffeetownpress.com or
www.reedbunzel.com

Cover Design by Anthony Sands

Carolina Heat
2019 © Reed Bunzel

Library of Congress Control Number: 0002019943851

ISBN: 9781941890660 (trade paper)
ISBN: 9781603817691 (ebook)

Printed in the United States of America

•

This one is dedicated to my wife Diana,
for her unwavering patience,
understanding, love, and confidence.

•

Chapter 1

It was hot. South Carolina hot. Fried eggs and sidewalks hot, but right now Jack Connor had something else on his mind.

"Thirty-two feet per second per second," he said as he stared up at the hotel balcony seventeen floors above him.

"What're you talkin' about?"

Connor gave a quick glance over his shoulder at Lionel Hanes, who had come up to him from behind and now was standing just off to his side.

"Law of physics," he explained. "It's how fast the guy was falling when he went over the railing."

"Which one?" Hanes was gazing up in the general area where Connor was looking, the top two floors of balconies that defined the hotel's pricey high-up suites.

"Up there, the one with the yellow tape," Connor indicated with his eyes.

"And this thirty-two feet per second stuff ... you know this how?"

"Miss Benson's high school science class."

"No shit."

Actually, it was one of those facts Connor had always figured was useless knowledge but had memorized anyway when he wasn't staring at Miss Benson's deep blue eyes, her long legs, and everything in between. If it hadn't been for the goofy glasses with the thick frames and the way she wore her blonde hair spooled up on top of her head, he never would have guessed she could get so turned on by stuff like protons and electrons and gravitational pull. But get turned on she did, and when she started talking about Avogadro's number and Planck's constant in that measured, sexy voice, the rest of the class got turned on, too. At least the young men did, although mass times the speed of light came nowhere near equaling the square root of their rapt imaginations.

"So how long did it take him?" Hanes asked. "To hit the pavement, I mean."

Connor shifted his eyes from the balcony down to the sidewalk where they were standing, calculated that the seventeenth floor of the Cape Myrtle Hotel was one hundred eighty feet above the ground. He performed the quick mental math, then said, "Just about three seconds, give or take."

"Wonder what he was thinking," Hanes said as he pictured the guy free-falling as he pushed off from the metal rail. "I mean, did he suddenly miss his wife and kids, or maybe start thinking he really didn't want to do this, but it was too late?"

"Hard to say what goes through your mind right about then," Connor said.

"Yeah, except maybe a slab of rock-hard concrete."

Connor shot him a reproving look, then glanced at his watch, "You made good time, what with all that crazy traffic in Georgetown."

"Maybe, but you still beat me."

"I was already out at The Plant, doing the billing for the Blanchard job, so I had a good head start."

The Plant was the main headquarters of Palmetto BioClean, a small suite of offices located in an industrial park near the Wando shipping terminal in Mount Pleasant, just across the Cooper River from Charleston. The company was the only business in the Lowcountry that specialized in cleaning up death and contamination scenes, mostly those where blood and other fluids presented a hazard to the public. All of the company's certified technicians except Connor were part-timers and most of its services were conducted out in the field, so expensive office space was not a necessity. They needed just enough room for Connor to file reports, handle invoices, submit insurance claims, and generally take care of all the details that didn't involve blood but were critical to the daily function of the company.

"So where did the guy land?" Hanes asked. He was a couple years older than Connor, early thirties, a tall and beefy Georgia Tech grad who had done a short stint in the NFL before an ankle injury put an end to his career. Now he was raising two boys on his own, working fulltime as a physical trainer at a local gym, and the work he picked up at Palmetto BioClean helped make ends meet. But just barely.

"Pretty much where we're standing," Connor said. "What I was told, he jumped from that corner balcony up there and came just about straight down. You can see the cracks in the concrete here."

Big and hulking as he was, Hanes gave a shudder at the thought.

"Damn ... the guy really hit hard."

"Gravity does that."

"So, where's the blood?" Hanes asked as he kneeled down to get a better look at the spider web of cracks.

"Hotel already had the ground crew hose it off. Right into that storm drain there, you want my guess."

"The one that says, 'No Dumping—Flows Directly To The Ocean'?" Connor shrugged and said, "No one reads these days, I guess."

"Damn," Hanes fumed. "Blood's full of dangerous shit. HIV, herpes, hepatitis, hantavirus—all the H factors."

"Tell that to the sea turtles and red drum."

Lionel Hanes made a deep rumbling noise in his throat, then said,

"So, what the hell are we doing here? What's there to clean?" "You ever eat a chocolate covered cherry?" Connor asked him.

"A chocolate-covered cherry? What the hell does that have to do with anything?"

"Hard shell on the outside, crack it open and you find something else totally gooey and red on the inside. That's what we've got going on here."

"What're you talkin' 'bout, man?"

Connor grinned at him and said, "Our jumper may have cracked some pavement out here on the sidewalk, but apparently he made a gooey mess in his hotel room before he decided to see if he could fly. Hotel manager told me the guy sliced both wrists but must've done it the wrong way, across the veins rather than along them. Lost a lot of blood, but evidently not enough to do the job. Which I guess is why he went over the rail. Plan B, thought up on the fly. So, to speak. Anyway, the manager said the guy left a river of blood all over the place."

"So, what are we doing out here?" Hanes asked him. "Where's the truck?"

"It had a cracked windshield. D-Dub's got a buddy who owns an auto glass place, and he took it in this morning to get it fixed. That's where he was when I called him."

D-Dub was short for D'wayne Davis, an expert at drywall and taping who had bottomed out during the home construction bust. Still, his talents came in handy whenever the BioClean team had to deconstruct walls and floors in order to get to the blood that had soaked through and through. When he wasn't mopping up blood he worked at his wife's cupcake shop, but the money he made cleaning death scenes helped put food on the table.

"Is Jenny with him?" Hanes asked.

"The truck was all finished except for the paperwork, so D-Dub picked her up on the way."

Jenny—otherwise known as Jennifer, Jenna, Jen, Jenster, and the Jenmeister—was a young chick in her mid-twenties from Virginia whose first and only job had been to help embalm dead people in the basement of her family's funeral home. Somewhere along the way she had fallen in love with a bad boy who had moved her down to Charleston before ditching her for a pole dancer in Atlanta, but her yoga studies taught her to be resolute and accept that she was better off without the bastard. Alone and broke, she had answered an ad on Craigslist for an entry-level job at Palmetto BioClean and aced every exam and dress rehearsal Connor could throw at her. This was only her third time on a real job, and he was curious to see how she might react to the river of blood he suspected awaited them upstairs.

"You got an ETA?"

"D-Dub just called on his cell," Connor said, glancing at his watch. "They're about five minutes out."

The two of them stood there looking at the hotel for a moment, neither of them particularly inclined to venture upstairs until the rest of the crew was on-site. The Cape Myrtle Hotel was located nowhere near any kind of geological formation that even remotely resembled a cape, but it did stretch seventeen stories into the sky over a glaring white stretch of sandy beach. It was an abnormally hot afternoon, mid-May, not a cloud in the sky, just a whisper of an ocean breeze rattling the fronds of the palmetto trees planted around the base of the building. The summer season had not yet begun, but the hotel already had plenty of guests, many of them aging snowbirds who had not yet migrated back north.

The building was a relic left over from the 1960s, refurbished once in the '80s and then again in the early '00s. At that time the cracked stucco façade was replastered from top to bottom and repainted lime green with terra cotta accents. The three hundred feet of beach had been replenished with sand imported from an island in the Caribbean, and green-and-white cabanas had been erected on a wooden boardwalk that separated the pool from the sea. Connor could see boats out on the water: a few outboard runabouts, sport fishing boats heading out to deeper waters, and a few vessels with points of sail driving silently through the blue water.

The drive up from Charleston had taken Connor just under ninety minutes. He'd put the top down on the Camaro all the way and the powerful sun had bored through the tiny air holes in his River Dogs cap, burned six bright red spots into his scalp. He flashed back to his days in Iraq, the brutal sun baking the life out of him, and his squad trekking through the desert for reasons that were lost on them all. Despite the passage of time it seemed like just yesterday, and he absently adjusted the cap to move the holes so the sun would start blistering his skin in a different place.

Just then the Palmetto BioClean truck made a sharp turn off North Ocean Boulevard and bumped up into the parking lot. Two seconds later Connor's phone rang, a frenetic drum riff that grew louder the longer Connor didn't answer it. He pulled it out of his pocket and looked at the screen, which read "D'Wayne."

"Sorry we're late," D-Dub apologized as soon as Connor answered. "They're still trying to untangle the traffic down in Georgetown."

"Yeah, damned wreck slowed us all up," Connor told him. "Pull the truck around back to the service entrance. We'll meet you there."

"Copy that," D-Dub said as he edged the truck into the side parking lot and drove around to the rear of the hotel.

The Palmetto BioClean work vehicle was a used Ford E350 4x4 ambulance that had been refitted to carry everything a biohazard work crew would need to do its job. A bench seat was set along one interior wall, and the other was configured with Plexiglas storage bins that held the disposable suits, nitrile gloves, and other materials needed to decontaminate a scene. Other compartments located throughout the truck held an assortment of mops, buckets, sponges, disinfectants, enzymes, solvents—anything the team would require for the clean-up process. Two heavy-duty vacuums capable of sucking up blood and other fluids were attached with bungee cords to the front wall of the compartment, and a trio of portable lights on telescoping stands were stored under the upholstered bench.

Locked exterior compartments held a five-thousand-watt generator used to power the lights, as well as a supply of cardboard biohazard boxes and heavy-duty sterile bags. The emergency strobes had been removed from the top of the cab and the ambulance markings painted over, replaced with the words "Palmetto BioClean Services" and the company's logo, a serious-looking shield incorporating the international biohazard symbol that looked like a martial arts weapon right out of some Xbox video game.

Connor and Hanes met D-Dub and Jenny at the rear loading bay, where the truck now was backed up against a concrete loading platform. D-Dub was climbing out of the cab, while Jenny sat in the front seat with the door open, one leg hanging out, while she finished off a can of diet Cheerwine.

"So, what do we got?" D-Dub said as he hoisted himself up onto the platform. Jenny was right behind him, her head nodding to the beat of whatever was coming from the iPod buds jammed in her ears. "What do we know about this guy whose mess we're cleaning up?"

"Not much. He checked in the day before yesterday, stayed two nights, and checked out early this morning."

"'Checked out,' as in he offed himself?" Jenny asked, sensitivity for dead people not being one of her innate strengths.

"Seventeen floors down," Connor said.

"Total freefall," D-Dub observed. "No ripcord."

"Man … what leads someone to do something like that?" Jenny said, shaking her bald head. A close friend had just undergone chemotherapy for breast cancer, and Jenny—last name Flynn—had totally shaved hers off out of camaraderie and respect. And to donate it to a place that made hairpieces for survivors. "What can make a person so freakin' desperate?"

Fact was, Connor had lost several buddies in Iraq to suicide, some of them while they were still over in the desert and a couple after they got back stateside. It would have been easy for him to say that all of them seemed pretty normal, guys who took what they saw and did all in stride. But that would have been a lie. Or, to be more accurate, convenient denial. The recruiters never tell you about the atrocities that happen in wartime, not in Iraq, not in Vietnam, not even in Korea or the beaches of France or the islands in the South Pacific. Enlisting to serve the cause of freedom is a heroic thing to do, and only heroic men and women did it—at least according to the marketing folks in the crisply pressed uniforms. All that heroism and grandeur kept them from internalizing the pain and mayhem and fear and death that defines one's entire purpose and existence in the military. So went the theory, at least.

"Everyone's got their own demons," Connor said, quoting what Dr. Pinch at the V.A. told him whenever they talked about Iraq. Which was just about every week.

"So, if the guy took a dive from the tower out front, what're we doing here at the back of the hotel?" D-Dub said as he unlocked the back of the truck.

"Nothing's ever as simple as it looks." Connor took a moment and explained what he'd already told Hanes, that the jumper had taken his dive only after he'd apparently bungled his attempt to slit his wrists. "What I was told is he did a pretty fair job with a razor blade. Not quite good enough to turn out the lights, but he sprayed more than enough blood around the room so the manager lost his grits when he let the cops inside this morning. What the manager said on the phone was it looked like a convention of vampires totally rocked out the place."

Chapter 2

The manager wasn't far off the mark.

Anyone who doesn't spend a lot of time around blood usually isn't aware that it has a very distinct odor. Several of them, in fact, usually depending on how long it has been out of the body, as well as the person who's smelling it. Connor thought the odor was similar to that of wet iron or copper, until it began to decompose, at which point it took on the nauseating smell of dead flesh. Jenny, on the other hand, had sworn that new blood reminded her of fresh rosewater mixed with pomegranate juice. In any event, as the Palmetto BioClean team stood in the hallway outside room 1701, looking at the yellow police tape stretched across the doorframe, the smell of blood on the other side of the door was unmistakable and powerful.

According to the police, the occupant of room 1701 had died precisely at five-forty-one that morning. They knew this because a hotel guest had been walking her toy poodle in the grassy area that separated the front drive-through from the parking lot, and was about twenty yards away when the dead man had slammed into the concrete. She screamed, dragged Fifi over to see what had caused the noise, then screamed again when she nearly tripped over the mangled body. It was only after she regained her composure that she managed to call her husband, who told her to put the dog in their car while he called the front desk. At some point during the whole ordeal she had noticed that the clock in her iPhone said it was exactly 5:41.

That was just under ten hours ago, and by now the scent of rosewater and pomegranates definitely had shifted to putrid cat food and decaying fish heads. The hotel manager—a man named Erskine Hadley—politely declined to accompany Connor and his team up to the room, explaining that one look through the suite was more than enough for him. What he wanted was for Palmetto BioClean to clean every speck of blood from the premises and do whatever it took to prep it for rebuilding. The Cape Myrtle Hotel was totally booked with a convention of chiropractors the following weekend, and Hadley needed the suite back in rentable order by then. He had simply given Connor a key card and told him to report back when the job was done.

"We may want to put our masks on out here," Connor warned his crew as he gently pulled the yellow tape back and loosened the card the police had fastened to both the metal door and the jamb. He slipped the plastic key in the computerized lock, a little light flashed green as the bolt clicked, and he gave the door a tentative push. At that instant a rush of pungent air caused Connor to hold his arm over his nose and mouth.

He stepped inside and froze at what he saw.

Blood was everywhere. It started in the foyer, large dried spatters that seemed to trail in from the living room, puddled on the hardwood floor right in front of the door, then tracked back out to the living room again. Connor knew it was a living room because the manager had told him that "John Doe" had checked into the suite, top floor corner, with a rack rate of three hundred ten bucks a night in the off-season, five-oh-five during the summer. There was a central living room just inside the foyer, a wet bar off to the left, a wall of glass facing west, and a sliding door opening out onto a wide balcony. On the other side of the room double wood doors led to an inner bedroom and another door—this one opened just a crack—showed where the bathroom was located. But none of that mattered, since right now blood was the only thing on anyone's mind.

Connor moved further into the suite, stepping carefully around every red patch he found. All four members of the team had already put on their biohazard suits and pulled disposable booties over their shoes, but none of them wanted to track blood anywhere it wasn't already. Then again, from the looks of things, it already was everywhere.

Lionel Hanes was the first to say something. He'd been with Palmetto BioClean longer than anyone in the room, and had seen just about all there was to see. "What the hell went down in here?" he said with a shudder, his voice hardly more than a whisper.

"This guy was a walking geyser, that's what," D-Dub replied. "Floor, walls, ceiling. Windows, glass—"

"Even out on the balcony," Jenny said, gingerly stepping over to the sliding door. "He still must have been bleeding when he went over the rail."

Hanes just shook his head as he glanced around. "There's sprays all over the place … the guy was a Bellagio of blood."

"Especially over there, at the desk," D-Dub said, using his chin to indicate where a pool of blood had dried on the wooden surface, dribbled over the edge and collected on the floor.

"The manager said the guy wrote a note apologizing to the maid before he went over," Connor explained.

"How considerate," Jenny said, rolling her eyes. "Just imagine going in and finding this mess."

"And this is just the side show," Connor said. "What I hear, the main event is in the bathroom." He inhaled a deep breath through his face mask, then followed the dried, brick-red trail around the back of the couch to the other side of the room, taking care to avoid the dried blisters of blood as he went. He gently pushed the bathroom door inward on silent hinges, and peeked inside. "Oh, holy shit—" Of course, there was nothing holy about it.

From what Connor could see, this is where it all had begun. The way he figured it, "John Doe" had run a bath and climbed in, along with some sort of a sharp object, probably a razor blade. Whatever implement was used, the crime scene investigators had taken it with them. And judging from the pink slime in the tub, the guy had slipped into the warm water, drawn the blades across his wrists, and then lay there to die. The tile walls were sprayed where contrails of blood had spurted out, probably while he was waiting to lose consciousness. And when Mr. Doe finally concluded that he was not going to die, at least not right there or then, he must have reached for the stainless grab bar and pulled himself up and gotten out of the tub. At that point blood had pulsed all over the floor, sink, mirror, and walls, until the guy evidently reached for some towels in an attempt to stanch the flow.

From there Connor guessed the guy must have covered up—the manager said the victim had been found wearing one of the complimentary robes provided by the hotel—and dragged himself back out into the living room, where he scribbled his note to the housekeeper. Then, for some reason, he had gone to the front door before eventually going out to the balcony, where he had managed to haul himself up and over the railing. Just about three seconds later he was dead, and several seconds after that a woman walking her poodle was screaming her head off.

Connor made one last assessment of the mess in the bathroom, then moved back out to the living room and inhaled deeply. When he let the air out of his lungs he said, "No question—the guy was set on punching out, no matter what it took."

"What do we know about him?" Hanes asked.

"No more than we need to. Hotel guest, white male."

"But who was he?" Jenny pressed. "I mean, the guy just about bled out—"

"I'm sure the cops are all over it," Connor replied, to all of them. "That's what they do. And what we do is clean up once they're gone." "Aren't you at all curious if he's married?" Jenny pressed him. "Maybe his wife left him, took the kids. Maybe he lost his job. Or maybe he found out he has cancer or AIDS—"

"Which is why we're wearing these suits," Hanes reminded her. "All I know he lost is a lot of blood, and it's our job to clean it up."

"Exactly," Connor said. "C'mon, team … this is gonna to be a big job. Walls, tile, floor, everything. Let's let the man rest in peace. We all know what we have to do."

Yes, they all knew, but that didn't keep Jenny from offering a lower-lip pout and saying, "You're no fun."

They worked until one in the morning, hefting sledges to rip out drywall and tile, and using pry bars to tear down the ceiling and pull up the hardwood floor in the foyer and the carpeting in the living room. The hotel manager thoughtfully had moved the guests in the nearby rooms to another floor so the deconstruction noise wouldn't bother them. Not much of a problem, once word had gotten around about what had happened in room 1701.

Anyone who thinks blood can be removed with soap and water or covered up with a coat of paint has no concept of its nasty ability to penetrate just about any porous surface. Fortunately, none of the victim's blood had seeped past the carpet pad into the concrete subfloor, but virtually all the sofa cushions, drapes, and lampshades had been contaminated by the spray and were tossed in a discard pile in the middle of the room. The tile in the bathroom had been sealed properly, so none of the blood that had been smeared on the walls penetrated to the concrete drywall beneath it. But the grout around the edge of the tub and the base of the wall was porous, so it had to be chipped away and discarded.

At one-point Connor spotted a chunk of concrete with a dab of red smudged on one end behind the toilet bowl. He bent down and took a long look, then picked it up with his fingers. He wasn't really concerned with disrupting what cops and lawyers called the chain of evidence, since in any suicide the victim and suspect clearly are the same person. And the odds were that whatever this was, it had been sitting behind the john for a very long time. Still, he held it up to the light over the porcelain sink and took a closer look.

"What you got there?" Hanes asked him as he wiped the last bits of soiled grout away with a rag.

"Looks to me like a piece of cement, maybe the corner of a cinder block," Connor replied as he turned it over in his hand.

"Yeah, I found a couple of those," Jenny said as she poked her head in. "Little pieces, same stuff."

"What'd you do with them?"

"Tossed 'em in the box." She shrugged as she went back to cutting the carpet. "And I'm not about to go after 'em, either."

The box was any of the half dozen cardboard packing cartons lined with sterile plastic bags that were beginning to stack up in the foyer of the suite. Every scrap of drywall, tile, or carpet that was pulled up at a death scene was cut down and then went directly into one of these boxes, which then was sealed and loaded into the back of the truck. Tomorrow Connor would drive it over to the medical waste furnace, where it was turned into ashes.

"Forget it," he told her. "I'm sure it's nothing." Still, he slipped the chunk of cement into a plastic zip-loc bag in case it later turned out to be something.

By the time Connor and his team were finished, the living room and bathroom had been torn down to the steel studs and ceiling joists. The drywall and carpet and bloody furnishings had been sliced up and packed into the biohazard boxes, which then were double-sealed at every seam and escorted down the service elevator to the Palmetto BioClean truck that was still parked in the service bay.

"Think they'll all fit?" D-Dub asked after all the boxes were stacked on the concrete platform.

"They'll have to," Connor told him. "You didn't bring Moby Dick." Moby Dick was the big white trailer that could be hooked to the back of the truck to store the debris from large clean-up jobs.

"Didn't want to waste time, doubling back to The Plant," D-Dub said, by way of an explanation. Or at least an excuse.

"No problem. There's plenty of room in the truck, and I'll get rid of it all later."

Connor went back upstairs and made one last inspection of the suite, taking a couple dozen photographs of his team's work. Eventually he judged the suite to be decontaminated, then locked the door and re-attached the yellow police tape. The entire team walked in silence down the long hallway to the elevator bank, where they were greeted by a waiting car.

"That was a nasty one," D-Dub announced with a shudder only after the doors had closed and they were riding down the elevator shaft.

"Never seen one that wasn't," Jenny said as she jammed the foam iPod buds back into her ears.

"Anyone up for dinner, maybe an early breakfast?" Hanes asked, glancing expectantly at the other three members of the team. "I saw a twenty-four-hour joint on the way in, just up the street."

"You're kidding, right?" Jenny had a look in her eyes that said,

"Seriously?"

"On me," Hanes added, hoping someone would join him.

D-Dub glanced at his watch and shook his head. "Elaine's expecting me in the shop in four hours," he said. "Sorry."

Hanes turned his eyes expectantly to Connor. "C'mon, man … you gotta be hungry after all this—"

That's when Connor's phone rang, the feverish drum ringtone providing a convenient interruption. He dug it out of his pocket and glanced at the screen.

"It's the boss," he said to the team. "Jordan James."

"At this hour?" Jenny said. "Man, am I glad I'm not you."

Chapter 3

"Connor—where are you?" Jordan James asked when Connor connected he call. "Hope I didn't wake you up—"

"No, sir," Connor told him. "In fact, I'm still up in Myrtle Beach with the team. We just finished a job."

"Jon Hilborn?"

"Say what?"

"The Jon Hilborn thing," James said. "That's why you're up there, right? He jumped off his hotel balcony this morning. Yesterday morning now, I guess."

"If that's his name, then yeah," Connor replied. He mouthed the word *sorry* to the rest of the team, then wandered a few paces down the loading bay platform, as if that would provide him more privacy. "What's this about?"

"What it's about is a guy who owes me money. A good deal of money. And now it looks like I won't see a penny of it."

"Hang on a sec," Connor said. "You knew the guy who jumped?"

"That's what I'm telling you. Look—I want you to stay put until I get there."

"You're coming here? It's pretty late and we just wrapped up—"

"I want to see for myself what he did."

"He sliced his wrists and then took a dive," Connor said, laying it out for his boss. "And where he did it is now just studs and a subfloor."

But Mr. James didn't seem to hear him, saying instead, "I just crossed the tracks in Georgetown—I should be there in half an hour, tops."

There went any hope—threat—of breakfast with Lionel Hanes. "I'll meet you here at the hotel, then," Connor said, trying to stifle an exhausted sigh.

"Why would we meet there?" Jordan James asked.

"That's the 'where' part—where your friend killed himself."

"First, he's not my friend. He was a business acquaintance, just someone I made a few investments with. And second, at this point I'm more interested in the 'what' part."

Jordan James had two peculiarities. Many more than that, actually, but there were two that always seemed to affect the dealings Connor had with the man. One of

11

these was his fondness for exceptionally dry Beefeater martinis, up, with two olives. The other was his habit of speaking in riddles that usually made little sense. The first of these traits greatly influenced the other, and Connor was quite certain this was the case tonight. This morning, actually. James didn't exactly sound inebriated, but Connor was certain the man had poured himself at least one stiff drink after hearing about Jon Hilborn's suicide.

"So where do you want to meet?"

"The police station," James said, as if that made all the sense in the world.

"You're sure about that?" Connor asked, thinking that was the last place James should go with even a hint of gin on his breath.

"Damn straight," the boss man said, and then he was gone.

Connor took a rain check on breakfast with Hanes, whom he knew would probably pout halfway back to Charleston. He said a quick "good-bye" to his team and ten minutes later parked the Camaro under an oak tree in the lot in back of the Myrtle Beach Police station, about six blocks up from the beach on 10th Avenue North. He'd put the convertible top up and was dozing behind the wheel when a cop rapped his Maglite on the windshield.

"This ain't the La Quinta," the officer said when Connor rolled the window down. "Time to move on."

"I'm waiting for someone," Connor told him, checking his watch.

"Not here, you're not."

"Look, officer. This is police business—"

"Let me see your license and registration," the cop interrupted him, shining the Maglite in his eyes.

Connor thought on this a second, then opened the glove box and dug out the registration slip. He handed it over and waited patiently while the officer studied it.

The cop took his sweet time looking at it, then said, "The thing is, Mr. Connor, I ran your plates just now. Seems you were recently arrested on a felony charge of possession with intent to distribute."

Even with the glare of the flashlight in his eyes Connor could see a glint of arrogance in the officer's eyes, the glare of power. "Shit, man," he said. "That charge was dropped. Whole thing was bogus."

The cop moved a hand to the butt of his gun. "You do not swear to an officer of the law, understand? Now, like I said, I want you to move this car out of this lot. Before I arrest you for vagrancy."

Connor sat there a moment, assessing the situation. It hadn't even occurred to him that, even though the possession charge had been dropped immediately, it might still be on his record. He'd have to look into getting the damned thing expunged, if that was possible here in South Carolina.

"This is about the suicide yesterday, at the Cape Myrtle," Connor tried to explain.

"I don't care if it's about the return of Moses come to part the Intracoastal Waterway." The officer narrowed his eyes at Connor and added, "You're not from here, are you?"

"Michigan. And a year and a half in Iraq."

That's when the cop's attitude shifted, his eyes still a little wary but maybe—just maybe—showing a glimmer of respect. "Seriously? My brother did two tours, almost got his leg blown off."

"Yeah, I saw a lot of that. Where was he stationed?"

"Fort Hood, here in the states. But he spent most of his time in Fallujah."

"Kirkuk," Connor said about himself. "Your brother, where is he now?"

"Here in Myrtle. One of the lucky ones, came home and got himself a job in security at the Hard Rock. You said you're here because of the jumper at the Cape Myrtle?"

"That's right," Connor told him. "My team and I, we just now cleaned the death scene."

"Death scene? Shit … what I heard that thing was pretty damned mean. So, why're you here, waiting for your friend—?"

"My boss, actually. He's driving up from Charleston, guess he wants to make sure the dude is dead."

"Oh, he's dead, all right." The cop shined the light in Connor's eyes again. "Damn! I know you. You're the guy figured out what happened to that TV chick down in Chucktown, and that asshole blew out his brains because of it."

Connor didn't know if that was a good thing or a bad thing, but the truth usually was the best thing, so he said, "Wasn't my intent, but yep, that's me."

"I never seen a guy do that before. Die, I mean. Except on TV and the movies."

"Doesn't come close to the real thing. Just ask your brother."

"Oh, yeah … he seen plenty over there in I-raq." The cop appeared to think for a moment, something that seemed to be a bit of a stretch for him. Then he said, "Look, I s'pose I could let you stay here, seein' as you're not bothering anyone. Not really. When did you say your boss is showing up?"

Connor glanced at his watch. "Should be here any minute."

"Well, go ahead and stay put," the cop said. "But the police station don't open until eight, so you're going to have a long wait."

Half an hour later Connor was seated in a booth at Jimbo's Grill on Mr. Joe White Avenue. He was sitting across from Jordan James, who had not initially accepted that there wasn't a detective on duty who could talk to him about the Jon Hilborn case. But when the dispatcher at the front desk explained that if James didn't leave and come back after eight o'clock, he could find a small room with bars for him to stay in, James agreed it might be best to return when an investigator was on duty. Which for Connor meant spending three hours in a hard Naugahyde booth with a stack of pancakes and a bottomless carafe of coffee.

"This Jon Hilborn … you don't think he's dead?" Connor asked once their food was in front of them and it was clear they would be there for a long time.

"Oh, there's no question he's dead," Jordan James said. "That's Hilborn's way. Jump before you pay a damned dime on a debt."

"So why are you here?" The better question was *why are we here*, but Connor didn't want to get into that. If Mr. James wanted him here, here is where he would be.

"I just want to see him with my own two eyes," James said as he cut into a waffle slathered with syrup. A real waffle, he had pointed out, not one of those Belgian things.

"You really think they're gonna let you see him?" Connor asked him. "From the sound of it, this isn't an open casket kind of thing."

"I'm gonna try," James said with a shrug. "If they don't go for that, I at least want to see the pics."

Connor sat there and studied his boss for a minute, watched as he slowly chewed his waffle, then picked up a napkin and dabbed a drip of maple syrup from his lower lip.

"Closure," Jordan James said, as if reading Connor's mind. "If I have to write off half a million bucks, at least I want the satisfaction of seeing him in his final repose."

Repose? Connor had never heard anyone actually use that word before, although he'd seen it in books. "Half a million is a lot of money," he observed, chewing a bite of pancake that tasted like a kneeling pad.

"Damn straight," Jordan James said. "And all cash, too. No record of the transaction that way, which means no way to write it off the books."

Connor wondered what sort of transaction Mr. James would have wanted to keep off the books. Wondered what half a million dollars actually looked like, too. That was five hundred thousand bucks, which translated to five thousand hundreds, or twenty-five thousand twenties. Either way you stacked it, it was a lot of cash to be carrying around in a suitcase or a duffel bag, with the most likely objective being not to alert Uncle Sam or the South Carolina tax board to what was going on.

"Mind if I ask what this Hilborn guy was going to do with the money?" he asked.

"Nope, long as you don't mind that I don't tell you," James replied, a crooked grin etched onto his face. "It's best all around if you don't know."

"The sort of thing someone might kill for?"

James glanced up and fixed Connor with a hardened look. "People kill for a lot of reasons," he pointed out.

"So, you're thinking he might have been pushed off that balcony?"

"It really doesn't matter how or why he died," James said. "It just is what it is."

"So why did you drive all the way up here?"

"Just to see for myself. See that the bastard really is dead. Proof of death."

"If you want proof, I've got six big boxes of it sitting in the back of the truck," Connor told him.

"I'm sure you do," James said. "But proof, like beauty, lies in the eye of the beholder."

Connor had figured there was no chance in hell that Jordan James would get the eyewitness proof he was seeking, and it turned out he was right.

The Myrtle Beach cop who agreed to speak with James made it quite clear from the outset that there was no way he, Detective Ozzie Harris, was going to allow a civilian inside the county morgue just to satisfy his curiosity. Further, Detective Harris made it quite clear that he didn't give a shit who Jordan James was, nor did he give a rat's ass how many businesses the man owned down in Charleston, or who he knew up in Columbia. The good ol' boy network was not going to work for him up here in Myrtle Beach. In fact, the detective said, if James persisted with his arrogance and attitude, he might well find himself arrested for obstruction of justice, or tampering with a police investigation, or whatever charges he could think of that would make a judge toss him into a cell for a day or two.

"At least you can let me see the pics," James insisted anyway. "What harm can there be in that?"

Detective Harris thought on this a second, then tipped his head in the slightest of nods and said, "I guess that would work."

He swiveled in his chair to the desk behind him, picked a folder off the top of a pile, then opened it as he swiveled back. He pulled out two letter-sized sheets of photo paper and set them on the metal surface in front of him. "Okay, here we are," he said. "Print-outs of the digital photos. You can look at 'em once, right here, and that's it. No copies, no second looks. Got it?"

"Works for me," Jordan James agreed as he craned his neck to see the upside-down images.

The detective used his fingers to pivot the two printouts so James could see them better. Each one had a half-dozen photos on it, like an old photographic contact sheet. He stabbed a pudgy index finger at the sheet on the left and said, "These pics were shot at the scene, and these" —he pointed the same finger at the sheet on the right— "were taken at the cut."

Connor was trained to consider each clean-up job as just that, a job, but just like the rest of this team he often found it difficult to ignore the grim reality behind his work. In this case that reality was a dead man named Jon Hilborn, and the photographs clearly depicted a body that had landed head-first on the pavement with such force that the concrete had cracked and the victim's arms and legs twisted and buckled in ways that did not seem possible.

One of Connor's buddies in Iraq—a young kid who had taken business classes at a community college in Rhode Island before enlisting—had talked about the "dead cat bounce." As he had explained, it was a stock market term that derived its meaning from the old adage that even a cat that falls from a great enough distance will bounce when it hits. And so, had Jon Hilborn, by the look of things. The manager of the Cape Myrtle had said that Hilborn was wrapped in one of the hotel's white terrycloth bathrobes, which probably had billowed outward as it caught the wind during free-fall. This left a part of Hilborn's backside exposed, as well as the right side of his mangled torso. But post-mortem modesty clearly was not an issue here, since the focus of all six photographs on the print-out was the amount of blood that had poured from the man's body after he had collided with the earth.

Connor was no expert on the abrupt cessation of motion— that was a lesson he totally missed in Miss Benson's science class. But it seemed that the victim had landed on that side of his body first, then was repositioned by a short bounce so his face was bashed in. Hilborn's chin, mouth, nose, and eyes all had been flattened by the impact, which very likely had snapped his neck as well.

In any event, there was blood. Lots of it, although Connor knew that a good measure of it also had been left upstairs in suite 1701 before Hilborn had jumped. Or was pushed, if Jordan James' lingering suspicions proved to be true.

"Pretty gruesome," was all James said as his eyes moved over the sheet of images.

"Sixteen feet per second per second will do that," the detective observed.

"Thirty-two," Connor said.

"What?"

"It's thirty-two feet per second."

Detective Harris clearly didn't like to be corrected, and shot Connor a mixed glance of skepticism and annoyance. "Whatever. As you can see in the postmortem photos, there wasn't an inch of him that escaped bruising, bleeding, or worse."

The investigator then summarized the events of yesterday morning, described the blood in the hotel suite and Hilborn's hastily scribbled note that explained how slicing his wrists hadn't gone exactly as he'd planned, so he'd improvised with Plan B and the science of gravity.

"Certainly not an open-casket moment," James observed as he studied the photos shot during the autopsy.

"No, but that's immaterial," Detective Harris said. "Says here in the file the body's set to be cremated. In fact, it's already at the funeral home."

"Good thing, considering," James said as he looked up from the photos and slid them back across the desk. "Just out of curiosity, who identified him?"

Harris looked back at the file and read through an incident report. "Says here it was his brother, David Hilborn, lives down in Hilton Head. The victim left his name and address up in the room, next to the apology note. The brother drove up yesterday and gave a positive I.D."

James placed his hands on the front edge of the desk and pushed himself up into a standing position. "So, the official ruling is suicide?"

"Medical examiner says right here, 'cause of death is consistent with multiple self-inflicted wounds.' Pretty conclusive, you ask me."

James inhaled a deep breath, then let it out slowly. "Well, I guess that's that."

"Anything else?" Detective Harris said, the tone of his voice suggesting an answer in the negative would be the wise one.

"I think I've taken up enough of your time," Jordan James told him. "Thanks for the Kodak moment."

Detective Harris shot him a puzzled look, too young to remember the old marketing campaign. Then he stood up and led James and Connor back out of the squad room to the front lobby, where he said, "How long are you here in our fair city?"

Jordan James glanced at his watch and said, "About ninety seconds. What's the easiest way back to route seventeen?"

"Back down Tenth to North Ocean, and turn right," the detective told him. Then he looked at Connor and added, "And just for the record, it's sixteen feet, not thirty-two."

"Miss Benson said it's thirty-two, and I have five dollars says she's right."

"And who is exactly is Miss Benson?"

"Someone you don't want to mess with, although we all wanted to," Connor told him. "But if you need proof, that's why they invented Google."

A smug grin tightened Harris' face, and he said, "In your dreams."

But Connor only chuckled, because Miss Benson had already had been in his dreams since his senior year in high school. "Stand in line."

Chapter 4

"I've changed my mind," Jordan James said as they walked down the steps outside the Myrtle Beach Municipal Building.

It was a hot spring morning, the brilliant sky split by an evaporating jet contrail that looked like someone had dragged a giant eraser across the expanse of Carolina blue. There wasn't a hint of a breeze, and the day had all the early marks of becoming another scorcher. Someone somewhere was frying onions and potatoes in a skillet; probably the diner over on the corner, the one with the parking lot crammed full of F-150s and panel trucks and Chevys and Mercedes. You can always judge good food by the number and variety of cars sitting outside.

"Changed your mind how?"

"I want to see the place. The hotel where Hilborn did it."

"I thought you said you weren't interested in the 'where,' just the 'what,'" Connor reminded him.

"Since when did you start listening to me?" It was strictly a rhetorical question, so James didn't leave time for Connor to respond. "If you'd done that before, you never would have nailed that bastard who killed Rebecca Rose. Just one more thing for the cops to sweep under the rug."

"I'm starting to think there's a lot of shit under there," Connor observed.

James grinned and said, "That's South Carolina for you. History is a big deal down here, and everyone's trying to avoid it."

"Is that why you want to go to the hotel, to see where your friend's history clocked out?"

"Like I already said, he wasn't my friend. Jon Hilborn was just someone I did business with, once or twice. But yeah, I guess that's it. I suppose doctors would call it closure, but to me it's more like seeing the spot where half a million dollars of my money evaporated into thin air."

They rode to the hotel in Jordan James' midnight blue Bentley, white hides and walnut burl and a sound system that rivaled any music hall. Connor still had the plastic key card the hotel manager had given him, so it was easy to get past the yellow police tape and the crime scene ticket that was still affixed to the door. Two minutes later he and James were standing on the balcony that wrapped around the corner of room 1701, both of them looking down at the sidewalk one hundred eighty feet below.

"All that blood loss, you think he could have hauled himself up over this railing?" James asked. This time it was not a rhetorical question.

"You're still thinking he was pushed," Connor said. It was not really an answer, but it was where James' thinking was going.

James gripped the railing with both hands and thought a moment before he answered. "We both saw the photos. And you saw the blood. From the looks of what's left of that room in there, he lost a lot of it. So, I'm asking you, do you think he would have had the strength to hoist himself over this here railing?"

"Maybe if he used a chair, something to get himself up high enough so just a little shift in balance would take him over."

"But that's just it—I don't see a chair," James said, shaking his head "Did you find a chair when you were pulling that room apart? One

that would have had blood all over it?"

"No, sir," Connor answered. "Course, the cops might have taken it with them as evidence."

"But there was blood on the rail, am I right?"

"Absolutely. Right about there, and drops on the balcony itself, coming out from the slider." Connor motioned with his hand to illustrate what he was talking about. "I took pictures, for the files. I can show them to you if you want."

But Jordan James shook his head and said, "Probably inconclusive. And immaterial, in the long run."

He stood there at the railing, gazing off to the distance. From where they were standing they could just see the municipal building ten blocks to the west, along with the roller coaster and water slides and other honky-tonk kitsch that peppered the boardwalk that ran along the sand. The city was still several weeks away from hitting summer full-tilt, but the buzz of tourist season was in the air, even seventeen stories above the boulevards and beaches.

"Tell me … how would you do it?" James asked. Once again this clearly was not a rhetorical question. Far from it, in fact, since he turned away from the horizon and looked Connor directly in the eye.

"You talking about jumping or pushing?"

"If Jon Hilborn jumped, what's done is done. There's no changing that."

"Same thing if someone pushed him," Connor observed.

James cleared his throat. "Maybe the same result, but different means. Just work with me here."

Connor studied his boss, not quite sure whether he meant the "work with me" part figuratively or literally. He already worked for James, who just three days ago had offered him a different position at the security firm he owned in Charleston.

"How tall was Hilborn?" he asked. "It's hard to tell from the pictures."

"About your height, maybe. Six feet, or thereabouts."

"Not really a pushover, then," Connor said, unable to resist the pun.

Jordan James groaned, then glanced back down at the pavement below. "Not without incapacitating him first."

"You're thinking about all the blood in the room?"

"At this point I'm thinking about everything," James conceded. "I'm thinking about why Hilborn was here in Myrtle Beach, since he lived down in Charleston. I'm thinking maybe there was a reason he rented this particular suite, instead of one of the oceanfront rooms. And I'm still thinking, if it were you, how would you do it? How would you get him over this railing?"

"If I didn't want to draw attention to myself, avoid a murder investigation, I'd drug him," Connor replied. "Get him drunk, slip a roofie into his Scotch and wait until he passed out."

James considered the idea for a minute, then shook his head. "Drugs would show up in a tox screen."

"Doesn't matter," Connor countered. "It would make sense for someone who's about to slash his wrists to maybe pop some pills to make the whole deal easier. Or less painful. Once Hilborn's asleep your killer could do just about anything he wanted."

"Like put him in the tub, run him a nice, warm bath, slash his wrists and wait for him to bleed out."

"Except he doesn't bleed out, and the killer panics. Hauls him out of the tub, leaving blood all over the place, just for show. He even writes a note apologizing for the botched job."

James had started nodding, but now cocked his head as if something didn't add up. "Whose handwriting?"

"Doesn't matter," Connor suggested. He was nodding now as well, clearly seeing how this could have worked. "At this point Hilborn would've been going into shock anyway, so he'd have a serious case of the shakes. Besides, we don't know what the note said. It could be something as simple as 'sorry for the mess.' Not a lot of words or letters to go by."

"Then the killer wraps him in the hotel robe—I saw it in the photo—and drags him out here to the balcony." Jordan James paused for a moment, possibly for effect but more likely to dislodge a scrap of food from between his teeth. Then he added, "And over he goes. So that's how you would have done it?"

"I would've skipped the bath tub part, gone right from the pills to the push. The fall was sure to kill him. But yeah, that's how it could've happened."

"If he didn't jump."

"Right." Despite all the coffee Connor had poured down his throat at breakfast he was starting to feel the effect of thirty hours with no sleep. Except for a few minutes he managed to snatch in his car while he was waiting for Jordan James to arrive. "And that's a big if."

"You still don't see it that way?"

"I see answers to 'what' and 'how,'" Connor replied through a stifled yawn..

"And we already know the 'where' and 'when.' But there's still the questions of 'who' and 'why.'"

"You're talking about motive."

"If someone actually did kill this Hilborn guy, he had to have a reason."

"Could be he had half a million reasons." James laid it out there, pure and simple, waited to see if Connor would catch the implication.

"You're thinking a cash grab," Connor said. "Your cash."

"It's been on my mind."

"Mind if I ask when your ... transaction ... with Mr. Hilborn took place?"

"Day before yesterday," James answered. "About twenty-four hours before he went off this balcony."

"You're thinking he had that money with him when he checked in. And someone killed him for it."

Jordan James made a quick motion with his head, not quite a nod, maybe nothing more than a nervous twitch. Then he said, "Makes a lot more sense than Hilborn going off the high dive all by himself and leaving all that cash behind. And I'm betting the cops didn't find a penny of it."

Connor didn't say anything to that, not right away. He was thinking this through, absorbing everything James was telling him and even some of the things he wasn't. Clearly James hadn't driven up here to Myrtle Beach because of any personal compassion for the late Jon Hilborn; the man could just as well have been a bag of pickled okra that went over that rail. But the half million dollars—five thousand hundreds or twenty-five thousand twenties; it didn't matter which—well, that was another matter altogether. The point was that James had access to that much cash in the first place and had trusted it to a man who just twenty-four hours later had crashed into the parking lot of a Myrtle Beach hotel. Didn't matter if James ever saw Hilborn again, but he clearly would love to say "hello" to that pile of cash one more time.

Then it hit him, harder than a body falling at thirty-two-feet per second per second. "I know where you're going with this—"

"Damn straight you do," James said. "You're quick, even when you don't want to be. Driven, too. Stubborn, maybe even obstinate. And you get things done. You dogged the killer of that Rose woman until he went and shot himself."

"I appreciate your confidence, Mr. James, but you need a pro. Someone who's done this sort of thing before."

"That's just it. You have done this sort of thing before. And as for being a professional, you're already on my payroll. That's good enough for me."

"But it may not be good enough for SLED," Connor said. SLED was the State Law Enforcement Division which, among many other things within its purview, oversaw the licensure of all security firms in the state of South Carolina. "They have some pretty strict regulations, which means you can't just put a gun in my hand and turn me loose on the streets. Gil Redman already laid it out for me."

"Yes, I already spoke with Gil. About several things, in fact."

"So, he must have told you I turned him down." Gil Redman was the head honcho at Citadel Security who had interviewed Connor for a sweet job just a couple days ago.

"He mentioned it to me," James replied. "I told him you'd come around."

"I'm serious, sir. I like what I'm doing."

"No one can like cleaning up blood and gore for too long, son. You need to think about the future. Next month and next year, not just next paycheck."

"I'm looking at it quarter by quarter, year over year," Connor reminded him. "Billings and cash flow are up, and overhead is down. My future is tied to your future."

Jordan James gave him a hard look that reflected both his disappointment and understanding. "Can't argue with that," he said with a resolute shrug. "But let's get back to the matter at hand, shall we?"

"Look, sir…with all due respect, I am not a detective."

But the boss man wasn't listening, or at least was pretending not to hear. Instead he said, "I know someone who can light a fire or two up in Columbia, burn through the red tape. Use your military service to this great country of ours as part of your law enforcement experience. Meanwhile, there's a clause in those SLED regulations that says, and this is almost a quote, 'Notwithstanding any other provision of this chapter, a person who holds a security business license' —that would be Citadel Security, by the way— 'may use temporary employees for special events without registering the temporary employees if the temporary employment does not exceed ten days in a calendar year and the employees have no arrest authority and are not armed during the employment.' The way I see it, this is a special event, you aren't going to arrest anyone, and you don't need a gun. And you have ten days."

"You're serious about this," Connor said. It was an observation, not a question.

"Dead serious," Jordan James assured him. "Like I've been telling you, I have a half-million dollars at play here. And one way or the other, whether Hilborn jumped or got himself dropped, wherever my money went, I want it back. And I want you to get it for me."

"I can't just drop everything at Palmetto BioClean—"

"If that's where you want to be, I'm not going to stop you. And anyway, that didn't stop you from going after the shitbag who killed your TV friend."

Rebecca Rose had not been Connor's friend, not in the end, but he decided to let that detail fade into history. James was prodding him here, pressing his hot buttons, and the fact was, he was intrigued by what his boss was saying. It was true that Connor hadn't known what the hell he was doing, chasing after Rebecca's killer, but he'd done it anyway. So maybe it had gotten a bit messy in the end, but the chase itself—well, he had to admit that had been quite a rush. Adrenaline and all. And in the end, he'd nailed the bastard.

"Still, I can't just leave Hanes and D-Dub and Jenny in the lurch."

"Who are they?"

"My crew," Connor explained to him. "Those are their names. I can't just cut and run out on 'em—"

"Then don't," James told him. "Do your job. But you and I know how the blood business goes: one day it's up and the next it's down. Leaves lots of time to multitask. And prioritize. The bottom line is, cash money doesn't stick around for long. And I want you to find mine before it takes a permanent vacation."

Chapter 5

"There's still every chance that he took his own life," Connor had said as James drove him back to where he'd left the Camaro in the police parking lot.

Once Jordan James got an idea in his head it was difficult to change his mind, but he simply shrugged and said, "If that's how it works out, fine. But if it turns out I'm right, you get a percentage of anything you collect."

"I'm not in this for the money," Connor had told him.

"Maybe not now, but some day you will be." James grinned. "Meanwhile, get some sleep. Clear your head. We'll talk about it again later."

Connor promised he would do just that, then got out of James' Bentley and unlocked the Camaro. He opened the door and started to get in, but then looked back and said, "Just out of curiosity, was it hundreds or twenties?"

"Excuse me?"

"The half million. Hundreds or twenties?" "Can't see how that matters," James said.

"It would help to know what size package I'm looking for."

James considered this, seeing where Connor was going with his question. If Hilborn's killer—again, presuming there was one—had taken the money, it would help to know whether it was in a small valise or a large suitcase.

Then he'd simply said, "Big," and gunned the hand-crafted engine, a six-liter W12 turbocharged Continental that he'd already told Connor could do zero to sixty in four-point-seven seconds, top speed of one-eighty-seven. Then James touched his finger to an imaginary hat and burned serious rubber as he all but flew out of the lot.

Connor watched him until he made a right turn at the light at the corner, then slipped in behind the wheel of the Camaro and hit the button to lower the convertible top. The day was going to be another late spring scorcher, and he needed the rush of wind to keep him awake on the drive home. Gone were the days when he could plod through the desert all day and night, eat a little chow, get an hour's worth of shut-eye, and then start the routine all over again.

When Connor pulled out into traffic it had been his intention to follow the signs back to Highway 17, but an inner sense led him in the other direction, back to the Cape Myrtle Hotel. He pulled into the main entrance directly in front and edged the car up against the white curb.

"You can't leave it there," the valet parking attendant told him.

"I'll only be a minute," Connor replied.

"It's a fire lane—"

"Then why isn't the curb painted red?"

The guy didn't have an answer to that, but Connor decided to make it easy on him. He dug a ten out of his wallet—Jordan James' first expense in this case—and slipped it into his hand. "I'm just going to talk to the manager. Just finished a cleaning job and we need to settle."

"This have anything to do with the jumper?" "In fact, it does," Connor replied.

"Got it," the parking attendant said, slipping the bill into his pocket. "By the way, nice ride. What is that, a sixty-eight?"

"Sixty-seven," Connor said. "Three ninety-six under the hood." "Sweet."

Connor stepped into the lobby and found the manager standing by the concierge desk. He appeared to be in a serious discussion with a woman in white tennis togs, racket in her hand and gym tote on the floor. There was a lot of arm-waving going on, and it seemed as if directions were being asked and given. Connor waited at a respectful distance until they were finished with their discussion, then slowly wandered up, trying to recall what the manager had said his name was. Something Hadley. Erskine—that was it. Erskine Hadley.

"Mr. Hadley ... Jack Connor," he said as he stuck out his hand. "From Palmetto BioClean."

"Yes, yes—Mr. Connor," Erskine Hadley said, apprehension in his voice. He was on the short side, maybe five-seven, with thick arms and neck, and little black eyes that seemed to be everywhere, all at once. If one word could adequately describe him it would be nervous. "Is there a problem?"

"No problem at all," Connor assured him. "In fact, we're all done. My crew left a couple hours ago, and we didn't want to wake you up with a call. You want to go upstairs, have a look?"

That seemed to be something Mr. Hadley most definitely didn't want to do, and quickly shook his head. "Thank you, but I'll have maintenance check it out."

"No problem. Like I predicted on the phone, we ended up having to pull out some drywall and carpet, but you should be able to patch it all up pretty quick. So unfortunate what happened to ... to Mr. Hilborn."

"Suicide is difficult to accept," Hadley said.

"Absolutely," Connor agreed. "You know, I was wondering ... is there any chance that your surveillance cameras might have record-

ed his actions ... well, after he checked in?"

Hadley frowned at that. "What are you suggesting?"

"Not suggesting anything," Connor quickly said, lifting his shoulder in a casual shrug. "Just figured the police might've asked to review the video."

"Matter of fact, no one's asked anything about it," Erskine Hadley told him.

"And I'd be the one to authorize it."

"So, they're definitely thinking he took his own life?"

"Seems pretty clear-cut to me," Hadley said, evidently not aware of his pun.

"You think maybe I could have a look?" Connor asked, pressing his luck.

"A look?" Hadley asked. "At the room? You just left it—"

"I'm talking about the video."

Hadley shot him a dark look that had the word sicko written all over it. "That wouldn't be proper, Mr. Connor. Or ethical."

"I was just thinking—"

"And I'm just telling you, the answer is 'no.'"

Well, so much for that, Connor thought. "Of course," he replied. "I totally understand—"

"Good. Now. How do we deal with the bill? For cleaning up the … mess."

"Don't worry about it," Mr. Hadley," Connor said. "You gave me the name of your insurance company on the phone, and we'll deal with them. They pay us directly."

"Really?"

"Unless you enjoy reams of paperwork."

"You're done, then?"

"Looks like."

Connor's head was on his pillow five minutes after he pulled into his driveway, and it was about eight o'clock in the evening when he finally hauled himself out of bed and wandered into the kitchen. His usual routine was to make a pot of coffee and then go for his morning run on the sand, but the job up in Myrtle Beach—and Jordan James' subsequent appearance—totally screwed with his body clock.

He'd missed the sunset, but he took a microwave dinner and a glass of gin on the rocks out to the small grassy patch that served as his backyard. Even though the day had slipped past the horizon an hour ago the lawn was still warm from the searing sun. He sat down in the beach chair that faced the dark marsh and took a sip of the gin, savoring the taste of juniper berries as it slipped down his throat. He'd slept in fits and starts, images of jumpers and blood patterns and broken bones invading his dreams, more carnage than usual and certainly more than any time since he'd come back from the war. He had not known Jon Hilborn but, in Jordan James' mind, there was no question that this was a murder, not suicide, and the man did not appear to have a capacity for taking "no" as an answer. Especially when a great quantity of money was involved. So, Connor had said "yes," with the understanding there was no guarantee he'd find Hilborn's presumed killer.

Now as Connor wolfed down his meal—some sort of cheesy pasta thing that passed for food once it came out of the microwave—he reviewed what he knew about Jon Hilborn. Which wasn't much. James had been particularly tight-lipped about their business relationship and why so much money had changed hands. Connor didn't like to make snap decisions about people, especially the man who signed his paycheck, but he naturally assumed there was a highly suspicious aspect to whatever deal had gone down. No—change that to illegal, he thought as his eyes followed a cabin cruiser puttering down the Intracoastal Waterway, red and green running lights marking its path in the darkness.

That was the real issue here. Even though James had been vague about his deal with Hilborn, Connor couldn't shake the notion that, in an era of online banking and instant wire transfers, two grown men wouldn't exchange that much cash unless there was a need for secrecy. Which, in Connor's mind, left just a few possibilities. Drugs was the most obvious but, despite all of Jordan James' businesses, Connor just didn't see him as a dealer, trafficker, or user. James liked his Beefeater martinis too much to snort a half a mil up his nose.

That led him to gambling, which could have been the case. The NBA and NHL playoffs were in full swing, and the Preakness was coming up on Saturday. All that money spread around on a few choice sporting events could produce a nice yield, if James was lucky. Or if he had an inside line on the odds. Of course, the money simply could have been straight out of James' many cash registers, pretax profits headed straight to an offshore bank. Other possibilities came to mind, as well: guns, girls, maybe counterfeit goods coming through the Port of Charleston. James' security firm held the contract for the docks along East Bay Street, where massive cargo ships unloaded and loaded their big steel containers. Could he possibly have a clandestine business enterprise operating in the shadows of those huge cranes, right under the noses of the customs agents?

Whatever the truth was, wherever it lay, the late Jon Hilborn was at the center of it all, and Connor knew absolutely nothing about the man. James had suggested they meet first thing in the morning to establish a plan of action, but Connor preferred to operate under his own terms, on his own schedule. Besides, as James had said just that morning, if the money was at the root of all this, the longer they waited, the tougher it would be to track it down.

Connor stared at the ice in his glass, then dumped it out on the lawn and went back inside. He grabbed his keys, took a bottle of water out of the fridge, then made sure his door was locked as he headed out to his car. There had been too many incidents involving that door over the past few weeks, not to mention that a psychopath named Freddy Keener recently had sworn to Connor's face that he was going to put him in the ground one piece at a time, Jimmy Hoffa-style. Connor had good reason to believe that Keener had ended up in the ground himself, but he was taking no chances.

Fifteen minutes later he was sitting at his desk in the Palmetto BioClean offices. He turned on his computer, then clicked on Google and typed in the name "Jon Hilborn." He figured the name was uncommon enough to produce a few listings, and after he scrolled down through Facebook and LinkedIn hits, he found one for an organization called Charleston Enterprise Association with a listing that read, "Jon Hilborn SC Business Profile."

Connor clicked on the link, which took him to an official-looking page that included a two-paragraph bio and a thumbnail head shot of Hilborn. He looked a lot better in this photograph than the two sets of shots Detective Harris had taken out of the case file that morning. His face still resembled a face, no blood or bone or gray matter seeping out from where his skull had cracked. Connor could see that Hilborn's eyes were dark blue, and his black hair was graying slightly around the temples. He guessed the man's age at around sixty, something that was confirmed when he read the short profile that accompanied the photo:

Jon Hilborn, President/CEO, Hilborn Capital Ventures

Jonathan Lee Hilborn, 63, is the president and chief executive of the company he founded when he was in his late 20s. Hilborn Capital is an investment banking and development firm that provides a full range of corporate financial services. Mr. Hilborn's investment banking career spans nearly four decades and nearly 150 transactions. Clients have ranged from Fortune 1000 publicly traded companies to early stage technology ventures, and include Apogee Laboratories, Kelly Homebuilders LLC, Black Heron Automotive, Santee Boatworks, Carolina Creamery, and many others.

Prior to founding Hilborn Capital, Mr. Hilborn spent five years at Bloom, Jennings, Templeton & Company in Columbia, where he worked in the venture enterprise division. He received his Bachelor of Arts degree from USC, and an M.B.A. from Duke University. Mr. Hilborn is a member of the board of Coastal Carolina Medical Center and the Andrew Barron Hilborn Foundation.

When he is not closing business transactions he usually can be found in the Carolina skies, flying his Beechcraft King turboprop airplane.

Connor printed the page, then hit the "back" button and scrolled further through the listing for Jon Hilborn. From subsequent links he learned that the man had been the target of a benefit roast sponsored by the Charleston Enterprise Association, an event that included comedy monologs from the city's mayor, several area CEOs and banker types, his brother David—Connor assumed this was the brother who identified the body in the morgue—and two of his four former wives. Two of Hilborn's children—a son and a daughter—had been in the audience, along with his current wife, Caroline. Since there was no date accompanying the story Connor couldn't tell when it was written, and whether Caroline was wife number four, or possibly a fifth one. In any event, a good time was had by all, and proceeds from the evening were donated to the Andrew Barron Hilborn Foundation, which the story said provided funding for amyotrophic lateral sclerosis research. Lou Gehrig's disease.

Andrew Barron Hilborn turned out to be Jon's father, who had died from complications due to ALS almost twenty years ago. The foundation had been set up in his honor, and over the past two decades it had provided close to twenty million dollars to medical researchers who were working to find a cure. Along with explaining the nature of the disease and how it debilitates its victims, the organization's webpage also noted that, "in about 10% of cases, ALS is caused by a genetic defect. In the remaining cases, the cause is unknown."

Connor didn't know if ten percent was a high or low risk as far as genetics were concerned, but if Jon Hilborn had recently been diagnosed with ALS, it could be enough of a reason to jump off a hotel balcony. Especially if he had watched his father slowly deteriorate from the disease two decades before.

There were a few other references to Hilborn, most of them confirmation of what Connor had already read: That he was an upstanding member of the community, an honorable businessman and "entrepreneurial capitalist," a respected philanthropist, and an avid pilot who flew his own plane whenever he got the chance. He'd been married four times, divorced four times, and had four children and two grandchildren. He split his time between homes in the Charleston area, and Blowing Rock, North Carolina. He had season tickets to USC Gamecocks football, and because he was a pilot he almost never missed a game.

And that was it.

Connor finished up around midnight, shut down his computer and turned off his office light. That's when his phone "pinged" and he saw that he'd received a text message. He opened it, found just three words: Are you up?

That meant Danielle was still up, so he quickly texted back: Still at the Plant. Just leaving.

He stood there in the outer office, watching his phone with great expectation. Finally, there was another "ping" and a reply: Can you call me when you get home?

To which he responded: Give me 20.

Traffic was light and so was Connor's head, although he still felt an awkward, almost childish sensation as his mind drifted to thoughts of Danielle Simmons. She had entered his life in an outlandish and sudden fashion a little over three weeks ago, and then had left it just as suddenly. The fact that she still had a husband down in Orlando played a major role in that turn of events, and he didn't blame her for being cautious and somewhat guarded about their relationship. Plus, he wasn't even sure what their relationship was, since it was founded strictly on several evenings of conversation and a couple of modest kisses exchanged in a dark parking lot. That was all; no harm, no foul. Except for the fact that she suspected her husband was having an affair, and had flown back down to Orlando to figure out what to do next. Essentially, that meant pay either a divorce lawyer or marriage counselor.

Of course, there was also the fact that Danielle had booked a flight to come back up to Charleston for the weekend, which meant the day after tomorrow.

He made it back to his place on Sullivan's Island in under fifteen minutes, and five minutes later he was back outside, portable phone in one hand and a bottle of cream soda in the other. It was way too late for another glass of gin, but not for the bag of cheese puffs he dragged out to his chair overlooking the marsh and the cloak of night beyond.

That sense of nerves came over him again, took him back to high school when he tried to screw up the courage to call Suzi Delano, ask her out to the big game. Scared shitless that her old man might answer and give him the third degree, as he was known to do. Which may have been why he ended up with Bethany Bennett instead.

Connor punched in Danielle's number, then hesitated a moment before hitting the "talk" button. He heard Danielle say "hello" on the other end, tentatively, as if someone else might be in the room.

"So, I'm wondering why the animal doctor is still awake at such a late hour," Connor said, dispensing with any of the usual "hi, it's me, how are you" talk. "Did you have a house call at Mickey and Minnie's?"

"Funny." Danielle Simmons was a veterinarian at the Animal Kingdom Park in Walt Disney World. "Actually, I'm staying at a friend's house tonight."

Connor hadn't asked her about her living arrangements since she had returned to Orlando two days after he'd taken down her sister's killer. She had told him she was going to decide what to do about her husband, whether she should stick with him or pack her things and move out. And while he didn't like the idea of her crawling into bed with Mr. Simmons every night, it was her life and he had no right to make any demands on her. Or even ask her delicate questions. Sort of a "don't ask, don't tell arrangement."

But tonight, things seemed to be different. "I see," he said, curious to know who her friend was. Male or female. Colleague or bosom buddy. That sort of thing.

"I found out who she is," Danielle continued, a tentative hitch in her voice. "The other woman."

"You know for sure?" Connor asked.

"Richard told me. Not at first, of course. He denied everything, said I was just being silly. Then I was paranoid, followed by obsessive. When he got to deranged I pulled out the pair of pink thong panties I'd found under our bed—my bed—and asked him if he thought I was that dumb. Of course, he had no quick answer for that, so he just fell silent. And then he admitted it all. Even started crying, the slimy bastard."

Connor said nothing for a moment, wasn't sure what he should do or say next. Should he comfort Danielle over the phone, tell her everything was going to be good, that she had done the right thing in confronting her husband? Should he sound relieved, indicating that with the proverbial elephant no longer crowding the room he didn't need to tiptoe around his feelings. Or should he tap into his alpha male side, proclaim what a prick the man was to do this to such a beautiful, smart, funny, woman, and he—Richard—didn't deserve her?

In the end he simply said, "Let me guess—the panties were either Hello Kitty or My Little Pony—"

That made Danielle laugh, and even over the phone he could feel her release a reservoir of stress from inside. "Actually, they had little Tinkerbelle fairies on them; can you imagine that?"

Connor laughed too, and then he said, "At least now you know for sure. As they say, 'the truth shall set you free.'"

"And like the song says, 'freedom is just another word for nothing left to lose.'" There was a slight slur behind her words, and he got the distinct impression that her evening had involved a dirty martini or two.

"You did the right thing, Danielle. That took courage."

"Yeah, I know. Richard's an idiot, he messed up, and he doesn't deserve me. I keep telling myself those things, but—" "But?" he pressed her.

That's when she burst into tears, although he could still hear full words blubbering under her sobs. "She was nineteen, Jack! Nineteen! An intern in his office, for Chrissakes. Studying sports marketing at Full Sail University. My husband was screwing a child!"

"Peter Pan and Tinkerbelle," was all Connor could think of saying.

"That's right," Danielle sniffed. "Well, I hope they live happily ever after in Never-Neverland. You have room for a houseguest?"

"What?"

"A houseguest? You do remember I'm coming up there this weekend."

"Of course, I remember."

"Because I want you to know something." He knew Danielle would tell him what she wanted him to know whether he said anything or not, so he didn't. "Last time I was up there, that chivalrous, last-gentleman-in-Charleston thing you pulled?"

"I remember—"

"Well, not this time. You're going to take me in your arms and hold me and kiss me, and then we're going to go to bed and boink until the cows come home. That okay with you?"

"Works for me," he assured her. "Except there's just one thing." "And what's that?" she asked, suspicion in her voice.

"There hasn't been a cow here on the island in years."

"That's my point," she said. Then she made a little kissing sound and hung up, but not without first saying, "Good night."

Chapter 6

"So how do you know this Hilborn guy?" Connor asked. He was digging into a mound of biscuits and gravy, thick with big chunks of sausage floating in it. Enough to clog his arteries on the spot, but that's what Jordan James' housekeeper had prepared for breakfast. That and strong coffee, plus a pitcher of freshly squeezed orange juice.

"We went to USC together," Jordan James said. "Jon came in as a freshman when I was a senior, but we still took a class together. Some sort of mathematics course, I think, but don't hold me to that. Anyway, it was obvious he came from money, down to the way he spelled his name. J-O-N. Who does that? Wore blazers with emblems from some pricey private school, drove a Corvette that attracted girls like bees to honey. Anyone who knew him also knew that anything he was going to touch would turn to gold. Success was his middle name." "Money begets money," Connor observed.

They were sitting in the glass-roofed gazebo in the back garden of James' house in Charleston, a place called Broadview, set on a large lot on Murray Street, which ran along the seawall. The Greek revival house was very much old South, with lots of brick and columns and ornate iron grillwork, flickering gas lanterns, and a lily pond stocked with orange and white Japanese koi the size of fireplace logs.

"So ... any idea how we're going to proceed?" James asked him. "It's already been forty-eight hours ... the more time slips by, the farther away my money gets."

"What's this 'we,' kemosabe?" Connor said, reciting the punch line of an old joke. "I work alone."

James took a sip of coffee, then set the china cup back on its matching china saucer. "Of course, you do. And I have no problem with that. I just want to help you as much as I can. Believe me."

Connor wasn't sure if he believed him or not, and it didn't matter. He still wasn't convinced he was the right person for this job, and that Jordan James really needed a seasoned private investigator to chase down his half million dollars—and Jon Hilborn's theoretical killer. But since he didn't really have much choice in the matter, he needed to lay some ground rules—and the first was that he couldn't have

James second-guessing every move, or feeding suggestions to him at every turn. He could deal with regular progress reports and would welcome leads or ideas that would assist in the search, but he didn't want to be quizzed on how things were going or whether he was getting close. Which is what he told him now.

"Sometimes you just don't know until you do know," he explained.

"Totally understand," James agreed. "But do you mind if I ask you where you're going to start?"

"Already did," Connor said. "I've got a nice little file on him, and as soon as we wrap up here I'm heading down to Hilton Head." "What's in Hilton Head?" James asked him.

"His brother, David Hilborn. He identified the body, and I want to see what he knows, then work my way backwards from there."

"Sounds like a plan," James said. He piled a bite of a gravy-slathered carbs into his mouth, then said while he chewed, "By the way,

Gil Redman called just before you got here."

"I hope you told him I say 'hi.'"

"I told him I hoped you would say 'yes'," James continued. "He said he ran a thorough background check on you—references, military record, mother and father and all that—and you passed with flying colors. He wants to offer you the job, but wanted to get back with me first."

Connor knew he would have to deal with this issue at some point, and he figured it would be soon. But not necessarily this morning, over a plate of the best biscuits and gravy he had ever tasted.

"He might want to hold off until we see how this Hilborn thing goes," he said. "If I screw it up you'll probably fire my ass."

"Don't sell yourself short," James replied. "You're a natural. I can spot 'em a mile away. And I know you're gonna take this wherever it goes. Naturally."

"I appreciate your confidence, Mr. James," Connor told him. "So, I hope you understand if I just eat and run. The clock is ticking, and it's ticking for thee."

"You've read Hemingway?"

"Had to, in high school. Don't know what all the fuss was about; the writer used the word 'said' too much."

James grinned at that. "Speaking of the word 'said,' Shirley said to remind you about the thing on Saturday."

The "thing" was the welcome-home party James and Shirley—his first ex-wife—were throwing for their son Eddie, who was the reason Connor was here in Charleston to begin with. Except Jordan James insisted it was the other way around, that it was because of Connor that Eddie was still alive, since Connor had single-handedly saved his life after their HumVee had been blown up while on patrol over in Iraq. It was a long story, one Connor didn't care to think much about, but he'd used his own bloody shirt to tie off Eddie's severed arm and then held him until a chopper arrived to take him out of there. Just another day in the middle of a long war, but it was a day that never seemed to end.

"Wouldn't miss it for anything," Connor assured him.

"Good. And feel free to bring your girl." James emphasized his point by staring Connor in the eyes, leveling him with a knowing look.

"What girl?"

"You think I don't know everything that's going on in my little corner of the world?" James asked, a mischievous gleam in his eyes.

Truth was, Connor didn't know what Jordan James knew, or how he knew it. But the man definitely had his ear glued to the street, and probably anywhere else there was a rumble of a rumor.

"Like I said, I wouldn't miss it," Connor said.

"I'll put you down for two."

One call to Citadel Security, the company from which Connor had turned down the job offer, told him that David Hilborn—the dead man's brother—lived at the Calibogue Sound Country Club near Hilton Head. A second call placed to a phone number provided by the first call was answered by a man who conceded that he was, indeed, David Hilborn. He was understandably guarded and suspicious, and it was only after Connor explained that he was a representative from an insurance company handling Jon Hilborn's term life policy that David—with some reluctance—agreed to meet with him.

"I have to drive up to Charleston tomorrow," David Hilborn explained. "We can meet then, if that works for you."

"Actually, I have another appointment in Hilton Head this afternoon so I'm already down here," Connor countered. He actually was calling from his car on Highway 21 just outside Beaufort, but Hilborn didn't need to know that. "What do you say we meet at your place at one?"

"Uh … I guess that would work," David Hilborn agreed. "Keep in mind it's pretty soon after my brother … well, you know. I'm dealing with a lot of things right now."

"I understand," Connor told him. "I'm sure this is all very difficult for you, so I won't take any more of your time than necessary."

"Thank you," Hilborn said. "See you at one."

• • •

On the drive down to Hilton Head Connor played a mental ping-pong game with the job offer he'd just turned down.

He knew he was supposed to be excited about the prospects of a future with Citadel Security, and equally flattered that Jordan James had enough confidence in him to take such a leap of faith. All assurances to the contrary, however, he still couldn't see himself as an armed guard walking a midnight beat down at the shipping port, or watching surveillance video on split screens in a stuffy office somewhere. He didn't have a P.I. license, and—except for recently solving a grisly murder case—he had no background in that sort of thing. He'd had no background in cleaning death scenes, either, but a quick OSHA training program had taken care of that. The blood and brains didn't bother him, the hours were solid, and the pay was a lot more than he'd been making in the Army. He had a nice pad at the edge of the marsh, a cool set of wheels powered by a 396 V8, and a girl who just last night had told him she wanted to boink until the cows come home. For someone who'd spent three years marching through a desert blast oven and now jumped every time a car backfired, he was doing okay.

Besides, if he ever changed his mind, he was pretty sure Mr. James would make a place for him in his fiefdom.

Connor breezed through the speed traps heading south on Highway 17 and arrived ten minutes early. With a little time to spare he decided to do a drive-by, to check out Hilborn's residence and the lush golf course behind it. It was one of those designer courses that rolled through the dunes and palmetto trees and sweetgrass, crafted by a famous pro who had retired into a second career in golf architecture. Connor had only picked up a club a couple times in his life, just enough to know he wasn't cut out for chasing a white ball with dimples for four hours. He didn't have the patience, the focus, the time, or the money. Especially the money. And as he guided the Camaro beside a long stretch of beautifully manicured fairway he figured those four hours here would cost him maybe a buck and a half. Which to him was one week's rent.

David Hilborn's house was a rambling contemporary set on a large wooded lot with lots of pines and elms and oaks. A circular drive led from the street up to a parking area near the front door, where a red Jaguar convertible was parked with the top down. A bronze fountain with a pair of dolphins was set in the middle of a neatly trimmed lawn, and as Connor pulled into the driveway he realized that the grass actually was a putting green with several sand bunkers carved into it.

Connor cut the gas and got out of his car, an accordion file fastened with an elastic tie clenched in his hand. His muscles still ached from being up thirty hours straight the day before, so he stretched against the stiffness for a couple seconds before walking up to the double front doors. A concrete frog holding a golf club was standing sentry at the front brick walkway, and a plaque fastened to wall read, "Old golfers never die—they just exist on greens."

He hit the button next to the door and somewhere inside the house he heard the chime of a gong, something like those church bells that ring every fifteen minutes. Or the Addams Family movie. He half expected Lurch to pull the door open and say in that low, guttural voice, "You rang?"

But the man who opened the door didn't look anything like a bell ringer or any Charles Addams creation. He was about six feet tall, thin salt-and-pepper hair, and a weathered face that suggested he spent a considerable amount of time outdoors. Just as any avid golfer would. He was wearing a green Ralph Lauren Polo shirt and yellow slacks that could have come right out of a PGA tournament.

He extended his hand and said, "Jack Connor? David Hilborn. Damn, but you have a lot of tattoos."

"I get that a lot, Mr. Hilborn. And I appreciate you seeing me like this, on such short notice."

"Well, you made it sound like I didn't really have a choice." He kept staring at Connor's arms and neck, all the art-covered skin that was visible, as if he were thinking, *you work for an insurance company?* "Should I know you from somewhere?"

"I get that a lot, too," Connor replied, not wanting to get into the Rebecca Rose thing. "The thing is, I thought you might want to be done with all of this" —he let it hang there, emphasizing that "all this" meant his brother's death— "as quickly and seamlessly as possible." Seamless was a word that his squad leader used a lot over in Iraq, as in, *we want to make this mission as seamless as possible.*

"Of course, but—"

"And I do want to offer you my condolences. I understand your brother was a very fine man, well-thought of and respected in the community."

"Thank you," David Hilborn said, averting his eyes to the floor for a minute. "It's very difficult to accept that he's … well, that he's gone. You said this was an insurance matter, so please—come in and have a seat."

Connor followed him into the living room, which was one step down from the wooden entryway, the floor of which had been stained two shades of green to resemble the fairway and the rough of a golf course. The living room was bright and cavernous, polished wood walls with a stacked stone fireplace on one wall and large built-in glass case opposite it. Inside the case were all kinds of trophies and gold cups and medallions and other memorabilia of the kind that were won, not bought. A separate wall of glass looked out over a sparkling blue pool in the backyard, and the golf course beyond that.

David Hilborn ushered him past the trophy case which, naturally, had everything to do with golf. "While my brother Jon was becoming a master of commerce, I learned how to swing a club," he explained. "Played the pro circuit a few years, picked up some junk along the way."

Junk wasn't the word for it. These were trophies and plaques and awards from some of the biggest pro tournaments. Connor saw the names Pebble Beach, Baldesrol, and Augusta National as he followed Hilborn past the case to a corner of the room where two chairs had been placed to take in the entire backyard vista.

"Have a seat," Hilborn said. "Can I get you something to drink? Tea, maybe a beer?"

The afternoon had grown warm and a beer sounded perfect, but Connor said, "Tea would be good."

"Be right back."

Connor surveyed the room while he heard David Hilborn out in the kitchen, running ice into glasses and then pouring tea out of a bottle. It was a room that had a man's touch, no doilies or lace or dainty frames highlighting needlepoint-by-number. Golf was the central motif, with framed photographs of what Connor assumed were particular holes or fairways of famous golf courses of the world. A large painting over the fireplace was by a famous painter whose name he couldn't quite place, but whose abstract work he had seen in books. Next to the fireplace was a rack of antique golf balls, some of which had aged to the shade of fine Scotch.

"So, what's this all about?" Hilborn asked as he set a glass of iced tea on a coaster on the table that separated the two chairs. "Do you have papers for me to sign?"

Connor looked at the glass, a wedge of lemon and a spring of mint in it. "Papers? No, no … nothing like that. I just have a few questions, is all."

"Questions? What sort of questions would an insurance company have about my brother's … death?"

"Insurance companies always have a lot of questions when it comes to benefits," Connor explained, shifting into his best insurance-speak. "Especially in cases like your brother Jon's."

David Hilborn shook his head. "I'm not sure I follow."

"Then please let me explain." He opened the accordion file and took out a thin manila folder, pretended to sort through a few pages of forms. "Ah … here we are."

David Hilborn looked at him expectantly, then took a sip of tea and waited.

"This sort of event … well, when it happens so suddenly, no warning, it's quite difficult to comprehend," Connor continued as he took a page from the stack. "And it may come as cold comfort, but if there's anything my company or I can do for you or your family, please … all you need to do is ask."

"That's very generous," Hilborn said, a steady somberness in his voice. "But I still don't understand what sort of questions an insurance company could have about the death of my older brother."

Connor shifted in his chair as he glanced at the dummy page in his hand. "Then let me get straight to the point," he said. "As you are aware, the Myrtle Beach Police Department has ruled that your brother … took his own life."

"Yes, so I've heard. And your point is?"

"My point is that in all cases where suicide is suspected, we at Moultrie Life and Casualty conduct our own investigation. You see, it appears your brother had taken out a life insurance policy about a year ago, and named you as the sole beneficiary."

A look of confusion crossed Hilborn's face, and he said, "That's absurd. And if you think I had anything to do with his death—"

Connor put up his hand and stopped him right there. "Absolutely not," he said. "Nothing of the sort. But you see, the policy had a … well, a suicide exemption. Meaning that if the policy-holder takes his own life, the terms of the policy are null and void. And thus, there is no payout."

"So basically, you're here to tell me that because Jon killed himself, whatever policy you're talking about is a moot point." Hilborn said, a note of irritation edging into his voice.

"Exactly. If that is, in fact, what he did. And our corporate policy dictates that we must determine—beyond a reasonable doubt— whether he took his own life. Or if someone else did."

Hilborn gave up a look of exasperation, one that involved a lot of head motion and rolling eyes, and said, "Look, Mr. Connor. I don't know about any insurance policy. Jon never told me about one, and I'm really not interested. And I find it hard to believe that he would have named me the beneficiary when he had four children, one by each of his former wives. I don't know how much money you're talking about here, but look around. I really don't need it. Not his, and not yours."

"I understand, and I'll be out of your way in just a minute," Connor said. "What I really need to ask you is whether you know of anyone—anyone at all— who would have wanted your brother dead."

Hilborn fixed his eyes on Connor and said, "I haven't got a clue. We really weren't particularly close."

"Still, he named you in this policy—"

"If you say so." There it was: disbelief at Connor's story, and he really didn't want to linger long enough for Hilborn to demand to see the wording of the policy itself.

"From what I understand, he mentioned your name in the note he left."

"That baffled me as much as anyone."

"Why is that?" Connor pressed him. "Why you were baffled."

"Like I said, he was married four times. Had four kids. I'm just surprised he didn't put one of their names on that note."

"Still, you drove all the way up to Myrtle Beach and identified the body," Connor pointed out.

"Yeah, I did. Four hours up and four hours back." As if taking that much time out of his day had been a total inconvenience. "It was like identifying a tray of lasagna. I'm sorry, but this whole thing was Jon's last joke on his little brother."

Connor picked up his glass of tea and took a long gulp, then said, "So you can't think of anyone who might have wanted to kill him?"

"Like I said, we weren't all that close. He was three years older than me, which doesn't sound like much when you're my age. But back when we were kids, he was the brainy one. Studied his ass off in high school and college, while I hung out on the golf course. 'You're never gonna make anything of yourself as long as you have that club in your hand,' is what he used to tell me. 'Only the top pros make a decent living.' So, he went his way, moving money from here to there, buying and selling companies, marrying and divorcing women. And I went my way, chasing a golf ball down fairways and knocking them into tiny cups."

Connor glanced over at the trophy case and said, "Looks like you ended up being pretty good at it."

"Like Jon said, 'The top pros make a decent living.'"

"Looks like," Connor agreed. "I know this is a sensitive question, but can you think of any reason why he might have ... taken his own life?"

David Hilborn shook his head at that. "Like I keep telling you, we weren't that close, so I wouldn't really know what might have been bothering him. Could have been one of his wives, or money issues. I really don't know. But the last time we spoke he did tell me that he'd been seeing doctors. More than one."

"Did he say why?"

"No, and I didn't ask him. Figured he'd tell me if he wanted to. But I do know he was worried about the hereditary factors of ALS."

"Lou Gehrig's disease. What your father died from—"

"That's right. After watching Dad pretty much waste away to nothing, Jon became obsessed with the symptoms and the genetic risk."

Connor took another slow sip of tea, then said, "But you don't know if that had anything to do with why he was seeing a doctor."

"No idea," Hilborn said. "I don't know when Jon took out this insurance policy, but there must have been a physical exam involved."

"You're right about that," Connor explained as he closed the manila folder and slipped it back in the accordion file. "And all it showed was high cholesterol."

"Southern fried cooking will do that to you." Hilborn said, the words coming out stiff, almost regretful.

Connor nodded as he slowly rose from his chair. "Again, I want to thank you for your cooperation, Mr. Hilborn. I understand this is a difficult time for me to intrude on your privacy."

Hilborn was on his feet now, moving toward the door. As long as Connor was making ready to leave, Hilborn seemed eager to speed the process. But when they got to the foyer he turned to Connor and said, "You really think there's a chance my brother was murdered?"

"Honest opinion?" Connor asked. "Not really. The autopsy report says the cause of death was extreme trauma caused by self-inflicted injuries. The tox screen is pending, but the results probably won't change any minds. I'm here asking you questions only because it's protocol. And my job."

"Of course," David Hilborn said, as if he understood.

Connor moved toward the open door, then stopped and said, "Is there going to be a service for your brother?"

"Not unless someone does something against Jon's wishes," Hilborn said. "His lawyer called me this morning and made it very clear. With so many wives and children, a public display of remembrance could get a little ... problematic."

"I can see what you mean." Connor handed Hilborn a fake business card that listed him as an information analyst for Moultrie Life & Casualty. "If you think of anything else, you'll give me a call?"

"If I think of anything," Hilborn confirmed, in a voice that told Connor that wasn't likely to happen anytime soon.

Chapter 7

Aside from demonstrating that the top pros can, in fact, make a decent living playing golf, the visit with David Hilborn told Connor very little he didn't already know. The man was polite enough, even gracious in the way he had accommodated Connor on such short notice, and so soon after his brother's death. Still, Connor sensed a distinct edge in him that hinted at a deeper knowledge of his brother's life and, quite possibly, the reason for his death.

His mind drifted to the notion of Occam's Razor—he'd learned about that one in Miss Benson's class, too—which essentially said that, when comparing theories or hypotheses, the one that requires the fewest assumptions usually is the correct one. If that was true in this case, Miss Benson would point out that Jon Hilborn most likely had jumped from his hotel balcony, as opposed to being pushed. And taking the "razor" one step further, he had jumped because he had recently received word that he had been diagnosed with ALS.

Connor knew Jordan James would not be comfortable with that reasoning, not when he had half a million reasons to prefer an alternative hypothesis. But sometimes reality is reality, and razors are razors. Miss Benson had been quite clear in her definition of the principle, but she had never explained what a razor had to do with anything. Or maybe Jack Connor's attention had been focused on something else during that part of her lecture.

In any event, it was after four in the afternoon when Connor pulled the Camaro into the parking space in front of Palmetto BioClean. Oddly, the space next to it was occupied by an SUV, a bronze-colored Lexus with a woman sitting behind the wheel. She was talking on her cell phone and was so distracted that she didn't even notice Connor until he was unlocking the door to the BioClean office suite. That's when he heard the car door open and a voice call out, "Excuse me! Hello!"

He turned around to find the woman climbing down from the SUV. She was still holding the phone, but now she was waving it to get his attention. "Do you work here?"

"That's right," he replied warily. The last time a strange woman had approached him he'd ended up being hit with a massive dose of pepper spray. "May I help you?"

"I sure hope so," the woman said. She was short—Connor figured she couldn't have been much taller than five feet, slender except for a big bosom that was accented by a tightly stretched designer T-shirt punctuated by red and blue sequins. Neatly feathered blond hair hung to just above her shoulders, and she was wearing too much mascara and eye shadow. She transferred the phone to her left hand and held out her right. "My name is Linda Loris."

Connor shook her hand. "Jack Connor. You're here to see me?"

"I am if you were up in Myrtle Beach the day before yesterday," she told him in a soft accent that suggested she was from North Carolina.

"The Cape Myrtle Hotel."

"Is that why you're here?"

Linda Loris nodded and said, "Is there someplace private we can go to talk?"

"Of course." Connor stood aside and used his hand to motion her inside. "My office is as private as we're going to get."

She followed him into the bare room and quickly surveyed the faded white walls, the small metal desk, the worn carpet, and the ficus tree lurking in the corner. Then she lowered herself into the straight back metal chair that was set in front of the desk, neatly crossed her legs, and folded her hands in her lap. Connor sat down across the desk from her and said, "May I get you something. Water, coffee—?"

"I'm fine," she said. "And I suppose you're wondering what this is all about."

Connor picked up a pencil and began rolling it between his thumb and index finger. "You mentioned Myrtle Beach."

Linda Loris studied Connor for a moment, taking in all the visible tattoos and probably wondering how much of the rest of him also was inked.

"I told you my name was Linda Loris," she began. "And it is. But fifteen years ago, I was Linda Hilborn."

"You were married to Jon," Connor finished for her.

"He was my first husband, and I was his second wife. We were married eight years, and we had one lovely daughter. We named her Connery, since she was conceived while we were watching an old James Bond movie while we … well, that's probably already too much information. Anyway, you're probably wondering why I'm here."

Connor stopped rolling the pencil, tapped the eraser on the desk's bare metal surface. "Actually, I think I have a pretty good hunch. But go ahead and tell me."

Linda Loris inhaled a deep breath, then let it out between blistering white teeth that looked too perfect to be natural. "Jon—my ex-husband—did not kill himself," she said matter-of-factly.

This was where Connor thought she was going and replied, "Then I think you need to speak to the police."

"I did that," she told him. "I spoke with a nice young detective who told me that the autopsy was consistent with a self-inflicted injury, and that the case was likely to be closed as a suicide."

"But you don't buy it."

"No, I do not. That detective was not married to Jon, didn't spend eight damned years with him. Which means he has absolutely no idea that the bastard would never think to take his own life."

A swirl of questions filled Connor's mind, but the first one that came out was a natural. "Why is that?"

"Lots of reasons," she said. "First, he was too full of himself to ever think about getting off in the middle of the ride. He just loved himself too much for that. The ultimate narcissist—that was Jon. He loved women, far more of them than I ever knew about when we were married. He loved money—again, way more of it than I ever knew about or saw back then. Cheap sonofabitch. He loved the thrill of the hunt, the power of his work, the cocktails at his club, and betting big on a straight royal flush. But he loved that damned airplane of his more than just about anything. Certainly, more than me and more than our daughter."

"And when you were married you took out an insurance policy on him," Connor ventured, cutting right to the proverbial chase.

She shot him a look of irritation, then lowered her head in a slight—almost guilty—nod. "Actually, he took it out himself," she explained. "When we got back from our honeymoon. He said he wanted to make sure that if anything ever happened to him, I'd be taken care of."

Connor was curious how much money that would require, but decided not to ask. Instead he said, "And when you got divorced you kept paying the premiums?"

"*He* did. It was stipulated in the settlement."

"But there's a suicide clause in the policy, am I right?" he guessed. Actually, it was much more of an educated deduction, since he had just used the same bit on David Hilborn.

"You catch on quick," she said, any hint of guilt now gone from her eyes. "And the damned Myrtle Beach cops are going to royally screw everything up."

"So why did you come to me?"

"Because you were there," she told him, her words coming out like Carolina honey. "The cops wouldn't tell me much, but the hotel manager told me plenty. Mr. Hadley. The poor man saw all the blood and everything, something I don't think he's going to forget for a long time. I asked to see the room, but he said it had already been taken care of. So, I told him this was important, both to me and my daughter, and that's when he told me your company was involved with the clean-up."

"That's right—we were. But I still don't know what you want."

"Of course, you do, Mr. Connor," Linda Loris said, her red lips turning up in just the slightest of smiles. "You were there. You took pictures. Lots of them. And I want to see them."

What she was saying was correct. He had taken five or six dozen high-resolution digital photographs, documenting every stage of the clean-up. Almost all insurance companies required photographic documentation before they would pay out on a claim, and Connor preferred to over-deliver rather than argue with an adjuster because there wasn't enough visual proof that a job was performed correctly, or even at all. Still, he had never had anyone other than an insurance agent or a police officer ask to see them, nor was he aware of any law that allowed or prohibited it. None of that client privilege stuff.

Still, he said, "Mrs. Loris. I really can't just turn over our photographic files. They're quite graphic, and there's a sort of confidentiality involved in cases like these."

"Horseshit," she said. "You shot 'em. My husband is dead, so he won't care. The hotel manager … well, he won't ever want to see them. And the cops? They've already closed the books on this whole thing, pending new evidence. So those photos— they're just going to sit on a hard drive until you forget about them, and then one day you'll delete them to make room for more photos you'll end up forgetting about. Meanwhile, my daughter and I will miss out on two million dollars, just because you're too chickenshit to let me have just a little peek."

There it was: two million dollars. Four times as much as Jordan James stood to lose if Jon Hilborn's death remained a suicide rather than a homicide. "It's not about shit, whether it's chicken, horse, or any other kind," Connor said. "But it is about keeping a crime scene private. These days any photo can go viral within seconds if it gets into the wrong hands."

Mrs. Loris smiled at that and held up her smooth palms, as if she were in an old liquid soap commercial on TV. "Tell me honestly, Mr. Connor. Do these look anything like the wrong hands?"

He grinned at her, gaining greater respect for her persistence. Then he studied her eyes, which were fixed tightly on his.

"Tell you what I can do," he said. "I have some paperwork to wrap up, which means my computer will be free for the next ten minutes. But only ten minutes. I can pull the photos up on the screen here and you can look at them, as long as you don't try to copy them to a thumb drive or anything." "Deal," she said.

Of course, Linda Loris had absolutely no idea of the graphic nature of the photographs and the extent of the blood in the hotel room until Connor opened the first image and the computer screen filled with a deep, crimson red.

"Oh, dear God!" she gasped, clamping a hand to her mouth. "This is gross."

"You can see why we try to keep them private," Connor said.

"Damned straight."

Still, she studied the image intently, and Connor could see her eyes slowly take in the different facets of the shot. All of it highlighted by the blood on the floor, the walls, the furniture, even the ceiling. Then she clicked through to the next photo, this one just as bloody, and again she drew in a sudden breath as the image filled the screen. But this time she didn't appear quite as shocked as she was with the first one, and by the time she had gotten through the first half dozen photos she seemed as if she had grown hardened by the carnage.

"The detective said my ex-husband lost a lot of blood in the room," Linda Loris said as she clicked mechanically to the next photo. "But what in the name of God happened in there?"

"They didn't tell you?"

She slowly shook her head. "Just that his first attempt failed, so he jumped off the balcony."

What you don't know can't hurt you, was probably what the cop had been thinking—the same kind of Army-think he and his squad had experienced over in Iraq. They'd get orders in the middle of the night to get ready to ship out, and then at oh-six-hundred they would set out into the desert. Then they'd trudge around in hundred-plus heat for a week, packs that felt like bags of dry concrete strapped to their backs, not really knowing what they were looking for or what they were supposed to do once they found it.

So, Connor told her what she hadn't been told, how her husband had slit his wrists in the bathtub, but apparently didn't quite do it the proper way so he decided to go over the railing.

"Pretty messy for a suicide, don't you think?"

"Not my specialty," Connor told her. "I just clean up afterwards."

"Well, it doesn't seem like Jon to me," she said, her words starting to come out rushed, even nervous. "I remember toward the end of our marriage, back in 2001, middle of September, we were watching the news right after nine-eleven, and they showed the footage of people jumping from the towers because of the flames. And Jon, he said, 'I could never bring myself to do that.' And I asked him even if a fire was right behind him, ready to swallow him up? And he said, 'Not even then.' And there sure as hell wasn't a fire in that room."

It was clear that she was looking to open up to someone about this, and he was the only other person in the room. "So, you don't see him jumping?" he asked her.

Mrs. Loris thought hard on that one. "A day or two after that awful day in September he'd had a couple of Scotches on the rocks, and became very contemplative. Just about everyone was around that time. And he said to me, out of the blue, 'If I was going to ever end it all I'd take this bottle here up to Alaska in the middle of winter and drink myself to sleep in a blizzard.' That was Jon: never had much taste for pain."

"I don't know anyone who does."

"No. But you didn't know Jon. He was a high lord of enterprise. His words, not mine. I told you he loved the power of his work. Well, he was a man of power, all right, and he controlled everything in his world."

Connor could read in her eyes that she meant *including me.* "So, with all that power, he must have had some big enemies," he observed, almost as if it were an afterthought.

"Comes with the territory," she replied. "Jon was always talking about 'return on investment.' Well, there's also such a thing as 'risk on investment,' and let me tell you: a lot of Jon's friends took some heavy risks when they put money into his schemes."

Interesting choice of words: schemes. "From everything I've heard, Mr. Hilborn was an upstanding citizen who helped a lot of companies get their start," Connor said, just letting it sit there like low-hanging fruit.

Mrs. Loris picked it quickly. "Upstanding? Ha! That's what the Enterprise Association and the bankers' groups and the city chambers want you to think.

Politics and business and schmoozing and monetizing and ball-scratching. That's all that shit is." The smooth honey-like Carolina sweetness of her voice suddenly had turned a little sour. "That bastard could pour it on like nobody's business. When you get down to it, Jonathan Lee Hilborn was no better than his father—a no-good, arrogant-opportunist-hillbilly-racist-chauvinist bag of horse manure."

It was a lot to unload on a man who was no longer around to defend himself, but Connor had been divorced himself, so he knew how the venom could ferment. And then spew uncontrollably. "But you married him," he pointed out.

"Love is blind, and lust is just plain dumb."

"Ain't that the truth?"

It had been four years since Connor had signed his divorce papers, the last three of those years spent in the employ of Uncle Sam. A lot of muddy water had traveled over the dam since then, but every once in a while—maybe for half a minute once a month—his mind would drift back to how things had been in Michigan before his entire world turned upside down. His father, his marriage, his murdered niece, the whole bag of dirt. But he was not about to let any of that cloud his memory right now, so he forced his brain to focus on the matter at hand.

"So—what are you thinking?" he asked her.

"Thinking? What do you mean?"

"Well, you seem pretty convinced your husband was murdered. So, you must have some idea of who might have done it and why."

"Oh, Mr. Connor, you don't seem to understand," she said, and he realized the smooth Carolina honey had seeped back into her voice. "I don't just have an idea about it—I already know who it was who pushed my husband off that balcony."

Connor hesitated, waiting to see if she would volunteer the information that he knew she was dying to divulge. But when she did not, he said, "And this person, does he—or she—have a name?"

"He most certainly does, but he's no one you want to meet."

Damn, but Carolina women can be coy. "Try me."

She seemed to think hard on his request, but Connor could tell she'd already made up her mind. "Bodean Barr, but he just goes by the name Bo. He's a real slimeball, has his fingers in more shit bird pies here than a kid with a sweet tooth. Did a lot of deals with Jon over the years, none of 'em good."

"Jon owed him money?"

Linda Loris shook her head at his question. "Jon never owed anyone anything. 'Debt is a scar that never heals,' is what he used to say. No, it was Bo who owed Jon, big time. And eventually Jon turned off the tap."

"So, what makes you think he killed your husband?"

"Ex-husband," she corrected him. "And I don't just think it, I know it. It's how Bo takes care of problems. He has a sheet a mile long, did three tours upstate, twice in Bennettsville and once in Ridgeland." "Those would be prisons?" Connor guessed.

"They would. Why in the name of God Jon hooked up with him I never could figure out."

"Has this Bo Barr ever killed anyone before?"

"Not that anyone could ever prove." Mrs. Loris seemed to have lost total interest in the digital photographs, but now she nodded at the screen in emphasis. "But people sure do have a habit of dying in close proximity to the man."

"Do you have any idea where he might be?"

"Long gone, I suspect. Along with all the money."

There it was again, almost begging him to ask the question, so he kindly obliged. "And what money are we talking about?"

"Two suitcases full of it," she told him, as if it were an everyday occurrence. And then, as if she were anticipating Connor's next question, she added, "Mostly hundreds."

"You saw it?"

"What do you think? Of course, I saw it. Jon was practically showing it off."

Connor stared at her, as if he might possibly be missing something here. "And when was this?"

"Three nights ago, in Myrtle Beach."

"You were there?"

"Of course, I was there."

"At the hotel? I'm afraid I don't understand—"

Mrs. Loris was almost smiling now, as if she had deftly steered Connor to where she wanted him all along. "Like I said, Jon was a narcissist and a sonofabitch, but in bed … well, you know what they say about sleeping with your ex. The sex is better because you don't have to worry about the break-up."

No, Connor did not know that—and it was not something he'd ever considered with Melissa, his ex-wife. Not in a million years. "This was the night before he … died?"

"The afternoon he checked in," she confirmed. "He'd called me the day before, asked if I wanted to meet him in Myrtle Beach. It was only a three-hour drive, and it had been months since I'd been with him—"

Connor raised his hands: way too much information, again. "You said he had two suitcases full of cash?"

"That's what I'm telling you. Had to be millions."

"And did you ask him why he had so much money?"

She shot him a look that said stupid question. "Of course, I did. In fact, I asked if I could have some. But he just laughed and said it was all part of an important deal."

"An all-cash deal—"

"That's what I asked him. And what he told me was, 'The less you know, the better off you'll be.'"

Connor leaned forward, as if they were sharing some deep conspiracy here. "So, what makes you think this dirtbag Bodean killed your husband and stole the money?"

"I've already told you, he was my ex-husband," she corrected him. "And I know it because as I got off the elevator in the lobby afterwards, Bo Barr was getting on."

Chapter 8

One more call to Citadel Security told Connor there was exactly one Bodean Barr living in the state of South Carolina. And, just as Linda Loris had told him, the man had quite the rap sheet: Two petty thefts; charges dropped both times. Three domestic batteries; all charges dropped. Two drunk and disorderlies; charges dropped. Five arrests for forgery; two convictions. Two separate sentences to the medium security prison in Bennettsville, three to five years each, both reduced to two years for good behavior. One theft of commercial property and robbery, one conviction and one five-year stint at Ridgefield, reduced to twenty-two months for good behavior.

"Last known address is in Walterboro," Caitlin Thomas, the voice that answered the phone at Citadel, told him. "Looks like his license is suspended on account of a second DUI, involving a hit-and-run with a bicycle."

"Does Mr. Barr have a job?"

"The file doesn't say."

"How 'bout an address?"

"Yeah, there's a 'last known,'" Caitlin Thomas said. "You got a pencil?"

Connor scribbled the address down on the back of an envelope, said a quick "thanks," then hung up. The only thing he knew about Walterboro was what he'd seen on the local news, and most of it wasn't good. Murder, meth, and overall mayhem seemed to be the town's major exports, and Connor wasn't particularly thrilled with the prospect of going there. Especially at night, which it now was.

The sun would be coming up soon enough, he told himself as he turned off the lights and locked the office. He was halfway across the causeway on his way home to Sullivan's Island when he realized this was Thursday night, which meant it was reggae night at Jimmy's Buffet down in Folly Beach. He hadn't expected the interruption with Linda Loris, and now the dashboard clock told him it was twenty minutes to eight. For half a second he considered skipping the show, telling the rest of the band that he just couldn't make it. But he'd done that last week, and if he missed two in a row the Jamaican Jerks might just boot him out. So, he turned the car around at the Toler's Cove Marina, put the canvas top down, and raced back toward Charleston.

The Jamaican Jerks were to music what a pair of twos was to poker night: better than nothing, but far from memorable. The group had two rhythm guitars, one bass, one drummer, and Connor on congas—not a necessary component in order to achieve the pure reggae beat but, because he had his own drums and was an Iraq vet covered with tats, the other Jerks had made him an honorary member of the band. The bass guitarist was a native of Jamaica, and was the band's only legitimate tie to the Caribbean. Even after moving to the states when he was twelve his words still carried the island accent of Bob Marley and Bunny Wailer.

His name was Dotan Bradley—DB for short—and as Connor loaded his congas onto the stage he said, "You hear the news?" "What news would that be?" Connor asked.

"We got a gig. A real one."

"What do you mean, 'a real one'?"

"The Lowcountry Rockin' Blues Festival," DB told him. The excitement was almost pouring out of his eyes. "We're opening for the
Bar-Kays."

"You're shittin' me, right?"

"I'm serious, man. One thirty-minute set. And we're getting paid."

"Paid? Back up a second—"

"It's just two hundred bucks, forty apiece. But it's a gig, man. A real one."

"When are we talking about?" Connor asked him.

"It's a last-minute thing," DB said. "This Saturday night. Someone must have dumped out of the program. But hey, a gig's a gig."

Saturday: That was the day after tomorrow, the same day Danielle was coming into town. The last thing he'd figured on was taking her to a music festival, asking her to hang around back stage like a groupie while he went out there in front of all those people and pounded on his congas.

"Listen, you guys are the band. I'm just taking up space up here on the stage—"

"That's bullshit, man, and you know it," DB told him. "You're as big a Jerk as the rest of us. And unless you're chickenshit, you're playing with us on Saturday."

How could he say "no"?

Jimmy's Buffet was thick with the regular beach crowd eager to get an early start on the weekend, and when the band took its first break Connor pressed his way up to the bar and snared the owner's attention. His real name was Jimmy Page, no relationship to the guitarist of Led Zeppelin fame, and the "buffet" was locally famous for its smorgasbord of two-dollar shots that could be drunk straight or blended with about a hundred different mixers. Those who thought it was an "all you can drink" place were quickly dissuaded of that notion, and Jimmy made it quite clear that no one entered or left the place too intoxicated to drive home.

As much as Connor wanted a glass of gin, he knew he had a long drive back, so he asked Jimmy for the usual: a tonic and lime.

"Missed you last week," Jimmy said as he set the plastic cup on the bar. He raised his hand in a gesture that said "on the house." "Thought maybe you'd gotten too big-time for the Buffet."

By "big-time" he was referring to Connor's take-down of a crooked politician and all the news coverage and media hype that had followed. "The last couple of weeks were totally out of control," he explained, without saying much. "But I'm thinking it's all blown over now."

Jimmy nodded, popped the caps off four Coronas and handed them to a young chick in a halter top and short denim cut-offs. "Heard you boys got yourself a gig at the Blues Fest," he said after she disappeared back into the smoky haze.

"Yeah … playing for a mom and pop crowd that's not wasted is going to be a new experience," Connor replied. His cup of tonic really needed a shot of gin—something his V.A. shrink had forced him to think about—but that was just going to have to wait.

"Don't sell yourselves short," Jimmy said. "You guys are better than you think."

"But keep our day jobs, is what you're really saying?"

"Well, now that you mention it." Jimmy grinned as he slowly ran a terrycloth rag over the polished wood counter, then said, "Hey, what's the deal with that chick was here with you a couple weeks back? Over and out?"

"Nope, just out of town," Connor said. No need to tell him anything more, that she was still married and had gone home to sort things out but was coming back into his life the day after tomorrow.

"Yeah, well, you ask me, she's a keeper. As in keep her real close, and don't take your eyes off her."

"I hear you." Connor checked his watch. "Hey, I gotta get back on stage. There's a buffalo soldier calling me."

Jimmy topped off Connor's tonic and lime. "Break a leg, Marley. After Saturday's gig I'm probably gonna have to pay you guys."

Late-night reggae led to late mornings after, which meant Connor had to skip his regular three-mile beach run. On his way in to The Plant he stopped at Café Medley on Sullivan's Island to grab a large cup of black coffee and had completely gulped it down by the time he pulled the Camaro up in front of Palmetto BioClean. The radio jock had said today was going to be as hot as yesterday, fueled by an extensive heat wave that seemed to have no intention of moving out of the area anytime soon. Connor's plan was to spend an hour finishing the electronic paperwork for the "death scene remediation" up in Myrtle Beach, then head out to Walterboro to see if he could track down Mr. Bodean Barr.

But that plan was going to have to be put on hold, at least for a while. Just as Linda Loris had ambushed him in the parking lot the afternoon before, this morning he found a midnight black Porsche Boxtser with the top down parked in the space directly in front of the BioClean door. The same space that had the word "reserved" painted in big white letters on the curb.

A woman was sitting behind the wheel, studying something on her iPhone, and even as Connor slipped the Camaro into the space beside her, she didn't bother to look up. A flood of wavy blonde hair spilled out from beneath a pink baseball cap, and as Connor got out of his car he saw she was wearing a tank top that loved curves as much as her car did. She seemed fixated on the screen of her phone and didn't look up even when he closed the Camaro door.

"May I help you with something?" he asked her as he edged between the two cars on his way to the front office door.

"Huh?" The woman suddenly looked up from her phone. "Oh … I didn't even see you drive up. Um … yes. I'm looking for a Mr. Jack

Connor. My records show this is where he works."

"Well, your records are right," Connor said. "May I ask what business you might have with Mr. Connor?" "That's confidential," she told him.

"May I tell him your name?"

"Kat Rattigan. Please tell Mr. Connor I'm a private investigator."

"I'll let him know when he gets in," Connor said as he turned back to the front door.

It took ten minutes before she realized she'd been had, and he heard the single bell chime that told him someone had entered the front lobby.

"Hello?" she called out.

"In here," Connor said, smiling mischievously as she appeared in the doorway to his office. "I understand you're looking for me?"

Kat Rattigan shot him a glance designed to let him know she was not amused, then stepped inside. "You're Jack Connor."

"Last I checked," he confirmed. "Please … come in. And I apologize for putting you on like that. In my line of work, you never know who you're going to run up against."

"My line of work, too," she said. "Mind if I sit down?"

"Please do. Would you like some coffee or tea?" He hoped the answer was "no," since all he had were packets of instant and a hot water tap in the bathroom.

"I'm good, thanks." Kat Rattigan settled into the stiff metal chair on the other side of the desk and crossed her legs, which were encased in a pair of tight black jeans. The white tank top he had noticed outside was tucked into the waist, stretching the material in all the right places. She looked to be in her thirties and was carrying a brightly colored purse, which she placed in her lap as she studied Connor for a moment. "I should have recognized you," she said. "The shaved head and all the tattoos. You've been all over the TV lately."

"My fifteen minutes of fame," Connor said, not knowing exactly what that meant except that someone famous had said it. "So, you're a detective?"

"Yes, and you can keep the 'private dick' jokes to yourself."

"Yeah, I guess you've heard them all."

Kat Rattigan rolled her eyes. "You have no idea. Listen … do you mind if I ask for some identification, just to make sure you are who you say you are?"

"You show me yours and I'll show you mine," Connor replied.

"I get that one a lot, too."

I'll just bet, he thought. She showed him her private investigator's license and he produced his driver's license and a business card. Once they were satisfied they both were who they said they were, all cards went back in their respective wallets.

Connor picked up a pencil and began rolling it between his finger and thumb. "So …. please tell me what this is all about," he said, trying to sound polite and businesslike. "Outside you used the word

'confidential.' I assume you have questions?"

"More of a request, at least to start," she replied. "Your company cleaned up the crime scene at the Cape Myrtle Hotel earlier this week, correct?"

Connor studied her, then shook his head in obvious amusement. "Go ahead … take a number."

Kat Rattigan stared at him, looking like she didn't quite get what he was telling her. Then a crestfallen look swept across her face. "You mean I'm not the first?"

The corners of his mouth turned up in a grin, and he said, "Now there's a question I haven't heard since high school."

Chapter 9

"Let me start again," Rattigan explained, after recovering from her embarrassment—and her clear disappointment that someone had beaten her to Palmetto BioClean. "All I can tell you is I represent someone who is closely connected to the deceased."

"But you can't tell me who."

"As I believe I told you outside, it's confidential."

"My guess is it's one of the wives," Connor ventured.

"Like I said, I can't talk about that," the blonde detective said. And now that he looked closely, he saw that she had arctic blue eyes that seemed almost iridescent under the fluorescent bulb set in the ceiling.

"Some sort of insurance policy is my guess," he continued. "But there's a suicide clause, so your client hired you to see whether Mr. Hilborn actually might have been bumped off."

Kat Rattigan was not amused, not in the slightest. Her lower lip turned out in a visible pout, and she simply sat there and stared at him. "I take it you've heard this before," she said eventually.

"Mr. Hilborn appears to be a very well-insured man," Connor said. "And while I'm on a roll, let me make another guess. You want to see the pictures."

"You have pictures?"

Me and my big mouth, he thought. "That's what everyone seems to think," he said, quickly covering the slip-up. "Look … you came to me, so tell me what you're after."

Kat studied him a moment, lost in thought, a nerve in her brow twitching from concentration. Then she said, "Okay. Here's what I can tell you. Yes, there is an insurance policy. And yes, it does have a clause that voids the payout if the insured takes his own life. And since that's what the Myrtle Beach medical examiner has ruled, it's in my client's best interest to get a second opinion. Now it's your turn."

"My turn for what?" Connor asked.

"I showed you mine, now I want to see yours."

"That was only for the I.D.," he told her. "And besides, you didn't show me anything I didn't already know."

Kat Rattigan fell silent for a moment, thinking things through. Or at least trying to make it look that way. Then she said, "You were there, right? You saw the room. And the blood."

"One of the perks of my job," Connor said dryly.

"So, what do you think? Did Hilborn kill himself, or did someone help him over that balcony?"

"Look, Ms. Rattigan—"

"Please … call me Kat."

"Okay. Kat. When we go out on a job we don't play 'CSI.' We just wait in the shadows, then clean up after everyone is gone. I'm not trained to collect evidence and analyze blood spatter, but I can clean blood like nobody's business."

"Still, you must have an opinion," she pressed him. "Everyone does."

Of course, he had an opinion. He had lots of them, but few people ever asked him for them. And more than once when he'd coughed one up it had gotten him in trouble. He sat there for a moment, then said, "If I tell you mine, you tell me yours."

"Sure. You first."

So, he told her. He explained how he and Lionel Hanes had stood on the concrete sidewalk outside the Cape Myrtle Hotel and checked out where Jon Hilborn had hit the pavement, hard. At thirty-two feet per second per second, he said, leaving out the part about Miss Benson or her legs. He then described the hotel suite on the seventeenth floor, the blood spattered on the walls, the floor, the ceiling, and the furniture. He talked her through what he had found in the bathroom, how it *appeared* to have been a suicide attempt gone wrong, so Hilborn had gone to Plan B and heaved himself over the balcony rail. Leaving behind a thoughtful but messy note apologizing to the housekeeping staff.

"How considerate," Kat Rattigan observed when he had finished. "The least he could have done was left a tip."

Connor reflected on the five hundred thousand dollars Jordan James had given to Hilborn, for whatever investment scheme he didn't want to talk about, and the money that wife number two had seen packed in suitcases. Just one of those bills would have gone a lot further toward an apology than a blood-stained note. Of course, Rattigan probably had no idea about the money, and there was no way Connor going to tip his hand on that.

"Would have been a nice touch," Connor said instead. "But I'm not sure a murderer would have even left the note. A suicide note, maybe. Maybe even forged. But not that one."

Rattigan fell silent, apparently sorting through what she knew. Maybe comparing it against what Connor was telling her.

When it appeared, she wasn't going to say anything anytime soon, Connor continued, "So this client of yours—does she have any idea who might have wanted to kill Mr. Hilborn?"

"Why do you assume my client is a 'she'?"

"Tell me I'm wrong."

Kat Rattigan stared at Connor, her look almost a glare. Then she said, "What I've been told is that Jon Hilborn was not all he said he was. On the surface you saw an outgoing, successful, type-A businessman, with the world as his oyster. But tear away that top layer and all you had was a house of cards ready to fall."

Connor knew from the English composition class he'd taken at night school that this was what Mrs. Jinks had called a mixed metaphor, but Rattigan's eyes were too perfectly blue for him to even think about mentioning it. Instead he said, "What did he do? For a living, I mean," not letting on what he already knew about the man.

Again, she seemed to ponder something, probably how much information she actually should share with him. "He's what you might call an investment banker and vulture capitalist," she explained.

"But—" he prodded her.

"But he had few investments and very little capital."

"You mean he was broke."

"Look … I've already told you too much," she said. "I mean, I didn't betray any client confidence, since anyone who did even a small bit of research into the man's background would find this all out. But yes—Jon Hilborn was pretty much under water in everything."

"So, if he was murdered, it wouldn't have been for his money," Connor suggested.

"But it might have been for what he owed."

Jordan James' words came back to him, how he had mentioned Jon Hilborn would "jump before he paid a damned dime on a debt." But Linda Loris had countered that, insisting he wouldn't have jumped for anything in the world. In any event, it was clear that Kat Rattigan was trying to tell him something.

"You think he was into someone, and that got him killed?"

"I can't answer that because I don't know," she said. "But there's reason to believe he got into trouble with the wrong sort of people."

Connor was familiar with that sort of person. His Uncle Bobby up in Detroit had gotten himself in deep with a couple of them and ended up with a broken jaw and a busted elbow. Several months later he lost his house and car and had to move his family into a two-bedroom roach coach infested with rats the size of shoes and gang tags sprayed on the fake brick walls.

"Your reason to believe this—it's solid?" he asked her.

"I wouldn't be talking to you if it wasn't. Look … was there something— anything at all—you found in that room that seemed out of place?"

He thought for a moment, then shook his head. "I'm sorry. It was all pretty much routine."

"Okay. I'm really sorry to trouble you with all this. I've already taken enough of your time. But—" she fished a glossy business card out of her purse of many colors and put it on his desk "—if you think of anything, please let me know."

He picked the card up and gave it a quick glance as she rose from her chair. "I promise you, I'll do just that."

"Thank you," she said as she moved toward the door. "I can let myself out."

Connor waited until he heard the bell signal that she had opened it, then heard the click as it closed. When he was sure she was gone he opened the file drawer built into his desk and took out the plastic bag that held the chunk of concrete he had found in suite 1701. Thinking, *maybe there was one thing after all.*

It wasn't very big, less than an inch square, with a ragged edge where it had broken off from a larger piece of concrete. Connor gently shook it out of the bag and used a pencil to move it to the center of the calendar pad on his desk. Now he could tell it was a chunk of cinder block, with several brick red smudges that looked like dried blood. Of course, Connor had seen so much blood on this job that almost anything even remotely similar in color looked like it.

Connor had found it behind the toilet, and really didn't give it much thought at the time. Even after Jenny said she'd collected a few similar pieces and chucked them into a disposal box. Experience told him that you never knew what you might find in a motel or hotel room, especially the kind where dead bodies show up. In the six months he'd been working at Palmetto BioClean he'd come across everything from used condoms to girlie magazines to feminine hygiene products. So, a few pieces of cinder block with dried blood on them didn't mean all that much.

But now he looked at it in a different light. Literally. The chunk could have been part of the everyday detritus that collects in a rented hotel room, but—aside from all the blood—suite 1701 of the Cape Myrtle Hotel was as clean as any room Connor had ever seen. Spotless was the word that came to mind. So even if Connor's chunk of cinder block had been hiding behind the toilet, he doubted it could have been there for long. And the fact that Jenny had found a few of them, as well, seemed to reinforce that notion.

As he slipped the chunk back into the plastic bag he made a mental note to ask Jordan James if he wanted to spring for a DNA test. Even if he got the go-ahead, he'd still have to find a way to match it to Jon Hilborn's own DNA, which probably would prove difficult. He doubted the Myrtle Beach medical examiner would release a sample voluntarily, which meant he would have to find an alternate way to find a match. Or not.

Then there was the time factor. Unlike on television cop shows, a DNA test takes much longer than a two-minute commercial break, and Connor doubted James would want to wait days—maybe weeks—before the results came back from a lab. Unless the man owned his own lab or knew someone who did.

In any event he placed the call, catching James in between mouthfuls of steak and eggs at the All-American Diner on James Island, another of the fine eateries he owned in the Charleston area.

"You want to do *what?*" James grumbled into the phone, and Connor pictured him sitting there in a red leatherette booth with a fork perched directly in front of his mouth.

"Test the DNA on something I found at the scene," Connor repeated.

"What in blazes for?"

"To see if it's Jon Hilborn's blood. If it is, then that chunk could be evidence that someone actually did hurl him off that balcony."

"Proof?" Jordan James said as he bit into another piece of stringy rib-eye. "Why in God's green earth would we want proof?"

"It might be useful in helping find whoever killed him," Connor said, stating what to him was the obvious.

Connor heard James chewing on the other end. Then he swallowed and replied, "You may recall that I didn't ask you to find out who killed Hilborn. If that is, in fact, what happened, and for my sake I hope it is. What I told you was I want you to get my money back. You don't have to build an airtight murder case as you go."

James had a point, but Connor didn't necessarily agree with it. If that was the victim's blood on the chunk of cinder block, it could go a long way in convincing the police that Hilborn maybe hadn't committed suicide. But Jordan James had hired him to find the half million dollars that somehow had gone missing in the forty-eight hours leading up to Hilborn's death. Nothing more than that.

"Yes sir," Connor said. "And I'm on it."

"Any leads?" James asked, expectation in his voice.

"A couple. Not sure where they'll go, but I'll let you know when I get there."

"Good to hear." James made the sound of another bite of steak being chewed, then said, "Keep me in the loop." "Ten-four," Connor said and ended the call.

An hour later he was parked fifty yards down a dirt road off Henderson Highway outside Walterboro, studying an unpainted, wood frame shack, looking for dogs or raccoon traps or anything else that might back up the sign posted on the top strand of a barbed wire fence that encircled the property. The sign read:

Absolutly No Trepassing!
Violaters Will Not Be Proscuted
They Will Be Shot

Spelling mistakes and all.

Jack Connor sat there, determining whether he felt like a violator, or just a blue-collar guy doing a simple job, asking simple questions. *What the hell*, he thought as he touched his foot to the gas and edged the Camaro between two unpainted wood posts that marked Bo Barr's driveway. *It couldn't be worse than Iraq*, he told himself. *This is America.*

He half-expected the powerful roar of 12-gauge shot ripping through the side of the car, or an improvised explosive device to lift the vehicle off the driveway in one massive fireball, just as he'd experienced in those shit bag villages outside Kirkuk when you never had a friggin' idea where the next shot or blast was going to come from. But nothing like that happened, and he slowly nosed the Camaro in between a rusted field tiller and an old icebox, the kind with the round compressor on the top. The door was missing and it was lying on its back, looking like it had been used as watering trough, or maybe a hillbilly hot tub.

"Anybody home?" Connor called out. He warily opened the door and swung his feet out, then stood up slowly. "Mr. Barr?"

But there was no voice calling back, no blast from a sawed-off 12-gauge or the telltale crunch of a Browning pump. Just the hum of dead silence, the sort of thorough quiet that allows you to hear the crackle of pressure in the inner ear. Not a bird in the nearby oaks, not the whir of tires out on the highway. Nothing. The sort of nothingness that was almost worse than something.

"Mr. Barr?" Connor said again, knowing he would get the same reaction, and he did. Just making sure. Didn't want anyone to think he was a violator who would die before he was prosecuted.

The wood shack was little more than a hovel that at some point probably was a sharecropper's residence. A decrepit door made of wide planks hung on tired shingles, and old wood-frame windows seemed to sag on either side of it. The roof was rusted tin and seemed to carry the weight of the whole world, and it extended out over a porch that drooped from age and exhaustion. What yard there was had been reclaimed by weeds and tires and vehicles on blocks. Clumps of Carolina creeper twisted up the trunks of pines and sweet gum trees.

Connor tested his weight on the front steps, gingerly taking them one at a time. He made it to the top, checked to make sure the porch boards could hold him, then knocked on the decaying door. There was no response, so he knocked again. A third time told him that even if he was a violator, no one was around to kill him.

He tried the knob, found it turned easily in his hand. He gave it a push and the door swung inward on protesting hinges.

But it didn't swing very far, about a foot and a half. Then it caught on something on the other side, something heavy but with a little give. Connor tried pushing it harder, but whatever was back there wasn't moving.

So, Connor stuck his head in, the smell of death and decay erupting into his nose as his hand instinctively flew to his mouth. He waited for his eyes to adjust to the dim light, then poked his head around the edge of the door—that's when he saw what was blocking the door from opening any further.

It was a body, lying face down in what appeared to be a massive pool of dried blood. At least, it would have been face down, if there had, in fact, been a face.

Or, for that matter, a head.

Chapter 10

Connor was faced with a dilemma: edge his way inside and have a quick look around the shack, or call nine-one-one. He thought about it for about two seconds, then decided to do both. Just not necessarily at the same time.

There was barely enough room for him to squeeze through the gap between the door and the jamb without having to disturb the position of the body. He found himself in a small living room, sparsely furnished with a couple ladder back chairs and a table that held an old television, the kind that needed a digital converter in order to work. But the trappings of the place didn't matter at that moment; what instantly caught his eye was the head that at one time had been attached to the body lying by the door. Or at least it was part of the head, blown to pulp by the blast of a shotgun fired at what Connor assumed was very close range.

The rest of the head, in the form of blood and gooey strings of gray matter, was dried on the walls and the ceiling. Flies had gathered, buzzing and laying eggs and otherwise doing what flies do.

It didn't take a forensic investigator to determine that the dead man probably had been standing just inside the door when several hundred pellets ripped through his head. Connor figured this meant the victim had opened the door for his killer, and then had been surprised by a sawed-off barrel in the face, a surprise that lasted only a moment.

It also didn't take a huge leap in logic to figure that the dead man very likely was the man who lived here—Bodean Barr. Connor stared at the headless corpse for a second, then kneeled down and felt for a wallet in his pockets. He didn't find one, but still figured this was the man Linda Loris had called Bo.

From the looks of things, he had been dead for at least a day, meaning that whoever had killed Bodean Barr was long gone. It also meant that the shotgun blast probably had not been heard by any neighbors, if there were any, since there were no police swarming the property. Which, putting two and two together, told Connor he had a few minutes to take a quick look through the place before he called this one in, since it didn't look like the police were going to come by on their own.

It didn't take long, and he didn't find much.

The house was small, just three rooms and a bath equipped with a tin stall shower. Connor couldn't tell how long Bo Barr had been living here, but from the looks of things the man didn't have a lot of personal possessions. Just the sparse furnishings Connor had already seen in the living room, plus a faded poster of saltwater fish of South Carolina taped to one wall. The kitchen was just as empty, except for the pile of pizza boxes and fast food bags with dried food stuck to them. A black trash bag was jammed full of empty beer cans, and another bag gorged with trash was sitting next to it in a corner.

The bedroom was small, with only enough room to move sideways around the double bed that was pushed up against one wall. To someone who had been Army-trained to make a tight bed every morning, this one was a disaster. Sheets and a thin blanket had been pushed to the floor, and the bare mattress was covered with stains of every color and origin. Dirty jeans and t-shirts and tighty-whities were scattered everywhere, and a black duffel bag was jammed under a grimy window that was missing a dagger of glass. Connor kneeled down and pawed through the contents, finding nothing of interest except a receipt from a barroom called Maccaws up in Myrtle Beach.

But in the end, there were no suitcases and certainly no sign of the cash Linda Loris had mentioned. Which didn't mean it hadn't been here, and whoever blew off Bodean's head had taken it with him. Or her.

Back outside Connor paused for a second, looking at the place, trying to figure how this had all gone down. It was easy, really: guy pulls up in the driveway, goes up to the front door. Knocks. Bo Barr opens it, maybe because he knows the guy. Doesn't know he has a sawed-off shotgun, though, and only has a second to think before his brains are decorating the living room. The man with the gun goes through the house; maybe he finds something, and maybe he doesn't. Either way, he hustles back out to his wheels and makes tracks down the dirt road.

Connor pulled out his cell phone and started to punch nine-one-one. Then he thought better of it, figuring there was no need to get himself messed up in this. The police would be asking a lot of questions about why he was out at Bo Barr's house, how he knew the man, what business Connor might have had with him. Cops were like that, and he wanted no part of it.

He had to pull off the road five times on his way back through town before he finally found a gas station with a functioning pay phone. He kept his head low, avoiding whatever surveillance cameras might be lurking, and dialed the Walterboro police, telling the woman who answered there was a dead man in a house on Huger Road, off Henderson Highway. Head blown off, looked like it had been that way a long time. No, he would not hold a moment, he told her in a thick Georgian accent he had picked up from D-Dub, then gave her the address of the place and hung up.

Two minutes later he heard the first siren, and just as he was pulling back onto the road a big Crown Vic with flashing blues screamed by him.

One call to Caitlin Thomas—interrupted by two minutes of on-hold music courtesy of Citadel Security—told Connor that Jon Hilborn's last known residence was located in a neighborhood known as Raven's Run in Mount Pleasant.

She texted him directions that led him to a gated cloister of mini-mansions that simply oozed money, and Hilborn's was no different. The huge iron gate had been left open, so Connor drove right in and two minutes later found himself parked in front of a massive home, three stories of red brick with tall dormers set into the slate roof, a wide verandah with white columns and fans hanging from the blue ceiling, and a large lawn that gently sloped down to the marsh. An attached three-car garage stood at the head of a driveway made of irregular pavers and closed off by a pair of wrought iron gates fixed with matching gas lanterns that long ago had stopped flickering. Massive pines and oak trees clumped with Spanish moss defined the edges of the lot, which was large enough to give the property a stately feel. Mercedes and Jaguars and BMWs were parked in driveways up and down the street, but not in front of the Hilborn home.

There were two reasons for that: One was that Hilborn obviously was not at home, and there was no telling where his car might be. The second reason was the big sign hanging from a metal post firmly planted in the grass, about six feet from the curb. It read:

For Sale

And hanging from that sign was a smaller one that simply said:
Foreclosure

Connor sat there in his car, studying the property, thinking the place appeared not to have been lived in for quite some time. It had that lonely look: no outdoor furniture, no signs of kids or dogs, grass that was longer than that of the neighbors. Flower beds that this time of year should have been a carpet of color had been filled in with pine straw, and the crepe myrtle trees had not been trimmed for the new season.

There was a name and a phone number on the "For Sale" sign, so Connor punched it into his phone and waited for someone to answer.

"Carolina Castles," a woman said on the other end. "How may I make you feel like a king or a queen today?"

"Maybe deal me an ace?" When his joke didn't bring the intended laugh, Connor said, "Actually, I'm sitting outside a house on Omni Boulevard in Raven's Run, and it has a sign with Sue Clement's picture on it. I was wondering if I might speak with her."

"I'm sorry, she's not in right now, but I can forward your call to her cell," the castle gatekeeper said. "It will only take a minute."

"Let's do it." Connor heard a click, then thirty seconds of silence, followed by another click and another voice.

"This is Sue Clement." The voice on the other end was bright, perky, accented with the laziness of a South Carolina afternoon. "I'm told you might be interested in one of my listings?"

Connor introduced himself and gave the address on Omni Boulevard. "How long has it been on the market?"

"About a year," Sue Clement told him. "It has five bedrooms, four bathrooms. Two en suite. Way more room than the owners needed, since they only had one child. A girl. But I guess they did a lot of entertaining. Would you like to make an appointment for a look-see?"

He pretended to think for a minute, then said, "Five bedrooms is a bit too large," he finally told her. "Right now, it's just my wife and me, although we are expecting our first in September. I was just driving through the neighborhood and thought I'd call. And I'll tell Cindy about it. If she wants to see it, I have your number."

One more call to Caitlin Thomas told Connor that the Andrew Barron Hilborn Foundation was housed on the third floor of a converted brick mansion on Charlotte Street, a block off East Bay in Charleston. A twin set of curved stairs led from the front walkway up to a large deck, and a massive oak door opened onto a lobby decorated with leather furniture and paintings of old dead men. A sign said the Foundation offices housed exactly two people: a receptionist and the executive director, whose name was Jillian Pritchard.

Connor climbed two flights of stairs to the third floor, where the receptionist told him that Ms. Pritchard was busy with a phone call, and asked if he could come back at another time. That turned out to be a minor fib, because two seconds later a tall black woman with very short hair poked her head through the doorway of an office and said, "No, I'm not."

Which was how Connor found himself seated in a stark white office with rented furniture and plants, the only personal touch being a framed portrait of what he assumed was Ms. Pritchard's family sitting at the corner of her desk. Several neat stacks of folders were squared perfectly at another corner, and a desk calendar displaying daily pictures of cats sat next to a land line telephone.

"So, you're a former client of Jon's?" she asked him after they were finished with opening pleasantries. The weather, the sudden rain, how the sun was beginning to poke through again. That sort of thing.

"Yes, ma'am," Connor lied. "Mr. Hilborn helped put me in business here in Charleston, and I owe him big time."

Her eyes drifted to his tattoos, no doubt causing her to wonder what kind of business that might be. "I see," she said. "So, what caused you to pay us a visit in person?"

"Well, you see, I heard about Mr. Hilborn's death, and I thought … well, he was so helpful to me when I got started that I wanted to pay him back. Or at least pay back his kindness. I knew he started this Foundation in memory of his father, and I wanted to take a personal look. See what it's all about, maybe make a donation."

Ms. Pritchard tapped a finger on her desk as she thought about this. Then she said, "It's very touching that you thought so highly of Jon that you even considered such a thing. Especially considering what happened to him. But you see, we're being forced to close our doors."

That would explain the Spartan furnishings and the skeleton staff. "Why is that?" Connor asked. "I'm sure Mr. Hilborn would have wanted the Foundation to keep going without him—"

"Unfortunately, our contribution to the world of medicine has been cut short by circumstances not related to Mr. Hilborn's passing," she explained as if she were reading directly from a news release. "So, unless your intended philanthropy is of such a grand nature to keep us afloat, we will be moving out at the end of this month."

"You've run out of funding?"

"I prefer not to explain the nature of our resources. All I can say is the Andrew Barron Hilborn Foundation has encountered unforeseen fiscal complications."

"For real? The way Mr. Hilborn was talking before he ... well, the last time I spoke with him, he made it sound like the Foundation was in the process of considering where this year's grants were going to go."

Jillian Pritchard crossed her arms and leaned back in her chair, a defensive position that didn't require a course in body language to interpret. "Jon was serious about the Foundation, and could be slightly ... well, aggressive in the way he approached potential benefactors." "Was that your approach, as well?"

She unleashed a scowl at him, and said, "It was his organization. If he showed enthusiasm in the way he built it, who was I to question him? Almost ninety percent of what we took in went to the programs we supported. Go ahead and check the nine-ninety if you want." "The nine-ninety?" he asked.

"It's the IRS form every five-oh-one C-three has to file every year. Shows exactly where every penny comes from, and where it goes."

"And this form, will it tell me about these unforeseen financial complications?"

"We haven't filed for this year yet," Ms. Pritchard said.

"So, no one really knows where the missing money is, then?"

Connor was making a huge accusation here, and it was clear Jillian Pritchard was not going to take it sitting down. She practically jumped from her seat, planting both hands firmly on her desk.

"No one said anything about any missing money," she snapped at him. "And I don't like what you're implying."

Connor took his cue and also rose from his chair. "Look, Ms. Pritchard. Jon suggested I contribute a sizeable amount of money to this foundation. Which, it seems, is running dryer than a Texas lake bed. And since you either can't or won't explain how that possibly could have happened, I have to assume your outgo was much less than your income."

"Have you ever run a non-profit, Mr. Connor," Jillian Pritchard said in a voice that sounded suspiciously like a growl. "In fact, do you know anything at all about cash flow and spread sheets and pro formas?"

Connor handed her his business card from Palmetto BioClean. "This is my company," he lied again. "It's a small business, but Jon Hilborn helped me with the start-up funds. I'm familiar with gross income and line items and cash flow."

Ms. Pritchard said nothing for a moment, just kept staring at his tattoos. Then she said, "Wait a minute—I know who you are. You've been all over the TV—" Ooops.

Connor closed his eyes, just enough to suggest that the question brought back a distant memory. "My uncle," he told her. "He had ALS—"

"Cut the bullshit, Mr. Connor. You're not here because of the Foundation. My guess is you're just on another one of your crusades. Jon Hilborn was an honorable, respectable man, and I won't have you tear him up like you did that congressman."

"That congressman was a rapist and a murderer," Connor pointed out.

"Let me put it this way, then," Ms. Pritchard said. "You have two minutes to get the hell out of here before I call the police."

Abrupt and to the point, no ambiguity. "Thank you for your assistance," Connor told her as he moved toward the door. "I can show myself out,"

He flashed a contrite smile at the receptionist as he headed for the stairs, felt her eyes linger on him just long enough to cause him to turn and look back at her. She obviously had been watching him, but now she hurriedly glanced down at whatever magazine she was reading. Then she looked back up at him a second time, this time letting her eyes study him for a moment.

Then she mouthed the words, "He was just diagnosed." "Excuse me?" Connor replied, his voice a whisper.

The receptionist glanced back toward Ms. Pritchard's door and said in a voice that was mostly air, "Mr. Hilborn. He had ALS." "You're sure about this?" Connor pushed her.

The receptionist gave him a quick nod, then looked back at her reading material just as a chime indicated the elevator had arrived. "He didn't tell anyone, but you know how it is," she said, without looking up. "Word gets around."

When he was back in his car Connor punched in the number for Citidel Security.

"Tat Man!" Caitlin Thomas answered after several rings. Her voice was high-pitched, sort of nasally, and made Connor think of a TV cartoon character. "Let me guess … you need me to crunch another address."

"Something like that," he said.

"I hope this one doesn't turn out like that guy you had me run this morning."

"What guy are you talking about?" he asked, knowing where she was going but not wanting to play his hand.

"You mean you don't know?" "Know what?"

"Don't you have a radio in that car of yours? It's all over the news. The cops found Bodean Barr gunned down in his house, at the address I gave to you. Got his head shot clean off. If I were you, I'd stay away from that place."

"Damn!" Connor swore. Best not to let on that he'd already been there, done that. "Thanks for the heads-up. The cops have any idea who pulled the trigger?"

"No, but a neighbor says she saw an orange Chevy Camaro pull into the driveway, then rush back out in a cloud of dust not ten minutes later."

Ooops again.

Chapter 11

The rain started again just as Connor headed up the entrance ramp to the Ravenel Bridge over the Cooper River, and he battled thick drops and slick pavement all the way home to Sullivan's Island. Friday evening commuter traffic didn't help much, and by the time he pulled into his short driveway the sun had dipped below the marsh, leaving only a faint pink afterglow in the seams of the dark clouds that were rolling offshore. He cut the engine and the headlights, then climbed out of the car and blindly fingered through his keys to find the one that fit the front door. He was just starting to insert it in the lock when a voice called out to him from somewhere in the shadows:

"Hey, Connor. You just going to ignore me?"

He froze at the voice, remembering the first time he had ever heard it, just a few weeks ago. Except that time a can of mace and two burning eyes were involved. A grin crept across his face as he turned around.

"Danielle?" he called out. "Is that you?"

"You drove right past me," Danielle Simmons replied through the open window of a car parked out on the street. "I guess it's true what they say about 'out of sight, out of mind.'"

"Actually, absence makes the heart grow fonder," he said as he moved forward to meet her. A little awkward, not quite knowing how to go with this, since he'd figured he had at least another twelve hours before she flew in from Orlando. "It's just been one helluva long day. Plus, the fact that I wasn't expecting you until tomorrow."

"I changed my flight," she said as she got out of the car, wrapped her arms around him and gave him a warm hug. Her body felt comfortable against his, so he held her just a moment longer than he needed to, but a whole lot less than he wanted to. "I should have called—"

"Hell no! Damn … what a surprise!"

"I hope you like them. Surprises, I mean."

"Ranks right up there with an extra dry martini watching the boats go by on a warm spring evening."

"It's why I'm here. One of the reasons, at least."

The last time they had seen each other had been under strained circumstances clouded by unanswered questions and confused intentions. But now that Danielle was here all those questions got swept aside just as quickly as the distance between them quickly disappeared. Their arms slipped around each other again, more tightly than the first time. Then their lips met, just a flicker of a taste at first, exploring lightly as some of those questions found answers, then more intense as the answers became comfortable.

Danielle was the first to pull back, just enough to get a quick gasp of air. "I think we'd better go inside," she suggested.

"If we have to," Connor said.

They kissed again, just a quick peck before he took her hand and led her to his front door. He had left the key in the lock, and now as he turned it their lips touched again before he swept her inside.

He had imagined this moment many times, starting several weeks ago when they had just met, but husbands and former girlfriends and murder had gotten in the way. His mind had played tricks on him since then and he'd wondered how this moment might unfold, not certain that it even would. Would it be instantaneous upon seeing each other again for the first time, or would it be slow and tentative, drawn out over cocktails and dinner and candlelight? Connor had figured he still had one more night to think this through, to make sure he said and did the right thing, whatever the right thing happened to be. But Danielle had hit him with the element of surprise by flying up from Florida a day early, so now as he edged the door closed with his foot it felt like a first high school date all over again.

Danielle gently draped her hands over his shoulders and peered up into his eyes. "Have you been pondering the possibilities?" she purred, referring back to the first—and last—time they had kissed.

"Every hour of every day," Connor told her, and this was the truth. He kissed her again, more passionately this time, since they were out of view of prying eyes. "Can I get you something to drink?"

"You think I came up here tonight for a cocktail?" It was a rhetorical question, confirmed when she slipped her fingers through his and gave his hand a slight tug. "You never gave me the full tour before, but it appears the bedroom is this way."

"Please accept my apologies," he said, squeezing her fingers lightly.

"How can I make it up to you?"

"It'll come to you," she whispered.

Those were the last words spoken for quite some time, as they moved into the bedroom, leaving the lights off, the only illumination coming from a half moon that was beginning to poke through the clearing clouds. They stood near the open window that looked out over the marsh, the rustle of the palmetto fronds and the whir of distant tires on the swing bridge the only sounds in the night. Although if either of them had listened closely they very well might have made out the beating of hearts, slowly at first, then building in rhythm as they began exploring each other with a passion that was both raw and full. Fingers, lips, tongues, skin—everything came into play, and by the time they were finished it was as if they had rafted down a mountain stream, leaped out of an airplane, and managed to ride out the eight-second clock at an Oklahoma rodeo.

Then: silence, except for heavy breathing, underscored by the plaintive call of a boat horn somewhere out on the waterway. It was Danielle who broke the spell.

"What … was that?" she said, gasping for breath.

"That, my dear, was an eight-point-oh on the Richter scale," he replied as he kissed her lips in the dark.

She giggled and softly nestled her head into the crook between Connor's shoulder and neck. "Better sound the tsunami alarm and close down all the nuclear reactors," she purred. "But I was serious … what was that? Didn't you hear it?"

"Hear what?"

Then he heard something that sounded like a heavy car door slamming, and she said, "That."

"I'm sure it's a neighbor just getting home," he replied, trying to comfort her. He realized Danielle had reason to be a little nervous— after all, the last time she had been in his home a crazed man had barged in waving a gun around.

Still, he sat up and moved his feet to the floor, then pulled on the jeans and shirt he'd been wearing earlier. "But if it will make you feel better, I'll go check."

"I'm sure you're right—it's just a neighbor. But I wouldn't put it past that shit bag husband of mine to follow me up here."

"You're kidding me," Connor said. "I thought you'd kicked him out."

"I did. Forget it." She drew in a deep breath, and let it out in a long, lingering sigh. "He's off doing his thing, and I'm here doing mine.

But I think maybe I could use that drink right about now." "A dirty martini?" he asked her.

"The dirtiest."

But the martinis were going to have to wait, because just then there was a loud pounding on the front door. Three pounds, in fact. Then a pause, then three more.

"Oh, shit," Danielle said.

"You stay there," Connor told her as he padded out into the living room. He crossed to the door and called out, "Who is it?"

"Police!" barked a voice on the other side. "Open up."

"Do you know what time it is?"

"Time for you to open the door," the voice said. Connor could almost hear the implied *asshole* tacked to the end.

So, he did. He turned the three locks, then pulled the door inward and stared at the two police officers standing there, backlit by a distant streetlamp. One of the cops was dressed in street clothes, while the other was wearing a Sullivan's Island cop uniform. The one in street clothes looked vaguely familiar, but Connor didn't instantly place him.

"Bryan Hallam, State Law Enforcement Division," the plainclothes guy said, holding up his badge. "I didn't think our paths would cross again so soon, Mr. Connor."

That's when it hit him: this was the same SLED detective who had grilled Connor several weeks ago when he was being interrogated—or *strongly questioned*— as a person of interest in a murder investigation.

"Like a bad penny, I always turn up," Connor said with a shrug. "To what do I owe the pleasure?"

"Mind if we come in?" Hallam asked.

Connor hesitated only a moment, then stood back and ushered them inside with a wave of his hand. He hoped that Danielle would stay in the bedroom and let him deal with this—whatever this was— by himself.

Hallam came in as if he owned the place, and in his mind, he probably did, at least for the next few minutes. The local cop followed him, holding up his badge so Connor could see it.

"Brad Little," he identified himself. "Sullivan's Island Police."

"No shit," Connor said as he closed the door. "So—I'll ask again. To what do I owe the pleasure of this late-night visit?"

Detective Hallam narrowed his eyes and gave him a cold, hard glare. "Where were you earlier this morning, around eleven o'clock?" "Where do you think I was?" Connor countered.

"That's right, I almost forgot. You've got a belligerent streak."

"I also have patience that wears thin pretty damned fast. Why don't you just tell me what this is about?"

Hallam and Little exchanged glances, then the SLED detective said, "This is about an orange Camaro someone saw down in Walterboro this morning pulling out of a crime scene. And that same Camaro— with a plate matching the one on your orange Camaro parked right outside—was picked up on a gas station surveillance video just a few minutes later. The same gas station where someone used a pay phone to call the police and report a possible murder."

Damn, Connor thought. He had done his best to hide his face from Big Brother, but he had not thought about the license plate. Or the fact that an orange 1967 Camaro might actually stand out in a state that was overrun with pick-up trucks.

It didn't take Connor long to decide how to play this. There was no reason to be evasive, and no need to lie. So, he said, "I don't believe I said, 'possible murder,' Detective. I have a damned good memory, and what I said was, 'There's a man with his head blown off, probably a shotgun, in a house out on Huger road.' I even pronounced it right: hew-gee. Then I gave her the address and said I thought the body had been there for quite a while."

Hallam made an exasperated gesture with his hands and said, "Whatever. You admit you made the call."

"'Admit' is a strong word. But yes, I did perform my civic duty and report what I figured was a crime. And I assume I'm right about the crime part."

"An autopsy has been scheduled for tomorrow, but yes. We're obviously treating this death as a homicide. And yes, the body was there for at least twenty-four hours. Decomp and maggots, that sort of thing."

It occurred to Connor that Palmetto BioClean might conceivably get the call to clean up the death scene, but he dismissed that idea almost as quickly as it came to him. Despite the blood and brains that had decorated the walls and ceiling, it was probably not in anyone's interest—or bank account—to go to the effort and expense to clean it up. In this case he assumed the owner would either slap on a coat of paint, or just bulldoze the place. Either way it wasn't his problem until someone called and made it his.

"Did you I.D. him?" he asked.

"Maybe. But what we're here for is to find out why you were there this morning."

"I was looking for someone. Couldn't tell for sure if I'd found him."

"And just who were you looking for?"

"How 'bout you tell me who I found, and I'll tell you if that's the person," Connor countered.

Hallam rolled his eyes and shifted his weight from one leg to the other. "All right. The deceased was identified as a Mr. Bodean Barr, of Walterboro. Was he your guy?"

"That would be him. Bo Barr."

"So, what was your interest in him?" Officer Little asked.

Hallam shot the cop a nasty look, then decided the question actually was a valid one. "Go ahead and answer him."

"It's strictly a business matter," Connor explained. "His name came up in conversation, and I had a few questions for him." Questions like *what do you know about a couple suitcases full of U.S. dollars?*

"You're not making this very easy, Mr. Connor—"

"I forgot the meaning of 'easy' when I was in Iraq," Connor said as he looked from the state cop to the local one. For a moment his mind drifted to Danielle lying in bed in the other room, listening intently to what they all were talking about, probably wondering what the hell she had wandered into here. "There's really not much I can tell you, except that someone I work with asked me to help locate Mr. Barr. I came up with an address in Walterboro and drove out there to make sure it was the same guy."

"Who is this person you say you work with?" Hallam demanded.

"I'm not at liberty to say. It's a private matter." "Do you have a ticket?" Officer Little then asked him.

"A ticket?" Connor repeated.

"Private investigator's license," Hallam clarified. "It's against the law in this state to conduct an investigation if you're not licensed."

"True. But state regs say that a company with a security business license can hire temporary employees for special events, as long as their employment isn't for more than ten days."

Hallam narrowed his eyes and said, "What special event are we talking about?"

"The suicide up in Myrtle Beach."

"That rich guy with all the wives? How does that qualify as a special event?"

"He jumped off a balcony. If you ask me, that's pretty special."

Hallam started to argue, maybe explain that the "special events" clause probably applied to bluegrass concerts or Jesus revivals, that sort of thing. But he stopped himself and said, "Whatever. Thing is, you're meddling in an official investigation, and you're awful close to what a judge might consider obstruction of justice."

"The only thing I'm obstructing is bullshit," Connor responded. "In fact, if it wasn't for me, you wouldn't even have an investigation. Mr. Bodean Barr would still be lying out there on the floor of that filthy cabin, being nibbled on by maggots and rats and roaches."

Detective Hallam could see that this conversation was going nowhere, that questioning Jack Connor further wasn't worth the effort.

Or aggravation.

"You really are a pain in the ass," he said with a deep sigh of exasperation.

"Someone's got to do it," Connor replied, and then opened the door for them.

Danielle waited for the sound of the engine starting before she wandered out from the bedroom. She had slipped back into the curve-hugging dress that he'd helped her out of earlier in the evening. But from the looks of things as she stood there in the doorway it was clear she'd left her bra on the bedroom floor. Panties, too, most likely.

She grinned at him and said, "How do you ever get any sleep around here?"

"Who said anything about sleep?" He was across the room in one swift motion, his hands holding hers to her sides. He leaned in and kissed her, long and lingering, "But if you want I can still fix you that dirty martini."

"How 'bout we split the difference?" she replied. "Let's do the dirty part now, worry about the martini later."

"My kind of woman," Connor said as he led her back into the bedroom.

Chapter 12

Two minutes after Connor stepped into the shower the following morning his phone started ringing. Danielle handed it to him around the plastic curtain, and he saw that it was a call to Palmetto BioClean that was being forwarded to his cell.

"Shit," he said, fearing the worst as he turned off the water. The last thing he wanted today was a clean-up job. But his worst fear went unfounded, because the call was from Linda Loris. And she was sounding close to hysterics.

"Mr. Connor—did you hear the news?"

"What news would that be, Ms. Loris?" he asked, knowing damned well what her answer would be.

"Bodean Barr … he got his head blown off."

"Calm down, Ms. Loris. Please. Yes, I saw it on TV." No need to mention his trip out to Barr's cabin in Walterboro, or the visit from the police last night.

"Then you see, right? It's obvious. That piece of slime killed my husband."

Your ex-husband, Connor could have reminded her. Instead he said, "I'm missing something here. How does the fact that Bodean Barr got himself killed prove anything?" "But … I … you …" she stammered.

"You said it yourself, Ms. Loris. Bo Barr had a sheet longer than an Italian opera. He did three tours of South Carolina's finest jails, and there was a lot of other shit that didn't stick. All that tells me is that he made a lot of bad choices, and any one of those choices could have pulled a trigger."

"But … you have to admit the timing is suspicious."

"Suspicious, yes," Connor conceded. "But unless there's something you're not telling me, something that goes anywhere near that thing called 'reasonable doubt,' it's all just circumstance. Or coincidence."

"I don't believe in coincidence," Ms. Loris stated emphatically.

Connor had heard that line before, most recently coming from his own mouth. "Neither do I. But right now, I'd need to know more before I'm convinced Bodean Barr's and Jon Hilborn's deaths are connected."

There was a momentary silence on the other end, then Ms. Loris said, "Meet me this afternoon, three o'clock—"

"Today's not a good day for me," Connor told her. It was the truth, but he didn't feel the need to explain why. Then he heard a sigh of disappointment, so he said, "Make it five o'clock, at The Plant." "What's the plant?" she asked.

"Where we met before. My office."

She seemed to think this over, then said, "Okay, five it is. See you there."

"And bring some evidence," Connor added. "Proof of something. Anything that comes anywhere close."

But he was speaking to dead air, since Linda Loris had already ended the call.

"I get the feeling this might not have been the best weekend for me to come up," Danielle said two minutes later. "Looks like you've got a lot going on."

They were standing in the kitchen, waiting for a pot of coffee to brew. Most mornings Connor went for a three-mile sunrise run on the beach, then picked up a to-go cup at Café Medley. But this was not most mornings. And he certainly didn't intend to spend a single moment of it running on the sand.

"Looks can be deceiving," he told her. "It's just something I'm working on."

"Something like you were working on last time?" Danielle asked, referring to Connor's investigation into her sister's murder.

"A bit like that, yeah," he said, trying to sound ambivalent. "But it's nothing big, and this time I'm being paid."

"That's why the cops were here last night?"

After last evening's unannounced visit from Detective Hallam and Officer Little, Connor was far too distracted by Danielle to explain much, and she was way too preoccupied to ask any questions. But this was a new day, which brought a new light.

"They were here because my car was spotted over in a town called Walterboro," he explained, and then gave her a brief run-down of what led up to yesterday's events. He began with Jon Hilborn's suicide, and ended with the surveillance video that captured his license plate.

She listened closely and nodded a few times and then, when he was finished. "Is this where I can start calling you a private dick?"

"Only if it's a term of endearment." He poured her a cup of coffee and said, "You know, I'm just now realizing that I don't have a clue what you take in this."

"There you go—a private dick without a clue," she giggled as she trickled her fingers up his thigh. "Good thing is, I can always show you."

"I think I see where this is going," Connor said. And in just another minute, without a bit of protest, she proved him right.

Tiring Connor out in bed was not the only thing on Danielle's agenda while she was in Charleston. Her primary motive, should anyone ask, was to start the probate process for her sister Rebecca, who had died without a will. As she was finding out, that was defined as "dying intestate" which, in South Carolina, could end up in a messy, prolonged, and expensive process. Rebecca was single and did not own any real property except her car, but she had a purse full of credit cards and an apartment lease and a car payment that was more than the vehicle was worth. In any event,

Danielle explained that she had to go meet with the lawyers that her parents had hired, since they were concerned they might not get paid for their services.

"You'll be back by two?" Connor asked her. "We still have the thing."

"Wouldn't miss it for the world," Danielle told him, kissing him on the forehead.

The "thing" was the reception that Jordan James and his first ex-wife were throwing for their son Eddie, Connor's Army buddy who had lost an arm and part of his brain in an explosion in Iraq. The entire James family was convinced Connor had saved the young man's life by tying off his brachial artery and keep him from bleeding out when the IED had sliced off the base of his humerus. And it probably was true, although Connor didn't give it a whole lot of thought at the time, and tried to give it even less now.

"It's not exactly going to be a bunch of fun and games—"

"So, you keep telling me," she said as she grabbed her keys from the kitchen counter. "But I definitely want to meet this Jordan James guy and his son you saved."

"Let's not go there," Connor said. "It's going to be bad enough this afternoon."

"Still, I'm looking forward to it," she said. "See you back here at two."

That's how Connor ended up at The Plant, transferring biohazard boxes from the back of the truck into Moby Dick, the company's white utility trailer, and then driving everything to the medical waste disposal site located behind a nearby hospital. Palmetto BioClean had a standing contract with the company that trucked the waste up to an incinerator in North Carolina, and he knew a shipment was due to depart that afternoon. After signing all the proper forms, he returned to The Plant, unhooked the trailer from the truck, and went inside to his desk so he could finish the billing paperwork for the Jon Hilborn job.

But best intentions, and all that, intervened. Just as Connor sat down at his computer and began filling in the automated form, there was a knock on the outer door. He considered ignoring it but then figured it could be Danielle or a potential client, so he went out to the lobby area and reluctantly opened it.

A woman in her mid-fifties was standing there, both hands clutching a blue handbag in front of her. She had short hair that looked silver with wisps of platinum swept through it, and designer glasses with lenses that made her eyes look bigger on the top than the bottom.

"Is this Palmetto BioClean?" she asked in a voice that sounded as if it had been born and raised in Carolina hill country.

"Yes it is," Connor said, wondering if the company sign above the front door had blown away. "How may I help you?"

"I'm looking for a Mr. Connor."

He stared at her for a second, then said, "Does this have to do with the death of Jon Hilborn?"

The woman seemed startled by his question, then said, "Why, yes … it does. How did you know?"

"Lucky guess," he told her. He ran a quick mental assessment of what this was about and the chance that he would be able to just turn this woman away. Conclusion: the odds were not good. "I'm Jack Connor. Come on in."

She told him her name was Mary Alice Benton, then followed him into his office. She sat down in the chair in front of his desk, fidgeted with the clasp on her handbag a few times before she got around to explaining why she was there.

"I'm told you cleaned the … the room where Jonathan took his life," she eventually said.

"Me and my team," he conceded. "Why do you ask?"

He suspected he already knew why, but decided to let her tell this in her own way.

"Jon and I …" Ms. Benton hesitated, seemingly unsure what to say next. "Well, for the last six months we shared a home up toward Cape Lookout, near the Outer Banks. My home, actually. I'm a nurse at the hospital in Morehead City, and we met when he was admitted there. I'm sorry … I really shouldn't be talking about patients." "ALS?" Connor ventured, cutting through the chatter.

"What about ALS?"

"Lou Gehrig's Disease," he clarified. "It's another name for ALS."

"I'm a nurse—I know what it is." This time her fidgeting actually resulted in her opening her purse, from which she removed a packet of tissues. She peeled one out of the package and wiped her brow, which did not seem the least bit damp. "And Jon most certainly did not have it. Nor did he suffer from chronic fatigue, or Epstein Barr, Lyme disease, or fibromyalgia, or epilepsy, or any of the other things he went around telling people he had. In fact, all that sonofabitch had was a mouth full of lies, and look where they got him."

"I see," Connor said, although he actually did not. "So, you came down here to speak with me for what reason?"

"I would think that would be obvious," her voice now taking on a bitter, almost hostile tone. Connor knew it was not directed at him, but her words were still coming out like acid. Which added up to a woman scorned. "I want to make sure the man is really, truly dead." "You should speak with the Myrtle Beach Police," he suggested.

"You don't think I've already done that? Of course, I did. But just because we weren't married, they wouldn't give me the time of day. I spoke with a detective there, a Mr. … uh … Mr. Harris. He assured me it was a suicide, pure and simple."

"But you don't believe him?" Seemed fewer and fewer people were buying into the suicide thing.

"Nothing was simple with Jon Hilborn, and there was nothing even remotely pure about him. And before you say anything else, yes, I did speak with the medical examiner. She said the same thing.

Suicide. I even saw the pictures."

"But you don't believe her? Or your own eyes?"

She thought on that a moment, then jiggled her head in a rapid nod. "Look, I'm going to level with you. I get the Charleston news on cable up at the house, and I know who you are. Figured it out on the drive down. The whole 'painted soldier thing,' couple weeks back. But you also were there, at the hotel just the other day. You saw the room. And the blood. You must have an opinion of what happened."

Connor looked directly into her eyes, saw no moisture there, no signs of any grief from this woman who had spent the last six months sharing her home with a man who died just four days ago.

"My opinion is the man jumped."

"You sound pretty sure."

"Ninety-nine percent," Connor said, not wanting to mention that the remaining one percent was becoming bigger and bigger every day.

"Walk me through it."

"Walk you … what are you talking about?"

She smiled at him then, a broad smile that tightened the corners of her mouth. "Tell me how you think it happened. Not what the police might have told you, but what you saw with your own eyes."

He closed those eyes for a minute, trying to recreate Suite 1701 in his mind. He used to be pretty good at this, which was why he had provided the Lansing police such a good description of the man who had shot his five-year-old niece. Not that it had done a damned bit of good at the time. "When my team and I got there, I was the first in the room. It was taped off, so not much had been disturbed. The first thing I saw was all the blood. On the floor, the walls, the ceiling. Everywhere. I'm sorry, this must be hard for you—"

"Don't apologize … that scumbag doesn't deserve it," she said.

"But go on."

So, he went on, explaining how it appeared that Jon Hilborn had checked into the room and at some point, had fixed himself a bath. He didn't mention that Hilborn's second ex-wife, Linda Loris, had shown up and had sex with him, or that a man named Bodean Barr might have visited him, as well. But he did describe how all the evidence pointed to how Hilborn had taken off his clothes and slit his wrists, apparently had done it the wrong way.

"Well, that explains it," Mary Alice Benton said, sort of an ah-ha moment.

"Explains what?" Connor asked.

"Years ago, I worked in a mental health unit at a hospital in Raleigh, and one night about a month back Jon asked me how patients usually tried to kill themselves. I told him there was no 'usual' way, but that men typically acted with a more direct approach, like jumping in front of a train or shooting themselves, while women tended to be more passive in their attempt, like taking an overdose of pills. That's a gross generalization, but there are stats that back it up. In a general sort of way."

"You think he was researching how to kill himself?"

"He was always researching something," she said with a shrug. "It's how he was. But now that conversation makes sense, in a bizarre way. So, tell me, how did he get from the tub to the ledge?"

"Well, from what I could see, and what the cops said, the slitting the-wrists thing didn't work. So, he hauled himself out of the tub, wrote a note apologizing for all the blood, and then went off the balcony."

A deep crease formed in her brow and she said, "He wrote a note?"

"Two of them, actually," Connor explained. "One for all the blood, and a suicide note."

"I see," she said as she started gently rocking in her chair. Her eyes seemed not to focus on anything, just fixed blankly on nothing.

"You say you lived together for six months?" Connor asked her, if only to break the silence.

Mary Alice Benton stopped her rocking and nodded. "That's right. Like I said, we met at the hospital. It took me about five minutes to fall for him. A real charmer. Ten days later he moved in, started doing all sorts of things around the house."

"What sort of things?"

"He repaired the rain gutters, painted the front porch railing, replaced some boards in the back deck." For each thing she mentioned she extended a finger, as if tallying them up. "He even convinced me to re-do the kitchen, put in new granite countertops and floors and stainless-steel appliances. He found a contractor and a stone guy and started paying people out of my bank account." "You gave him access to your money?"

Nurse Benton's eyes took a big roll of stupidity. "I know, I was dense. Brainless. Lost in love, and all that. But I trusted him. He seemed so sincere, and we'd even started talking about getting married."

"Did you know he'd been married four times before?"

"Not until after he moved out, and I didn't check. I was in love with the shithead."

Connor leaned closer across the desk and fixed her with his eyes. "When was it that he moved out?"

"About eight weeks ago. And only after I confronted him about my finances. You see, in addition to paying the contractor and the workmen and the suppliers for all the remodeling work, he was also paying himself a tidy commission. Or at least that's what he called it when I confronted him."

Connor could see the dark fury brewing in her eyes, but decided to push forward. "How much money are we talking about?"

"All told, just under a hundred thousand dollars," she fumed. "And about two-thirds of that is unaccounted for."

"You're saying he cleaned you out," he summarized.

"Pretty much," Nurse Benton agreed. "Almost sixty grand of my retirement, right down the drain. Then he just seemed to fall off the face of the earth, until he wound up dead at the Cape Myrtle Hotel.

I can't say I'm all broken up over it, except I'd like my money back." *Take a number and stand in line,* Connor thought.

"And my gun," she added. "I almost forgot that. A real nice Sig Sauer .38 with rosewood grips and a Nitron slide. Only has a six-shot magazine, but that's more than enough for me."

"Did you report any of this to the cops?"

"The money, yes," she said as she started to rise from her chair.

"But not the gun, 'cause then I would've had to tell 'em how I got it."

Chapter 13

Shirley James was Jordan James' first ex-wife, and had never re-married after their divorce twenty years ago. Not that she hadn't come close once or twice, but she'd done well during the settlement stage and had walked away with a nice beach house on the Isle of Palms and a comfortable monthly alimony check that she didn't wish to give up.

So, she had remained a single woman, engaging in a little good ol' Southern sin from time to time, but that's how she liked it. And her ex-husband didn't complain—at least, not much. The cash flow from all his various enterprises made that monthly check just a small drop in a very large bucket, and he even managed to stay on peaceful terms with her and her occasional male suitors.

Above all else, she was the mother of his first-born son Eddie, who was the guest of honor at the party this afternoon. Despite the divorce they had seen to it that their son had a solid upbringing with private schools and tutors and music lessons and football and baseball practice. That was followed by full tuition, room, and board at USC, where Eddie had been on a solid business track when he was bitten by the military bug. It was something he never could explain to his parents, but he felt so strongly about it that he enlisted in the Army at the end of his junior year and ended up at Fort Drum in upstate New York. That's where he and Jack Connor met, and they shipped over to Iraq within weeks of each other.

Colorful signs planted in the front yard told Connor and Danielle that the party was unfolding around back on the lush, rolling lawn that extended down to the dunes. A couple dozen people Connor did not recognize were standing around in clumps, engaged in garden-party conversation that Connor never could understand. A waitress dressed in beige slacks and a yellow button-down shirt was circulating with a tray of drinks. Crepe paper and balloons and spinning pinwheels decorated the perimeter of the yard, and a big sign was stretched between two of the concrete pilings that lifted Shirley James' oceanfront McMansion off the sand. The sign read:

Welcome Home Eddie—Son Of The Century

"Steady Eddie," Connor called out now as he walked up to where his war buddy was sitting in a cushioned lounge chair with a sunshade stretched on a frame over his head. Despite the fact that this event was being held in his honor, he was partying all by himself. "How're you doin'?"

"Ja' Connuh!" Eddie said, the two words coming out labored in his throat. Months of occupational therapy up in Bethesda had gotten him back to talking, but just barely. "Goo see yuh."

"Good to see you, too," Connor said, trying not to stare at the large bandage wrapped like a turban around Eddie's head, or the padded stump where his arm once had been. "It's great to have you home again."

"Mih too. How Izbewwa?"

"Isabella's beautiful, as always," Connor said, referring to the 1967 Camaro with the 396 V-8 under the hood. Eddie had signed over the title to Connor when it became obvious he was never going to get behind the wheel again. "I only feed her the best oil, check all the fluids and air. She's the belle of the ball."

That made Eddie smile, but it was a smile that only used one-half of his face. The other half had suffered permanent nerve damage when their HumVee was blown to bits by the suicide bomber who plowed right into them.

"Hoo duh go-jess gir?" he asked, moving his head slightly to look at Danielle.

"Hell, where are my manners?" Connor said, quickly drawing his meandering brain back to the present. "Eddie, I would like you to meet Danielle, a … a very good friend of mine. Danielle, this is Eddie James, my best buddy in Iraq."

Danielle leaned forward and kissed Eddie gently on the lips. "I'm delighted to meet you, Eddie. Jack has told me so many great things about you."

"Doh' lissen twim," Eddie said with a grin. Then, still grinning, he drew his glance back to Connor and added, "Jus' wha kine o' goo fren?"

"We're figuring that part out," Connor said, managing a laugh. "Tell you what, Eddie. Maybe you and me, we could go for a spin with Isabella sometime. If your doctors say it's okay, that is."

"Fug-ged da docs," Eddie said, anticipation in his eyes. "Les go nah."

But they could not go now, because Jordan James chose that moment to walk up and clamp a massive hand on his son's shoulder. Not surprisingly, a martini glass was clenched in the other. "I see you've been catching up on old times," he said. Then he focused on Danielle, soaked in her thin, cotton sun dress, wide-brimmed hat, blue eyes, and everything else in one very long sip. "I assume this is the young lady I've been hearing so much about?"

If Jordan James was hearing anything about Danielle he wasn't getting it from Connor, but he'd learned that James had many ears to the ground and heard all sorts of things that weren't actually said. So, he did the introductions again, saying, "Danielle, this is Jordan James, the man who signs my paycheck. Mr. James, I'd like you to meet Danielle Simmons."

"I can't tell you how pleased I am to meet you," James said as he lightly took her wrist and kissed the back of her hand.

"The pleasure is all mine," Danielle replied.

"We'll split it fifty-fifty," James said. "But I hope you won't mind terribly if I steal your date for a minute. We have some urgent business to discuss, but it shouldn't take long."

Danielle glanced at Connor, then shot Mr. James a devilish look and said, "Take your time, sir. I believe your son and I have some things to catch up on."

Jordan James thanked her, then steered Connor to an empty corner of the lawn. They moved into the shade of a large pindo palm, and some sort of bird that Connor did not recognize shot out of a nest near the top of the tree and took flight. The gentle sea breeze drifting in over the dunes was shaking the fronds, but otherwise this part of the backyard was quiet.

James raised his martini glass to his lips and took a healthy gulp, and a glassy look in his eye told Connor this wasn't his first drink of the day.

"How are we doing?" he asked after loudly smacking his lips. "Are you any closer to finding my money?"

"At this point it's hard to say," Connor replied. "What do you know about a man named Bodean Barr?"

"Lowlife redneck was sure to get his number punched one of these days," James said. "How does he figure into this?"

"That's what I'm trying to find out." Connor didn't want to get into his talk with Linda Loris the other day, or his upcoming meeting with her later that afternoon. "How do you know him?"

There was another long sip of gin, followed by another smacking of lips. "I never met the man, but I knew who he was."

"From Jon Hilborn?"

"Way I understood it, the two of them were business associates," James said with a nod.

"Odd bedfellows," Connor pointed out. "Bodean Barr is just one level above Carolina roadkill, but Hilborn was an M.B.A. with millions of dollars chasing him. What's the connection?"

"Give it a sec ... it'll come to you."

"Well, it's the money, obviously. But there's got to be something more. I don't get the feeling Hilborn was in the business of handing those millions out to just any old junkyard dog."

"You're being kind to junkyard dogs." James chuckled. "Look ... you're right. Hilborn was a smart money guy, spun his clients' resources into some smart investments. Why would he be involved with a douche bag like Barr?"

"But he was," Connor said. "Involved, I mean. And now they're both dead."

"Yep, that is a bit suspicious." James' martini glass was dry, and he glanced around the yard in an almost frantic attempt to find another. Finally, he caught the attention of the waitress in the yellow shirt at the far side of the yard and tapped the rim of his empty glass. Then he held up two fingers, and she seemed to understand. "Look, Jack. I don't know the why, how, or what those two men had going on.

Maybe it was Bodean Barr who killed Hilborn. I don't know. All I know is they're both dead, and my money is still missing."

"Yes sir," Connor said. For a second his eyes drifted over to where Danielle appeared to be telling some sort of story to Eddie, who seemed captivated by her very presence. Then he looked back at James and continued. "Now, about your money, sir. It might help me cut through a few layers if you told me what it was for."

"I already told you, it's a private matter," James told him. "All you need to know is it's not drugs or numbers or girls or money laundering, nothing like that."

"A lot of your businesses are cash cows, sir," Connor pointed out.

"And all that cheese is accounted for. Ah … here comes my martini now. And one for you."

"I need to get one for my date," Connor said, using James' word for Danielle.

"Hell, where are my manners?" James said as the waitress handed each of them a glass. Then he told her, "Please, see the young woman talking to my son over there? Get one of these for her, too. And another lemonade for Eddie."

"Sir," she said, and trotted off.

When they were alone again, James held up his glass in a silent toast to Connor, and said, "I run a clean shop, Jack. Everything is above board. But in this world of wire transfers and online banking and identify theft, some folks still do things the ol' fashioned way.

That means cash on the barrel. I hope you can appreciate that."

"Not a problem," Connor replied. "But if someone killed Jon Hilborn and then snatched your money off that barrel, it would help to know who he might have been talking to in the days leading up to his death."

"Point taken," James agreed, still dodging the point. "And all I can say is that if Bodean Barr was involved with Jon Hilborn, we're looking for someone with close ties to both of them."

They left the party not long after that, Connor taking time to say goodbye to Eddie, telling him he'd drop by again sometime in the next few days for a longer visit. Most of the guests had left Eddie alone except to say a quick "hello," but the young man seemed exhausted by the afternoon's events, and just said "tha' goot." Then he seemed to lose his empty gaze to a vanishing point far, far away.

Shirl "The Pearl" Pinckney James, Eddie's mother, stopped Connor and Danielle at the backyard gate and thanked them both for coming. She also collected both martini glasses, which had been drained of their contents.

"Eddie is so lost," she lamented with great sadness stitched into her words. "Or maybe it's me who's lost. I know he's in there, but I just can't seem to find my boy in that empty desert his mind has become."

"Your son traveled all the way to hell and back," Connor told her, his words coming out hollow and without much comfort. "And along the way the world took a big part of him."

"Yes, it most certainly did." She sniffed. "But at least his heart is still ticking. You made sure of that."

Connor was reminded once again why he never felt completely comfortable around Jordan James or any part of his family. They all credited him with saving Eddie's life, when all he did was fail to see the old Ford van with the suicide bomber handcuffed to the wheel until it was too late. Sure, after the smoke and dust settled Connor had done what he could to stabilize the kid, stanch the flow of blood and protect his severed arm and dented skull. But he hardly considered that lifesaving, or heroic, or anything short of what anyone else would do.

"I'm just glad he's here," Connor said, hoping that the lameness of his words would be swept away in the ocean breeze. "I'm thankful he made it home."

"We're all glad," she said, and then she leaned up on her toes and kissed him on the forehead. "Thank you for making it possible."

Linda Loris was waiting for him when he pulled the Camaro into a parking space in front of The Plant. She was leaning against the front fender of her Lexus SUV, and pushed away from it as he cut the engine. He'd driven here directly from the party, stopping only at the Towne Center retail sprawl so Danielle could do a little shopping while he tended to business. Since the Lowcountry Rockin' Blues Festival was at Belle Hall Plantation on the far side of Mount Pleasant, it made more sense to stay on that side of town instead of making two trips back to Sullivan's Island. His conga drums were already in the trunk, Danielle was already dressed for the occasion, and time was already running tight.

Ms. Loris made a point of tapping her watch as Connor got out of the Camaro, then said, "Right on time."

"Hope I didn't keep you waiting long," he replied. "Do you want to go inside?"

She glanced around, convinced herself that no one was anywhere close to being within earshot. "This is fine," she said. "I'm only going to be a minute, and I hate to waste a beautiful afternoon."

"Me too," Connor told her as he settled in against his own fender. "So, tell me, Ms. Loris … what's this all about? You sounded pretty upset on the phone."

"Of course, I was upset," she said, almost defensively. "I'd just learned that someone had blown Bo Barr's head off. Which proves that this goes deep … much deeper than I thought. And please … call me Linda."

From where Connor was leaning against his car the sun was at just the right angle to be glaring in his eyes, so he adjusted his sunglasses, then slipped his hands into his pockets. "All right, Linda. Why does Bodean Barr's murder prove anything?"

"You said this morning, you don't believe in coincidences," she reminded him.

"I also said I'd need to know more about Barr and your ex-husband before I'd believe their deaths were connected."

She studied him then, not saying anything for what seemed like ages, but probably was no more than five seconds. "They were working on something," she finally said.

"What kind of something?"

"I don't know. But that's why Bo was at the Cape Myrtle Hotel. He went there to pick up the cash I saw."

"And you know this how?" Connor asked.

"I was married to Jon for eight years. I knew him better than most people. And I know he and Bo were in cahoots."

"*Cahoots* is a very strange word," Connor said. "What are you saying?"

Linda Loris took a long breath, then sighed with deep resignation. "Jon met Bo about ten, twelve years ago. I remember because there was all this paranoia about national security and radicalism and surviving the big Muslim assault that was coming. Bo had been in prison when the twin towers came down, and some of his friends in there began talking about the end times. Of course, there wasn't much they could do to protect themselves, but Bo—all he could talk about was how there was big money in personal security."

"You mean like home alarms, that sort of thing?"

"More than that," she said, shaking her head. "This had to do with guns, bunkers, food lockers, solar panels. *Going off the grid* is what Bo called it. He seemed convinced there was big money in survival." "And your husband ... what did he think?" Connor asked.

"Jon tolerated him. Maybe he even humored him. But he did not invest in Bodean Barr's scheme. That's what he called it, Jon did. The *scheme.*"

"What did Barr do when your husband told him *no*?"

"What do you think he did? He went ape shit. Kicked out Jon's headlights, threatened to kill our dog and make our daughter disappear. When Jon told me all this I started to freak out, but he went all calm-like and patiently explained that from an investment standpoint there was solid upside in the short term, but huge long-term risk. And that scumbag Barr was threatening our lives, and Jon was treating it all like an investment opportunity."

"I take it Bo Barr didn't just walk away—"

Linda Loris drew her head from side to side. "You got that right. But he never made good on his threats to our dog or our daughter. Instead he somehow got his hands-on Jon's corporate check register and wrote himself three separate drafts totaling thirty-two thousand dollars. Apparently, that's how much he needed for his scheme and to buy all the equipment."

"But Jon caught him and sent him back to jail," Connor finished for her.

"Exactly. And I never heard my husband mention him again, not while we were married and certainly not after we were divorced."

"Yet there he was the other day when you were getting out of the hotel elevator."

"There he was," she agreed. "I don't think he recognized me, but I sure remembered him. You don't soon forget the dog pile that threatens your family."

Connor said nothing for a minute as he let this all settle in. Then he asked, "So do you have any idea what the connection between them was? Or who?"

"No one specific," she replied, shaking her head again. "But when I saw Jon up in Myrtle Beach he seemed ... different."

"Different in what way?"

"Changed. Drained. Tired. In the past, whenever we got together—which wasn't all that often, let me assure you—he had this spark. Enthusiasm. Vigor. And I don't just mean in bed, either. But this last time he just seemed … beaten."

At that moment Connor's phone pinged in his pocket, telling him he had a text. Probably from Danielle, checking in to see when he'd be done with his errand. "Did he look physically ill, anything like that?"

"Not really. Jon was always worried about his health, I guess because his father died from such a horrible disease. But he would have mentioned it to me, if that was it." She thought a moment more, then added, "I think something else was bothering him."

"Money?"

"I can't imagine Jon ever having money problems," she said. "He was too careful to ever lose anything that could cripple him financially. Even when he bet on the horses, like the time we went to the Derby, he only bought two-dollar tickets."

The right side of Connor's brain flashed on Mary Alice Benton, complete with her platinum hair and dark glasses and the blue clutch purse. "Do you know anyone who could've taken advantage of him?" he asked her.

"There were always people trying to take advantage of him, but he was too shrewd to fall for any of that," she replied.

"Any idea where he went after his last marriage fell apart?" Connor asked, wondering how much she and Jon actually talked.

"Just that Jon said he'd been seeing someone, and it didn't work out," Linda Loris told him. "Which is what I'd already figured, since the only time he'd ever call to get together was when he was between friendships. That's what he called them: *friendships.*"

"Can you think of anyone who might know what your husband was involved with? Someone like a lawyer, maybe a business partner?"

A frown darkened her face and she said, "Jon had a whole team of lawyers, and good luck getting close to any of them. They're all assholes, especially the one who handled his end of our divorce. Same thing with his partners. Ex-partners, actually, since Jon went out on his own about seven, eight years ago."

"What about the agent who wrote your insurance policy?"

She scowled at that, the insurance still obviously a sore spot because of the suicide clause. "Ollie Hunter. Yeah, he might know. I'll have to look for his number, but I'll get it to you." She flashed him a hopeful look then, and added, "Does this mean you're starting to believe my husband was murdered?"

Connor's phone pinged again: another text. "Don't get your hopes up," he said to her. "All this means is your husband is still dead, and how he got that way is still anybody's guess."

Chapter 14

"Did you see how many people are out there?" Danielle said as she gave Connor a quick peck on the lips. "This is going to be so much fun!"

"Fun?" He stared at her as if she were out of her mind. "We've never played a gig like this before."

"Neither did Bob Marley, not in the beginning."

"The Jamaican Jerks are not Bob Marley," Connor said. "Why do you think we're called the *Jerks?*"

They were standing backstage at the Lowcountry Rockin' Blues Festival, which actually was an excuse for a lot of local bands to get together, jam, and make a little music, while several thousand folks of all ages and backgrounds ate barbecue and oysters and ribs, and drank beer. Lots and lots of beer. The fact that the musical acts on the bill riffed on rock, country, jazz, bluegrass, soul, and yes, even some blues, gave great testimony to the multicultural heritage of the central Carolina coast. And the fact that it all came together on the grounds of an old rice plantation provided further proof that, at least when it came to music, color was blind and history was tone deaf.

As far as definitions went, "backstage" was an overstatement. It actually was an area to the rear of the performing area, sectioned off from the crowd by orange construction fencing and two large sound trucks that seemed to stand guard on both sides of the stage. Fortunately, the weather front that had been predicted for the evening seemed to have stalled a few miles to the west, holding off the deluge that would have turned the entire festival into hog slop.

"I hope you'll still speak to me when this is all over," she said, a mischievous spark in her eyes. "All those groupies and big-time re-cord guys hanging around."

"You can always throw your bra up on the stage," he replied, going with it.

"I'll have you know I'm not wearing a bra," she told him, doing one quick spin to show him her bare back.

"Dressing room's right over there," he said, cocking his head toward a trailer. "We might have just enough time for a quickie—"

"Down boy, down," she giggled. "There'll be plenty of time after the show."

Someone had given Connor a beer when they arrived, and he took a long swallow now before it lost its cold edge. Up on the stage a jazz trio from Atlanta was performing a smoky-fusion rendition of Johnny Mercer's "Moon River," which then segued almost effortlessly into Elvis' "Blue Moon." The audience applauded at the seamless transition, and Connor took another sip.

"What if the audience doesn't like reggae?" he asked.

"Everyone likes reggae," Danielle told him.

"Not your husband," Connor reminded her. "At least that's what you told me."

"And he's not here, is he?" she pointed out, the not-so-subtle message in her voice saying, *let's leave him out of this, if that's all right with you.*

An hour later it was all over. The Jamaican Jerks made it through six songs and one encore, their usual rendition of Bob Marley's "Three Little Birds," which most of the crowd knew as "Everything's Gonna Be Alright." The applause continued until Connor and his band mates were well offstage, where there were no groupies or artist managers or record label guys waiting in the wings. But there was a table of food and beer and wine, so they dug in, giving each other high-fives just for making it through. No one would be signing them to million-dollar contracts, but they'd had two thousand music fans on their feet, and that was enough for the Jerks.

"I don't think I'd like the whole groupie thing," Connor told Danielle, maybe an hour after they left the festival. The rain had held off until halfway through the Bar-Kays' set of soul funk, and Connor had made the executive decision to rescue the Camaro before the parking lot turned into a sea of mud. Now it was parked in the drive-way of his apartment on Sullivan's Island, and Connor and Danielle were nested in the darkness of his bedroom, the only music being that of the thick raindrops pelting the grass out in the marsh. "You're plenty enough woman for me."

"You say that now," she said, her voice almost a purr. "You'll change your tune when all those room keys start flying up on the stage." "Not a lot of those tonight," he pointed out.

She said nothing to that, just gently nibbled his neck and made that gentle purring sound again. They lay that way for a long time— the rain and the darkness and the warmth of their own bodies—and then she said, "Tell me about my sister."

Her words snapped like a rubber band in the back of his mind, and he asked, "What about her?"

"You know what," Danielle said. "Did you bring her here?"

It was a loaded question, and now certainly did not seem the time to go into all that. Connor had met Danielle only after her sister Rebecca had been murdered, and the police had considered Connor a potential suspect in her death because of a fling he'd had with her shortly before the night she'd been found dead in the gutter. Danielle was fully aware of their history when she met him, so he knew the questions would be there, lingering on some back burner in her mind. He actually was surprised she had held off for so long in getting around to asking them.

"A gentleman never tells," he replied. "But I can honestly say that never in my life have I experienced anything so completely … complete as I have with you."

"Hmmm," her throat rumbled, a totally different kind of purr. "Good answer. How 'bout the other thing? Did you ever bring her here?"

"The answer is *no*," he said. Not one hundred percent truthful, but it was the sort of answer he would have wanted to hear. In fact, he had questions of his own, things like "does your husband know where you are" and "has he moved out?" but Danielle seemed to be doing just fine asking the awkward questions right now. He could save his for later.

"But definitely at her place?" Danielle asked. "Process of elimination," Connor conceded.

"Then we'll just stick to right here and right now, if that's okay with you."

"Sounds like a plan," he told her.

"In that case, I think we need to go over those plans again," she said. There was that purr in her voice again, low and subtle. The rain had passed.

"Now might be a good time," he suggested.

"My thinking exactly."

The next morning, they had breakfast at a small restaurant called Sea Biscuit on the Isle of Palms, the "tree hugger" yogurt and granola mix for her and biscuits and gravy for him. Plus, plenty of coffee, good and strong. When they were on their way back to the car Danielle announced she had to go over to James Island to sort through the rest of her sister's belongings before the landlord put them out on the front lawn. She only had until the end of the month, which was coming up fast, but Connor thought he detected a subtle excuse to have some time alone.

It was when he turned the key in the ignition that she added, "And I have to go back home tomorrow morning."

Connor had made a point of not asking Danielle how long she planned to be up in Charleston, mostly because he didn't want to know the answer. And now that he did know it, he was just as full of questions as she had been the night before.

"Will he be there?" he asked. "Your husband?"

"His name is Richard. And he'll probably be with … Tinkerbell. At least until he grows tired of her."

"Which means—"

"Which means I'll be sleeping alone."

"And what happens when Peter Pan does get tired of Tinkerbell?"

"Maybe he'll grow up and become a man, realize he's made his own bed and has to sleep in it," Danielle said. "Except he won't be able to, 'cause the first thing I'm going to do when I get home is burn it."

She was wearing a thin straw hat, holding it to the top of her head to keep it from blowing away. They were driving on the bridge over the breach between Isle of Palms and Sullivan's Island, the watery cut through which the Confederate Navy launched the Hunley submersible during the Civil War. Or, as it was commonly referred to in

South Carolina, the "war of northern aggression."

"He's going to want you back," Connor said, talking more to the wind than to Danielle.

"Tough shit."

"He'll beg and plead."

"You think so?"

"All men do."

"Would you?" she asked him.

"I'd never be so stupid to lose you in the first place."

She turned and looked at him then, and said, "No, I don't believe you would."

When Connor arrived at The Plant he checked his email and found a message from Linda Loris, who had the contact info for Ollie Hunter. He was the insurance agent who had sold Jon Hilborn the term life policy naming her as beneficiary, and she provided Connor with numbers for his office in Summerville, his home in Goose Creek, and a cell number, which could have been just about anywhere. Connor preferred not to disturb the man on a Sunday, but since insurance agents are on the job twenty-four seven, he figured one quick call wouldn't be much of a disruption.

Hunter answered on the fourth ring and quickly said "I'm afraid I can't talk about that" when Connor explained who he was and why he was calling.

"This'll only take a minute," Connor pushed. "I'm just looking for information on the Hilborn policy, and then I'll be done."

"Mr. Hilborn is dead," Hunter explained, as if this were news to anyone.

"Good thing you sell life insurance."

"It is my understanding that he took his own life," the insurance agent said. "Which means any such policy is null and void."

Connor thought he heard water lapping on the other end, maybe slapping against pilings or possibly the hull of a boat. "Don't they mean the same thing?" he asked.

"Excuse me?"

"Null and void. They pretty much mean the same thing. Anyway, it's starting to look like Hilborn did not, as you say, take his own life. In fact, there's a good chance someone killed him."

"That's news to me." Hunter sounded preoccupied, even impatient. "The medical examiner's report is quite clear in stating that his death was self-inflicted. Now, if you don't mind—"

"Would you happen to know if Mr. Hilborn was having money problems?" Connor asked him.

"Look, Mr. Connor. I don't know what this is all about, why you're calling, but I can't answer that. I was not involved with his personal finances in any way."

"But you would know if he stopped paying the premiums, right?"

"That's a private matter—"

"C'mon, Mr. Hunter. I'm sure Jon Hilborn had written more than one policy with your firm. Had he stopped paying his premiums?"

There was a long silence after that, followed by Ollie Hunter saying, in a slow and deliberate voice, "You're right. Jon had a number of policies with my company. As for whether he was paid up on any of them, all I can tell you is to go to hell."

Connor started to say something smart-assed, but Hunter had already hung up by the time he figured out what to say.

Before Connor had called Ollie Hunter, he had placed a call to Caitlin Thomas at Citadel Security, and it took her nine minutes to get back to him with the information he had requested.

It turned out that the small shack out in Walterboro where Bodean Barr had been shot-gunned was located on a large tract of land owned by ACE Property and Development, LLC. That particular parcel consisted of eighty-seven acres of woods and wetlands set on both sides of the Ashepoo River, and was only one of more than a dozen tracts of similar size that the company owned in that area of the state. The company itself was named for the three rivers that emptied into South Carolina's ACE Basin: the Ashepoo, the Edisto, and the Combahee. Connor thought it almost sounded like the words to an old folk song about trains.

A quick Google search of ACE Property and Development turned up hundreds of hits, the first one being the website for the company itself. In the "about" section Connor found that the company had been formed about ten years ago and was based in Orangeburg, South Carolina. Shortly after that the two primary partners—Mason Sanders and Miller Mundy—began acquiring undeveloped properties with the ultimate goal of "improving God's own work for the betterment of human progress." Whatever that meant. The website offered examples of this progress in other corporate projects, including one of the largest "big box shopping bonanzas in the South," located outside Augusta, Georgia, and a "family-oriented entertainment extravaganza" that had been built near Raleigh, North Carolina. There was no mention of why the company had acquired over seven hundred acres of wetlands along three of South Carolina's most pristine rivers, but Connor made an educated guess.

A tab with the notation "leadership" provided short bios on Mr. Sanders and Mr. Mundy, the company's co-founders. Both were in their early sixties and their write-ups were accompanied by headshots. Judging from his jowls and gray hair and sagging eyes, Sanders appeared to be the older of the two. He possessed a degree in economics from the University of North Carolina, and an MBA from Duke. He had established a long career in land development, and over the decades had built a number of commercial shopping centers and residential complexes throughout the South.

Miller Mundy still had a bit of brown at the temples, possibly applied every few weeks as needed, and had a bit of a smile, but very thin lips. His bio said he was a proud Georgia Bulldog, with a degree in marketing, and a Master's Degree in Economics from South Carolina. Most of his life had been spent working in the real estate industry, first as an agent negotiating commercial acquisitions, and later facilitating the sale of land to retail developers.

Connor was about to think he was chasing a wild horse when his eyes found their way to the bottom of the webpage. There he found the photo of an attractive woman with blond hair who appeared to be in her mid-forties. Her title was listed as Vice President of Marketing and Communications, and she had earned a bachelor's degree in, of all things, soils and sustainable crop systems at Clemson University.

Nothing outwardly peculiar about that, Connor figured, since it probably was what a lot of future farmers of America majored in. But what was odd—in fact, he almost missed it—was her hyphenated name: Marjorie Barr-Chambers.

The bio revealed that Marjorie was a South Carolina native, born to a family of farmers and raised in the town of Aiken.

After graduating from Clemson, she had found work in the fertilizer industry, serving as a marketing representative for a major supplier of "high-yield technologies and crop protection systems." She eventually worked her way into corporate marketing, experience she took with her when she moved to ACE. The blurb ended with the sentence, "Marjorie is married to Richard Chambers, an attorney, and is the proud mother of a daughter, who at age six is already scoring goals for her soccer team."

Which, to Connor, meant that Marjorie Barr-Chambers' maiden name had been Barr, a family of farmers from whose collective loins a reprobate and dirtbag named Bodean had sprung. And who had been living in a small shack on a piece of property owned and managed by ACE Property and Development. Connor took another look at Marjorie's photo, then realized he had nothing to compare her features to, since the only time he had come face-to face with Bodean Barr was after the man's head had been blown off.

Another Google search solved that problem. The *Charleston Post & Courier* website had run a story about the dead man found out in Walterboro, and had published a file photo of him that appeared to be a mug shot from one of his previous encounters with the law. Mug shots never are photographed during anyone's finest hour, and this certainly could be said for Bo Barr. His long dirty-blond hair had taken on the style of a tangle of kudzu, and he was sporting two black eyes. His nose was red, and he had a bad prison tattoo on the side of his neck. But as Connor studied the photo he found more than a few similarities between this man and Marjorie Barr-Chambers. Same brown eyes, same chin, even the same ears, except it looked like one of Bo's had been cut during a long-ago fight.

The article cinched the deal, ending with a short paragraph noting that "Mr. Barr is survived by his brother, Nathan Barr, of Aiken, SC, and a sister, Marjorie Chambers, of Orangeburg, SC."

The "contact" section of the ACE website offered both the corporate address and phone number, both of which Connor entered into his phone. He considered calling right then, but knew the office would be closed on a Sunday. Besides, Danielle would be almost done sorting through her sister's things and Connor didn't want to waste another second of the afternoon chasing the Jon Hilborn thing, at least not today. If Danielle was heading back to Orlando in the morning, every remaining second of this day and night belonged to her.

And as it turned out, not one of them was wasted.

Chapter 15

There's one non-stop between Charleston and Orlando, a Delta flight that leaves at seven-fifty-five in the morning. That was the one Danielle had booked, and in order to return the rental car and still check in through security, she was on the road at six thirty. Anything later than that and she ran the risk of being delayed by the swing bridge when it opened, which would add a good ten minutes to her trip.

"Is this where it gets awkward?" he asked her as she came out of the bedroom, pulling her roll-aboard behind her. He had fixed a pot of coffee and had set a cup for her on the small counter that separated the kitchen from the living room.

"Why start now?" Danielle replied with a half-smile.

"I don't like saying 'goodbye,'" he told her. "Never been good at it."

"I don't want you to be," she said. "I want it to be as tough as it can be, for both of us."

"That means you're coming back?"

"Yes ... and no."

Connor shot her a quizzical look. "Meaning what?"

"It means I'm finished with my sister's place, so I don't have to come back for that. But yes, I am coming back."

"So where does the 'no' come in?"

"It means I'll come back here only after you come to visit me in Orlando."

Connor took a sip of coffee and silently soaked her in. Every bit of her, from her black low-heeled shoes to her thin legs, nice ass, great curves all the way up to her beautiful lips and bedroom eyes. "How 'bout right now?" he suggested.

"'Now' could get a bit tricky," she said, for reasons she didn't need to go into. "Give it a week or two?"

"I think I can manage that," he told her. He came around the counter and moved close to her. Eye to eye, just inches apart. Close enough to see her, just distant enough to lose focus. Then he leaned in and gave her a kiss, solid and real and raw, enough to make her shudder before he pulled away.

She sighed, then let her eyes slip to her wristwatch. "I have to go."

"I know. I'll walk you out to your car."

Which only prolonged the inevitable, but he didn't hear a word of protest. Just the opposite, in fact. He kissed her one more time as she was sliding in behind the wheel, and then she said, "Can I keep it for a while?"

"Keep what?"

"Your heart." She closed the door, then rolled down the window and looked out at him. "Remember what you said in that email you sent me, just a little over a week ago?"

"Yeah … sorry about that. I'm not much of a writer."

"I thought it was sweet. And as I recall, you said something about really missing me, and how all your words were coming directly from your heart."

"Something like that, yeah," he said with an embarrassed laugh.

"And I wrote back, and I think this is pretty much word-for-word, 'if it's all the same to you, I think I'll hang on to your heart for a while.' So … may I keep it?"

"As long as you keep it warm and safe and dry," he agreed. "I have no use for it as long as you're not here."

"See you soon?"

"That's way too long, but it'll have to do," he said, and then he watched her drive away.

Despite the fact that Bodean Barr had been brutally murdered, Marjorie Barr-Chambers had come into her office that morning, which told Connor that Bo either wasn't actually her brother, or she wasn't very troubled by his death.

Either way, she evidently had told the receptionist at ACE Property & Development that she was busy all morning, a message Connor didn't want to hear, since he had driven all the way up to Orangeburg. "You need an appointment," the young woman behind the desk told him. She looked to be no more than twenty, maybe twenty-two, African American, with short curly hair and large black eyes. A name plate on the desk said her name was Leanna Hendrix, and a large styrofoam cup had a smudge of ruddy lipstick on the plastic to-go lid.

"Can't you make an exception, since I'm already here?" he asked, almost pleading with her. "It was a long drive."

"I'm sorry, but it's company policy," she apologized, offering him a closed-mouth smile. Then she looked at the tattoos on his arms and said, "Lordy, all that ink must have hurt."

Connor lifted his shoulder in a shrug and said, "I didn't get 'em all at once. You're sure Ms. Barr-Chambers can't spare just five minutes?"

"First, it's just Chambers. She dropped the Barr part a year ago.

And second, you really do need an appointment."

Connor stood there and stared at her, but he could tell Leanna Hendrix wasn't going to budge. Rules were rules, and policy was policy.

"All right," he finally said, then turned and pushed his way back outside into the building Carolina steam. It wasn't even June yet, but the weather reports were calling for temperatures in the low nineties again. With humidity to match.

ACE Property & Development was located at the end of an aging strip mall that was anchored by one of the Kmart stores that hadn't shut its doors in the latest wave of closings. A hunting supply store was located next to it, and the words "Super Blow-Out Gun Sale" were painted in large letters on the plate glass window. Further down the line of storefronts was a coffee shop, not one of the big chains but a place that looked family-owned. The sign overhead simply read "Carolina Coffee."

Connor walked over to where he had parked the Camaro and started to unlock the door, then stopped as a thought came to him. He crossed the sticky asphalt to the coffee shop and went inside, where he ordered two large coffees with creamer and sweetener to go. He paid the young woman at the cash register, emptied his pocket change into the tip jar, then went back outside and marched down the sidewalk to the property company's reflectorized front door. He used his hip to open it, and pushed his way back inside.

"I told you, you need to make an appointment," the young receptionist repeated as he approached her desk, a cup of coffee in each hand.

"Everyone needs a coffee break," Connor explained to her, offering a polite smile as he set the cups down. "One for you and one for Ms. Chambers."

Her eyes traveled from Connor's face to the coffee, then back. "Bribery works every time," she said with a grin as she pulled one of the cups closer to her. "I'll see what I can do."

Marjorie Chambers, without the Barr-hyphen, did not drink coffee, but she was suitably impressed by Connor's persistence to grant him five minutes of her valuable time. She almost balked when he told her he was there to discuss her brother Bodean, but then she uttered an exasperated sigh and said, "Have a seat."

Her office was large enough to be equipped not only with a desk, chair, and computer extension, but also a grouping of three chrome and vinyl chairs situated around a table in one corner. It was cheap but functional, the sort of furniture that comes from Office Depot or, in this case, the Habitat for Humanity Restore. The floor was covered with stacks of folders and binders, and Connor had to use care when pulling out his chair to make sure he didn't knock over one of the piles.

"I'm sorry about your brother," he began as he drank from the cup of coffee that had been intended for Marjorie Chambers. "I'm sure the news of his death must have been a shock."

She shook her head and said, "Not really. In fact, I'm surprised he made it this long. What's your interest in him?"

"I was the person who found him," Connor explained. Since the cops had already shown up at his apartment and questioned him about Bo Barr's death, there was no reason to keep it a secret.

"I see," she said, although it was clear she didn't. Her eyes surveyed the tats on his arms and neck, and then she added, "You were on TV.

I saw you. That dead Congressman thing." "Guilty as charged," he admitted.

"Were you a friend of Bodean's?"

Implied guilt by association. "I'd never met him," Connor told her.

"But I went to his place hoping to talk to him."

"What about?"

"About another man who's also dead," Connor explained. "An investment banker named Jon Hilborn."

If she recognized the name her eyes didn't betray her. "Why would my brother know anything about an investment banker?" she asked.

"Exactly what I wanted to know," he said. "But I didn't get the chance."

"I heard he was shot in the head." She said it very matter-of-factly, no remorse or sadness in her voice.

"Close enough. From what I could tell, someone came knocking at his front door and surprised him."

"That would be Bo," Marjorie said, her voice wistful and distant. "What's your interest in him?"

"Just something I'm working on," Connor replied, trying to stay vague. "Did you know he was living on property owned by your employer? ACE."

Her head went through the motions of a nod, and she said, "It was family land. My father's, actually, and his father's before that. When my folks were killed—car accident—we were forced to sell it. Bo hated the idea, said we needed to hang on to it in the name of the Barr family and the pride of the Confederacy, or some such shit. But the taxes and insurance were too steep, so it had to go. I figured if we sold it to ACE it wouldn't be developed for years, and Bo could forget about the whole thing."

"Did he? Forget about it?"

"He was living there, wasn't he?" Marjorie Chambers said. "As long as no one made him get out of the house, he probably figured it still belonged to family. And you still haven't told me why you're interested in my little brother."

"Loose ends. This investment banker I mentioned. It appears your brother may have been the last person to see him alive."

Her eyes instantly turned dark and she fiercely gripped the edge of the table with both hands. "Are you saying my brother had something to do with that man's death?" she snapped.

"Not at all," Connor quickly assured her. "The medical examiner said Hilborn took his own life, and that's good enough for me. I'm just trying to figure out why, and I thought Bodean might have known something."

Marjorie Chambers seemed to relax, just a bit. "And now we'll never know."

Connor liked the "we" part of what she was saying, possibly implying that she was might be softening to his questions about her brother. He really didn't want to be kicked out on his ass.

"You remember the last time you saw him?"

"Not for months," she replied without having to think. "We traveled on separate paths, and it seemed like his always led to problems. I don't know what he did for money, or who his friends were. Nor did I care. I know that may sound cruel, but Bo was trouble with a capital 'T' ever since I remember. Just about killed Mom and Dad, and probably would've, 'cept a drunk driver got them first."

This was the second time she had mentioned the car accident, so Connor said, "I'm very sorry about that. Was it recent?"

She shook her head. "It's been about a year and a half now. They were coming home from Augusta, visiting friends. Both of them were killed instantly. Anyway, their deaths put Bo into a real tailspin. He'd been there before, the downward spiral thing, but this one seemed to hit him hardest."

"I bet it did," Connor observed. "He ever mention any friends. People he hung out with?"

"Like I said, we didn't really talk much. But there was one guy, a real scumbag if you want my two cents. Leland, I think his name was. Don't remember his last name. Had a bald head, with prison tats etched into it. Not like yours, but real nasty stuff. Swastikas, pentagrams, SS lightning bolts, the number four-nineteen—"

"Waco and the Oklahoma City bombing," Connor told her.

"And the Covenant siege in Arkansas," Marjorie Chambers said. "Anyway, this was a few years ago, and he had a big influence on Bo. Who was easily influenced to begin with, given that he was about as sharp as a brick. Anyway, Leland was convinced the blacks and Muslims and Jews were going to take over the world, so he was on this survival kick. Even spent some time out in Idaho at a training camp, getting prepared. When he came back he hooked Bo on the idea of selling survival kits and underground bunkers for when the second holocaust comes, although it was pretty damned clear from their rhetoric they didn't believe in the first one."

This seemed to jibe with what Linda Loris had told Connor on Saturday, so he said, "And your brother tried to raise some money for the cause."

"He did," she agreed. "I didn't know how, and I didn't want to know. But whatever Bo tried, it failed. So, he went and forged some checks, and just like that he was back in jail. And Leland, he just up and disappeared. You think maybe he's the chickenshit bastard blew my brother's head off?"

"Looked to me it was someone he knew. Probably trusted. A friend."

"Worst kind of enemy there is."

Chapter 16

Back in the car Connor punched the speed dial number for Citadel Security just as a squirrel tried to play chicken with the Camaro. Connor swerved sharply around the suicidal critter just as his call was answered.

"Tat Man!" Caitlin said, her voice almost a yelp. "Heard you had quite a weekend of adventure—"

"Just what did you hear, and how did you hear it?" Connor asked warily.

"Citadel hears whatever there is to hear," she reminded him with a giggle. "We're the big brother you never had."

"How did you know I never had ... oh, never mind," he said.

"So ... you've got another number you want me to run?"

"I'm that obvious?"

"Like a hickey on a schoolgirl's neck. Give it to me."

Connor gave it to her, beginning with the local Charleston area code. There was a short silence on the other end, and then Caitlin came back on the line.

"That's the number for Kat Rattigan," she said. "Runs her own P.I. shop. Mostly does background checks. Citadel feeds her some business now and then. Why are you backgrounding her?"

It was really none of Caitlin's business why Connor was looking for her address, but since they ostensibly worked for the same company he said, "She called me the other day, and I need to follow up on something. Face-to-face is better than the phone any day."

"So, when are you going to drop by Citadel, Mr. Tat Man?" she asked him.

"Soon as you tell me how you know about my body art."

"You know the answer to that," Caitlin said, her voice almost a squeak. "Here at Citadel it's our business to know everything about everyone. Like the NSA, it's what we do."

The address turned out to be for a dump of a place out near the closed Navy Base, an area where the federal government and the city of Charleston were pushing hard to finish what the Pentagon had begun. Internet start-ups, graphic arts companies, and even a motion picture company leased office space out here, but in the case of K.R. Investigators, the regentrification thing didn't appear to be working. Then again, Connor knew the old adage about judging a book from its cover, so he pulled the Camaro into the parking lot and cut the engine.

Kat Rattigan's detective agency occupied the smaller half of an office duplex that squatted at the far end of a partially paved lot that had seen better years. Situated next door was a joint that looked like a hundred other neighborhood taverns Connor had seen, except for the large sign fastened to the roof. There was just one word on it: "Billiards." The parking area was pocked with deep sinkholes, and chunks of pavement had crumbled from the ravages of time. There were no marked spaces, so he pulled in next to the black Porsche he recognized from the investigator's visit to The Plant last week.

Connor sat behind the wheel for a moment, assessing the irony here, the apparent squalor of the storefront and the shiny Boxster parked alone in front of it. Either business was very good or very bad, or something else was at play here.

He got out of the car and walked up to the door that had K.R. Investigators painted on it in neat block letters. It was locked, but beside it was a doorbell with a plastic sign that read: "Please Buzz For Service." Connor rang the buzzer, then waited in the searing Carolina sun for someone to answer. When that didn't happen he rang it again, laying on the button until finally he heard a voice through the tinny speaker.

"All right, already—hold your horses." It was a woman's voice, matching the one Connor remembered from Kat Rattigan's visit to

Palmetto BioClean last week. "Who is it?"

He lowered his mouth to the tiny hole he figured was the microphone. "This is Jack Connor," he said, tugging on the damp bill of his River Dogs baseball cap. "You came by my office the other day, had some questions about Jon Hilborn."

"Right, right, Mr. Connor. I'll buzz you in."

Five seconds later Connor found himself in Kat Rattigan's office suite defined by white walls, industrial carpeting pocked by coffee stains and mildew. Brown moisture clouded the drop ceiling and plastic reflector film was peeling back at the edges of the mirrored windows. The outer room, the one he entered when the lock had buzzed, held a metal desk with a computer on it, a few chairs for clients, a wall of shelves stuffed with files, framed certificates and licenses hanging on another wall. No one was sitting behind the desk, but a handbag on the floor suggested that whoever belonged to it was somewhere close by. Probably the ladies room, if there was one.

Then a door on the far side of the empty desk opened and Kat Rattigan stood there, white jeans with a bright pink top, auburn hair cut just below the ears, lipstick the color of white zinfandel. Silver earrings, not too dangly, silver watch on her left wrist, no ring on the finger that counted. Connor mentally slapped himself, since it had only been a few hours since Danielle had driven herself to the airport.

Bad dog, he told himself.

"Mr. Connor ... good to see you again," she said, extending a hand to him. "Belinda had to step out for a moment, otherwise she would have let you in. Why don't we meet in my inner sanctum?"

Connor politely shook her hand, then followed her through another doorway, where he found more white walls, a metal desk identical to the one in the outer office, a large computer set squarely on top. Mountains of files reached from the floor almost to the ceiling, and one wall was stacked high with books. Set into the opposite wall was a door with a laminated sign that read "No Exit."

"Please, sit down," Kat invited him, indicating the chair in front of her desk. "Just put those folders on the floor."

Connor did as he was instructed and took a seat. He glanced around at what appeared to be utter chaos, pretty much the way his ex-wife had kept their apartment up in Lansing.

"Sorry for dropping in like this, but I really was in the neighborhood and … well, I had a couple of questions. Thought I could steal a minute of your time."

Kat slipped into her desk chair, then opened a small fridge that Connor hadn't noticed until now. "You look like you could use some water." She took out two plastic bottles and handed him one before he could answer.

"Thank you." He twisted the cap off and drank almost half of it in one gulp. "Damn, but it's hot out there."

"It appears we skipped June and July and went straight into August." She took a sip of her own water and seemed to settle into her chair. "You're not from around here, are you? Originally, I mean."

"It shows that bad?"

"Only when you talk," she said. "If I were to guess, I'd say upper Midwest. Ohio, maybe Michigan."

"You're good," Connor told her. "Lansing, born and raised. Just moved down here last fall. And again, I want to thank you for seeing me like this. No warning."

"We're even, then. For me just showing up last week. The thing is, I usually don't do this. Meet with clients face-to-face."

"I'm not a client," he reminded her. The straight-back chair in which he was sitting was metal with a worn vinyl seat, designed to make people anxious to leave as soon as they sat down. If that was its purpose, it was working. His ass was already hurting, but he wasn't about to let her know that. "And I kinda figured it, anyway, since there's no conference room, nothing like that."

She nodded. "Most of my clients are just voices on the phone or emails in my inbox. Generally, what I do is background checks. Employment, usually, but I'm seeing more and more women checking up on their boyfriends and fiancés and husbands. And most of that is done online these days. You just have to know where to look."

"Then why did you take this case? You already knew from your client that her husband was dead." Connor just put it out there, making a huge assumption that was based on nothing but pure bullshit.

"Whoa!" she said, raising both hands in protest. "I never told you who hired me to look into this—"

"No, you didn't. But I figured whoever hired you probably has the most to lose. Ex-wife number four already lost her house and her neighborhood and probably whatever alimony her husband was paying. But then he goes and sets up shop with another woman just weeks after the divorce is final … well, that really had to hurt."

Kat Rattigan fixed him with her eyes, but they were way too blue to be menacing. "I am not going to talk about my client." She tapped a nervous finger on her desk. "You said you had some questions. If that's the truth, ask them. Otherwise, you can leave now."

He hesitated only a second, showing her that he meant business, then asked, "Does the name Bodean Barr mean anything to you?"

"Should it?"

Connor figured her response was either rhetorical or a tactical stall. "How about Mary Alice Benton?"

This name brought an instant reaction, one of apprehension and alarm. "How do you know her?" Rattigan asked.

"She popped in the other day, just like you," he explained. "In fact, a lot of people seem to be crawling out of the woodwork because of

Jon Hilborn's death."

"What did she want?"

"Ms. Benton did not have particularly kind things to say about Hilborn," Connor said. "As I'm sure your client doesn't, either." "My client stays out of this," she cautioned him.

"Of course, she does. I don't even know her name. But you might want to ask her if she ever met someone named Bodean Barr."

She tilted her chair back and laced her fingers together. "The name has already come up, and not in a good way. My client thinks someone may have been blackmailing Mr. Hilborn."

Connor's brain flashed for a second on the murder he had recently solved, the scam a young hooker and her narcissistic boyfriend had been running on rich businessmen. "What would give her that idea?"

"Oh, I don't know," Rattigan said, almost too wistfully. "Maybe the fact that their bank accounts dried up, and he started selling their assets. Bonds, mutual funds, stocks. Even pieces of their art collection began to disappear from the house."

"This would be the house in Raven's Run," Connor said, for no other reason but to let her know that he was already in the loop. "The one that's now in foreclosure."

She studied him over her laced fingers, her thumbs battling each other like the Rock 'Em-Sock 'Em robots he played with when he was a kid. "Why do you think Bodean Barr is involved?" she finally asked.

Connor spun for her the brief version of Barr's survivalist scheme and how he tried to get Hilborn to invest in it. "That was a long time ago, long before your client came into the picture. Sorry. But I get the sense that if Bodean Barr was anything, he was like a mosquito. Persistent and annoying as hell. And someone took a swipe at him last week, smacked him real hard."

"I heard about that. They identified him positively?"

"Fingerprints," he told her. "Look, Ms. Rattigan. If your client thinks someone killed her ex-husband, she's got to have an idea who it was. Or at least why."

"Keeping my client's possible relationship to Mr. Hilborn out of this, what makes you say so?"

"Wives tend to know what their husbands are up to."

"Speaking from experience now, are we?" she prodded him.

"Mine watched too much Jerry Springer," Connor said. "Put too many nasty thoughts in her head. But if your client happened to notice money disappearing from accounts and paintings flying off the walls, she damned well suspected what was going on. And I think you do, too."

Detective Rattigan crossed her arms and leaned forward over her desk. "What makes you say that?"

"Because I think your client contacted you before her husband died," Connor said, cocking his head to reflect a point in the past. "When she first suspected something was wrong, she hired you to do a background check on him. Now that he's dead, she contacted you again."

Her left hand went for a shiny ball that was resting near the phone on her desk, black and white with the number "8" painted on in. Probably from the pool hall next door. She began rolling it back and forth between her hands on the flat surface.

"What I can tell you is that I'm inclined to agree with my client," she finally said. "I think someone was blackmailing him, for a large sum of money. Eventually he ran out of cash, so he took off."

"And Mary Alice Benton took him in," Connor finished for her.

"Something like that, yes," Rattigan said. "The blackmailer probably sent some muscle that tracked him down to the hotel in Myrtle Beach, demanded more money for his silence. And when Hilborn couldn't pay up, he was thrown over the railing."

"After the blackmailer slashed his wrists."

She stared at him a moment, then said, "It's a working theory."

The thing was, there was a grain of validity to her theory. Linda Loris had already explained she had seen the boatload of cash in her ex-husband's room, and not long after that she had run into Bodean Barr as he was getting into the elevator. Even with more than four hundred rooms in the hotel, there was no question he was on his way up to Suite 1701 to visit the man she had just left.

"So, who was blackmailing him?"

Kat Rattigan shook her head ruefully and said, "Don't have a clue. Everything I've pulled up on the computer points to an upstanding citizen and businessman, if not necessarily a good husband."

"Did he have a record?"

"Nothing, not even a parking ticket. There was one warning from the FAA last year for failing to file a flight plan, but other than that he was as clean as a boy scout."

Connor had been a boy scout and knew a couple of them who turned out to be pretty dirty. One of them was in jail up in Michigan doing time for attempting to kill a cop. But Kat Rattigan had intended it as a metaphor, and he got the meaning.

"Everyone has a back story," he said. "Find Hilborn's, and we find his killer."

Chapter 17

The fact was, for every reason someone would have wanted to kill Jon Hilborn, there were an equal and opposite number of reasons for him to want to kill himself.

Connor played it out in his head as he drove back across the bridge to Mount Pleasant, realized it sounded like one of Miss Benson's laws of physics—the one that talked about equal and opposite reactions. The way he looked at it, if someone was running a blackmail scam, and if Hilborn had run out of money, the blackmailer could have made good on some sort of physical threat and killed him. Or had him killed.

But the opposite theory that carried equal weight went something like this: if Hilborn had drained his bank accounts to keep this hypothetical blackmailer off his back, he also might have gone so far as to clean out the Andrew Barron Hilborn Foundation in the process. And then when the money ran out he could have felt so desperate and helpless that he decided the only way out was to end it all. So, he checked into a luxury suite that he never intended to pay for, called in his ex-wife for one last little roll in the sack, then ran a warm bath and slit his wrists. The fact that Hilborn had messed up his first attempt didn't matter, since there was a Plan B right out there on his balcony.

But three things didn't add up in that scenario, which led Connor to believe Jordan James might have been right. The first was that Linda Loris had seen the two suitcases loaded with cash. Lots of cash. The second thing was that five hundred thousand of it might have belonged to Mr. James. And the third thing was Bodean Barr, who somehow figured into all of this.

There was something else that bothered him about all of these scenarios, one that a quick conversation might clear up. He took out his phone, used one hand to punch in a number while he kept the other hand on the wheel.

Mary Alice Benton answered her phone on the third ring. Her voice sounded hushed, and she didn't seem to recognize Connor's name when he told her who was calling.

"You came down to Mount Pleasant last Saturday, stopped by my place of business for a visit," he explained stiffly. "Palmetto BioClean."

"Oh, yes … I remember now." Her voice was low, hardly more than a whisper, and he heard other voices in the background.

"I'm sorry … I must have called you at the hospital."

"It's okay—I'm due for a break. What's this about?"

Connor thought for a second, framing in his mind what he was going to say. "The other day you said Jon moved out of your house about eight weeks ago. Is that right?"

"Give or take a few days, yes. Why do you ask?"

"Do you happen to know where he went after that?"

"Excuse me?"

"When he moved out, he must have gone somewhere," Connor pointed out. "Do you have any idea if he stayed around Morehead City?"

"Shit, he split town faster than a priest running from a whorehouse," Ms. Benton said, emphasizing her point with a huffing sound. "Slick bastard could've gone just about anywhere, but I just naturally assumed he went down to Myrtle Beach."

"Why is that?"

"That's where his girlfriend lives," she said as if it all made perfect sense.

"His girlfriend?" Connor repeated, thinking *you gotta be shittin' me.*

"I guess I left that part out, huh?" she said. "That's the real reason I booted his ass out. That and the money he stole."

"This girlfriend, does she have a name?"

"Charlene Marks. That may not be her real name, since she works in one of those sleazy bars where they make you wear nothin' on top 'cept a bra. And I admit it—I was snooping through his phone one day and found her name, but only after she called him one time, and he was out in the driveway washing my car." She sounded as if she needed some sort of justification for checking up on him.

"You don't happen to remember the name of the place, do you?" he asked. "This sleazy bar …"

"Coogers," Mary Alice Benton said with a sniff of disgust. "Spelled with two 'O's, little nipples painted in 'em. I know this cuz I checked the place out when I was down there the other day. It's a coupla blocks back from the beach, near the boardwalk."

"Did you talk to her? This Charlene Marks?"

"She wasn't there … day off," she answered quickly. "And no one would give me her address. But that's where he went—I know it."

Connor made a mental note of the name and her description, then thanked her for her time and promised he wouldn't call her again at the hospital.

"What's this about, anyway?"

"It's about a hundred and one things that don't quite add up," he told her, and then ended the call.

Caitlin Thomas hit the ball out of the park twice, once when she gave Connor the location of Coogers in Myrtle Beach, and a second time when she gave him the address for Charlene Marks' apartment. "Titty bars for the Tat Man," she said with a high-pitched giggle.

"Tit for Tat."

"It's work," he said. "That's all."

"And someone's got to do it."

"That's how it goes."

"Remember, all work and no play make Jack a dull boy," Caitlin told him.

"That explains everything."

"Ma gumby piz choo."

Connor glanced over at Eddie James sitting in the passenger seat, an Army baseball cap jammed on his head and looking like it was going to take off in the wind blasting over the windshield. He was wearing dark shades, but a tight grin suggested he was enjoying this quick spin in his old Camaro. His words came out only in truncated bits of vowels and consonants, but Connor eventually figured out what his old buddy was trying to say.

"Your mom's going to be pissed at me?"

Eddie attempted a slight nod but said nothing.

"Why would she be pissed?"

Forming complete words was not something Eddie was able to do yet, so he cocked his head and flashed Connor a look that, without even removing his sunglasses, obviously meant *what do you think?*

"She's going to be pissed at me for taking you out for a ride with a top down at seventy miles an hour without checking with her first?"

Eddie's grin expanded just a notch, and his head seemed to move forward in the slightest of nods.

"We're just going over the bridge and around the barn," Connor said. "Twenty minutes."

"Sti gumby piss."

Connor guided the car along the road that tracked parallel to the Intracoastal Waterway, then crossed the bridge at the Breach—recently renamed the H.L. Hunley Bridge—that connected the Isle of Palms to Sullivan's Island. He and Eddie said nothing for a long time, Connor still feeling an odd sense of guilt for being in one piece and of relative sound body—although his V.A. shrink might have something to say about that—while Eddie James could barely talk. Or even engage in just about any kind of physical activity.

He hung a right at Route 702 and gunned the engine as all 396 cubic inches of Detroit power launched them onto the causeway that led to the swing bridge. Connor checked his watch, saw they were just going to miss the back-up that formed when the span opened on the hour, every hour. A van pulling a garden trailer loaded with lawn mowers caused him to slow down, and that allowed him to hear what Eddie James was now trying to say in the seat next to him.

"Remba Leesa Toh?" It was a question, but barely.

Connor tried to figure out what he was saying, came up with "Remember Lisa?"

That seemed to be an acceptable translation, because Eddie again tried to nod before saying. "Lisa Sto."

"Lisa Stone? The girl in supply?"

Lisa Stone had been a private who handled inventory in the transportation unit at their Forward Operating Base outside Kirkuk.

"Yeah … I remember her. Cute, short dark hair—"

"She commie."

"She's what?"

"She. Caw. Me."

"She called you? You mean, on the phone?" Eddie lowered his head in another nod.

The car hit the metal span of the bridge and Connor waited until they were on the other side before speaking again. Then: "When was this?"

"Yessay."

"Yesterday."

"Mah hel fo."

Connor worked on this one, then said, "Your mother held the phone."

Another yes.

"How's she doing?" Connor asked, wondering why Lisa would have called Eddie and why he was mentioning it now.

Everyone at the F.O.B. knew what had happened to him, that his life had been shattered by the roadside bomb that had taken his arm and screwed up his head. He'd been hanging on by a thread when the chopper carried him out. Then again, maybe that was the reason she had reached out to him.

Eddie attempted a slight shake of his head. "Try kissef."

That one didn't take much figuring, but what he said sent an icy rattle down Connor's spine. "She tried to kill herself? Why on earth—"

"Ember Sarja Tura."

This one took a good twenty seconds before Connor could figure out what Eddie was trying to say, but eventually it came to him. "Sergeant Turner?"

Even with the dark shades Connor could see the anger in Eddie's eyes. "Bassud."

Yes, Connor had to agree: Sergeant Turner was a bastard, on many levels and for many reasons. In fact, the first thing Connor had tried to do when he rotated back to Fort Drum was try to put the shithead out of his mind. It didn't work.

"What did he do?" he asked warily, already knowing the answer before he was even finished with the question.

"He. Raped. Her."

Shit. "When was this?" he asked, then clarified the question and said, "I mean, when did she try to kill herself?"

Eddie lifted his shoulder in a shrug. "Dunno. Slih riss."

She slit her wrists. "Damn, Eddie. This war screwed so many good people."

He gave an almost imperceptible nod and said, "Bick clussah fug."

Connor picked up an order of ribs and coleslaw at Publix on the way home, fixed himself a martini, and carried it all out to his chair at the edge of the marsh.

He watched as the sky shifted from blue to pink to orange, and then finally to a deep purple that caused a bank of clouds to fade into the night. At one point a fast-moving squall raced across the marsh, pummeling the sweetgrass and pluff mud for about two minutes before it slipped across the island and fell out to sea. Connor retreated inside to fix another drink, then came back outside and inhaled the evening while the steam rose from the ground and a swarm of bats squeaked through the twilight.

But mostly he sat there, thinking. Thinking about who had caught up with Bodean Barr at the front door of his shack up in Walterboro and fired a shotgun into his face. And why Barr had gone up to visit Jon Hilborn at the Cape Myrtle Hotel just thirty hours before Hilborn had jumped to his death. Or got himself tossed over the rail. And why Hilborn had stolen sixty thousand dollars and a gun from a nurse up in North Carolina, and why he had invited one of his four ex-wives to his hotel room for one last round of hide the salami.

But mostly he sat there thinking about Danielle, how her flight had gone, when she had landed, how her day had been. She had told him there was a lioness that might need assistance in the birthing process, and he wondered if that had been part of her afternoon. He thought about her going home to a house that she had bought with her husband, but which now was going to be empty, since she had kicked him out. And he wondered if she was thinking about him as much as he was thinking of her, and what he had told her about his heart—that he had no use for it as long as she was down in Orlando and he was up here in Charleston.

At some point, when he finally was through with all the thinking, he picked up his phone and punched in her number, waited for it to ring. Once, twice, three times…

"Connor!" she said, sounding rushed. "I just got home. What a day!"

"I missed you," he told her.

"I missed you more. Listen—can I call you right back? I literally just walked in and, well, a girl's got to do what a girl's got to do."

Connor told her that would be fine and not to rush, then watched the lights of a trawler sliding south along the waterway. He could hear music, some sort of rhythmic beat that he recognized but could not place. About a half dozen people were on the deck, laughing and drinking and generally having fun in the night as the boat chugged toward the harbor, where the captain would probably find a marina and tie up for the night.

Danielle called him back two minutes later, sounding less desperate and rushed. She explained how her flight had landed right on time and she had arrived at work only ten minutes late, and the lioness had not gone into any sort of labor over the weekend, and all was quiet in the land of Mickey and Minnie. Then she said, "Let me guess: you're sitting in your chair out back, martini in one hand, phone in the other, watching the marsh and the boats and the bridge."

"That pretty much sums it up," he admitted. Then, pushing things a little bit, he asked, "Any sign of Peter Pan?"

She laughed at that, and said, "All is very quiet here in Neverland. And truth be told, I'd rather be right there beside you, watching the night and inhaling the smells of the marsh. And a bit of gin. But it's been a long day, and I have to be at the clinic early in the morning—"

"To be continued," Connor finished for her. "I just wanted to hear the sound of your voice, make sure the weekend wasn't all a dream."

"Trust me, it was real. Have a good evening."

And it was a good evening, as good as they make them in Carolina. A gentle breeze was beginning to kick up as a front moved in across the lowcountry, pushing out the sweltering heat. The party trawler had disappeared down the waterway but Connor still could hear music coming from the bars several blocks away in the tiny downtown area of Sullivans Island. An owl in a nearby tree hooted softly, and in the distance, Connor heard the rhythmic clang of a bell indicating that the Ben Sawyer Bridge was opening.

On evenings like this Connor left the windows open. He watched a few minutes of *Breaking Bad*, then clicked off the light and immediately was lost in the darkness. It was perfect sleeping weather, and the three martinis and the lingering sound of Danielle's voice allowed him to slip into a comforting sleep.

There was a time when he dreaded the prospect of sleep, when his dreams conjured up images of men without arms or legs trapped in their Army vehicles, or Iraqis dressed in dirty robes and masks or hoods aiming guns out windows, firing at anything that moved. Or a woman in a burqa he had seen walking into a crowded market, then screamed in horror as she pressed a switch that wiped the area clean of anything living. Or Connor firing his M4 into the head of a person whom the Army told him afterward was an insurgent, but whom he saw as just another person. A husband, a father, a son who, because of the irony of geography and oil, simply had a different outlook on life and God. And death.

Except more often than not they weren't dreams, and even now— on a night when he felt the quietest calm and his dreams were of lions and planes and cartoon mice with big black ears—he rode that narrow ridge between sleep and wakefulness, his hair-trigger reflexes leaving him ready to grab for a gun that wasn't there.

That's when he heard the distinctive cha-chunk of a bullet being jacked into the chamber of a gun. His brain registering with instant clarity that this was not a dream; it was for real.

Chapter 18

Connor bolted upright, reached under his pillow, realized he was not in Iraq, and said in a calm, measured voice, "Put the gun down. No one gets hurt."

"Don't move," said a voice in the darkness. Succinct, stern, deep, and very much scared. "Hands in the air."

"Get the hell out of my house!" Connor snapped back at him. Wondering first if this was a home invasion, some asshole who'd gotten some bad intel on where to find drugs or cash or weapons. Or maybe this was connected to the Jon Hilborn thing, possibly the same dirtbag who'd blown Bodean Barr's brains all over the wall. Except this weapon sounded more like a semi-automatic handgun, like a Glock or a Sig, rather than the shotgun that took off Barr's head.

"On your feet!" The voice was trying to sound menacing, but Connor detected a hint of uneasiness in it, too, the gunman maybe questioning his own resolve.

"Whose orders?" Pushing the edge.

"Just get up!" the gunman barked at him. "Slow, feet first. And keep your hands where I can see 'em."

The room was dark still and Connor doubted the gunman was wearing night vision goggles. He'd probably just come in through the glass slider, which Connor had left partly open to the evening breeze.

"You don't want to do this," he said. "It's not too late to be smart."

"I said 'get up.' Move!"

Connor could see the man's shadowy outline now. He appeared tall, a little more than six feet, broad shoulders. Big but not built, most of that size probably coming from fat rather than muscle.

"I'm moving." He was already sitting up, but now pivoted so his feet found the floor. "Just be careful with the gun."

"*I'm* giving the orders here!" the man growled.

"If you're after drugs or money, you came to the wrong place—"

"Shut up. And *get* up. Nice and slow. Like I said."

Connor pushed off from the mattress and stood beside the bed, keeping an eye on the man's shadowy form the entire time. Calculating, guessing, anticipating. "Now what?" he asked.

"Now we go into the other room. Real slow, no funny moves. Understand?"

"Loud and clear," Connor said, also understanding that the gun was pointed at his chest, maybe five feet away. Just a bit more than an arm's reach. not much chance of missing at such close range. He slowly made his way around the foot of the bed toward the door.

"Nice and slow," the man warned him, stepping back a foot or two to make room for Connor to slip past him into the hallway.

"That's me," Connor assured him. "Nice and slow."

Miss Benson once had used the term *nanosecond* in science class, and at the time Connor really hadn't known nor cared what it meant. But now it could have been used to describe the speed with which he used the base of his right palm to jab upward and shatter the gunman's nose, coming close to pushing it upwards into the cranial cavity, as he had been trained to do in the Army. But at the last moment he stopped himself, since that move could have been lethal, choosing instead to slam the man's head backwards into the wall, resulting in a loud *crack* and a gush of blood. Then: silence.

Connor flipped on the overhead light, got a good look at the intruder for the first time. He was crumpled on the floor, bleeding from the nose and the back of his head, but he was still conscious. He was dressed in black jeans and a black T-shirt, with black smears rubbed under his eyes, and a black cap—it looked sort of like a French beret—was lying next to him. Definitely dressed for the part, whatever role this asshole was playing.

The gun had clattered to the floor, and Connor stepped over and retrieved it, ejecting the round that was in the chamber. It was clear this guy wasn't going anywhere fast, so Connor slipped into his small kitchen, where he soaked a wad of paper towels in cold water and brought them back to where the injured man was groaning.

He pressed the wet towels against the busted nose, then lifted the man's hand up so he could hold the wad in place by himself. Connor was well-acquainted in the properties of blood and all the nasty things that can live in it, and he now went into the bathroom, where he pulled out a pair of nitrile gloves and snapped them over his own hands. When he came back out he reached down and felt through the man's pockets, pulling a wallet from his black jeans. He opened it to the driver's license and gave it a good, hard look.

"Oh, shit," he mumbled under his breath.

"Geddit?" the man said, the broken nose making it sound as if he had a cold.

"This was real stupid, man. Breaking and entering, armed assault—"

"You attagged me," Danielle's husband—*estranged husband*— mumbled.

"After you broke in and jammed a gun in my face," Connor explained. "Look … can you stand up?"

The answer was a slow, painful "yes," but two minutes later Richard Simmons—no relation to the aerobics guy on TV—was sitting in a wooden chair at the kitchen table. Connor had given him a new wad of wet paper towels, but most of the bleeding had stopped. Not the pain, however.

"You … my wife … she …" He was shaking his head, as if he couldn't get the image of what he was trying to say out of his mind. "Where's … Danni—"

"She's not here," Connor told him.

"Da hell she idn't—"

For all Danielle had told Connor about her husband—what a prick and a dirtbag he had been—he still felt sorry for the man. Maybe a little. Okay, not much at all.

"She went home this morning," he said. "You'd know that if you weren't such a douche bag."

"Wadge id," Simmons snorted. "She still my wife." "What about Tinkerbell?" Connor asked him.

Simmons gave him a puzzled look, then winced as a wave of pain stabbed through his head. "Who?"

"Your office intern. Yes, Danielle told me all about her."

Simmons closed his eyes and hung his head until his chin just about touched his chest. "Big middake," he muttered. "It wud jus' one o' dose digs. You work wid sub-wud and all of a sudded you just feel dat spark. You doe how id is."

Simmons had a point: Connor knew exactly how it was. He knew that spark, the giddy high-school feeling he got when he thought about Danielle, knew how his legs grew weak at the very sight of her. Except in his case it wasn't a 19-year-old intern from the local university; it was Mrs. Simmons, and she just happened to be married to this man who had brought a gun into his home.

"Were you really going to shoot me?" he asked.

Simmons shook his head. "No. At least, I dod't thig so. I jus' drobe ub here to scare you. Mostly. Six hours od da road. Didn't know you'd been to jail, man."

"Jail?" Connor asked. Then he realized he was still naked from the waist up, and Simmons was eyeing all his tattoos. "Not jail … U.S. Army. I could've killed you."

"Probably be a good thing," Simmons said, and Connor realized he wasn't talking through his nose anymore. "This isn't going to look good."

"Breaking into a person's home and pointing a gun at him never does," Connor agreed. "Cops usually don't like it."

"You going to call 'em?"

"What would you do if I don't?"

"Shit, man … you do that, you'll never see me in this state again. Ever."

"What about Danielle?"

Simmons wasn't so quick with an answer on that one, but finally gave a little nod of comprehension. "I blew it totally. She said as much when she kicked me out."

"Doesn't answer my question," Connor told him. "You can't go near her."

"You do this for me, let me go? I promise."

Connor knew from experience that promises were cheaper than bullets, but he really didn't want to send this man to jail tonight. Even though Simmons had pushed his way into Connor's house and threatened to kill him. It would raise far more questions for him and for Danielle, and neither of them needed that. Neither did Simmons, who obviously had made a poor judgment call. Still, there was always the possibility that he could head right back down to Orlando and do the murder-suicide thing.

"I think we need to bring Danielle in on this," he said.

"Do we have to?"

"She's your wife. You can't keep this from her."

"Shit." Simmons lowered his bloody face to his hands, took a deep breath, then let it out. "You're right. But now?"

It was a good question. Danielle had already told him that she needed to get to bed early because she had to get up early, deal with animal emergencies in the morning. A two-a.m. call informing her of what her husband had done would not do anything except keep her from going back to sleep.

"Tomorrow," Connor said. "You stay on the couch tonight and we'll call her in the morning. If you're gone, I call the cops. If I hear your car start, I call the cops. If you try to take the gun, I call the cops."

"It's my gun."

Connor was ready for that, and plucked a dollar from his wallet. "Not anymore," he said, handing it to Simmons. "You just sold it to me. You have a problem with that, I call the cops."

Connor did not have to call the cops. He found Richard Simmons still sound asleep on the couch the next morning, a flimsy cotton sheet tucked up under his chin. The sheet was spotted with blood stains from his nose and scraped scalp, and probably was destined for the trash. But the fact was, he had slept through the rest of the night, probably aided by the shot of bourbon Connor had given him once they got the rules straight. By contrast, Connor slept in fits and starts, waking to each little noise or bump, instantly sliding his hand into the gap between the mattress and the wall and grabbing the gun, which had turned out to be a Glock.

"This is damned awkward," Simmons said when Connor handed him a mug of coffee, asked if he took cream or sugar.

"It is what it is," Connor replied. He had made a show of popping the loaded magazine from the grip of the gun, which he then placed on the kitchen counter. "I think we need to call Danielle and get this over with."

"She's going to be damned pissed."

"Count on it."

"And she'll never forgive me."

That's what Connor was counting on. He used his own phone to dial the number, and when Danielle answered he said, "Good morning," being careful not to use any terms of endearment. Simmons was already on edge from the whole situation, and Connor didn't want to set him off. "There's somebody here who wants to talk to you."

"Damned pissed" turned out to be nowhere near the way to describe it.

Chapter 19

Connor's plan was to head up to Myrtle Beach, look in on Charlene Moxie at Coogers and see what she could tell him about Jon Hilborn. That was the plan, at least, but ten minutes after he'd packed Simmons into his car and sent him on his way back to Orlando, telling him he needed to get his act together, his phone rang. The man on the other end identified himself as the manager of a restaurant in downtown Charleston, a trendy joint right near the Marketplace that had caught the bloody end of a knife fight the night before. He told Connor that two men had been involved in the clash, both of them seriously injured and now guests of the Medical University, with arrests pending once they were released.

"We have a lot of blood," the manager, whose name was Denny Something, told him. His voice was shaky, as if he'd never seen so much of it in one place. "All over the floor, ceiling, and walls."

"Blood is what we do," Connor assured him. "Don't touch anything. We'll have a team there in thirty minutes."

The clean-up job lasted a good six hours, and by the time Connor got back to The Plant the clock on the dash was already pushing four o'clock. By the time he got everything properly stored and the camera images downloaded it was closer to five, and then if he added another ninety minutes onto that, it would be close to six-thirty by the time he got to Myrtle Beach.

Springsteen kept him entertained the entire ride up, singing about glory days and union cards and hungry hearts. The stop-and-start traffic sludge south of Myrtle Beach slowed him to a crawl, and by the time he pulled the Camaro into the gravel lot behind the place known as Coogers it was closer to seven. Still early by the standard of any drinking establishment, especially because the sun was still slipping toward the retail sprawl to the west. The only real indication that night was approaching was the neon that was glowing in the plate glass window. Corona, Heineken, Red Stripe, Budweiser. And, for those really living on the slippery slope of time, Camels and Marlboros.

Mary Alice Benton had been correct in her description of the Coogers sign, with nipples painted inside each of the "O's," except the sign on the roof was so massive that the sexual imagery appeared far more intimidating than tantalizing. A wild cat motif with piercing eyes and a menacing glare completed the look, a large thick tail curling beneath the word "Coogers" as if to underline and emphasize it.

Connor put the top up and locked the doors before heading inside. Most of the other vehicles in the lot were (naturally) F-150s and Dodge Rams and Chevy Silverados, and the Camaro's bright orange paint job and aftermarket chrome rims were sure to draw interest. The later the hour, the more interest. He knew from experience that, in places like this one, interest often took the form of a busted lock or a smashed window.

A thin girl dressed in black shorts and a red bra greeted him just inside the door. "You're early," she said to him. "Show doesn't start until nine." Then she jerked her eyes toward a tiny stage built into a corner, a microphone and amps squeezed tightly up against the wall and a basic set of drums looking like it might tip onto the floor

"Who's playing?"

"The Moxies," the girl said.

"Don't know 'em," he said, trying not to react to the name of the band. Maybe Mary Alice Benton had gotten her wires crossed about her ex-lover's girlfriend.

"Rock and blues cover band," she explained. And now that Connor got a good look, he saw that thin wasn't the word to describe her. Emaciated was more like it, her arms about the size and firmness of a roll of refrigerator biscuits. Same color, too. "Hendrix, Zeppelin, Janis, Prince, Aretha. Even a little Blue Oyster Cult. The lead's a chick, name of Charlene."

"They go on at nine, you said?"

"About then. And just so you know, happy hour's over. Why no one's here."

Connor peered through the dimly lit club, saw that all of the tables were empty, and only two guys were seated at the bar, a couple of stools between them. "Can I just get a beer?" he asked.

"Suit yourself. But there's a five-dollar cover for the show, unless you order at least ten bucks in food. Then it's free."

For such a loose joint there seemed to be a lot of rules. Connor took his time meandering over to the long row of stools pushed up under a long plank of oak, initials and dates and doodles crudely etched into its polished surface. He edged up on a stool at the end of the bar, ordered a draft beer even though he felt like having a double gin on the rocks, then slowly swiveled around and took a good hard look at the place.

He'd been in joints like this before, more than a few times. It wasn't quite a strip club with the requisite brass pole and disco lights, more like a country roadhouse except there was a busy four-lane street out front rather than a rural highway. The main attraction seemed to be an array of Victoria's many secrets—bras and panties and thongs and garter belts, and more bras and panties—all of them apparently removed by female customers and then stuck to the walls and ceiling with colored push pins. The place was totally littered with them, thousands of undergarments pinned right on top of others, layers and layers of lingerie collected in a trend that probably started years ago and apparently continued right up to today.

The plate glass window was clogged with the neon signs so there was almost no natural light, and the thick aroma of chicken fried oil meant palmetto bugs probably were lurking in every corner. The only illumination came from the ceiling, where recessed bulbs gave off just about as much light as a distant star. Connor's shoes stuck to the floor when he walked over to the bar, and he decided to avoid the men's room, if there was any way possible.

"Getcha?"

The word came from the bartender behind him, a thin dude with red hair combed up in a peak at the top of his head, sort of like the Rhodesian ridgeback Connor had seen on the beach the last time he went for a run. He interpreted the single word to mean, "what can I get you," so he replied, "Coors Light," something he'd always figured was redundant.

The bartender grunted something, then slapped a bar menu down on the counter and went off to fetch Connor's beer. He was back in less than thirty seconds—a whole lot of nothing keeping him busy— and set the bottle down with a clunk.

"Three dollars," he said.

Connor fished a twenty out of his wallet and pushed it toward the bartender. "Take it out of that, and keep it open," he said.

"Sir," the bartender replied, leaving out the word "yes."

Connor picked up the menu and studied the five items priced at ten dollars or more. He ordered the chicken fried steak with potatoes and gravy, just the thought of it causing his arteries to constrict as he settled in for what he figured would be a long evening. After giving a moment's thought to how he might get home, he figured the motel across the street with the "Vacancy" sign might prove to be the answer to that question. Especially since Jordan James was covering his expenses on this recon mission.

Ninety minutes later Connor experienced first-hand what had drawn Jon Hilborn down to Myrtle Beach. Charlene Marks swept through the front door with what he later would learn was a Gibson Les Paul Axcess electric guitar hanging from a shoulder strap, a beautiful maple and mahogany six-string with a rosewood fingerboard. But it wasn't the guitar that snared Connor's attention, nor that of the other patrons who had begun to fill the place in anticipation of the show. It was Charlene herself, a stunning black-haired woman with eyes to match, intense and piercing but sensuous and luxurious and captivating, all at the same time. She was wearing a pair of painted-on black jeans and a black tank top that screamed *dangerous curves*, while a black leather choker elicited a sexy bondage look, exaggerated by a pair of handcuffs that dangled from a belt loop.

Connor watched her as she moved straight for the stage, where she propped the guitar against a metal stand and then pulled the bottom of her shirt tight. That move drew almost a hundred inaudible gasps, half of them from the men in the room whose collective breath had been taken away by the mere sight of Charlene and what she must be capable of. The other gasps came from the women who were with the men, wondering how they could ever compete with this goddess whose image was sure to linger well into the darkness of their own bedrooms long after the show had ended.

Two other musicians appeared shortly after her entrance. One was a man who appeared to be in his forties with a Pabst over-the-belt belly and a polished Mr. Clean head. He was carrying a flat, oblong case that he set down on the snare drum and opened, to reveal a dozen pairs of sticks fashioned from different kinds of wood. He carefully selected one of the pairs, then closed the case and set it on the stage. The other musician was a scrawny black kid who couldn't have been more than a couple years out of high school, with long dreads that he kept trying to shake out of his face. He was carrying a black bass guitar covered with scratches and nicks and filled, Connor guessed, with plenty of old stories and memories.

They huddled with Charlene up on the tiny stage, reviewing the set list and taking a look at the gathering crowd. Coogers was a small joint, but it was filling up fast. A waitress carrying a tray of drinks came over to the stage and deftly handed glasses to each of the musicians, then skittered off to another table. Charlene whispered something into the young bass player's ear, then they both plugged their guitars into the small amps stacked like orange crates in the corner. They spent the next five minutes tuning up, and then Charlene turned and faced the audience.

She stood there a few seconds, slipping into the moment, then the drummer landed a single beat on his snare, followed a second later when Charlene picked out a familiar riff that caused the entire joint to erupt in applause. Then the bass player began fingering a deep reggae current straight out of Muscle Shoals, followed by electric piano and sax generated by a beat box Connor hadn't noticed before. At that point Charlene moved to the edge of the tiny stage and began swaying her hips as she sang out to the crowd, her gravelly voice resonating with the throaty intensity reminiscent of the great Mavis Staples: "I know a place…ain't nobody cryin'…ain't nobody worried… no smilin' faces lyin' to the races—"

In a flash the joint was pumping with the iconic bass guitar riff, Charlene calling up every ounce of soul in her body, her voice as sultry as a pharaoh's harem, yet as forlorn as the call of a mourning dove at dusk. The SRO crowd— equal parts black and white, Connor noticed—was on its feet now as Cooger's was filled with the improbable sound of gospel on a Friday night as Charlene belted out "I'll take you there…!"

Then someone in the back of the joint called out, "More cowbell!"—*a non sequitur* from an old *Saturday Night Live* skit—and the spell that had fallen over the place was broken.

She followed the Staples Singers classic with Jimi Hendrix, Led Zeppelin, Prince, Whitney Houston, Otis Redding, and Etta James. An hour later Charlene Marks—her face soaked with perspiration, hair wild like she'd just stuck her thumb in a socket—announced to the crowd that she and the band would be back in fifteen minutes.

Connor was unsure what to do next, so he decided just to let fate take its course. There was no dressing room, and he knew from one quick trip that the restrooms didn't invite much lingering. Charlene could always step outside for a smoke or some fresh air, but either way she would have to move from the stage in one direction or another. Then luck crossed in front of him in the form of the waitress who had brought the band their drinks at the beginning of the set, and Connor quickly slipped her a portrait of Andrew Jackson and a business card and asked her to deliver it to Charlene. The waitress balked for a second, then gave him a single nod and quickly made the twenty disappear.

Connor watched as Charlene chatted with fans who were seated closest to the stage, then gave a cursory glance in his direction after the waitress told her something he could not hear. Charlene asked her a question, the waitress lifted her shoulder in a shrug, and Charlene responded by shaking her head in a way that hinted of exasperation. But she eventually edged her way over to where Connor had taken up residence at the bar, absorbing kudos and praise from her adoring fans as she moved.

"Do I know you?" she said as she stopped in front of him.

"No, and now's probably not the time to change that," he said. "But I'd like a word with you when you have a minute." "About what?" she asked, her voice thick with suspicion.

"A mutual acquaintance." He sensed the suspicion shift toward distrust, so he added, "His name is Jon Hilborn."

She didn't move, didn't say anything for a good while, then said, "Jon is dead."

"That's why I want to talk with you."

"It's only been a few days since—" Charlene said, her voice trailing off.

"And I only want a few minutes," he pressed. "Just a couple questions."

She stood there, chewed her lip a second as she thought this through, a smear of lipstick transferring to her lower teeth. She gave a backward glance to the stage, then flexed her shoulder in slight shrug and said, "I'm always starved after the show. I know a place serves great sushi."

"I'll take you there," he told her.

Charlene grinned at the reference to the song she had sung earlier and said, "They have great sake, too."

"I won't move from this stool," he promised her. "Great show, by the way."

"Great tats," she replied.

Connor didn't catch the name of the sushi joint when they entered it just a little past midnight. It was a small place, just a few tables, lighting that was way too bright for this time of night. An odor of stale soy sauce and sesame oil and raw fish seemed to be everywhere. But Charlene Marks was right—it served great sushi, and she ordered a lot of it. California rolls, spider rolls, spicy yellowtail roll, even sea eel and cucumber roll.

Jordan James paid.

"Look," Connor began, "I appreciate you coming here, agreeing to talk to me. I'm sure you're still in shock—"

"More like confused," she said. "You think you really know someone, and then ... they do something like this." She applied a dab of wasabi to a piece of the spider roll, piled on a sliver of ginger, and dunked it in a dish of soy sauce. "So how do you know Jon?"

He watched her as she popped the spider roll in her mouth, couldn't figure out if she was in shock or denial, or maybe just trying not to think too much about Jon Hilborn. "I know him through a friend down in Charleston," he eventually said, not totally a lie.

"Is that where you're from?"

"Not originally. Moved there last September."

"Thought so. You don't have the accent."

That's when Connor noticed Charlene didn't have one, either, at least not one from this part of the South. Maybe Florida or the Gulf. "Neither do you," he said.

"New Orleans, born and raised. Came up here three years ago, part of another band doing an east coast tour. The promoter screwed us and ran off with our money, left us high and dry. It was the middle of winter and I couldn't see myself going north, and I wasn't ready to head back home where everyone I knew were just dyin' to say, 'I told you so.' So, I stayed on and formed a new band. What do you think?"

"I think you're great," Connor said, the words coming out as lame as they possibly could. "I mean, fantastic. Vocals, guitar, drums, everything."

"But not enough cowbell?" she said with a laugh.

"That wasn't me," he protested. "So ... what can you tell me about Jon Hilborn?"

"What exactly is it you want to know?"

"Well ... how the two of you, well, hooked up," he said.

She cocked her head ever-so-slightly and shot him a quizzical look. "Hooked up in what way?" she asked as she sipped from a cup of hot sake.

Connor was pretty sure he blushed at his question, and said, "Well, you know. Like they do on Animal Planet—"

Charlene almost spit out the sake as she laughed at him. "Jon and me? You thought we were like ... boyfriend and girlfriend? Now, that would be totally hilarious if it wasn't so absolutely disgusting."

Chapter 20

Maybe we should start over," Connor suggested, feeling his face grow red as he realized Mary Alice Benton had had it all wrong, and maybe that was why Charlene didn't mind talking. As long as there was sushi involved. "What I heard was the two of you were living together—"

"Look ... I'll save you the trouble," Charlene said. "Jon came to one of my shows last winter sometime. He was in town on business and said he was a real 'blues and soul' kind of guy. That's how he put it. He also was a Jack Daniels kind of guy, and by the time the show was over he couldn't remember where he was staying, let alone his own name. He reminded me a lot of my dad before he died—couldn't hold his liquor for shit, but he loved good music—so I took him back to my place and let him sleep it off on the couch."

Connor watched her eyes while she talked, tried to figure out if she was telling him the truth or feeding him a line. "Probably not the safest thing," he said.

"Yeah, I know that." She went through the motions of fixing another bite of sushi, wasabi and ginger and soy sauce all over again, and slipped it into her mouth. "Forgive me for talking while I chew—I know it's rude. Anyway, next morning when I woke up he was whistling his way around my kitchen, frying bacon and eggs, like nothing happened. And he was a pretty good cook, you want my opinion. That's when he said he noticed I had a spare bedroom no one was using, and if he paid me five hundred a month could he stay there from time to time, rather than some big hotel where a room service breakfast was twenty bucks."

"Not bad rent for one room," Connor pointed out.

"And I needed the money." She glanced down at the table of sushi. "Go ahead— help yourself."

Connor started to say "no," but realized he was hungry and had never tasted eel. He followed Charlene's lead with the fixin's and used his fingers rather than chopsticks to slip it into his mouth. When he was finished he asked her, "When was the last time you saw him?"

"Six, eight weeks ago," she said. "He was there a few days, then just disappeared. Never saw him again."

"He didn't leave a note?" Connor asked.

She shook her head and said, "No. But he did leave five Benjamins under a salt shaker in the kitchen. Eventually I figured out it was his last month's rent."

More questions tumbled around in Connor's head than he could sort through, and he mentally grabbed one as it went drifting by. "Did Hilborn ever tell you what brought him through Myrtle Beach?" he asked.

"Work, was all he said." She poured another small measure of sake from the porcelain container the waitress had brought, then took a slow sip. "He never let on what kind, but I got the feeling he was in some sort of high-end sales. Usually he'd just show up, stick around for a few, then pretty much drop off the planet again."

"What about friends?" Connor asked. "Anyone he knew here in Myrtle Beach, maybe someone he talked to on the phone?"

She appeared to give the question some thought, but Connor wasn't convinced that she wasn't putting on an act. "Jon was always on the phone, but usually when he talked he was out on the patio or in his room," she said. "But no one ever dropped by, not that I ever saw. He kept pretty much to himself."

Connor stole a quick glance at his watch, saw it was well past midnight, and figured Jordan James was going to have to spring for a hotel room tonight. "The last time you saw him, how did he seem?"

"In what way?"

"Was he up or down? Healthy or sluggish? Depressed?"

"My opinion, he'd changed," she answered. "He seemed down, sort of like some kind of light had gone out in him. The only time he went out was at night, and then only for a short trip to Walgreens or CVS." "Was he on medication?" he asked her.

Charlene mustered a slight shrug, her eyes solidly fixed on her sushi. "Coulda been," she replied. "I know Jon talked to his doctor a few times, usually very hush-hush. And yeah, it occurred to me he might've been sick."

"What makes you say that?"

She set her chopsticks on the edge of her plate and looked at him. "I know it was wrong, but one time I went looking through his room and found some books."

"What sort of books?" Connor pressed.

"They were about some sort of disease with a long name. Began with A, and had to do with a baseball player." "Lou Gehrig?".

"Yeah, that's him." She picked up her chopsticks again. "I wanted to ask him about it, but then he'd know I'd been snooping."

Connor studied her a moment, couldn't stop thinking that he'd just witnessed a pretty decent stage performance. "Did he ever give you any reason to think he might try to take his own life?"

She shook her head. "It never came up. But he did seem desperate, maybe depressed at times."

"Understandable if he thought he was dying," Connor replied, going along with it. "You think he was depressed enough to go down to the beach, check into a hotel, and jump off his balcony?"

Charlene closed her eyes, as if she were trying to blink the memory from her mind. "I wouldn't know," she finally said.

"Does the name Mary Alice Benton mean anything?" he asked, abruptly changing direction to see how Charlene might react.

"Not that I remember," she said, maybe just a little too quickly.

"Who's she?"

"No one important," Connor told her. "How about an ex-wife?"

"He said he'd been married before, but he seemed to want to put a lot of distance between himself and his past," she said. "Are we almost done here?"

"Just one more name, okay?"

"Go ahead," she sighed, sounding tired. "But I doubt it'll mean anything."

"Bodean Barr."

Charlene flinched at the mention of the name, obviously not part of any act. It was instinctive, a reaction to something she didn't see coming and certainly couldn't control.

"That's it," she said. Gone were the throaty rhythm and blues in her voice, replaced by a growl that reminded Connor of the movie "The Exorcist." "We're done here."

"What do you mean, done—?"

"What the word means. Get out."

"But—"

"I said 'get out.' Please."

So, he got out. But he did not leave.

He and Charlene had taken separate cars to the sushi joint, and now he pulled the Camaro out of the near-empty parking lot and turned right onto North Kings Highway. He traveled about a hundred yards, then pulled into the parking lot of a pizza restaurant that was closed, wedged the car in beside a blue dumpster.

Traffic was light and the night was dark, and the Camaro was pretty well hidden, so he wasn't too worried about being rousted by cops or some nervous nut itching to draw a concealed gun and jack his car. He didn't want to become part of tomorrow's news cycle, but he also figured he wouldn't have to wait long until he saw Charlene Marks' Jeep Cherokee bump its way out of the sushi place and race off in one of two directions. Just enough time for her to make a phone call, pound down the rest of her sake, and split. About five minutes, max.

Turned out it was just under four. Then the light from a pair of headlamps hit his eyes from just up the street, and he could hear the engine sputter to life. Connor's sister had owned a Cherokee years ago, drove it all the way out to Reno when she got out of Michigan, and he knew the sound of the Jeep pistons chugging to life. He heard the wide tires spin on loose gravel, and waited for the vehicle to race past him, heading north. If it didn't that meant she was headed in the other direction, and Connor would just have to change his plan.

But Charlene Marks made it easy on him and evidently didn't see his car parked beside the dumpster as she roared past. He waited patiently until she was a good fifty yards past him before he turned on his lights and edged out onto the highway behind her.

At first, he thought she might be going home to her apartment, at which point all bets were off. He wasn't about to stalk her to her front door to see who she might have called. If she'd called anyone. In fact, Connor wondered if he might be just a little paranoid here, thinking it was the name "Bodean Barr" that had set off that look of panic in her eyes.

But ten minutes later he could still see her taillights ahead of him, heading north on Highway 17 out of town. Eventually he saw the bright red glow of her brake lights flash on, telling him she was getting ready to either stop or turn. It turned out to be the latter, and she cut a hard right onto a two-lane state highway and continued until the roadway climbed up over a body of water that a sign said was the continuation of the same Intracoastal Waterway he saw from his own backyard.

Not long after that the Jeep made one more turn, this time a sharp left onto a narrower strip of roadway that had no discernible shoulder, and then one final right turn into a patch of dark woods made even darker by the fact that Connor had no idea where he was, or what was going to happen when Charlene got to whatever she was going. From the way the roads kept getting progressively smaller, he suspected that moment was going to come very soon. A set of headlights behind him disappeared up a narrow drive, and with that in mind he pushed in the knob on his dashboard and instantly the road ahead of him went completely black. The Jeep was still thumping along in front of him, a good hundred-fifty yards ahead, so he knew he was heading in the right direction.

Then the lights stopped their motion, and a moment later they went out completely. Connor edged the Camaro as far down the narrow road as he felt comfortable, until he was maybe thirty yards from where Charlene had parked. He realized she had led him right into a trailer park, not the kind with mobile homes set side by side like shoeboxes on the floor at Rack Room, little gardens nicely hoed and planted with roses and foxgloves and snapdragons. No, these homes were more spread out through a dense forest of pines and cypress, old single-wides dropped on cinder block foundations with rusting pick-ups and long-wheelbase Detroit sedans, and an occasional motorcycle. And those were just the vehicles that weren't missing wheels or engines.

Connor thumbed the chrome dashboard knob that controlled the interior lights, then slowly opened the door and slipped out into the night. Charlene was still sitting behind the wheel of the Jeep, pulled in behind an old truck that was parked in a dirt track in front of one of the trailers. As he slowly moved closer in a low crouch he could hear her still talking on the phone.

"Look, I'm not waiting out here all night," she said in what she probably thought was a whisper. "Get your ass out here."

Less than a minute later the door to the trailer opened, spilling a faint glow of light out onto a hard-pack dirt yard cluttered with old boat motors, mounts, mooring lines, and a utility trailer with a flat tire. A man's head poked through the doorway, looked out at the Jeep for a minute before the rest of him came out onto the wooden steps, revealing a body of pasty white skin just about everywhere except for the pair of blue boxers that cinched his waist. He shuffled down the stairs, then scuffed through dry leaves that hadn't been raked in years.

When the man got to the Jeep he opened the passenger door and slid inside. As he did the dome light went on and for a moment Connor caught a better look at him: snarled black hair, thin cheeks with deep eye sockets, a tiny patch of beard under his lower lip that served no purpose except to catch stray crumbs. Then the door closed, the light went out, and all Connor could hear were muffled voices of a conversation that oddly seemed both urgent and calming.

It was dark enough that Connor was able to make his way around the Jeep to where the truck was parked, and he could see that it was an older F-150, black with mud caked everywhere: wheels, fenders, bumper, license plate. He glanced over his shoulder at the Jeep, figured that unless Charlene or this mystery man looked directly up the driveway to the trailer he was in good position to get closer to the truck. So, he did, one cautious foot at a time, until he was within a yard of the truck's tailgate.

That's when the Jeep door opened again, and the man in boxer shorts said something like "what's done is done," and then closed it again. Now he was moving back up the driveway toward his front door, so Connor slipped around the side of the truck as quietly as anyone can on a dark night with a gravel driveway under them. The man seemed to stop once as if he'd heard something, then continued toward the front door of the trailer, opened it, and disappeared inside.

Behind him Charlene started the Jeep, and the headlamps cut a swath of light across the driveway as she threw it into reverse and backed out to the narrow road. For a moment Connor wondered if he had pulled the Camaro far enough off the road to not block her way, and then he worried that she might remember the car from earlier in the evening when they had driven to the sushi place. But she had been in the lead, and when he joined her at the door of the restaurant she hadn't commented on the orange paint job or the roar of the muffler.

Once he knew she was gone and the man with skin the color of a marshmallow was back inside, Connor again slipped around to the rear of the truck. Then, using the flat of his hand, he brushed away just enough mud to make out the numbers and letters on the license plate. He punched them into his phone, along with the address of the trailer home, figuring Caitlin Thomas would find it first thing in the morning and run it all through Citadel's computers.

That's when he heard the unmistakable cha-chunk of a pump-action shotgun, followed by the words, "Freeze, sucker. Your life as you know it is over."

Chapter 21

This sort of moment was like *déjà vu* all over again. He'd experienced it many times in Iraq, when he and his squad had pushed their way into rock-hard mud hovels or bombed out storefronts in search of rebels fighting for their cause, whatever that cause might be. He'd had guns fired at him, knives thrown at him, and all manner of slurs hurled at him from man, woman, and child. During his sixteen months in the desert he'd dodged more than his share of bullets, managed to be broad-sided by a suicide bomber, and he'd killed two men. He wasn't sure they deserved to die, but it was either them or him. Plus, he'd been armed, which made everything that much easier.

But this was America, and Connor was damned sure he wasn't going to die at the hand of some redneck with the I.Q. of a mullet. The fish, not the hair-do.

Still, he said, "I'm froze."

There was silence behind him, and Connor could almost swear he heard air whistling through Marshmallow Man's ears. Then: "All right. On your feet."

Connor slowly stood up from where he had been crouching and just as slowly raised his hands in the air. "Okay, I'm on 'em."

"Now, turn around."

This was the tricky part, because as soon as Connor started doing that the man with the gun no longer would be accused of shooting him in the back. In fact, he could claim Connor tried to attack him first, and since this was private property Connor had set foot on in the middle of the night, he'd have a good argument.

Connor turned around. Very slowly, very cautiously. But the man didn't shoot him.

Which told him several things: The man with the gun was planning on shooting Connor later. The man with the gun intended to torture him before he killed him. The man with the gun wanted to know who he was and what he was doing out here in the forest, wiping the caked-on mud from his license plate. Or—and Connor gave a lot of hard but quick thought to this—the man with the gun didn't want to attract attention. No neighbors, no cops.

He suspected it was all of the above, but the primary cause was the last one: no attention. Which on its own raised a whole lot of questions.

"I ain't got what you're lookin' for," the man said, making a small stabbing motion at Connor with the shotgun for emphasis.

"I don't s'pose you do," Connor replied.

"What's that s'posed to mean?"

"It means you're right." Connor lowered his hands a few inches.

"Cuz I'm lookin' for my wife, and you don't appear to be her type."

"Your wife? What the hell's she got to do with this?"

"I don't know what you mean by 'this,' but my brother-in-law, Matt—he's Merilee's brother—he said she got into a black Ford pickup earlier tonight, down to Myrtle Beach. He got the tag number, but now I can see it don't match yours."

This seemed to pose a bigger quandary than it should have, because the man with the gun clearly was expecting a different story, something that would give him good reason to just go and fire a blast of pellets through Connor's gut. Something it was obvious he was itching to do. But the story about the wife getting into a pickup—now, that made a whole lot of other sense, sense that he could sympathize with. Any red-blooded son of the Confederacy could.

"What do you mean by she ain't my type?" he demanded, making that little thrusting motion with the pump-action again.

Connor knew Marshmallow Man would zero in on this, as soon as the implication registered in his brain. "She's more into the NBA these days."

"NBA? What's that mean?"

"It means I go over to Iraq and when I come home I find she's been in and out of the sack with about half the entire league," Connor explained. He hated to use the race card, but he figured this shithead was playing with a full deck of them. All right, maybe just half a deck.

Finally, Marshmallow Man got it, and lowered the shotgun. "Shit man, that's rough. You go over to rag-head city to fight for our freedom, and your old lady is spendin' her time over here bagging herself some coons."

For a second Connor thought the shitbag was going to use the "N" word, but "coon" was just as bad. Whoever he was, whatever his name, Connor was on him in one of those same nanoseconds it had taken him to flatten Danielle's husband's nose. *Thank you, Ms. Benson.* One right fist in the stomach, a left uppercut to the face, and one arm wrenched behind his back and the guy was lying face-down on his hard-pack front yard, Connor standing over him with the shotgun jammed into the base of his skull.

"That's how it's done," he said. "And for your information, she likes 'em tall. NBA tall."

Connor left the guy in the living room of his trailer home, legs and arms bound to a kitchen chair with strips of a terrycloth towel he'd found in the bathroom. He'd soaked them in water to make them that much more difficult to untie, the objective here to keep him out of commission long enough for Connor to make it back to the main highway before the guy got himself free. He also shoved an old sock in the guy's mouth to keep him quiet, but not far enough to choke him. Then he checked the man's driver's license in order to spare Caitlin Thomas the task of running the plate through the system.

Jacob Wheeler.

It was well past two by the time he rolled back into Myrtle Beach. He knew he could have been back home in his own bed in ninety minutes, but there were several other things he wanted to look into as long as he was up on the "grand strand," so he checked into a room at the Cape Myrtle Hotel and turned the lights out five minutes later. It was as good a place as any for him to get some sleep if either Jacob Wheeler or Danielle's husband made any effort to track him down.

Still, Connor did not sleep well. He rarely did when he wasn't at his own place, and now he woke up every hour on the hour, trying to remember where he was and why he was there, hearing the sound of a round being chambered in a semi-automatic or the pump of a Remington slide-action repeater. And to make matters worse he'd been given a room near the elevator shaft, which was all right at two in the morning, but not as the first guests began to stir and the housekeeping crew started to do their thing.

He gave up a little before seven and took a shower, then put on the same clothes he'd worn yesterday and went downstairs to find a toothbrush and a plate full of breakfast. When he was done with both he called Citadel Security and was greeted warmly by Caitlin Thomas.

"Jacob Wheeler?" she repeated when he told her what he was looking for.

"That's right," Connor said, then recited the license number address he had punched into his cell phone the night before.

"I'll get back to you," she told him, and then hung up.

Myrtle Beach was two weeks away from full-tilt summer season, so the streets were still quiet. Connor figured nothing much happened until hangovers wore off and the sun was high in the sky, but he ventured outside anyway and headed down to the beach. He'd gone several days without his morning run, but neither his shoes nor his clothes were suitable for slogging through the sand, so when he reached the edge of the ocean he turned north and started walking.

Thirty seconds later he removed the shoes, and a minute after that the shirt was gone, as well. This brought a lot of stares from people coming the other way, including one little boy who couldn't stop gawking at all his body art as his mother dragged him off.

"I don't ever want to see you do that!" she warned him as she practically picked him up by one arm. "Tattoos can only lead to prison, and worse."

Connor eventually circled back to the hotel and made another attempt to grab a stretch of sleep, but it just wasn't in the cards. He came back downstairs a half hour later to check out, and then asked the desk clerk if he knew of a place called Maccaws. That was the name of the restaurant printed on the receipt Connor had found in Bodean Barr's shack down in Walterboro, and it was stamped with the same date Linda Loris had said she had seen Barr getting into the hotel elevator. It looked like it had been a cash transaction, no credit card and no signature involved. Connor figured as long as he was up here in Myrtle he might as well check it out, see if there was any discernible connection to Hilborn's death. Which, if anyone were to ask, Connor would still say looked much more like a suicide than murder.

The desk clerk gave Connor a curious eye, then said, "It's up on Withers Avenue, between 9th and 10th. But there's lots of other places to grab a burger."

"Maccaws came highly recommended," Connor explained.

"By who?"

"A friend."

The desk clerk raised his brow. "To each his own."

The place was right where it was supposed to be, a single-story stucco storefront painted yellow and lime green with large plate glass windows set on either side of the double front doors. There was a large neon sign with an oversized tropical bird reaching up from the roof, with the name "Maccaws" written in large, cursive lettering. Because it wasn't yet noon the neon was not lit, but Connor imagined the street probably looked a bit like Las Vegas did back in the 1960s, before craziness took over.

A sign in the window said the restaurant was open, so he gave the door a push and stepped inside. He had not really noticed how warm it had become until a blast of air conditioning hit him as if he had just stepped into a walk-in freezer. The place had to be twenty degrees cooler than out on the street, and he briskly rubbed his hands on his arms as he gave a quick look around the place.

Then a voice asked from behind him, "Just one?"

Connor turned around and found a thin young man with a shag mustache holding a small stack of menus in his arms. "Please," he told him. "I can sit at the counter, if you have one."

"That would be the bar, and we don't serve lunch there. But it's still early, and as you can see we have a lot of tables open." He emphasized his point with a gallant sweep of his arm, then added, "Do you have a preference?"

"Over there by the window," Connor suggested, pointing to a small table set in a corner.

"Certainly," the host said, and led him across the dining room.

Connor followed him, trying to absorb the décor as he followed the kid through a maze of tables. The walls were covered with framed photographs, album covers, and movie posters depicting Hollywood's greatest stars: Judy Garland, Barbra Streisand, Cher, Lady Gaga, Elton John, Rock Hudson. The floors were unpolished pine, while the ceiling was an ornate floral pattern stamped into tin and then painted a color Connor was sure his mother would have described as mauve. An old bubbler jukebox plugged into a wall outlet was playing The Beatles' "You've Got To Hide Your Love Away."

The kid set a menu on the table as Connor slid into a seat, then glanced at his bare arms and said, "Cool ink job." "Thanks," Connor told him.

"Something to drink?"

He could have used one of Jordan James' Beefeater martinis right about then, but instead he ordered an unsweet tea, knowing that just ordering "iced tea" in South Carolina branded him as an outsider. Or even worse, a Yankee.

"On its way."

Connor was just about the first customer of the day, but over the next twenty minutes Maccaws filled up rapidly. By noon it was practically full, mostly tables of two but some triples as well, plus a crowd of men pressing up to the bar to order a lunchtime cocktail. And it was when he really studied the activity at the bar that it struck him: there were no women in here. Not at the tables, not at the bar, not behind the bar. None. Nowhere.

Just men.

Now he knew why the desk clerk at the hotel had sized him up when he'd asked how to find the place.

Before driving up here yesterday Connor had printed out several color photos he'd found on Google. Now, when his waiter—not the young kid who had seated him, but an older man dressed in tight jeans and a beige polo shirt—came over and asked how the Reuben sandwich was, Connor held up a photo of Bodean Barr and said, "Do you recognize this man?"

The waiter instantly shook his head and said nothing.

"He was in here just last week," Connor said. "At lunch."

"A lot of people come here for lunch," the waiter said. "As you can see. Now, if you don't need anything else—"

"He was here with someone else," Connor pressed. The receipt had been stamped not only with the date and time, but it also said two sandwiches and two teas had been ordered. "I understand privacy, and all that. And I'm not here to get into anyone's business. I just want to know who this man was with."

But the waiter simply said, "Sorry," and went on to his next table.

Maccaws obviously wasn't the sort of place that welcomed new customers asking a lot of questions, and Connor wasn't about to start mingling with the crowd and holding up Bo Barr's photograph. All he'd really wanted was to get a sense of the place where Barr had eaten, maybe see if he could find anyone who recognized him. But that didn't seem likely, given the clientele and what he assumed was a desire for privacy.

He took a bite of his sandwich and let his mind drift back to the events of last night, particularly Charlene's story. Connor had expected her to give him the brush off, but she had talked about Hilborn as if the man had just stepped out to the corner drugstore to get a pack of smokes, rather than taken a step off a hotel balcony. But now as he thought about it, he realized she really hadn't told him much at all, just that Hilborn had rented a room from her—and then she deftly led him down the base path with Lou Gehrig and her suspicion that Hilborn had been seeing doctors and taking medications. It had been a beautiful performance, right up until Connor had mentioned Bodean Barr—and everything suddenly changed.

He thought back to Jacob Wheeler, wondered whether he'd been able to free himself from the cloth ties, and that's when a rather large man wearing black jeans and a tie-dyed T-shirt came up to Connor's table.

"I hear you lookin' for someone," he said, the accent as distant from the deep south as it could get, more like something from Australia.

"Just aimin' to get a fix on someone who was in here last week," Connor said.

"A fix? What sort of fix?"

"Look … I'm not trying to cause any trouble." He wiped his mouth with a napkin and set it down on the table. "And don't worry—I'm not a cop. But this guy—" he held up the color photo of Bodean Barr "—he was in here last week, and I'm hoping someone might have seen him. That's all."

The man in the tie-dye looked long and hard at Barr's face, finally said, "Just so you know, this is my place. I own it. Name's Mack, from Sidney. The land down under. Oz, to you Americans. People used to call me Oz, so … Mack Oz. Maccaws. Get it?"

Connor extended his hand and said, "Glad to meet you, Mack."

"Pleasure's all mine. Now this guy in the picture, here—yeah, maybe he was in here, maybe he wasn't. But he's clearly out of his element." "His element?" Connor repeated.

The big man cleared his throat and said, "Look around you. Then tell me if this guy in the photo fits. You too, for that matter."

Connor understood what he meant, and said so. "That's what doesn't add up. But I know this guy was in here, most likely with someone else. Another man, I would presume."

"That presumption would be correct. But like I said, he doesn't fit.

So, if he was here, it was for a reason."

"The reason could've been his friend," Connor suggested.

Mack from Oz made a show of crossing his arms, showing off biceps hardened from years of heavy lifting. "Could be," he agreed. "But in here, the kind of questions you're asking don't go over too good. You hear what I'm saying?"

"I think it's pretty clear."

"Good. So, here's what you're gonna do. You're gonna finish that Reuben and those fries and that unsweet tea, and then you're going to leave. Take your time; no rush. Enjoy yourself. But when the bill comes don't even think of paying it—just leave it on the table, cuz your money's no good here at Maccaws. Just go out that front door, and be thankful for today and tomorrow, and the next day." "And don't come back," Connor added, just for clarity. "You learn quick," Mack from Oz said.

What still didn't add up, Connor thought as he stepped out into the late May heat, was what Bodean Barr was doing at Maccaws. Out of his element, the man had said. But the receipt was proof that he'd been there—unless, of course, it wasn't Barr's in the first place. Since there was no signature he couldn't be sure. But Connor had found it in the dead man's shack, which more likely than not put him inside the place, with someone else. The same day before he had been seen at the Cape Myrtle Hotel, heading up to Jon Hilborn's room.

He'd parked the Camaro on the street, two blocks up on 9th Avenue, and he took his time getting there. His business here in Myrtle Beach was just about wrapped up, but he realized he was in no real hurry to leave. The wind off the ocean was heavy with salt and filled with the sounds of gulls and petrels and the constant rattle of palmetto fronds. Somewhere in the distance he heard the clatter of a wooden roller coaster jolting toward the sky, then the screams of kids as it plummeted back to earth. Somewhere close by a siren squealed, followed by the loud horn of a fire truck blasting through an intersection not that far away.

The roar was so loud he almost missed his phone ringing, but he managed to pull it out of his pocket and hit the "on" button before it stopped.

"Jack Connor," he said, not bothering to check the screen to see who was calling.

"Tat Man," Caitlin Thomas said, her piercing voice not that much different from the siren. "I have that four-one-one you wanted." "Go," he said.

She went. "Jacob Wheeler, age thirty-two. Last known address was the one you gave me, on Seagull Court. Couple minor charges, including a B and E when he was a minor. Charged as an adult, got time served. Looks like there was another bust last year, this one a fed rap for trafficking, but it got kicked. Other than that, he's clean, or too smart for anything to stick."

"Trust me, he's not that smart," Connor assured her. "Anything else on him?"

"Has a hard time holding a job, and he's done just about all of them. Tree cutter, lawn cutter, stone cutter. He's cleaned septic tanks, cement trucks, and swimming pools. Did a stint in the Marines but washed out. Last known employer was at the beach boardwalk, fixing rides. That was last fall."

Connor thought a second about the kids squealing their hearts out on the roller coaster, then focused back on Mr. Wheeler. "Anything that ties him in with Bodean Barr?" he asked.

"Just that his older brother Leland did time at Bennettsville at the same time that Barr was there," she said.

Marjorie Chambers had mentioned that her brother had a prison buddy named Leland, and Connor would bet good money that Jacob's brother was one and the same. He remembered how she described the guy: bald head, jailhouse tats of Nazi symbols and lightning bolts. Sharp as a bowling ball.

"Don't suppose you ran Leland through the system," he said.

"It's what I do," Caitlin reminded him. "The guy's a real sweetheart, believe me."

"Got an address?"

"North Charleston, near the stinky plant."

That would be the paper mill on the Cooper River at the foot of the Don Holt Bridge. The plant produced everything from pet food bags to beer cartons, and when the wind was blowing just right, the smoke billowing out of its stacks could almost be seen from outer space.

"Can you text it to me?" he asked. "I'm just about done up here."

In fact, Connor had one more place to go before he left town, and that was back to Coogers. Last night he hadn't checked to see if the bar was even open for lunch, but some people always needed their alcoholic fix, and where there's a bottle, there's a way. Or something like that.

Business was slow, but at least it was business. Connor pushed his way inside and wandered up to the bar, where he took up a position between two stools and waited for the bartender to notice he was there. He was at the other end of the counter, chatting it up with a guy in jeans and a stained T-shirt, his ass spilling over the edge of his own stool, both hands protectively wrapped around a draft beer. Connor couldn't hear what they were talking about, nor did he care. This was just one of those quick in-and-out things, maybe involving a beer if he had to buy one in order to get what he wanted.

Finally, the bartender pushed away from the counter and made his way over to where Connor was standing.

"Get you somethin'?" he asked.

"What do you know about Charlene Marks?" he asked. "Nothin', less you're drinkin'."

Connor ordered a Coors Light and slid his butt up onto a stool. The bartender ran him a cold draft, brought it over and set it down on a cardboard coaster.

"Now do you know anything about her?" Connor asked.

"Hottest chick in this whole damn town," the bartender said.

"I mean something I don't already know."

"I don't know what you don't know."

Connor dug the photo of Bodean Barr out of his pocket and laid it on the counter in front of him. "You ever see her with this man?" The bartender actually studied it. "Don't rightly know. Maybe could've, but I'm not too good with faces."

Connor wondered if the bartender was maybe pushing for a tip here, something like a ten or twenty to help grease his memory. But he didn't bite. "You know where she might be?" he asked instead.

"Nope, and if I did, I wouldn't tell you. But it don't matter anyway, cuz she just up an' quit this place."

"What do you mean, she quit?"

"Jus' like it sounds. 'Bout an hour ago she came in, told T-Bone— he's the manager—she was headin' out, for good. T jus' 'bout freaked, cuz she an' her band was packin' 'em in jus' 'bout ever' night. Tried to get her to change her mind, but she said it was a family emergency and she was hittin' the road." Just like that.

The address Caitlin Thomas had given Connor for Charlene Marks turned out to be in an apartment complex known as the Gypsy Rose Villas, just a couple blocks off Highway 17. It was a clean and tidy place, with a swimming pool and trees and a nice view of a water tower, and it was quite clear that Charlene was not there. Her place was on the ground floor, and the last time she had been there—most likely less than an hour ago, after picking up her check at Coogers— she had left the curtain over the kitchen window open. That and the fact that no one answered when Connor hit the doorbell provided conclusive evidence that she was gone.

Still, Connor walked around to the rear of the building, where Charlene also had left the plastic horizontal blinds over the glass slider wide open. A card table was folded up and now leaned against a scuffed wall, two folding metal chairs set next to it. The carpet looked worn and dirty, and a bag of trash was tied up and ready to be hauled out to the dumpster. Other than that, the apartment had been cleaned out in a hurry, and Charlene and her Jeep Cherokee were an hour north, south, or west.

Connor hit the road about two minutes after that, and had just about made it back to where the main business spur connects with Highway 17 when his phone rang. The screen said it was Caitlin Thomas at Citadel Security.

"Where are you?" she asked him, a distinct sense of urgency in her voice.

"Just south of Myrtle Beach—"

"Well, you may want to pull over at the nearest gas station."

A sudden feeling of foreboding hit him as an icy shiver raked his spine. "What's going on?" he asked.

"You know that address you gave me?"

"The one where Jacob Wheeler lives? What about it?"

"Well, that's the thing. I'm not sure he lives there anymore."

"I just saw him there last night—"

"You'd better be careful what you say," she said, her tone shifting to one of deep concern. "Every call in and out of Citadel is monitored for safety and follow-up."

"Yeah, I know that," Connor replied. "So what—?"

"So, there was a fire out there early this morning. News I'm getting is his place went up like a propane tank. Police and fire marshals are still on the scene."

Connor sensed where this was going, and didn't like what it implied. "You're sure it's the same place?"

"Hundred percent. Old trailer home, Ford pick-up truck parked out front. License plate matches what you gave me."

"What about Wheeler?" he said, fearing the worst.

"Fire chief found him inside. Or what they think is him. It's going to be one of those dental records things."

Chapter 22

Holy shit, Connor thought. *If I hadn't tied his arms and legs to the chair he could have gotten out.*

"You there, Tat Man?" she asked him.

"Yeah, I'm here," he told her. He edged his foot on the brake and pulled into a gas station, steering the Camaro around to where the air hose and vacuum were located. "You said the cops and fire marshals are still at the scene?"

"As of twenty minutes ago. But if I were you—"

But Connor wasn't listening to her, or what she would do. He was already running the scenario through his head, trying to figure out how this had gone bad. Caitlin had said the trailer had gone up like a fireball—actually like a propane tank, which didn't make sense, because Connor hadn't smelled a thing. Pressurized gas is treated with a chemical that gives it an unmistakable noxious odor, and he hadn't caught one whiff of that. Nor was there the smell of gasoline in the place. If an accelerant had been used, which had to be the case, it hadn't been there when Connor was.

Still, he had tied Jacob Wheeler to the chair, and in all likelihood the guy had still been struggling to get out of it when the explosion blew the mobile home apart. He would have been fried to a crisp before the terrycloth ties had a chance to burn through, and that's when Connor wondered whether the fire had been so fierce that there would be any trace of them left at the scene. And whether anyone might have seen an orange Camaro nudging its way down the gravel road deep into the piney woods late last night.

"—So, it's really not a good idea to go back out there, if that's what you're thinking," she said. "Not without a lawyer."

"This is my fault," he said.

"We don't know that. All we know is that a body was found inside that trailer. It could have been Wheeler, or it could be someone else."

Connor killed the engine and stared through the windshield, both hands gripping the wheel. "I tied him to a chair," he said. "He might not have gotten free."

"We don't know that, either. And like I told you, all Citadel phone calls are recorded."

"Too late now, I guess," Connor said. "Look—I'm going back out there, check it out."

"I'd advise against it—" she told him.

"If you don't hear back from me in an hour, call Mr. James," he said. "I might be needing one of his lawyers."

"Tat Man—" she said, but it was too late. He'd already hung up.

The narrow road through the pines and cypress looked different during the day, but that generally was true of just about everything. Now Connor actually could see the individual two-rut driveways with aging mobile homes and rusted vehicles and trailered ATVs that he had trusted were there, but couldn't make out in the darkness. Clumps of Spanish moss hung from the trees like ZZ Top's beards, and beds of petunias and pansies were planted inside old tractor tires that had been painted white. A thick veil of steam hovered near the ground, and the rich smell of pluff mud told him a marsh was nearby, just through the pines.

He wasn't sure he would remember exactly where Charlene Marks had pulled off the road last night and summoned Jacob Wheeler from his home, but the blue and red strobes told him all he needed to know. He bounced the Camaro around a sharp turn and found the dirt road clogged with fire trucks and police units and other emergency vehicles. An ambulance was backed into the driveway, angled sideways with its rear doors open so whatever was wheeled out from the charred mound that had been the trailer could bypass the scorched pick-up that was still parked there.

Connor slowed as he approached the scene, but a cop in a North Myrtle Beach Police uniform motioned for him to keep going. "Official business," he said, as if that explained everything.

"What's going on?" Connor asked, trying to sound innocent.

"You live here?" the cop asked.

"My brother does, just up the road, there," Connor explained, nodding his head past the hood of his car.

"Then go there."

But Connor wasn't going to go there. Instead he turned and stared at the charred remains of Jacob Wheeler's trailer. It was just a pile of twisted black metal and a few wisps of smoke rising from still-smoldering cinders.

"Looks bad," he said, clearly stating the obvious. "Hope no one was hurt—"

The cop appeared torn between getting Connor to move on and wanting to tell *someone* what had happened here. A nameplate above his breast pocket read "Talbot." "One fatality, unidentified," he said in the best official voice he could muster. "Found him in the kitchen."

The kitchen, not the living room. "Homicide, you think?"

"What I think is you'd better go and visit your brother," was all Talbot said. Touching his hand to his gun for emphasis.

"Yes, sir."

Connor touched his foot to the gas and inched forward, trying to act casual as he pictured how this might have gone down. If the cop named Talbot was correct and Wheeler was found in the kitchen, he'd been able to free himself from the strips of wet towels Connor had used on his arms and legs. And he'd had plenty of time to do that—almost five hours—if the fire had started around seven.

Then there was Charlene Marks. Where was she, and how did she figure into what had gone down here? She had driven out here last night to … to do what? Warn Wheeler? Alert him to the fact that someone had come to Coogers asking questions about Bodean Barr? She hadn't stayed long, just a few impatient minutes before she was on her way. And out of town, as it turned out. So why the hasty exit?

Which brought it all around full circle to Bodean Barr, Jacob Wheeler, and his brother Leland. And, of course, Jon Hilborn.

Connor was itching to get home and take a shower, but he wanted to check out Leland Wheeler's place in North Charleston before doubling back to Sullivans Island. The wind was blowing from the west this afternoon, which meant that the stench from the paper plant hit him full force as he headed up the Mark Clark Expressway. He'd put the top down for the ride back from Myrtle Beach and he easily could have pulled over to the shoulder to raise it again, but there were too many eighteen-wheelers hauling shipping containers from the Wando port for him to do that without being clipped. So, he endured the disgusting odor, knowing that as soon as he had the plant in his rear-view mirror, his nose was home free.

Unless, of course, the wind shifted.

The address Caitlin Thomas had texted to him was easy to find, an old weathered shack several blocks off North Rhett Avenue with a dirt lawn and chain-link fencing that was hanging in rusted curls from its support posts. It clearly was a no-collar neighborhood, judging by the shirtless men nursing PBRs on their front porches, only partly keeping their eyes open while kids chased squirrels and dogs yapped at other dogs. Somewhere someone had poured what smelled like a whole can of lighter fluid on a mound of charcoal and touched a match to it. It gave off a rich and pungent smell, but in the long run it was better than the paper plant.

Connor pulled the Camaro off the street and coasted to a stop. The unexpected appearance of a 1967 classic with a scooped hood and loud pipes caused several of the neighbors to look up from their beers and broad bellies to catch a look. Even the dogs seemed to stop barking for a spell, at least until Connor cut the gas and listened to the clicking sound of the engine block starting to cool.

It was probably bad timing, Connor showing up like this the same day Leland Wheeler's brother was killed, but tomorrow or the next day wouldn't be any better. Besides, he didn't intend to stay more than a couple minutes, just long enough to get a sense of the man. So, he opened the door and slowly got out of the car, stretching out the cramps that had formed in his legs on the drive down from Myrtle Beach.

The lack of a vehicle of any kind told Connor that Leland Wheeler probably was not at home, but he still crossed the dusty yard toward the front door. Knobby tire tracks in the dirt hinted at a motorcycle of some kind, but it clearly wasn't there now. As he made his way up the wooden steps to the front porch he felt a half dozen pair of eyes keeping an eye on him from other porches nearby. Not exactly great entertainment, but probably more gripping than watching a rerun of *Ice Road Truckers.*

Connor knocked on the front door, then peered through the glass into the darkened living room. He couldn't see much more than a couch and a television, so he knocked again, just to make sure. Then he retreated down the steps and moved over to the living room window, where he had a better view of the interior, although there was not much more to see. The place was sparsely furnished, the sofa and TV he'd just observed, plus a couple chairs and a spindly table that still had a plate of pizza crust on it and an empty jelly glass. An ashtray with a mound of butts in it completed the picture.

Connor moved around to the side of the house, caught a glimpse of a bedroom with a double bed, the sheets kicked to the floor. Clothes were scattered everywhere, and a card table set in the corner was covered with mounds of papers and files, and more dirty dishes. In another corner stood a shotgun, its barrel pointing toward the ceiling, a plastic bag from a local sporting goods store set beside it on the floor. Probably held a couple boxes of shells, he figured.

The kitchen door around the back of the house was locked and a curtain was pulled over the grimy glass. Connor tried to peer through a crack but there wasn't enough light inside to see much of anything, so he gave up. He edged his way back around to the front, and that's when he saw the white Chevrolet Caprice with a blue light bar parked behind the Camaro. An officer dressed in black trousers and black shirt, gold badge pinned to his chest and radio pinned to his shoulder, was just climbing out.

"Stop right there," the officer said. He was black, a little too thin to have been on the job for very long, no sign of the typical donut spread forming around his gut. "What's your name?"

Connor stopped and said, "Jack Connor. I'm looking for Leland Wheeler."

"That so?" the officer asked, coming closer. Hand near, but not yet touching, the gun in his holster.

"He lives here," Connor said. "Least that's what I hear."

The officer studied Connor carefully, the tattoos and bald head obviously ringing an alarm in his head. "You try knocking?"

"Yep. Then I went around back, see if maybe he was out working in the yard. Maybe having a beer."

"You have some I.D.?" Suspicious, as if he didn't believe a word he was hearing.

Connor inhaled a quick breath, then dug his wallet out of his back pocket. He peeled out his driver's license and handed it to the officer.

"Jack Connor," the cop read from the card.

"Like I said."

The cop handed it back and said, "Here's the situation. We're keeping an eye on this house. No big secret; Leland Wheeler, he lives here, and he knows we're watching him. No sign of the guy or his bike since yesterday. So, when a pretty orange classic Camaro with a scooped hood pulls into the yard, it's bound to draw a little scrutiny. You follow what I'm saying?"

"Like GPS." Connor tucked the license back into his wallet, which he slipped back into his pocket. "So, what's he into, he's got police keeping a tight leash on him? Looks of this place, meth or crack would be my guess."

The officer shook his head and said, "Sorry … can't say. What's your business with him, anyway?"

"Something I'm working on, and people around him keep dying."

"You a private detective?" the cop asked. Then he did a double take and said, "Wait … I've seen you on TV."

"'America's Got Talent'?"

The cop grinned at that. "Hardly. You're the one took down that sicko a couple weeks ago, right? This thing you're working on, is it anything like that?"

"Nope … just tracking down something for a friend," Connor assured him. "Wheeler's name just came up yesterday, and I wanted to check him out."

The officer stared at him then, trying to get a sense of whether this man with all the tattoos was telling him anything near the truth. Finally, he pulled a small notebook out of a pocket, along with a pen, and said, "You mind giving me your contact info?"

Connor told him where he lived and offered him his cell number, as well. "Does this mean you'll let me know when you find him?"

"Nope. This means in case your story doesn't check out, you'll be hearing from us again. And it probably won't be me, either." "I'll keep that in mind," Connor said.

The officer left not long after that, but only after making sure Connor got into his car and started the engine. Then he backed out into the street, far enough so Connor could do the same, and waited until he was on his way before making a three-point turn and heading back to where he'd been parked before the pretty orange Camaro had showed up.

Connor was halfway back to Sullivan's Island when his phone rang. It was Caitlin Thomas, and when he answered she simply said,

"I have an update."

"Update on what?"

"The man who fried in the trailer," she told him. "Jacob Wheeler."

"So, what's up?"

"It wasn't you," Caitlin said. "You didn't kill him." "And you know this how?" Connor asked.

"The M.E. just did the prelim, found two entry wounds in his forehead. Matching exit wounds out the back." "Double tap," he said.

"That's what they call it, yes," Caitlin confirmed.

This was good news, but not quite good enough. "Still, if I hadn't tied him up in the first place, he might've gotten out before he got shot," Connor said.

"Ifs and mights are the little devils of the mind," she told him. "The fact is, Jacob Wheeler didn't have a very good day, and you only figured into a small part of it."

She was right, of course, but that still didn't make it any easier for Connor to erase the mental picture of Wheeler trapped in a flash fire rolling through his mobile home. He recalled the unspeakable desperation that folks who were trapped inside the twin towers must have felt when they elected to jump from ninety floors up rather than be hit by a wall of flames.

"They find any slugs or casings?" he asked her.

"No info on that," Caitlin said. "They're still sifting through ashes, and all that stuff."

Connor thanked her for the update and clicked off. A few minutes later he hit the causeway over to Sullivan's Island and saw the tide was way, way in, the tidal flow almost up to the roadway on both sides. It was a steamy evening, summer being just a few weeks away, and there was a warm sweetness in the air, almost like honey. When he pulled up to the rise at the Ben Sawyer Bridge the lights began to flash amidst the clanging of bells, and he knew it was the top of the hour. He braked to a stop three cars back from the barricade, which slowly lowered across the roadway.

As he sat there, the throaty 396 gurgling under the hood and the tip of a sailboat mast gliding past the lip of the bridge toward Charleston harbor, he couldn't help but consider how all this was connected. Jon Hilborn, dead. Bodean Barr, who had visited Hilborn in the Cape Myrtle Hotel, also dead. Charlene Marks, Hilborn's roommate—and who really knew what else—gone. After paying a visit to Jacob Wheeler, who also was dead. Then there was Leland Wheeler, prison pals with Bo Barr, who probably was still alive. He'd been gone for more than a day—not really that long, in the grand scheme of things—and even the North Charleston PD didn't appear to know where he was. Even though they seemed to care enough to have his house under surveillance.

More questions then flowed into Connor's brain: Who had gone to Bo Barr's house and pumped his head off with a shotgun? Was it the same person who had paid a visit to Jacob Wheeler and placed two rounds neatly between his eyes, then set the trailer on fire? And what was the point in that? The gunman couldn't possibly have figured the flames would hide the two bullet holes, so why bother tossing a match? Was he—or she—trying to cover tracks or destroy something, or simply make a vicious statement? Whatever it was, it circled back around to Jon Hilborn, whose death—and life—remained as much of a riddle as ever.

Connor didn't feel much like cooking dinner, so when the bridge closed again he grabbed some takeout at the local taco joint and brought it home to accompany a martini and a tangerine sunset over the marsh. As he settled into his chair his phone rang, and when he checked the screen he saw it was Danielle. Great timing.

"You really did a number on him," she said in a voice that was surprisingly terse. "I'm talking about Richard."

Connor already figured that, and said, "How was I supposed to know who he was? He was aiming a gun at me."

"He said he told you who he was—"

"Not until after I'd decked him," Connor said, thinking, what is this? "The guy broke into my home, Danielle. He woke me up with a gun he probably isn't licensed to carry."

There was silence on the other end, followed by a long, deep breath. Then: "I know, Jack. And I'm sorry. Really, I am. But his face … it's like a truck backed over his head."

"Yeah, I'm sorry about that. Something Uncle Sam taught me. But I'm telling you, I didn't know who the guy was, and I wasn't about to let him shoot me. And when he finally did tell me he was your husband … well, I got the feeling he was hoping he'd catch you here, too."

She evidently hadn't thought of that and said, "Oh, Jesus. This is really a mess."

"Did he tell you the gun was loaded?"

Danielle sighed again, then said, "He says he just meant to scare you."

"Mission accomplished. Look, Danielle—I don't make a habit of beating people up. I hope you know that about me. But one of the first things the army teaches you in boot camp is hand-to-hand combat skills. Fact is, if you get so close to the enemy that you're going at it *mano-a-mano,* you're already in big trouble, so most guys end up using their knuckles only when they get in a bar brawl."

"Or when a jealous husband shows up."

"Yeah, that too." Now it was Connor's turn to take a deep breath, which he let out very slowly. "Let me guess he told you he cut things off with Tinkerbell and wants you to give your marriage another try."

"You hit the nail pretty much on the head," Danielle conceded. "My guess is she took one look at what you did to him and booted his ass out."

"So where does that leave us?" Connor asked her.

"Where that leaves us is I have to think about what I'm doing. With Richard, and with you. This is one of those turning points in life where there's no map or owner's manual."

"I'd be happy to give you directions," Connor said, trying to sound lighthearted, even though he felt exactly the opposite.

Still, she giggled, then said, "It may come to that. But for now, I have to figure out where I am all on my own. And that may take a while."

"How long is *awhile?*"

"That part's a little hazy," she admitted. "I'm thinking it's located somewhere in between a jif and an eon. But Connor—?"

There was something in her voice that felt like a knot being tightened around his heart, if just for a moment. "Yes?" he said, cautiously.

"There's something you really need to know. For what it's worth, I think I'm probably falling in love with you."

"Is that a fact?"

"Fact," she assured him. "And probably not just probably."

Chapter 23

One martini turned into three, not a healthy thing for a work night—or any night, for that matter. Something Dr. Pinch at the V.A. kept telling him. But Danielle's call had led directly to a second glass, and then everything that had started racing through Connor's mind quickly fed into a third. And at the bottom of that glass he learned a new equation about gin, a painful one that Miss Benson never mentioned in her physics class: $V = QG \times n$. Or, in more understandable terms, vision equals the quantity of gin in your glass, multiplied by the number of glasses.

The next morning the entire formula translated to a brain-hammering headache, which was only partially solved by a run on the beach. A dome of high pressure had settled in over the lowcountry, meaning that even at seven o'clock the sun was already making its presence felt, the air hot and thick and sticky as he pounded his way down the sand. The waves lapped gently at his feet while a small pod of dolphins humped their way through the surf just a short distance from shore. At one point a chocolate lab raced by him in pursuit of a tennis ball, the dog's paws sounding like the hooves of a race horse rounding the clubhouse turn at Pimlico. He caught the ball on the second bounce, snaring it like Connor had seen Derek Jeter do once in Comerica Park in Detroit, although he was pretty sure Jeter hadn't used his mouth.

A large coffee from Café Medley helped pack down the hangover, and by the time he arrived at The Plant his brain had lost the bass drum effect, although there was still a hint of reverb. He spent the first hour catching up on Palmetto BioClean business, filing insurance claims for the last couple of jobs and following up on older cases that were still being disputed by the various underwriters. Most homeowner and business policies included a provision for cleaning up blood and other toxic substances, but some claims adjusters still balked when they saw the actual damages.

When he was finished with official business he clicked on Google and ran a search on Jacob Wheeler. That yielded countless Facebook and LinkedIn entries, plus a link to a bass fisherman, an author, and a character in a western movie. He refined the search by adding "South Carolina" to the search terms, and found there were four people with that name living in the state. He made a mental note to have Caitlin Thomas narrow that down, then changed "South Carolina" to "Leland Wheeler" to see what the search engine came spit out.

Turns out, not much, except for a few genealogical searches that appeared to list every possible member of every Wheeler family in the history of the world. Connor scrolled down through the short list of results, none of it making much sense until he clicked through to the second of two pages. That's when he saw a single entry with a summary that read:

> **WHEELER**—U.S. Attorney General's Office…DEA uncovers smuggling scheme … that undercover sources believe moved thousands of pounds of cocaine a year. Two brothers…**Leland Wheeler** and … **Jacob Wheeler** … reported ties to organized crime…

Connor clicked on the link and was forwarded to a webpage for a newspaper up in the city of Augusta. The story was dated ten weeks previously and recounted a DEA sting operation that had netted a dozen suspects in what the feds believed was a major east coast trafficking ring. It read:

Feds Arrest Drug Suspects In Early Morning Raids

ATLANTA—Federal agents arrested a dozen men and women early this morning in what was described as a major sting operation that covered four cities in Georgia, Tennessee, Mississippi, and South Carolina. Prosecutors allege the suspects were involved in trafficking cocaine, methamphetamines, and heroin from the port of Charleston to Atlanta, Nashville, and Biloxi, and had ties to organized crime.

DEA agents say the operation was initiated 18 months ago after police in Berkeley County, SC, pulled over a rental truck transporting cocaine and assault weapons. South Carolina authorities arrested the driver of that truck, Jacob Wheeler, as well as his brother Leland, who was providing an escort in a separate vehicle. The two men reportedly cooperated with prosecutors in the federal investigation, during which at least one alleged drug trafficker negotiated to buy an undisclosed quantity of narcotics from undercover agents.

The article went on to name the men and women who had been rounded up during the pre-dawn raids, all of them scattered across the south in communities located along the major interstates. He read the story again, paying close attention to the names and time frames involved with the events leading up to the sting. It seemed that after the two-Wheeler brothers were nabbed with the load of drugs and guns, prosecutors made it clear they both were facing serious jail time. Connor hadn't run a sheet on either of them, but he knew Leland Wheeler already had done at least one stretch in Bennettsville, where he had met Bodean Barr. He'd probably be looking at twenty years, and Jacob likely would have been facing at least the same amount.

But prosecutors apparently had given them a deal. With the combined I.Q. of a Hostess Twinkie the Wheeler brothers obviously were not the brains behind this outfit, so they were released back into the wild. With the feds looking over their shoulders the two of them helped lay the groundwork that eventually would snare a dozen suspects, two tons of drugs with the street value of eighteen million dollars, several crates of assault rifles, and close to a million dollars in cash. That had been just over ten weeks ago, and somehow—maybe through a glitch in the system, maybe the witness protection plan— Jacob and Leland were still on the street.

Correction: One of them was dead, and the other one was missing.

And that's what just didn't add up. First, if the sting had occurred a full ten weeks ago, both Wheelers would have either disappeared or shuffled off to a federal prison where their identities would not be known. Even if they were inducted into the Witness Security Program, as it was officially known, they wouldn't still be freewheeling around the Palmetto State. They'd most likely be selling pizzas in Minnesota or farming potatoes in Idaho. But here they were, Jacob almost living out in the open in a trailer in North Myrtle Beach, and Leland blending into a white trash neighborhood just outside Charleston. Now one of the DEA's key witnesses was dead, and his brother apparently had eluded whatever surveillance team had been put in place to babysit him.

There was one other thing at the bottom of the article that caught Connor's attention, and now he found himself reading it again for a third time:

At a news conference organized to announce the arrests, federal agent Andrew Corliss said the DEA sting interrupted one of the largest drug and weapon trafficking operations in the U.S. in the last decade. "We watched these individuals for well over a year, and we have full, comprehensive knowledge of how they worked," Mr. Corliss said. "We know how the goods entered the country, where they came from, where they were going, and— most important—who was involved with their purchase and delivery. We are still searching for two primary suspects who are involved on the financial end of the operation, but with the evidence we have compiled, apprehending them is just a matter of time."

The story went on to quote Agent Corliss as saying that an additional individual believed to be involved with the transportation of U.S. currency to offshore locations also was being sought by U.S. Treasury agents.

Connor printed out the article, then quickly Googled "Andrew Corliss + DEA" and came up with dozens of hits. Many of them dealt with other cases the agent was involved with, but several were follow-up reports on the drug sting. There wasn't much new information except that all suspects had been arraigned in federal district court, and the unnamed suspect who was mentioned by Corliss still had not been apprehended.

When Connor finished with Google he dialed Caitlin Thomas at Citadel, asked her if she could track down an agent at the Drug Enforcement Agency.

"This is still about the Hilborn case?" she asked him.

"One and the same," he said. "And probably a long shot. The agent's name is Andrew Corliss."

"I'll see what I can do," she told him. "And by the way, the autopsy confirmed the preliminary exam. Jacob Wheeler definitely was killed by the two pops to the head."

Probably fired by someone who wasn't too happy about his role in the DEA sting.
"Good to know," he said. "Although it doesn't do Wheeler any good."

When Connor hung up he sat at his desk a minute, cracking his knuckles, then turned back to his computer and brought Google back up on his screen. He typed in "Charlene Marks" and waited a few seconds for the search results to appear. It hadn't occurred to him that she might have her own website but there it was, right at the top of the search results, her stunning eyes staring out at him from the screen. He studied the homepage for a moment, with separate tabs for her bio, upcoming gigs, recent press, her music, videos, and photos. He moved the cursor over "Bio" and a moment later a page full of text, accompanied by another but equally stunning photo, filled his screen. It read, in part:

Anyone who has heard Charlene Marks perform in any music venue, large or small, knows the passion and conviction with which she sings whenever she's on a stage. The only daughter of a medical supply salesman and a music teacher, Charlene began singing professionally at age 4, when she was paid $10 to perform Kool and the Gang's hit song "Cherish" at a family wedding.

Born and raised in New Orleans, Charlene—who was known as "Babe" as a child—began taking her music seriously during a singing competition in high school, and when she was 15 she received a waiver that allowed her to play in establishments that served alcoholic beverages. She recorded her first album at the age of 16, and since then has produced six more, including one that reached #88 on the Billboard R&B album chart. She prefers to perform live, however, and has played in nightclubs throughout the Gulf area and up and down the East coast. In addition to her albums and digital tracks, which are available on iTunes and Amazon, she has half a dozen videos posted on YouTube.

Connor clicked on the photo tab and found a full archive of images that began when she was just a child, and continued up through her appearances at several Bourbon Street clubs, and most recently at Coogers. He recognized the small stage but not the two musicians performing with her, and he realized that the bassist and drummer were just as disposable as a light bulb.

What was it about the mention of Bodean Barr that spooked you? he wondered as his eyes drifted from one dazzling photo to the next. *Why did you run to Jacob Wheeler's place, and where are you now?*

"This makes seven weeks in a row you haven't cancelled," Dr. Pinch said as Connor settled into the leather chair across a scuffed coffee table from him. Pinch was the V.A. shrink who had drawn Connor's case, and they had been meeting once a week in this stale little office since last fall. Except for the times Connor called to cancel, or simply didn't show—something Pinch told him was standard operating procedure for a lot of returning vets who didn't want someone messing their heads up any more than they already were. "Seems to me you're making progress."

"Could be I've got nowhere else to be," Connor suggested as he unconsciously picked at the cuticles of his thumbs. It was a nervous habit he'd acquired when he was young and his parents—usually his father—sat him down in the living room and grilled him about his latest blunder. Denting the front fender of the family car, or quitting the baseball team without telling anyone. Things that these days were long-forgotten, but back then seemed like class A felonies.

"Or maybe you're learning to live with yourself again," Dr. Pinch said. "Re-entry takes some time."

Pinch was a large man, mid-sixties, with a gray U.S. Marine buzz cut covering his scalp like a moldy peach that's been left in the fridge too long. His upper body was strong, arms and neck thick from regular workouts with weights, but his legs had atrophied from decades of inactivity. After three tours of duty in Vietnam, a bullet had sliced through his spine in the waning days of Desert Storm and put him in a chair, and that had made him want to put a bullet in his head. He'd had to work through his own anger and resentment and bitterness, a personal journey that had been long and difficult but now allowed him to understand what the person sitting in that chair opposite him was thinking and feeling.

"I think I'm doing pretty well, considering what some of my buddies are going through," Connor told him.

"That's a fact, and you should be encouraged by how far you've come," the doctor said, trying not to sound condescending. "But you're still shredding your thumbs and squirming as if your nads are in a vice."

This was the way their appointments usually began, Connor behaving as if he'd rather be anywhere else on earth than here. Well, certainly not the killing grounds of Iraq, but just about anywhere else. He studied Dr. Pinch for a long moment, and stopped picking at his thumbs.

"I learned some tough news the other day," he said. "It didn't sit well."

"What sort of bad news?" Pinch asked, leaning forward and pushing his thick black glasses further up on his nose.

Connor quickly told him what Eddie James had said about Private Stone, how she had tried to slit her wrists. And how he, Connor, then made a few calls to make sure she was all right.

The V.A. doctor let out a weary sigh and said, "I'm terribly sorry to hear this. I really am. I believe we discussed this sort of thing in our very first meeting."

"'Cutting through the bullshit,' is what you said," Connor agreed. "You weren't going to sugarcoat the crap most veterans get hit with.

Depression, divorce, booze, drugs, suicide—"

"Exactly," Pinch said. "Coming home can be tougher than an astronaut re-entering the atmosphere. War is hell, and no one really is prepared for life on this side of it."

Connor couldn't help but notice how drab the small office was, just as it was the first day he walked through Pinch's door. Stark white walls with framed certificates hanging on them, rows of books shoved into bookcases, and a withered Ficus tree lurking in the corner.

"Private Stone was raped, Doc," he said. "By one of our own."

Dr. Pinch didn't say anything, not for a while. When he did, his words came out slow and deliberate. "Let me guess: either she didn't report it or no one listened to her. Or maybe it just got swept under the rug."

"Sounds like you've heard this sort of thing before," Connor said.

"More often than I care to think," Pinch replied. "And I suspect I know where you're going with this."

"Please enlighten me, cuz I'm pretty damned confused. And pissed."

"C'mon, Mr. Connor. You can't fight everyone's demons for them. In fact, despite all your progress, you're still having trouble facing your own."

Connor crossed his arms and said, "I'm doing just fine, thank you.

And stop calling me Mr. Connor. My name is Jack."

"Okay, Jack. Are you still having night sweats?"

"Thanks for bringing that up—"

"And the dreams?"

Connor glared at him but said nothing.

"And the gin … how's that going for you?"

"Okay, so I still drink a bit. And I still wake up ten times a night. But not nearly as much as when I got out. Look, Doc. I know I'm not perfect. But at least I've got all my body parts and my brain's pretty much what it was. I've got a good job, and I go home to the same bed every night. That's more than most of my buddies can say. And Private Stone … shit, she was living under a bridge in Baltimore, until she found a shelter. Or rather a shelter found her."

"She needs to go to the V.A.," Dr. Pinch told him. "They're equipped to help people who are having coping issues."

"You don't get it, do you?" Connor said, trying to suppress his growing frustration. "The V.A. isn't her friend, it's the enemy. It wasn't just a bastard sergeant who raped her over there, it was the entire military. The whole friggin' Army, Doc. They screwed her in Iraq, and they screwed her when she got home."

"Let me blunt with you, Jack," Dr. Pinch said. "She got screwed. You got screwed. We all got screwed. I'm not making excuses, and I'm not trying to minimize what happened to your friend, Private Stone. The fact is, war sucks. And the people who make war don't much worry about what happens to the men and women in the trenches. That's why I'm here."

"To unscrew me?"

"No one can do that except yourself, Jack."

"So, then what? What is it you really get paid to do, Doc?"

"To help you figure out how to loosen your own screws. Like you said, you're doing better than a lot of soldiers when they come home.

Like your friend, Eddie."

Connor had told Dr. Pinch about Eddie during his first visit, explaining how the kid had lost an arm and suffered brain damage when their vehicle was rammed by a suicide bomber. Connor had been declared a hero for saving Eddie's life, but he still blamed himself for not seeing the suicide bomber handcuffed to the wheel of the Ford van until it was too late. Pinch had called it "survivor's guilt," but to Connor it just felt like total shit.

"I took him for a ride," Connor told him. "Top down, wind in his face."

"That was a really nice thing to do, Jack," Pinch said. "I'm sure Eddie enjoyed it thoroughly."

"Damn straight. But man, did I ever catch hell from his mom when we got back."

Half an hour later Connor pulled the Camaro into the dusty parking lot off Morrison Drive near the old Navy yard.

Kat Rattigan's black Boxster was pulled into a space in front of her P.I. firm, and an old GMC Suburban with a cracked taillight and a bad case of orange peel was parked in front of the billiard hall. He pulled in between the two vehicles and cut the gas, took one last sip from a cup of cold coffee, then got out and walked over to Rattigan's door.

Just like last time it was locked, so he pressed the buzzer and waited. No answer, so he pressed it again. After a third time he gave up, wondering why her car was there while she was not. Connor could have called ahead to make sure she was in the office, but he preferred the instant of surprise when a person doesn't have a chance to speculate on motive or agenda. He started back to his car, then decided to pay a visit to the billiard joint. All that coffee had to go somewhere, and right now it was being very insistent in telling him it wanted out of his system.

Connor figured the Suburban out front belonged to whoever owned the place, which meant that business had to be slow. Or maybe it didn't open until later, even though the sign in the window was glowing. But the door opened easily, a rush of cold air smacking him in the face as he stepped inside, one look telling him it was a classy joint. Classy by pool hall standards, anyway, no smell of beer hanging in the air or cheap aftershave mixing with bourbon or body odor. No peanut shells on the floor, no video game cocktail tables in the corners, no aging street signs or pawn shop memorabilia nailed to the walls.

Most pool halls Connor had ever been in essentially were honkytonks with billiard tables scattered around, but this place was set up like a swanky club with an elegant bar and beveled mirrors and lots of top-shelf booze. Sure, there were beer signs hanging on the walls, but they were tastefully arranged like pieces of art, no strands of dust or cobwebs dripping from them, and the lights that hung over the tables—six in all—looked right out of a decorators' catalog.

Then there were the tables themselves: gone was the green felt, the coin slots, the ball returns, the metal rails, drink stains and gouges on the felt where players had tried to jump the eight and scraped the table instead. No, these tables were all solid hardwood with inlaid pearl markers and maroon felt that looked brand new. And real leather pockets collected the balls, the theory here being that players were on the honor system to pay for a game, no stacking quarters on the rail to lay claim to the table. This clearly was a place where serious players had serious fun, no amateurs allowed.

Kat Rattigan was leaning over one of the tables in a far corner, her body extended over the rail, her very nice ass thrust out as she lined up her shot. Then there was a sudden motion, followed by a loud thwack as the cue ball did its thing.

"Yes!" she said, her voice like a whisper with an exclamation mark at the end. Without looking up, she circled the table to where the cue ball had come to rest near the opposite rail, then leaned over to get a fix on the seven.

Connor watched her, then took another look around the place: photos on the wall, a glass case full of trophies in the back, an unmarked door along the wall that was shared with K.R. Investigators next door. He edged over to the photographs, found himself looking at Kat Rattigan standing in front of an ornately carved table and holding a red, white, and blue three-tiered trophy. The bottom of the photo read "Ladies' 8-Ball Invitational, Caesars Palace, Las Vegas. "Another photo showed her using her outstretched arms to hold up a giant check made out to her in the amount of two hundred thousand dollars. "North American 8-Ball Championship, Phoenix," the printed caption read.

This time the cue ball hit its intended target with a much softer clack, and Connor looked up just as Kat Rattigan sank her target.

"Nice shot," he said.

That broke her concentration and she looked up, a peeved look in her eyes. Then she said, "Jack Connor?"

"I was in the neighborhood, thought I'd stop by for a quick question," he said. "You never said you were a pool champ—"

She said nothing for a moment, then said, "Ancient history, but yeah, I played a little 8-ball in my day."

"Looks like you still do," Connor said, glancing around the billiard hall.

"Once it's in your blood you can't get it out," she explained. "Sort of like heroin, what I'm told. So, what brings you to the seamier side of town?"

He considered her question for just a second, figuring there was no reason not to just come out with why he was there. "The name Charlene Marks mean anything to you?" he asked.

"Should it?"

"C'mon … a 'yes' or 'no' answer would do fine."

A smile seeped into her face and she said, "Buy you a beer?"

Not exactly what Connor expected, but a little hair of the dog couldn't hurt right about now. He checked his watch. "What the hell … it's past noon."

Kat Rattigan led Connor over to the bar, then used her chin to invite him to take a seat on a stool. No cheap bar stool, either: this one was polished steel, with two crossed cues cut into the seatback, the whole thing covered with a bright red powder coat that matched the tables. She raised a hinged section of counter, stepped behind the bar, and lifted the lid to a stainless-steel beer cooler. She pulled out two Sierra Nevada's and popped the tops, slid one in front of him.

She clinked her bottle against his and said, "Cheers. So, let me guess. Charlene Marks would be the young chick Jon Hilborn took up with after he ran out on his girlfriend up in North Carolina."

"So, what do you know about her?" Connor pressed. The beer was ice cold, and the first sip went down easily. "Charlene, I mean."

"I don't know shit, and Mary Alice Benson didn't want to talk. She's the woman up in N.C.—" she said it exactly that way, enn-cee "—but then you already know that. Said she's totally over what Hilborn did and is trying to move on with her life. We are talking about the same girl here, right? This Charlene Marks?"

"That would be her," Connor said, and then he launched into a heavily edited version of his trip up to Myrtle Beach the night before last. He explained about the club called Coogers, and the blues and soul music and the sushi dinner after the show, and how Charlene had insisted she and Jon Hilborn had just been friends, nothing sexual or intimate between them.

"You believe that?" Kat asked him.

"Probably not," he replied, mostly because there was a lot about Charlene's story that he didn't believe, so why hang on to that one piece. "Actually, she put on a good act. But then I asked her about Bodean Barr, and she freaked."

"She knew Bo Barr?" Kat asked, the wrinkles of a frown creasing her brow as she looked at him from across the bar.

"She didn't say so, not in so many words. But when I mentioned his name her eyes went dark, and then she stopped talking. She said our little chat was over, and to get out. So, I did."

"Do you think she knew Barr was dead?" Kat asked.

"She didn't say, but I figure she had to," Connor told her.

He wasn't about to go into how he had followed Charlene Marks and witnessed the exchange between her and Jacob Wheeler, whom he then beat the shit out of and tied up. All before someone else came by and tapped him twice in the head, then chicken-fried his ass.

"What's the connection, you think?" she asked.

"You said your client thought someone might be blackmailing Hilborn," Connor pressed. "You think it could have been Charlene and Bodean?"

"Anything's possible," Kat said with a shrug, but the doubtful look in her eyes told him she didn't think so.

"How about Leland or Jacob Wheeler?"

"Who are they?"

"Couple of dog turd brothers who knew Bo Barr and Charlene Marks," Connor explained. "Seems they got themselves mixed up in a DEA sting, ratted out a few of their fellow dog turds. That sort of thing doesn't go over too well with some folks."

"Where are these dog turd brothers now?" Kat Rattigan asked.

"One of 'em now is just fried shitlin'," he said, thinking he was being pretty clever. "And the last I heard, the other one's gone missing."

He took a long sip of beer while she considered what he had told her. Finally, she said, "It's obvious Hilborn was mixed up in something, and I doubt any of it was good. Could be these Wheeler brothers were mixed up in it, too. Now, do you mind if I run a name by you?"

Connor realized that the reason he had come inside the pool hall in the first place was to find the men's room, and the beer didn't help much in settling that need. But he didn't want to break the flow of the conversation, so he just pushed the urge to the back of his mind. "Go ahead," he said, taking another sip.

"Malcolm Nickels, spelled like the coin."

He'd never heard the name but didn't want to be too quick to admit it, so he turned it over in his brain for a second before saying, "Maybe, can't be sure. Why?"

Kat Rattigan took a big gulp from her bottle before answering. "Let's just say he was an acquaintance of Hilborn's. They did some deals together, things had to do with property development and business investment."

"It's what Hilborn did."

"Exactly. But what I hear is Nickels took a big risk, right about the time the economy crashed, and lost a large chunk of change. Blamed Hilborn, who'd lost a lot of his own money in the same deal. Things got pretty ugly, lawyers got involved, and marriages ended." There: that was Kat Rattigan's closest admission yet that her client was one of Hilborn's ex-wives.

"And where is this Malcolm Nickels now?"

"That's just it. No one seems to know. Last time anyone saw him was a little over a week ago. There was talk he might have gone down to Mississippi to see a cousin of a cousin named Babic, try to raise some cash to cover his debts."

"Wait—did you say Babic?" Connor said, raising his hand as if he were stopping traffic.

"Yeah, but I don't know his first name."

"Anywhere near Biloxi?"

"I think so," she said. "What's the connection?"

But Connor didn't hear her question, his brain traveling back just a few weeks to what a retired deputy sheriff had told him about an old Croatian thug named Max Babic from Biloxi who the kingpin behind a loose-knit crime ring was known as the Dixie Mafia.

"C'mon, Connor ... what is it? Don't hold out on me ..."

He pounded back the rest of his Sierra Nevada, set the bottle down on the bar. "I know that name," he told her as he slid off his stool.

"Babic. And what I hear, nothing good is connected to it."

"Jack Connor! Don't you just walk out of here—"

"Give me twenty-four hours," he said as he dug a card out of his wallet. "You don't hear from me, call me. All my numbers are right there." "And where will you be?" Kat Rattigan demanded.

"Sorry, Kat. But this Babic guy ... well, I've gotta go talk to a man."

Chapter 24

Several men, as it turned out. But not before using the rest room down the street at the Hess station.

His first call was to Andrew Corliss, the DEA agent who had set up the sting that two months ago had netted a dozen drug traffickers in four states and millions of dollars in drugs, guns, and cash. The phone number Caitlin Thomas had turned up came with an Atlanta area code and, as Connor expected, he was given the federal runaround for a good ten minutes before someone figured out he: A— wasn't some crackpot putting the shine on a federal agent, and B—he really did only need a minute of Corliss' precious time.

"What's this about?" Corliss almost barked into the phone when he finally answered.

"It's about the Wheelers," Connor told him, figuring there was no point in making small talk. "Jacob and Leland." "Jacob's dead," Corliss said.

"So, I heard."

"So, I'm asking you again, what's this about?" "Max Babic," Connor replied.

That brought a distinct silence, and in the background, Connor could hear the Doppler effect of eighteen-wheelers roaring by on a freeway somewhere. It was another thing he remembered from Miss Benson's classroom, a loose fact that at the time he was sure he would never, ever need to know. Then Corliss said, "Babic's been in the ground a long time."

"But I'll bet he has a big family."

"What is it you think you know?" The DEA agent asked, driving straight to the heart of the matter.

203

"I'm looking for someone," Connor said. "Man by the name of Malcolm Nickels. Ever heard of him?"

"Who'd you say you were?" Corliss' tone almost instantly had changed from almost insolent to guarded.

"Jack Connor. I clean crime scenes."

"So, what's your interest in this one?"

"I'm still trying to figure that out."

"Tell you what, pardner." *Pardner.* Connor could hear the thick condescension in Corliss' voice, same as officialdom everywhere. Even the army. Especially the army, now that Connor thought about it. "You leave this to the pros and go back to watching NCIS."

Good thing this was only a phone call, or Connor would have done to the DEA agent just what he'd done to Danielle's husband and Jacob Wheeler. Okay, probably not, but it was fun to just think about it.

The second man Connor talked to was Chandler Smoak, a septuagenarian felon, thug, and all-around crime boss with a history of corruption and offenses, and no thumbs. Connor neither knew nor cared about the long laundry list of crimes Smoak and his progeny had committed, outside of a recent incident that had come way too close to home. But a retired deputy sheriff once told Connor that Smoak had lost his thumbs to Max Babic, and that's what interested him now.

Connor and Smoak were nothing close to what anyone would call friends, but they were on speaking terms, and Connor even had the old man's number on speed dial. That's the number he punched now.

"Mr. Smoak?" Connor asked.

"Maybe," a gravelly voice said on the other end. "Who's asking?"

"Mr. Smoak ... it's Jack Connor."

There was a second of mental calculation, after which Smoak said, "Connor. Shit. Last person I thought would be calling me." There was no animosity or warning in his voice, just an honest element of surprise.

"Me, too," Connor told him. "Look ... I know you're busy, so I'll keep this short."

"Short is good. What's on your mind?"

There was no easy way to ask him subtly about Max Babic or what he'd done to Smoak's thumbs, so he just got into it and said, "Tell me about the Babics—"

"You're no match for them, Connor," the old man replied, almost instantly. "Whatever you think you're doing, drop it. Now."

"So even with the old man gone, Babic's still a bad name?"

"You really don't want to know. Like I said, leave it alone."

"That's what I'm thinking," Connor said. "Just one more question?"

"Make it quick."

"Does the name Malcolm Nickels mean anything?" "Not anymore, it don't," Smoak said.

"What's that mean, not anymore?"

"What I heard, he's worm food. Got himself into Babic's boys in a big way."

"How big—?"

"Eight figures. Some real estate deal went sour. Just more proof."

"Proof of what?"

"What they say: you don't mess with Babic."

Connor wondered how Chandler Smoak had messed with the man that got his thumbs chopped off. But now was not a good time to mention it, or ask how he knew about Malcolm Nickels. "I appreciate your help," he told him.

"Don't make a habit of it," Smoak replied, and that was it.

Before heading back across the bridge to Sullivan's Island Connor detoured back through North Charleston, drove by Leland Wheeler's house again. He wasn't sure what he'd find except probably a whole lot of nothing, and that's pretty much what he got. Same tiny house with the same dirt yard, the dusty driveway as empty as before. Still, he pulled the Camaro off the street and sat for a minute with the engine running, looking for something—anything—that was out of place. Tire tracks, fresh cigarette butts, empty beer cans. Even the fluttering motion of a curtain in the window. Anything.

He glanced in the rear-view mirror and started to shift the car into reverse when he heard a sharp bang. At the same time the driver's side mirror disintegrated in an explosion of metal, plastic, and glass, a combination of sounds he'd heard before, mostly in Iraq. Within seconds he was lying flat across the twin seats, keeping his head as low as he could.

"That wasn't a miss!" came a voice from the edge of the yard. A woman's voice, gritty from cigarettes and allergies. "Just so's you know."

Connor lay there across the seats, not moving, trying to get a sense of all this. Didn't take much thinking, really; he was trespassing and she was shooting at him. And the wonderful laws of South Carolina were on her side.

"You get outta here right now, you unnerstand?" she yelled again.

"You got no binness here."

Connor hesitated just a second, then called out, "Can I sit up?"

"How should I know?" the woman said. "You ain't wounded."

It wasn't much of an answer, but he sat back up and raised his hands in the air even though he wasn't told to do that.

"Name's Jack Connor," he called to her.

"Don't give a shit if it's Robert E. Jefferson Davis Lee." She spat. "Yo' ass ain't wanted roun' here."

Connor already figured that, so he slowly turned around and put his hand on the door handle. "You Mrs. Wheeler?" he said to her.

"You shittin' me?" she snapped, and now he could see her there, standing at the edge of a rotting garden shed overgrown with Carolina Jessamine. She was about the size and dimensions of the old wringer washing machine his grandmother had in her basement in Lansing, and oozed just about as much style. A dress about the shape of a camp tent clung to her, and her hair was done up in curlers, with some sort of turban holding them in place. A pump action rifle was crooked between a massive breast and her shoulder, but right now it was aimed at the ground about halfway between her and him. "Jus' keepin' an eye on Leland's place, while he's gone."

"Gone where? Connor ventured, wondering where she was yesterday.

"Don' know, and don' wanna know," she said.

"Why'd you shoot out my mirror—?"

"Easiest thing on a car to replace."

Which was probably true, but it didn't answer his question. So, he tried another one, assuming this woman with the gun was the lady of the house.

"You seen him lately?" he called to her, already knowing the answer. "Leland?"

"What you want with him?" she shot back.

"I want to talk to him."

"You think I give a crap? Like I said, Leland's gone. An' if you was smart, you'd get your ass gone, too." With that she raised the rifle, pumped it as she raised it toward Connor. "Now'd be real good a time."

Connor gave it about a second's thought, figured his chance of getting anything useful out of this woman was about zero, so he raised his hand in a polite gesture to indicate he was leaving. Then he shifted into reverse and slipped back down the driveway, leaving a ghost of dust in his wake.

Chapter 25

"Isabella's been nicked," Connor found himself confessing an hour later.

"Nick? How … happen?"

"Side mirror got shot out."

Eddie James was sitting in his wheelchair on his mother's screened porch, a radio pounding out a steady hip-hop beat, the kind of music that seemed to charge up all the grunts Connor had known over in Iraq. The steady thump-thump of the rap beat coupled with the urgency of action kept blood pumping and adrenaline flowing at all hours of the desert night. And while nothing seemed to be pumping through Eddie's system right now, except maybe a dose of Percocet, Connor was pretty certain the music created a connection to times not too long ago when the kid still had full use of his arm and his brain.

"Shot?" he managed to say.

"It's just a flesh wound," Connor said. "But she needs a good doctor, and I thought maybe you could tell me where you used to take her."

"Duck's cussum cars." Eddie's words were almost drowned out by the rap music, but Connor wasn't about to mess with that.

"Duck?"

"No. Duck. D. O. U. G. Wes' Ashey."

Doug's Custom Cars in the West Ashley section of Charleston. Probably out on old Savannah Highway, with all the other auto body shops. "Thanks, buddy," Connor said, gripping Eddie's shoulder, not too hard. "She'll be right as rain in a few days."

There was an awkward silence as Eddie stared past the dunes out to the beach, where he would never again be able to walk, and the ocean beyond that, where he would never again be able to swim. Connor stood there a moment, his eyes drifting from the blaring radio to the bandage wrapped around Eddie's head, then to the *haint blue* porch ceiling. Painted that way to ward off spirits trapped between the world of the living and that of the dead. The symbolism was not lost on him.

"Dat pizz," Eddie finally said.

"Your dad is pissed?" Connor translated for himself. "Because I took you for a drive?"

150

Eddie shook his head and said, "Nah. He pizz cuz he bah pain'in'," he said, a booming song by Fifty Cent almost drowning out the words.

"He's in pain?"

"No. *Paintin'*," Eddie said again, this time trying to get the word out right.

Connor tried to piece the words together, then asked, "Your dad bought a painting?"

"Yeh. Uh Doll."

Connor knew this was difficult on Eddie, not being understood, but he figured it must be important. "A painting of a doll?" he asked.

"No. Doll. E."

That's when Connor's night course in art history kicked in, and he said, "Dali. You mean Salvador Dali?"

"Yeh, Pay lozz cash."

"He paid lots of cash?" Connor asked.

"Dass rye. Half me-yun."

Total translation: Jordan James had bought a painting by Salvador Dali for a half million dollars. And now he was pissed.

"Did your father say who he bought the painting from?" Connor asked, even though he was pretty sure he already knew the answer.

"Dead man," Eddie said. "An' he pizt."

Connor thought back to what Kat Rattigan had told him about pieces of the Hilborns' art collection beginning to disappear from the walls of their house.

"Because he still doesn't have the painting, right?"

Eddie managed a nod, then said, "An' man dead."

So that's what this was all about, at least for Jordan James. He'd paid five hundred thousand dollars cash for a painting that never got delivered, and the man he bought it from had jumped off his hotel balcony. Or was pushed. Take your pick, since Connor still wasn't that much closer to an answer.

All the talking had pretty much tired Eddie out, and now his chin slowly lowered to his chest as his eyes slipped closed like those of the baby doll that Connor's sister used to play with up in Michigan. One moment they were open, the next they clicked shut.

Connor stayed there on the screen porch for a few minutes, making sure Eddie was still breathing. The steady rise and fall of his chest indicated he was, and his brain had shipped off to dreamland, despite the music that was still pounding. Not necessarily conducive to quality sleep, but in Eddie's world all the rules seemed to run backwards, and Connor wasn't about to interfere. Eventually he slipped down the back stairs, easing the screen door closed on a weary spring.

"Can you ask your client whether her husband—excuse me, whether Jon Hilborn—had any artwork by Salvador Dali?"

Connor had put the Camaro's top up and now was driving on the connector that led from Isle of Palms back to Mount Pleasant. He had dialed Kat Rattigan as soon as he pulled out of Eddie's mother's driveway, the sound of pool balls clacking in the background telling him that Kat was next door at the billiard parlor. When he told her this was urgent, she told him to give her ninety seconds and she would call him back.

"Salvador Dali?" she repeated now that she had used the unmarked door in the back of the pool hall and was back in her office. "What's that got to do with anything?"

"Maybe nothing, maybe a lot," he told her. "Either way it's important."

"Okay, I'll ask. Meanwhile, did you check out Malcolm Nickels?"

"I asked around. General thinking is, the guy's probably buried somewhere between here and the Gulf. He owed a lot of money, and his debt got canceled. Same as him."

"What about this Babic guy? Nickels' cousin." "Leave it alone," Connor said.

"I'm just asking—"

"No. I mean, that's what I was told, by someone who should know. He said 'leave it alone.' I think it's good advice."

"So, are you? Leaving it alone, I mean?"

Connor considered her question seriously, realized he had inched his way into something that was beyond what Jordan James had intended and could end up getting burned. Or worse. "I'm just nibbling at the edges, no big bites or anything."

"Right," Kat Rattigan said, doubt in her voice. "Thanks for the update. And I'll call my client, see what I can find out about that painting."

When the call ended Connor placed another one, this time to Jordan James' cell phone. With all the businesses the man owned throughout the lowcountry he could be just about anywhere, but Connor wanted to meet with him. Now, if possible.

"Jack!" he said when he answered the call. "Have you found my money?"

"Not exactly, but I think I know where it might've gone. Can we meet?"

"Is this important, or can it wait?"

"It's your money," Connor reminded him.

James said nothing for a minute, then said, "Meet me in a half hour, Aaaardvark Bail Bonds, up on Leeds Avenue. Spelled with five

'A's, four of 'em in the beginning. It's right next to the jail."

"I'll be there."

Thirty minutes later Connor was sitting by himself in what he presumed was a client conference room. No windows, drop ceiling with fluorescent lights, wood laminate table with six chairs pushed in around it. The smell of stale smoke and Old Spice and perspiration lingered in the air.

Eventually the door opened and Jordan James pushed his way in. He instantly dominated the room, wearing a dark blue double-breasted suit with white silk shirt and yellow tie, monograms on his cuffs. His salt-and-pepper hair was combed back and held in place by a smear of gel, and he wore a large gold ring on his left pinkie.

"Jack, my boy," he said, vigorously pumping Connor's hand. "Good to see you. Sorry to have you drive all the way out here, but the aardvark is missing one of his ants." Connor gave him a blank look, so James added, "One of our quote-unquote clients has skipped out, and there's a lot of dough riding on him. I'd send you to find him, but you are otherwise engaged at the moment. So—why don't you tell me what you think you know."

"You paid Jon Hilborn a half million dollars for a painting he never delivered," Connor answered, getting right to it.

Jordan James studied him hard, then took a seat opposite him at the table. He interlaced his fingers, the gold pinkie ring glowing in the fluorescent lighting. "Yes, I did. Good job. I don't suppose you found it or my money, did you?"

"Not yet, but I think I'm getting close."

Connor spent the next five minutes filling James in on the last couple months in Jon Hilborn's life, how his house had been foreclosed, a major business deal had soured, he may or may not have been diagnosed with Lou Gehrig's disease, he'd stolen money and a gun from a nurse up in North Carolina, and he'd been hiding out in a crash pad up in Myrtle Beach. There was no need to mention Bodean Barr or the Wheeler brothers, or Malcolm Nickels, or any possible connection to one of the dirtiest crime families in the deep South.

When Connor was finished James just sat there, his eyes staring down at his hands as what he had just heard had a chance to settle into his brain. Then he said, "You can never judge a peanut by looking at its shell."

"Seems this one got pretty well boiled," Connor observed. "You want me to keep looking for your money?"

"No. It's long gone, and it's my own stupidity. Like they say, if something looks too good to be true, it probably is."

"You're talking about the painting—"

"Of course, I am. Look, since you got this far, I'll tell you what happened. But it's between you and me and God, if He's listening. Got it?" James didn't wait for an answer because he wasn't expecting one. Instead he said, "Jon Hilborn figured himself a connoisseur of fine things. Cars, wine, women, and art. Mostly art, despite what his ex-wives might think. Over the years he'd bought a lot of it, and his house was jammed full. Each time he got divorced his new ex got a few pieces, and he'd go out and replace them. It got so it was almost an obsession with him. And sometimes when he acquired a new piece, he couldn't display it. Not where it could be seen."

"You're saying he was stealing them?"

"Not himself, no. But when you're in the art world, you hear things. A few paintings become available here, a few more there. Some of them are acquired on demand, a collector who's looking for a specific painting or sculpture. And some of them are acquired on what they call spec. Hilborn couldn't afford the direct contract route, so he was into speculation."

"And this Dali painting. You paid Hilborn in cash because it was in his private vault. Meaning it was stolen."

"He didn't say, and I didn't ask."

Rich men's games, Connor thought. "So, what happened? You gave him the money, but he didn't give you the painting?"

"Actually, it turned out to be a cheap knock-off that I couldn't get appraised."

"And he knew you couldn't."

"Buyer beware," Jordan James said, letting out a deep sigh. "There's outfits all over the world that will hand-paint any piece of art in any style you ask them to. What I paid a half million dollars for would fetch twenty bucks out at the Ramada Inn."

"How big was this painting?"

"About like this," James said, using his outstretched arms to indicate a canvas that would be about thirty inches by forty.

"Was it in a frame?"

"No. it was a loose canvas. The day he showed it to me he took it out of a cardboard tube and unrolled it."

Connor nodded, then remembered something Charlene Marks had told him. "When was this?" he asked.

"Two, maybe three weeks ago."

"And when did you pay him for it?"

"Just a few days before he died," James said without having to think about it. "We had dinner in Charleston and made the exchange. Which gave him plenty of time to have a copy made." "Maybe more than one," Connor suggested.

"Sonofabitch!" Jordan James' face was turning red and deep creases were forming in his forehead. "I hadn't thought of that. The bastard probably sold it more than once!"

"Does that sound like someone who was planning to kill himself?"

"Maybe if he was desperate," James said. "Like if someone threatened to punch his ticket if he didn't pay what he owed."

That's when Connor's mind went from Charlene Marks to Linda Loris, and what she told him about seeing the suitcases stuffed with cash. Just before Bodean Barr showed up.

"The painting's still out there," Connor said.

"Yep," James concurred. He played with his pinkie ring for a few seconds, then said, "What I said earlier about finding my money? Like I told you, give it up. It's long gone anyway. That painting is what I really want."

"Kinda figured," Connor said. He started to stand up, but it was clear James wasn't quite through yet.

"How'd you know it was a Dali?" he asked.

"I dunno. Maybe you told me."

But Jordan James shook his head and said, "Not me. You put it out there first. So, what I want to know is how'd you come to know it?"

It was just a simple question, no accusation in his voice. But it still made Connor uneasy, so he decided to go for the truth. "Your son, sir."

"What does Eddie have to do with this?"

"Mr. James, your son may have a hard time making words come out of his mouth, but he doesn't have any problem with them going into his ears."

"Guess what I found." Caitlin Thomas had called Connor about five minutes after he'd left Aaaardvark Bail Bonds next to the county jail. Her voice oozed excitement, as if she had just located Amelia Earhart's missing airplane. "You'll never guess, not in a million years."

"Dog years or human?

"Hah! Tat Man's tryin' to be funny. What I found is the county transfer records for a piece of property up in North Myrtle Beach. One hundred ninety-eight acres of primo land right on the marsh up there."

"And this is important why?"

"Because of who owned it. And who owns it now. You see, this parcel of land was sold by a company called Skipjack Development

Ventures, out of Columbia."

Connor was passing an eighteen-wheeler on the Mark Clark Expressway and glanced in his side view mirror to see if it was safe to pull in. Only there was no mirror, just a shattered mass of glass and chrome that had just been pulverized by a bullet.

"So, what's Skipjack?" he asked, because she seemed to be waiting for him to.

"Skipjack is a holding company. Offshore, in fact, with a banking address in the Bahamas and a U.S. office in Columbia, like I said. But I did some digging into this little enterprise, and it wasn't hard to find a name."

"And that would be?" Connor asked, again because she was waiting for him to pull it out of her.

"Jon Hilborn," she said.

Connor actually let out a low whistle, then said, "What else did you find?"

"Just that Hilborn was chairman of the board and the primary shareholder. There are a few other partners involved, but Hilborn ran the show."

"So, who did he sell the property to?"

"That's where it really gets interesting. The Congaree Corporation bought the entire tract for just over four million. And to save you the question, Congaree is a wholly owned subsidiary of ACE Property and Development."

"That's the company that owns the land that Bodean Barr's house was on," Connor reminded her. "So, when did the Myrtle Beach property close?"

"Last winter," Caitlin said. "The thing is, you already know this piece of land, because it's where you followed Jacob Wheeler the other night. Same place he got himself flash-fried."

"Damn—"

"But wait—there's more," Caitlin said, sounding like one of those TV infomercials. "The Congaree Corporation—which, by the way, is named after another river here in South Carolina—is an entity made up of the three partners in ACE, and another silent partner named Nickels. Malcolm Nickels."

And there it was: the connection that made the loop complete. Jon Hilborn, Bodean Barr and his sister Marjorie, the Wheeler brothers, Charlene Marks, Malcolm Nickels, and back to Hilborn again. Connor still didn't know what it all meant, especially when you tossed DEA Agent Corliss, the Babic family, and a missing Salvador Dali painting into the mix. But at least three men were dead, possibly four, if Nickels—as Chandler Smoak had so tactfully put it—was worm food. Maybe even five, given that Leland Wheeler hadn't been seen in days.

"Nickels? What do you know about him?" Connor asked, not wanting to let on that he'd already come across the name.

"Not much, at least not yet. One arrest ten years ago: violating a restraining order. Charges were dropped. Other than that, he seems clean."

"Do you have an address?"

"I knew you were going to ask me that, so I already texted it to your phone." She hesitated a moment, then added, "There is one thing, Tat Man."

"And what would that be?" he dutifully asked.

"This Nickels guy. Seems people who get too close to him … well, they have a habit of never being seen again."

He didn't ask her how she knew that but figured it was good intel to live by.

Chapter 26

The address for Malcolm Nickels was in Yemassee, a small town about twenty miles west of Beaufort, pronounced *Bew-furt,* as opposed to the North Carolina city by the same spelling that was pronounced *Bo-furt.* In any event, it was too late in the day to make the trip—and for all he knew the man was dead anyway.

Besides, it was Thursday, and that meant it was reggae night at the Buffet. The owner, Jimmy Page, had been talking about maybe moving the Jamaican Jerks to Saturday night, on account of their performance at the Lowcountry Rockin' Blues Festival. But the blues band that had the weekend gig at Jimmy's had six weeks left on their cocktail napkin contract, so for now the Jerks were stuck with Thursday. Which was just fine with Connor, who liked to keep his weekends free. For what, he wasn't quite sure, especially now that things appeared to be so iffy with Danielle.

In any event it was after midnight by the time he pulled into his driveway and cut the engine. He was still wired from all the driving and the reggae beat at Jimmy's, so he could have used a gin on the rocks. But he had started the day with a hangover and didn't want to end it heading in the same direction, so he passed up the gin—Dr. Pinch would have been proud—and grabbed a beer from the fridge instead. He took a long gulp, the cold brew icing his throat as it went down, then carried it out to the back lawn to settle into his chair at the edge of the marsh.

Only problem was, someone was already sitting in it.

The guy had to have heard Connor open and close the sliding door, but he hadn't budged. Not even one twitch. He just sat there, gazing out at the waterway, a blue baseball cap on his head, bill in front and the adjustable band in the back. Not the cool way, with the bill at the rear.

"Help you?" Connor said, slowly setting his beer on the small concrete slab that served as a back patio.

Still the guy didn't move, causing Connor to think maybe he was deaf. Or even worse, dead.

"My name's Connor," he said, a little bit louder this time. "And that's my chair you've got your ass parked in."

Finally, there was just a little hitch of movement, and the guy said,

"Nice place you've got here, Connor."

"I know you?"

"We've talked. Why no mosquitoes?"

"Man who owns the house sprays for 'em," Connor said. "I told you my name, you gonna tell me yours?"

"You're the guy playing private dick … you tell me," the man said. He still hadn't turned around, still was gazing out at the marsh and the waterway and the twin spires of the Ravenel Bridge in the distance.

He probably thought he was being cool, but Connor just figured him for arrogant, which—along with the dark blue cap and the ugly black sedan with the government plates he now remembered seeing parked out on the street—put it all together in a flash.

"You're Corliss," he said. "DEA."

The guy looked around, flashing Connor a mouthful of teeth that were just aching to be bashed in. "Not bad," he said. "Have a seat."

There was only one chair and Corliss was already sitting in it. And that, in Connor's mind, made it a bombastic comment, an indication of brash arrogance that quite often accompanied a badge and a gun. Connor had no way of knowing whether Corliss actually was wearing his service weapon, but he didn't seem to be the type to go anywhere without it, so he had to watch himself here. Still, Corliss was trespassing, so Connor had a bit of leverage.

It was just a cheap beach chair he'd picked up from Target, and in about a half a second he'd grabbed both sides of the metal frame and dumped the agent out on the grass, face-first.

Two seconds after that Corliss was in a crouch, turned around and facing Connor with a look on his face like Nicholson's in "The Shining." His gun—looked like a standard Glock—was in both hands, one finger through the trigger guard, barrel pointed at Connor's chest. "What're you gonna do now, asshole?" he snarled.

"Same question I was going to ask you," Connor replied, his voice calm and level. "You going to shoot an unarmed man in his own backyard after you came onto his property without being invited?" "Probable cause," Corliss said.

"Blow it out your probable ass. Are you here for a reason, or do you just like making yourself look like a bag of shit?"

"Listen, I—"

"Put the gun down, Corliss," Connor said, trying to sound bored even though his heart had almost doubled its pulse. Guns have a habit of doing that. "No one's shooting anyone tonight. You know that and I know that. So whatever reason you dropped by, get on with it. Or you can leave. Your choice."

This was not the way Corliss had envisioned this going; that was clear. But he really had no choice than to be smart, because he'd already played the stupid card, and it hadn't worked. He lowered the Glock, but did not yet put it back in the shoulder holster that Connor hadn't seen in the darkness.

"Get you a beer?" Connor asked then.

Corliss glared at him a second, then managed a slight nod. "Sure. And maybe another chair."

Sixty seconds later they were both sitting in chairs, Corliss in the aluminum one that now had a slightly bent frame, Connor in a wooden chair from the kitchen.

"You always such a douchebag?" Connor asked him.

"Bad day," the DEA agent said. "Shit happens."

"So why are you here?"

Corliss shifted position in his chair so he was facing Connor, looked him directly in the eyes. "I'm here because you've been asking about things you shouldn't have known."

Connor held up his bottle and looked at the moon through the brown glass. "Things like Nickels and Babic," he eventually said.

"Correct. You need to tell me how you know those names. And don't give me any of that Internet horseshit, either."

That caused Connor to grin. "Seems you ask enough questions around these parts with regards to certain elements, the name Max Babic comes up. Guy's dead, but what I heard is the family's still churning 'em out."

"Each one meaner than the next," Corliss agreed. "But that still doesn't answer how you know about him. Or them."

There were several ways Connor could play this, one being to fill the DEA agent in on the Rebecca Rose case, and how in the process of tracking down her killer he—Connor—had gotten mixed up with a Dixie mobster whose thumbs had been lopped off by Babic himself. Maybe Corliss already knew about that and was keeping his cards dry. Or he could explain that a private detective who, in a former life, was a ladies' champion eight-ball player had steered him in the direction of Babic and Malcolm Nickels. But Connor knew that Corliss didn't know what he knew, so he didn't have to take either of those paths.

So instead he said, "Nickels had a cousin named Babic," figuring that would be enough for now. "Paid him a visit not too long ago, and no one's seen him since."

"On the phone you said you were looking for him. Nickels. Why's that?"

"It's what you do when someone's missing."

Corliss glared at him, and unfolded himself out of the beach chair. "I can see this is going nowhere," he said. "I thought maybe you'd be cooperative on account you're a veteran and all that. But this is just a big waste of time."

"And I was just starting to enjoy it," Connor replied, holding out his bottle in a casual toast of friendship. "Glad you stopped by."

"You remember what I told you on the phone?"

"You told me a few things—"

"I told you to leave this to the pros, and you keep cleaning crime scenes."

"Actually, what you told me was to keep watching NCIS," Connor corrected him. "But you know what I'm thinking?" "Haven't got a clue," Corliss said.

"If you're such a damned pro, why're you wasting your time with me?"

Malcolm Nickels' place was a postcard right from the old South. It started at an open wrought-iron gateway, which fed into a long, winding drive lined with live oaks and magnolias and flowering plants that Connor didn't recognize. Tufts of Spanish moss dripped from twisted branches, and the scent of jasmine and what smelled like orange blossoms clung to the air. A limp windsock hanging from a pole a quarter mile off in the distance told him there wasn't a hint of a breeze except for the wash of hot air that came over the hood of the Camaro.

The house was yellow with white Greek columns and black shutters, three full stories of antebellum set up high, cloaked with shade from more oaks and elms and gum trees. The driveway hooked around in a lazy circle in front of a broad set of stairs that led up to a wide wrap-around porch, where several outdoor ceiling fans spun slowly while squirrels chased each other across the rail in a late-spring mating ritual. Somewhere music was playing, or perhaps that was just the theme song from a different era echoing in Connor's mind, back when a gallon of gas cost a quarter and the worst thing imaginable was commies putting fluoride in the drinking water.

Connor coasted the Camaro to a stop just past the stairway and cut the gas. Even the rumbling engine seemed to appreciate the theme of the past, the pistons gently coughing until all was silent, except for a vague sigh as Isabella took a deep breath and rested. He half expected to see Butterfly McQueen appear through the front door and come out onto the porch with a pitcher of lemonade and tall glasses, maybe ask him if he'd like to set a spell and have a sip.

But that's not what happened. Appearances definitely can be deceptive, and in the case of Malcolm Nickels' revered Renellswood Place—that's what the iron sign over the gate called it—that deception seemed deliberately designed. Because instead of an African American housekeeper, the person who pushed out through that front door was a man dressed in faux Army fatigues, a genuine automatic machine pistol aimed directly at Connor. And, by proxy, just about anything within firing range of it.

"What's your business?" he barked louder than a pit bull.

For a second Connor was at a loss for words, wondering if the gun was one of those Tek-9 things, then said, "I'm here to see Mr. Nickels."

"'Bout what?'"

Connor should have known to leave this alone, get out right now before he became part of the mulch that he now realized had been spread around a beautiful rose garden in the center of the circular driveway. But it was too late for that now; in for a penny and all that. "Max Babic," he said.

Wrong answer, it seemed, because almost instantly two more similarly clothed and armed men came out of the house, and now he had three automatic weapons aimed at him.

"Out of the car!" the first one ordered him.

Connor got out of the car, putting his hands on the top of his head just so they didn't have to order him to do it.

"We're cool here?" he asked. "I'm cool."

"Don't give a shit who or what you are," the first man out on the porch snapped. He obviously was the intellect of the three, which wasn't saying much. "Come here. Real slow."

Connor moved slower than slow. No point in giving an itchy finger a reason to scratch. He made his way around the hood of the Camaro, then edged up to the bottom of the stairs that led up to the verandah. He lifted his hands a couple inches off his head and said, "I'm not carrying." "What you want with Babic?" the gunman said.

"Nothing—you misunderstood me. You asked me what my business was, and I said 'Max Babic.' I don't know him, but I know who he is. Was."

"Quiet!" The gunman doing all the talking obviously figured himself for the brains of this outfit. "What's your name?"

No need to lie here, he figured, so he said, "Jack Connor. I clean crime scenes."

"Come back tomorrow, we may have a need for you." Brains glanced over at the other two gunmen, and they moved closer on the porch so they could have a small conference. "Which gets us all the way back to nothing. So, I'm going to ask you again, what's your business here?"

"I'm trying to find Mr. Nickels," Connor said. "I think one of the Babics might know something about where he is."

Brains looked at his two compadres, then back to Connor. "You are either one dumb shit-for-brains or one lucky sonofabitch," he said.

"Why's that?"

"Because you ain't dead yet, that's why. Get your ass up here."

Connor took the stairs one slow step at a time, silently counting to fifteen by the time he reached the elevated porch. When he got to the top Brains jabbed his automatic in Connor's ribs and said, "Stop right there."

Then he gave a quick nod to the other two gunmen, who cautiously approached and gave him a thorough pat-down. If they ever were in need of work they could always find a job with the TSA. When they finished they both backed away, one of them saying, "Clean."

"Check his car, both of you," Brains said. "Look everywhere." Then to Connor he added, "You're coming with me."

That meant going inside, through the eight-foot double oak doors that led into an entryway about the size of Connor's entire apartment. The ceiling went up about twenty feet, a gold chandelier with hundreds of chunks of hand-carved crystal and just as many bulbs dangling down to provide a sense of opulence and grandeur. To the rear a central staircase ascended halfway to a mezzanine, then split right and left to climb the rest of the way to the second floor. The walls were decorated with the sort of artwork Connor couldn't figure anyone would want, old dusty portraits of people long dead staring out from ornate gilded frames.

And now that he was inside, the temperature a good fifteen degrees lower than outside, he again was sure he heard music. Coming from somewhere on one of the upper floors, gentle trills echoing down the stairwell to the foyer. Piano music played slowly but with emotion, a melody he recognized but couldn't quite place, except that it seemed oddly out of kilter here.

"I'm afraid your presence has created a bit of a problem," Brains said.

"I can leave," Connor suggested. "Mr. Nickels obviously isn't here."

"Obviously. But you're here, and therein lies the problem."

"Seems to me I got lost, never got where I was going—"

"GPS does have a way of crashing out here in the boondocks," Brains agreed. "People get lost all the time. Thing is, you've still seen more than you should."

"I haven't seen a thing," Connor assured him, hoping ignorance might get him out of here. "And my short-term memory sucks, on account of the war. V.A.'s even treating me for it."

"Afghanistan?" Brains asked then, showing a momentary spark of interest.

"Iraq. Went over as part of the surge."

"Shit," Brains swore under his breath. "My little brother was in Iraq. Were you infantry?"

Connor nodded. "3rd Brigade Combat Team, 10th Mountain Division out of Fort Drum. Spent most of my time north of Kirkuk."

"Double-shit," Brains said this time, lowering his weapon. "You was in the same squad. Had to be. You know a kid named Jimmy Winthrop?"

Connor brightened; all was not lost yet. "Yeah … we called him Jimmy Throw-Up. He was from down here, right? Georgia, I think he said—"

"Dalton," Brains said. "Our family's been around those parts since before the war. The big one, I mean."

"Good kid. He come home when the Prez pulled us out?"

Brains shook his head. "Never made it. Car bomb."

Now it was Connor's turn to say "shit," and then he just stood there shaking his head. "Hey … I'm sorry, man. Your brother was a good kid. Played a mean game of Texas Hold 'Em. What happened really sucks."

"Yeah, it does that. Jimmy, he had a girlfriend he was gonna marry, even a job lined up at a local farm supply store. You ever see what a dog packed with grenades can do to a Humvee?"

Connor stood there awkwardly, then nodded slowly and said, "It's why I've got short-term memory loss. 'Cept in my case it was a suicide driver, instead of a dog."

"Damned war," Brains said.

That's when Connor realized the music upstairs had stopped, and now he heard a pair of feet descending the stairs. Slowly, hard heels, tap-tap as one foot hit the polished marble steps, then the other. A woman, he could tell, not just from the footsteps but from the sudden wash of a scent that smelled like a mixture of a summer garden and a department store perfume display. In other words, floral but almost overpowering.

Since Brains had lowered his gun Connor turned to see who it was, found himself staring eye-to-eye with Charlene Marks, who was holding a book of sheet music in one hand.

"You—!" she blurted out when she recognized his bald head and tattooed arms. "What the hell are you doing here?"

"Charlene Marks," he replied. "Or maybe I should call you Babe."

She shot a glare at Brains and said, "Kenny … how did this asshole get in here?"

"He just drove up and started asking about Mr. Nickels," Brains— now known as Kenny—explained to her.

"Seems to me the two of you are old pals," she snapped at him. There definitely appeared to be a pecking order here, and Charlene seemed to be well above Kenny Winthrop on it.

"He knew my brother, in Iraq," Kenny explained quickly. "And, you should know, when he mentioned Mr. Nickels, he also said something about Max Babic."

Charlene Marks turned to Connor. "Max Babic is dead."

"So, I've been told," Connor replied. "And as far as I can tell, so is Nickels."

"I have no idea where Malcolm Nickels is," she told him.

"Didn't say you did," Connor told her. "What about Mrs. Nickels?"

"There isn't one. Malcolm never married."

Connor considered this for about a half a second, which was all the time it was worth. "So why are you here, Babe? Last time I saw you, you were meeting Jacob Wheeler in the middle of the woods. Just a few hours before he fried to death in that tin can he lived in."

Her jaw literally dropped open, just enough for a little gasp to come out. "You followed me out there?"

"Wasn't that hard," he said. "Funny thing: all I did was mention Bodean Barr, and you were out of the gate like Sea Biscuit."

She did it again this time, visibly flinched at the sound of Bo Barr's name. She glanced from Kenny Winthrop to Connor, then back to Winthrop, and said, "Put him in his car and get him out of here." Then to Connor she added, "Next time I see you, you are going to know the full Babic experience." "Yes, *Babe*," he said.

"What can I say? It's my name. My mother was Max's niece."

Chapter 27

As the crow flies, Hilton Head is about 10 miles from Beaufort, and another 20 from Yemassee. But neither crows nor highways travel in a straight line, especially when they have to go the long way around the barn. All those marsh inlets, rivers, bridges and, of course, Parris Island, where every new Marine east of the Mississippi River goes to have his or her hair cropped and their lard-ass bodies whipped into shape.

Since Connor already was down in this neck of the woods he figured a little drive out of his way couldn't do any harm. He already had David Hilborn's address in his cell, and the GPS app helped him out the rest of the way. He managed to elude a short military convoy he encountered on the Robert Smalls Parkway and twenty minutes later he was crossing the bridge to Hilton Head Island. Ten minutes after that he was slowing down at the entrance to David Hilborn's driveway at Calibogue Sound, the same red Jag parked close to the front door, and the same bronze dolphins still splashing in the fountain.

But that's where any similarities to his last visit ended. Because now three Beaufort County sheriff's cruisers, an unmarked Crown Vic, and an ambulance that was the same model Ford truck as the one he drove at Palmetto BioClean were parked in the drive behind the Jag.

Connor edged the Camaro to the side of the road and got out. Billows of dark clouds were beginning to lumber in from the west, and the temperature had dropped a few degrees since he'd left the Nickels Plantation half an hour ago. That meant a cold front was set to move up from Georgia, but Connor figured that whatever was going on here—and it didn't look good—he had enough time to get in and out before the rain started coming down.

The front door was wide open, but Connor didn't get anywhere close to it before he was stopped by a uniformed cop.

"That's as far as you go, sir," the officer said, planting himself directly in Connor's path. He had a square jaw and matching shoulders, and had his fingers tucked into his belt as he moved. A brass tag pinned to his shirt said his name was Deputy Lange.

Connor stopped, peered past the cop at the door, then said, "What's going on here?"

The cop ignored his question, and asked one of his own. "Who are you?"

"Name's Connor," he said, digging a card out of his wallet. "I'm with Citadel Security, down from Charleston."

Officer Lange eyeballed the card a minute. "This here says you're with Palmetto BioClean. 'Full-service biohazard clean up service,' in fact."

"Well, technically, you're right. I wear a couple of hats."

"Uh-huh." He studied Connor with a suspicious look. "You know what I think?"

From Connor's limited experience with cops he didn't find them capable of doing too much thinking, but decided not to express that opinion right here, right now. So instead he said, "Couldn't possibly imagine."

"I'm thinking you heard about what went down here, now you're poking your nose around to get yourself a clean-up job."

"No ... it's nothing like that," Connor said, trying not to roll his eyes. "In fact, I'm here to talk to David Hilborn."

Deputy Lange had no response to that, not right away. Instead he glanced down the driveway to the orange Camaro that Connor had just gotten out of, then studied the tattoo sleeves on his arms. "'Bout what?" he finally asked.

"That's between me and Mr. Hilborn," Connor said. He tried to keep his words even and steady, trying not to lose his patience.

"Well, that's gonna be difficult now, considering what happened."

The ambulance and all the sheriff's cars suggested what Lange was getting at, but Connor tried to keep his brain from jumping ahead of things. "And what would that be?"

But it was another cop, one dressed in blue slacks and a button-down short-sleeved shirt, who answered Connor's question. But only after another round of questions, plus an exchange of business cards and a thorough inspection of Connor's driver's license.

"Mr. Hilborn is dead," the plainclothes cop said, after explaining that he was Detective Porcher, of the Beaufort County Sheriff's Department.

Shit ... this was getting more and more twisted. "Dead?" Connor asked.

"That's what I said. So ... what was your business with the deceased?"

Connor hesitated, figured there was no reason to avoid the truth, so he again explained that he worked with Citadel Security up in Charleston, he was here on business, a follow-up to a conversation he'd had with David Hilborn about a week ago. Porcher's eyes narrowed when Connor said that, and he asked, "You're sure it was a week ago?"

"Give or take," Connor said, figuring anything more specific than that might encourage the start of an interrogation. "We talked briefly about his brother Jon, who had just died up in Myrtle Beach. I'd only met him that one time, and we only talked for a few minutes. If you don't mind me asking, how did Mr. Hilborn die?"

Porcher studied Connor, mostly his tats and shaved head. Then he said, "It appears Mr. Hilborn was murdered. But maybe you already knew that."

Connor suspected this was coming, but the truth—and Porcher's clear insinuation—still took him by surprise. "What are you implying—?"

"I'm not implying anything," Porcher said. "We've got an apparent homicide here, and a lot of unanswered questions."

"And just because I had business with Mr. Hilborn you think maybe I'm involved?"

"We're talking to everyone, is all," Porcher said. "Now's your turn. So, help me out here."

So, Connor helped him out, without helping too much. He explained how he was quietly looking into the suicide of Jon Hilborn up in Myrtle Beach, and had driven down to Hilton Head last week to talk to David Hilborn, who had been the person who'd identified his brother's body. He just happened to be in the area today and thought he'd drop in, see if David Hilborn had anything else to add to what they'd discussed earlier.

"That's your story?" Detective Porcher asked.

"It's the truth."

"I see," Porcher said, nodding slightly. "Sounds simple. Plausible, even."

"Of course, it is. The truth usually is."

"Most of the time, yes. The thing is, there's a problem with your story." It was a statement designed to make Connor squirm, but he let any insinuation fly right over his head. "Your version of the truth."

"How do you figure?"

Porcher rubbed the back of his neck and said, "It's a horrible thing, what happened here. Death always is, especially when it comes so suddenly. The thing of it is, David Hilborn comes home after being away for a while, and someone puts a bullet in his head not three days after he gets back."

Connor's brain was on time-delay, and it took about a half a second for what Porcher said to register. "What did you say?"

"I said that Hilborn had been out of the country, helping a friend sail a boat back from France. One of those multi-hull things. Couple days after he gets back, this happens."

"When did he get home?" Connor asked.

"This past Saturday," Detective Porcher said. "I know that because there was a party at the Yacht Club that evening. Kept us busy all night."

"And you're saying he was gone for a month before that?" Connor pressed.

"Close to."

It was about ten seconds later that it all clicked together, like an old pocket watch that just had a new replacement gear popped into place.

Detective Porcher let Connor go about ten minutes after that, and as soon as he was back in the car he called Caitlin Thomas, asked her if the Citadel computers had a tie-in with the Federal Aviation Administration.

"We can't access their servers directly, but I can file a request. Shouldn't take more than a few minutes for a response."

"That'll do," Connor told her. He'd put the convertible top up before pulling back out onto the road and now, just a few minutes later, the first large plops of rain began to hit the windshield, splattering into large star patterns on the glass. "Let me know when you're ready." "What's this about?" Caitlin asked him.

"I want you to locate an airplane," he told her.

"What kind of plane?"

Connor thought back to the Google listing for Jon Hilborn he had found on the Charleston Enterprise Association website "A Beechcraft King. Registered to Jon Hilborn." "I'm on it," she said, and clicked off.

DEA agent Andrew Corliss was tired of Jack Connor, and he made that quite clear when he answered the phone.

"Just hear me out," Connor insisted. "Just a couple of questions and I'm out of your life forever."

"Somehow I doubt that," Corliss said, resigned exasperation in his voice. "What is it this time?"

"Tell me what you know about Jon Hilborn."

"I don't believe I know that name. Now if you don't mind—"

"Sure, you know it. He was part of your sting until he screwed you over and disappeared."

"You know what, Connor?" Corliss paused as if he really expected an answer, then said, "You have a true Hollywood imagination, with plots and conspiracies and villains and all that shit. But like I said, I don't know any Jon Hilborn. Now, are you done?"

Connor ignored him and continued, "Hilborn and Nickels got in way over their heads with the wrong people and tried to deal their way out. Literally. This whole thing with the Wheeler brothers, and the other guys you hauled in—they were just the cogs in the wheel. Nickels was the brains that pulled it all together, and Hilborn provided the wings that helped him do it."

"You're grasping at thin air, Connor," Corliss snarled at him. "I told you, use your head and stay out of this."

"Just tell me one thing, Agent Corliss. Was Hilborn on your side and outsmarted you, or did he play everyone for a fool?"

"You're the fool, if you don't let this go," Corliss told him. "Now good-bye."

Connor started to ask another question, but he heard the silence of dead air and he knew Corliss was already gone.

The drive from Hilton Head back to Charleston took about two hours, and Connor spent the time thinking how this all must have come together. The stream of drugs from Charleston to Mobile, and maybe back again. The piles of cash that had to be involved, and nowhere to stash it. The Wheeler brothers, who had been nabbed by an alert South Carolina highway patrol officer. Jacob Wheeler, turned to ash inside his single-wide, and Leland Wheeler, who was nowhere to be found.

Same thing with Malcolm Nickels, who was either dead or had disappeared, maybe with the help of the feds. Bodean Barr, who maybe had stumbled in on Jon Hilborn counting a mountain of money and then killed him before walking out of his suite with it. Only to be relieved of that very same money in a bug-infested shack in Walterboro after having the front of his face shot off. One of the Wheelers? Nickels? Maybe even Charlene Marks?

Connor took the 526 spur around Charleston, out past the airport where a massive Boeing 787 was laboriously lifting off over the trees. He had just passed the pungent paper plant and was pulling onto the Don Holt Bridge when his phone rang. It was Caitlin Thomas, and she said, "It wasn't Hilborn's plane."

"Say again?" Connor told her, as if he was out in the Iraq desert and the field radio had garbled a command.

"The plane you asked about. It wasn't really Hilborn's. He leased it from a company called Palmetto Avionics, based here in Charleston. Apparently Hilborn defaulted on the payments last winter and they repossessed it."

"Where is it now?" Connor asked.

"Sitting on the tarmac," Caitlin told him. "Apparently, it's been used for a few private charters, but otherwise it hasn't moved."

He thought for a minute as he passed an eighteen-wheeler in the slow lane of the bridge. Then he said, "Do you have an address for this Palmetto Avionics?"

"It's right on Aviation Avenue, off Rivers. Head left toward the airport, and when the road comes to an end, there you are."

Caitlin's directions were perfect. He'd had to make a U-turn at Clements Ferry Road and make another swing past the paper plant, but ten minutes later Connor was pulling the Camaro into a space in front of a one-story glass-and-steel building with a half dozen corporate logos fixed to the wall. He cut the engine and got out, pushing his way through the tinted double-glass doors that served as an entrance for the private aviation terminal.

Palmetto Avionics consisted of a single small office with a glass wall that opened out to the main terminal, much like the airline kiosks that are found at baggage claim where lost luggage is reported and, on occasion, reunited with its owners. Connor knocked on the doorjamb and a young woman with dark skin and very short black hair glanced up at him. A fake wood plaque on her desk identified her as Sh'landra.

"May I help you?" she asked.

Connor explained who he was and said he was curious about the Beechcraft King that until recently had been leased to Jon Hilborn.

"I'm sorry, sir, but I can't discuss our clients," she said. "Privacy, and all that."

Connor wasn't sure what "all that" might entail, but it wasn't important. "I'm not interested in Mr. Hilborn," he assured her. "I was just hoping I might be able to take a look at the plane." "Are you a pilot?" Sh'landra asked.

"No, but the man I work for ... well, from time to time he's required to charter a plane for business purposes," Connor said, figuring what he said probably was true. "He had a chance to fly with Mr. Hilborn on several occasions, and he liked the plane. I'm here to check it out."

"Of course," Sh'landra said, rising from behind her desk. She was wearing white slacks and a black sleeveless top, lots of bangles on both wrists and fingernails that had little designs painted on them. "I can let you have a look, if you want."

"That would be great," he said. "Has it been out much since ... well, since Mr. Hilborn turned it in?"

Sh'landra confirmed what Caitlin had already told him, that the plane had been used on several charter flights in the past few weeks, but nothing of any duration. Both engines and the hydraulics were inspected on a regular basis, and the instrumentation was up to FAA specs.

"In other words, it's ready to fly at a moment's notice," she assured him.

Connor really didn't know what he was looking for. To him a plane was a plane, although the aircraft he had flown in while in the army were considerably less comfortable than a commercial jet at thirty-thousand feet. But this Beechcraft was the one Hilborn had leased and he wanted to get a sense of the man in the cockpit, maybe hopping from Charleston to Charlotte or Atlanta or New York. Or the islands.

"What's the range of this thing?" he asked as he followed her across the tarmac toward the dual-prop aircraft that was parked at an angle to the terminal.

"About two thousand miles, depending on the number of passengers and weight of the cargo," she told him. "Both engines are original and have about twelve hundred hours on them. Everything was completely inspected when we took possession. Seating is two plus seven, meaning two in the cockpit and seven passengers in the cabin. As you'll see, there are four cabin tables, an aft-side electric flush toilet, and a lot of built-in storage."

By now they had arrived at the plane, and Sh'landra pulled down the aft cabin door and motioned for Connor to step up inside. Like most people Connor had never flown in a private aircraft, and he was duly impressed by the leather seats, the polished wood paneling, and the copious legroom. Still, the aisle seemed a bit cramped and the seating in the cockpit was more like that of a Formula 500 race car, plus the full array of gauges gave him a renewed respect for the guys who actually climb behind the controls and fly these things.

"What about luggage space?" he asked her as he made his way down the steps to the tarmac. "Is there a separate hold?"

"The baggage compartment in the Beechcraft King is heated, pressurized, and fully accessible during flight, in addition to external lockers to carry additional baggage," she said, as if reading from a sales brochure. They were walking around the exterior of the plane now, but Connor refrained from kicking the tires.

"Full instrumentation and autopilot?"

"Of course. Do you think your employer would want to check it out?"

"I assume it can be stocked with alcohol?" Connor said.

"Pretty much whatever the client wishes," she told him. "You'd be surprised what some of our customers ask for."

"I'll let him know and give you a call."

"Please do." Sh'landra handed Connor her business card and pointed to her direct number at the bottom. "And use that phone line. We work on commission here."

"Got it," Connor said as he slipped the card into a pocket. They stopped at the terminal door, and he held it open for her. "This may be a stupid question, but are there any restrictions on where this plane can go?"

"Restrictions?"

"What I mean is, can it be taken out of the country?"

"It can fly anywhere within that two-thousand-mile range I told you about," she explained. "East coast, west coast, Canada, the Caribbean. Anywhere except Cuba."

"How 'bout the Caymans?"

"Oh, definitely the Caymans," she replied with a knowing twinkle in her eye. "A lot of our customers like to go there."

"People are starting to talk, Tat Man," Caitlin Thomas said, a grin in her voice. "I spend more time on the phone with you than my boyfriend."

"Something to think about," Connor replied. He was pulling into a parking space in front of a Publix supermarket, answering a craving for the best fried chicken in the South Carolina Lowcountry. "Listen … I was wondering if you could check on one more thing for me."

"It's why I get paid the big bucks," she told him. "Shoot—"

"Is there any way you can run a check on missing persons?" he asked her. "Someone who disappeared about ten, twelve days ago. Most likely up in the Myrtle Beach area?"

"Just any old person, or can you narrow it down for me?"

"Try white males, about sixty years old. About six feet, hundred ninety pounds. Possibly gray hair, could be black."

"Yeah, I'm sure there's only one man fits that description in all of South Carolina," she said, her voice thick with sarcasm. "Anything else as long as I'm at it?"

Connor let his brain work this through, then said, "Yeah. Could be a long shot, but the guy might be gay."

"This still the Hilborn thing?" Caitlin asked him.

"Just working on a hunch. I know it's late and you're probably done for the day, but—"

"But what else have I got going on, right?"

"That's not what I meant—"

"I'm just messin' with you, Tat Man." She giggled. "I'll give you a call when I find whatever it is I find."

He thanked her but she had already hung up, so he climbed out of the Camaro and started toward the automatic door that separated him from his fried chicken. That's when he saw the Chevy Caprice with the flashing blue light bar and the words "Mount Pleasant Police Department" painted on the door. An officer in a black uniform was making his way toward Connor, the new leather of his gun belt squeaking like a hamster on a flywheel.

"Hold it right there."

Connor held it, looked the cop directly in the eyes. "I do something?"

"License and registration, please," the officer said.

"What is this …?" Connor caught himself mid-sentence, realizing it was best just to go along with this. He had to go back to the Camaro and retrieve the registration from the locked glove compartment, then handed it and his license to the cop.

The officer studied both documents carefully, then handed them back, almost reluctantly. "You're missing a side view mirror, Mr. Connor," he finally said. "That's a violation of the South Carolina motor vehicle code—"

"Someone vandalized it," Connor explained, not wanting to go into how Leland Wheeler's neighbor had shot it off with a rifle. "New mirror's on order. Should be in, in a day or two." "Mind if I have a look?"

"Excuse me?" Connor asked.

"Improper equipment on a moving vehicle constitutes probable cause," the officer said. "I called your plate in and the computer spit back a hit from SLED. Seems you were arrested a couple weeks back for possession with intent to distribute."

"Does your computer say the charges were dropped and the whole thing went away?" Connor said, refusing to give in to the frustration—no, anger—that was building inside him.

"No, it does not," the cop said. "And I don't give a rat's ass. Technically, I don't have to ask your permission, so if you don't mind I'm going to take myself a look."

"Knock yourself out," Connor said, thankful that he'd made the snap decision to take Jacob Wheeler's pump-action out of his trunk as soon as he'd returned from Myrtle Beach.

The officer obviously must have thought he'd stumbled upon something that could elevate his status from patrol duty to detective, because he spent a good ten minutes inspecting the car thoroughly. Floor mats, ash trays, glove box, door panels, engine compartment, trunk: everything that possibly could hold even a microbe of a controlled substance was checked. Connor stood by, looking bored and confident that this search would yield nothing.

Eventually the officer pried himself away from the Camaro and said, "Get that mirror fixed. I could give you a ticket for that, but I'm going to be lenient on account of this is such a bitchin' car."

"Thanks," Connor replied, knowing he was expected to show the cop eternal gratitude and respect. "You out here alone?"

"My partner, he's inside the store, gettin' us some dinner," the officer explained. "I was just waitin' out here for him when you pulled in. Easiest stop all day."

Just then another cop in a matching black uniform emerged through the automatic glass door. He carried a grocery bag in his hand.

"Good timing," the cop said as his partner wandered over. "Got the last pieces of chicken in the store."

Connor felt a slow burn. "You're shittin' me—"

"Nope," the cop with the grocery bag said. "Say—did you know you've got a busted mirror?"

"Thanks for pointing it out," Connor said, thinking he'd better get out of there before the mirror wasn't the only thing that got busted.

In the end dinner was a pizza from a local joint down the street, lots of pepperoni and veggies, washed down with a glass of gin on ice and another blood-red sunset view over the marsh. Connor knew the gin was becoming an all-too-frequent thing, but he excused it by the day being a long one, including the news of David Hilborn's murder in his Hilton Head home. Dr. Pinch at the V.A. kept telling him that returning vets turned to alcohol as the first plan of escape, and while Connor had dismissed the warning as psycho-pop counseling, he knew it contained more than a grain of truth.

Besides, the gin had given him the resolve to make the one phone call he had been thinking about all day when he wasn't trying to unravel the tapestry of Jon Hilborn's death. So, when he finished his first glass, he fixed himself another, then hit the number in his "favorites" and waited for it to ring.

"Connor!" Even though it was just one word, he could hear a sense of relief and hope in Danielle's voice. And maybe just a touch of nerves, as well. "I've been thinking about you."

"In a good way, I hope," he said in a voice that was more tentative than he intended.

"A very good way," she assured him.

"So, have you figured out yet how long 'a while' is?"

"Longer than I wanted, shorter than I expected."

Connor watched as a large bird took flight from a limb high up in a pine tree and soared off over the marsh. "Which means—?"

"Which means I'm glad you called."

There was an awkward pause that lasted almost too long, and then he asked, "How's Richard doing?"

"Richard is fine. He's seeing someone."

"Besides Tinkerbell? That didn't take long."

"No, I don't mean *seeing* in that way. He's seeing a therapist."

"You mean like a marriage counselor?"

"No, as in every other kind of counselor. Richard has a lot of baggage involving anger, control, alcohol, and sex. And that's all you need to know."

Connor thought back to last weekend when he and Danielle were tearing up the sheets in his bedroom, just a few feet from where he now was sitting.

"How's your African cat?" he asked. "Did she have her cub?"

"This morning, actually. There were a few complications, but she gave birth to a healthy young lion king, weighed in at five pounds. We named him Regis."

"I can't wait to see him," Connor said, putting the issue—if not the question—out there in the open.

"When?" Danielle asked.

"As soon as you give me the all-clear."

"Consider it given. And I promise you, Richard won't be an issue." "Does he know that?" Connor asked.

"He will," she assured him. "So … when can you come to Orlando? Are you done with that suicide case you were working on?"

"Just about," he said. "Another day or two and I'll be all wrapped up."

He had no idea at the time just how prescient his words would prove to be.

Chapter 28

The drive to Myrtle Beach the next morning took the usual ninety minutes, but because it was his third trip up there in just over a week the miles seemed to drag.

He set out after the morning swell of traffic, nursing a cup of strong coffee from Café Medley as he drove. His conversation with Danielle had gone much longer than he had expected but just as long as he had hoped, which powered him through his second glass of gin. At the time it felt good, his head softened just enough by the juniper berries as the tone of her voice eased the anxiety that he realized had built up around his confrontation with her husband. The last time they had talked things had not gone well, and could have gone either up or down from there. Fortunately, the current direction was up, and that's what occupied his mind now as he edged from Route 17 onto the business spur that would take him into the heart of the resort town.

A few minutes later he pulled off the highway at a Kangaroo gas station and went inside to get another cup of coffee. When he came back outside he made a quick call to Citadel Security and asked Caitlin Thomas if she'd had any luck with her search.

"Nothing," she replied. "No one who comes close to matching the description you gave me has gone missing anywhere near Myrtle Beach. Or Wilmington, Charleston, or anywhere in between. Looks like sixty-year-old white men usually don't just drop off the face of the planet."

Unless the Babics are involved, Connor thought as he took a small sip of steaming coffee and said, "I know it's a stretch. Let me know if anything turns up, okay?"

"Ten-four, Tat Man," Caitlin said.

The last time he had come up to Myrtle Beach, Mac from Oz had made it clear he didn't want to see Connor's face again. Not in Maccaws, not anywhere. There was no implied threat of violence in his words, but the meaning was clear: you're not welcome here, so stay away. Which is what Connor would have done this morning, except that the question he needed to ask was not good for a telephone that could be disconnected. So here he was, pushing his way through the glass door and feeling the instant chill of the air conditioner.

"Table for one, or are you meeting someone?" It was the same thin young man with the thick mustache who had greeted him the last time. "It's early, so you can have your pick."

"Actually, I'm looking for Mac," Connor said. "Is he in?"

In fact, Connor already had established on the phone that Mac was in the kitchen, something Thin Man confirmed with a cautious look. "He's here, but he's busy," he said.

"This will only take a minute," Connor pressed.

Thin Man hesitated a second, as if he were considering Mac's reaction to being interrupted. Then he said, "Will he know what this is about?"

"As soon as he gets out here," Connor said. "Tell him we spoke a few days ago."

Again, Thin Man looked hesitant, but eventually said "wait here" and disappeared through the swinging doors into the back.

Thirty seconds later Mac from Oz pushed his way out from the kitchen and stopped mid-stride when he recognized Connor standing near the "Please Wait To Be Seated" sign.

"You!" he snapped. "I thought I made it pretty obvious that neither you nor your money was welcome here!"

"That you did," Connor said. "And I'm not staying. I just wanted to show you another picture—"

"What is it about protecting my customers' privacy that you don't understand?" he demanded in that thick accent from down under.

"I don't think this gentleman is a customer anymore," Connor said. "Please— just take a quick look."

He unfolded a color photograph he had printed off a website and handed it to Mac, who just glared at him. But eventually he caved and glanced down at the creased image. The look of recognition in his eyes told Connor all he wanted to know.

"That's Hilly," he said, handing the photograph back without refolding it.

"Hilly?" Connor repeated.

"Jon Hilborn. He wasn't a regular, but he came in every once in a while, when he was in town. Till he died, that is."

"Hilborn was married four times, with four kids," Connor said.

"Not my fault," Mac said with a shrug. "Lot of my customers are like that, you catch my drift."

Connor considered what he was implying, then said, "Do you recall anyone being with him the last time he was in here?"

"I don't keep tabs on everyone who comes in here, Mr. Connor."

"But—?"

Mac glared at him, then took another look at the picture. "But yeah, I remember him being with someone, since usually he came in alone and left alone."

"You wouldn't happen to remember who he might have been with," Connor said, really pushing his luck now.

"I'm not the Gestapo. Not like some folks in this country who have an irrational fear of what they don't know. I don't ask names, and I don't keep records."

"Can you at least describe him?"

Mac's eyes bored into him, and eventually he said, "White male. Clean shaven, just like Hilly. Early sixties. Again, just like Hilly. In fact, you ask me, he bore a strong resemblance to Hilly. Similar nose, chin, eyes. Maybe an inch shorter. And now, if you don't mind, I want you to get the hell out of my establishment and never show even the shadow of your face in here again. You got it?" Yep. He got it.

Detective Ozzie Harris was no more pleased to see Jack Connor than Mac from Oz was, and he had just as good a method for exhibiting his displeasure.

"I remember you," he said with what sounded like a growl. "You were up here from Charleston with that rich dink, asking about the suicide at the Cape Myrtle."

"Thirty-two feet per second per second," Connor said, as he handed over a page he'd printed from Wikipedia. "Says so right here. You owe me five bucks."

"What the hell're you talkin' about," the detective asked, as his eyes drifted to the print-out. Connor had used a yellow marker to highlight the section that read:

Near the surface of the Earth, use $g = 9.8$ m/s^2 (metres per second squared; which might be thought of as 'metres per second, per second,' or 32 ft/s^2 as 'feet per second per second').

"There it is, in black and white," Connor said. "And yellow."

"You drove all the way up here to collect on a bet?" Detective Harris blurted, shaking his head.

"Or you could let me take a look at the autopsy photos again, we call it even."

Harris stared at him, not sure if Connor was pulling his leg or simply crazy. Eventually he said, "You're serious. You really want to see the pics?"

"Five minutes and you save five dollars," Connor told him.

It was a bargain at any price, although it took Connor almost ten minutes to review the entire file of photos. He looked at the crime scene pics first, those that were taken of Hilborn's body where it had come to rest on the pavement, where the woman with the dog named Fifi had practically stumbled upon him in the pre-dawn darkness. Next came the pictures that were snapped by the medical examiner, Jon Hilborn lying naked and gray on the stainless-steel table before she had cut him open, and then again after she had stitched his chest cavity shut. Both sets of shots told the story of a man who had failed in his attempt to slit his wrists, then hauled himself out of the bath tub, stumbled around the living room of his suite, and eventually managed to drag himself over the balcony, where he fell to his death.

And in the end, they told him everything he needed to know. Well, almost everything.

Ten miles south of Myrtle Beach, just past the entrance to Brookgreen Gardens, Connor's phone rang. He didn't recognize the number, and the rush of wind over the scooped hood coupled with the fact that the convertible top was down made it difficult to hear.

"Is this Palmetto BioClean?" asked a voice that sounded tentative and uncertain. And decidedly female.

Connor realized he'd answered the phone just by giving his first and last name, and now clarified that she had, indeed, called the right number.

"You people clean up blood?"

"That's our specialty," he confirmed for her. When he first got hired he used to add, "no job is too big or too small," but when he learned he usually was dealing with bereaved relatives of the recently deceased, he realized the levity was not appreciated. "How may I help you today?" he said instead.

"I ... we ... well, my brothers and I ... we need to hire you," she said. "There's blood everywhere ... in the foyer, the living room, the kitchen. It's more than we can deal with ... so the police suggested I give you a call."

Connor eased his foot onto the brake and pulled the Camaro into the entrance of a driveway that cut off to the right. "They gave you good advice," he assured her. "Now, I hate to ask you this, but this blood—how long has it been there?"

The woman on the other end sniffed back some tears. "The cops said two, maybe three days," she told him. "Does that matter?"

"It might, depending on what surface the blood is on, and how long it's had a chance to permeate that surface," Connor explained. "When would you like us to start?"

"As soon as possible," the woman replied. "I can't stand to look at it, all that blood all over the place."

"You won't have to," he told her. "Depending on where you're located I can have a crew there today."

"Good," the woman said, letting out what sounded like a huge sigh of relief. "Can you come all the way to Hilton Head?" *Wham!* There it was.

"That's well within our territory," Connor said. "I'll dispatch a truck as soon as you tell me where it's going."

"Calibogue Sound Country Club, in Hilton Head," she said. "And by the way, my name is Carol Hilborn. My father was David Hilborn, and ... well, it's his house you'll be coming to."

Coincidence. Serendipity.. Synchronicity. Those words and more stirred Connor's mind for most of the drive down to Hilton Head. After getting the phone call from Carol Hilborn he'd reached out and found Lionel Hanes at his gym, where he'd been showing a young kid with a big bully problem how to punch a body bag to a pulp. Hanes said he could make it down to the death scene in a couple hours, if D-Dub was able to pick up the truck. A call to D-Dub confirmed that was possible, and he agreed to hook up Moby Dick and stop for Jenny on the way downstate. Connor told all of them he was still an hour out from Charleston, on his way back from Myrtle Beach, and suggested they start the clean-up before he arrived on-site. He also warned them this job could go well into the night, maybe even into the next day, judging from how long the blood had been there and the surface on which had pooled and then dried.

"You still working that thing for Mr. James?" Lionel Hanes asked him.

"Almost done," Connor said.

"You want, we can handle this one ourselves, so you don't have to go all the way down to Hilton Head."

"No problem—the drive will do me good," Connor assured him. Thinking he wouldn't mind a good look around David Hilborn's house, considering what fate had just dropped into his lap. Adding the word *ethics* to all the others that were spinning around in his brain.

The police had finished their initial investigation of David Hilborn's murder, and a mound of yellow crime scene tape was piled where the Palmetto BioClean team had put it when they'd entered the house. A Beaufort County Sheriff's car with a uniformed officer was waiting for them, along with David Hilborn's daughter, who had driven up from St. Augustine when she had learned of her father's death. By the time Connor arrived on the scene both of them were gone, placing their trust in Lionel Hanes and the rest of the BioClean team to leave the place just as they had found it, except for the blood.

David Hilborn's body had been found in the kitchen, and the good news was that the blood had not seeped through the travertine flooring, to which the builder apparently had applied a generous layer of sealer. By the time Connor walked in Hanes had scrubbed up virtually every dried speck of it, and an application of protein indicator confirmed that the blood had not penetrated to the subfloor. The bad news was that Hilborn somehow had left a trail of blood across the living room from the foyer, and none of that hardwood—teak and two types of cherry—had been sealed at all, which meant that all of it had to be torn out. D-Dub and Jenny initially pulled up only those boards that had come in direct contact with David Hilborn's blood, but then discovered that some of it had even seeped into the wood beneath that, which meant that a section of subfloor had to be ripped out. Carol Hilborn did not sound happy with that prospect on the phone, but when she came back to inspect the damage she agreed that all of her late father's blood needed to be removed from the house.

"Just do what you have to do," she told them as she got back into her car, her eyes moist from the tears she was trying not to let out.

Connor was pretty sure Carol Hilborn's offer did not include going through her father's personal things. But as Hanes, D-Dub, and Jenny were loading the scraps of flooring into the big white trailer he allowed himself a quick tour of the house, ending with a room that had all the appearances of a study. The golf motif that defined the house was even thicker in here, with almost every square inch of wall space cluttered with photographs of Hilborn with other golfers, politicians, Hollywood stars, and men and women of the sporting world. A fireplace was set squarely in the wall opposite a mammoth desk, which again was a mass of ordered confusion, and all of it golf-related. Balls, tees, figurines, pens, clocks—if it had to do with golf, it had had a place on David Hilborn's desk. Above the fireplace mantle was a large oil painting of a stone bridge spanning a stream on a golf course, pink and red azaleas in bloom all around.

He slowly moved around the room, peering at the smiling faces in a photograph or lifting a knick-knack from its resting place and examining it. Every surface appeared to have been dusted recently, and not by an evidence collection team looking for fingerprints. The green carpet still had the tell-tale marks on it that suggested a vacuum had recently swept across it, disturbed only by several sets of footprints that seemed to have made the same journey around the room that Connor was making now. Most likely the police, who had checked the room out but probably realized that David Hilborn's killer had not come in here.

But they were wrong, and Connor figured this out the moment he saw the scrap of paper lying on the floor behind the heavy mahogany door. He bent down, realized it was a business card with a hand-scribbled number on it. The card was for a man named William Barber who worked for Regal Air in Brunswick, Georgia, at an address on Glynco Parkway and a phone number that began with a 912 area code. Interestingly, the number handwritten in blue ink at the bottom carried a different area code.

Connor stepped outside to dial the 912 number and a man answered with a curt "Regal Air."

"Do you lease airplanes?" Connor asked him.

"We do," the man said. "Or at least we did."

"Are you William Barber?"

"Last time I checked. Who's this?"

"Name's Jack Connor. And I'm not sure I understand what you mean when you said you *did* lease airplanes"

"Look: it's easy. We had an airplane that we leased out for charters. With a licensed pilot, or fly it yourself. But we don't do that anymore."

"Why not?" It was the question William Barber had intended for Connor to ask, so he dutifully obliged.

"Because we only had the one plane, a twin-engine Beechcraft,"

Barber replied. "And it went missing a week ago." "How do you mean, missing?" Connor said.

"How things usually go missing. One minute it's there, next minute it's not."

"You mean someone stole it?"

"It didn't fly off on its own. Sorry I can't help you—"

"Well, maybe you can. Does the name Jon Hilborn mean anything to you?"

There was a genuine silence on the other end, and eventually Mr. Barber said, "Can't say that it does."

"Did anyone come by your place asking questions about your plane?" Connor asked. "Before it was stolen, I mean."

"We get a lot of questions, most of 'em from wannabe pilots."

"But no one that stands out, maybe a guy in his sixties who knew all about Beechcraft Kings?"

Another silence followed, as William Barber considered the question. "Afraid not," he said in a tired voice. "Look, it's awful late—"

"Yeah, sorry 'bout calling at this hour," Connor apologized. "You're still working?"

"Something like that," Barber replied. "Can't do anything about my missing plane, not till it shows up or the insurance company sends me a check. But I'll be damned if anyone's gonna get my chopper."

Chapter 29

The next morning Connor was parked in Kat Rattigan's lot, waiting for her to arrive in her midnight black Boxster. He'd pulled up at nine o'clock, and a half hour later was about to give up when the car bumped into the lot, throwing up a cloud of brown dust in its wake. It came to a stop just a few feet from where he was standing, and Rattigan flashed him a broad grin as she untied the scarf that was bound to her head.

"Well, look what the cat dragged in," she said.

"Straight from the litter box," he said, still feeling tired from the three hours' sleep he'd managed after driving back from Hilton Head. "Late night?"

"Early morning," she replied as she opened the door and got out.

"Eight-ball marathon down in Beaufort, closed the place down." "You win?" he asked her.

"They don't call me Carolina Slim for nothing," she said, a big grin showing her perfect white teeth. "This a business call, or do you have time for a game?"

"I'm nowhere near your league," he told her.

"That's what I'm counting on," she said as she unlocked her office door and waved him inside. "So, what's this about?"

"I have a question about Jon Hilborn."

"Of course, you do. What gives?"

"Did your client ever mention to you whether ... well, do you happen to know if Hilborn swung both ways?"

"Huh?"

"It's a baseball analogy. It means, do you think he was ... bisexual?"

"I know what it means, Connor. My 'huh' was short for 'you've gotta be nuts.' Jon Hilborn was the number one hound dog in South Carolina. A true ladies' man. The Sultan of Swat. That's a baseball analogy, too, if I'm not mistaken."

"Yes, it is. But do you think it's possible he ever played for the other team?"

"I've done two background checks on the man, and both times he came up as straight as a Kansas highway. What's this about, anyway?"

Connor had already considered how to play this, since his question was bound to circle around to the one Kat Rattigan had just asked him. "There's evidence that Hilborn occasionally ate at a restaurant that caters to a ... homosexual crowd."

"For Chrissakes, Connor—it's okay to call a gay bar a gay bar," she said, bursting into laughter. "So what gay bar are we talking about?"

"A place called Maccaws, up in Myrtle Beach," he explained. "And like I said, it's possible that he went there a time or two. Nothing verified."

"And if he did?" she asked him. "What would that mean?" "Depends on why he was there, and who he was with." "Maybe the guy who killed him?" she pressed.

"Something like that," Connor told her, learning more and more the power of being vague.

Half a mile down Morrison Avenue from Kat Rattigan's office Connor pulled over and called the number that had been scribbled at the bottom of William Barber's business card. The fact that Barber's company, Regal Air, had just experienced a theft of Jon Hilborn's favorite type of aircraft was far more coincidence than Connor could accept. He wondered if the handwriting on the card would match up to that on the note Hilborn had left for the housekeeper at the Cape Myrtle Hotel.

The call clicked through and was answered before Connor even heard it ring.

"Sapelo Island Inn," a woman's voice answered in a thick accent Connor was now beginning to recognize as rural Georgian.

"I'm sorry, did you say Sapelo Island?" Connor asked. He'd never heard of the place, and had absolutely no idea where he was dialing.

"That's right," the woman said. "Are you calling to make a reservation, or to contact a guest?"

"I'd like to speak with Jon Hilborn, if he's registered there," Connor told her as he shifted his phone to his other hand.

"I'm sorry, there's no one here by that name."

"You're sure about that?"

"We only have four guest rooms, sir," the woman told him. "And Mr. Hilborn isn't in any of them."

Connor thought for a moment and said, "How about Malcolm Nickels? Spelled like the coin."

"Again, there's no one by that name staying here at the moment, but it does sound familiar. Hold on a moment." There was a momentary pause, and Connor thought he could hear her turning pages in a book. "Yes, here it is. A Mr. Nickels, spelled like the coin, just as you said. Looks like he was here a week ago. Stayed for just one night."

"Are you expecting him to stay with you again?"

"Not that I can tell you," she replied. "And I've already said too much already. If you're not going to make a reservation, I'm going to hang up."

When Connor arrived back at The Plant he ran a Google search on "Sapelo Island," then clicked on the official listing from the Georgia Department of Natural Resources. The web page told him that Sapelo was a small barrier island with long, barren beaches and beautiful marshes on the state's "Colonial Coast," just a 30-minute ferry ride from the Georgia mainland and then only about a half hour from Brunswick.

Bingo!

He sat there at his desk, reading about the nature walks and visitors' center and mansion tours, as everything slipped neatly into place. When he had read it all twice he picked up his phone and dialed Linda Loris' phone number from his contacts menu.

"Did you or your husband ever vacation on the Georgia coast?" he asked her after they exchanged brief small talk.

"In fact, we did," she said. "Several times in fact. He loved Tybee, near Savannah, and one other time he surprised me with a weekend trip to some small place out in the middle of nowhere. It was an island, the name of which I can't for the life of me remember. It had beautiful beaches and an old black community that was named after pigs, I think."

"Sapelo Island?" Connor suggested.

"Why yes, I do believe that was it," she replied. "Sapelo sounds right. A very lovely place. Why do you ask?"

"Give me twenty-four hours and I'll let you know," he said.

This time the Mount Pleasant police hadn't rounded up the last of the fried chicken at Publix, so Connor asked the man behind the counter to box up a few pieces and add in a container of mac and cheese. Yeah, the fried grease was no better for him than the glass of gin he'd planned to go with it, or the next one that inevitably would follow, but what the hell—it certainly seemed programmed for more longevity than keeping company with Jon Hilborn did.

Connor's brain had become so tangled in the web of death that surrounded Hilborn that he didn't even see the silver Acura when he pulled into his short driveway. Not until he had gotten out of his car and was fumbling to unlock his front door. That's when he saw a shadow move across his line of vision, causing him to drop the box of fried chicken from his left hand and pull out the Glock with his right. In the same rapid moment, he spun around to see what had caused the momentary blur of motion.

"Holy shit, Connor—put that thing down!"

It was Danielle, and she was carrying her own bag of groceries.

Connor went rigid, then slowly lowered the gun until it was pointing at the ground. "This whole thing's got me a bit jumpy," he explained to her. "I was just thinking how many people are dead, all because of Jon Hilborn."

"Yeah, well, I don't want to be added to the list," she said. Then the deep scowl in her eyes shifted to a smile, and she said, "Aren't you even going to ask me what I'm doing here?"

He glanced at the bag of groceries she was still holding and said, "Nope. But I'm thinking maybe you can just come inside and show me."

It was at least another hour before they got around to the grocery bag, which contained all the fixin's for pasta and a salad, and a bottle of wine. They also had the chicken and mac and cheese Connor had bought at the store. But by the time they got to it neither of them felt much like cooking, so Danielle said, "I could sure go for one of those thick burgers at that place you took me last time." *Last time* in this case referring to the night she had shown up at his door, apologizing for blasting him in the face with pepper spray.

"Poe's," Connor said, identifying the restaurant. "That's the place. And a good, stiff martini." "Just one?" he asked her.

"You may not have noticed, but it's Sunday," she reminded him. "That car out front is Rebecca's. After we talked last night I decided on a whim to fly up here and drive it home. Among other things."

"I assume I'm one of those other things?"

"You know it. And after we have dinner I'm going to help myself to seconds."

It was just under a seven-hour drive from Sullivan's Island to Orlando, and Danielle was expecting the arrival of two wildebeests at the animal park the next afternoon. That meant two things: she really was serious about only having one martini, and she was equally serious about leaving at first light in order to get back down to the animal park in time to give each of the new arrivals from Africa a thorough physical exam.

She also kept her promise about having seconds after dinner, not to mention a midnight snack a little later as a gentle breeze rustled the palmetto fronds outside Connor's window.

Once Danielle was back on the road it had been Connor's plan to hit the sand for his regular three-mile run, which had become less than regular due to the events of the past several weeks. But as he watched her brake lights flash as she hung a left at the corner, a gust of warm wind blew in from the waterway, lifting a pair of snowy egrets into the air. Lowcountry angels, is what they called them down here. He watched the birds as their long, graceful wings took to the sky, naturally banking into the wind to increase their lift. And that's when it hit him, something he'd totally missed.

Something right there in front of him, if he'd only been looking.

Ninety minutes later Connor touched his foot to the brake and slowed the Camaro almost to a stop directly in front of the gated entrance to Rennelswood Place. Just as he did the other day, he followed the winding driveway back through the bearded oaks and magnolias toward the yellow house with the white columns and black shutters. Today the windsock in the distance indicated a slight breeze out of the south, and some dark clouds carried a serious threat of rain. As he neared the circular pull-through section of the driveway he expected to find the same armed guard standing on the porch, the same outdoor ceiling fan lazily spinning in the warm, still air. But on this morning, there seemed to be no hustle of activity, and except for the birds singing in the trees there were no signs of life at Malcolm Nickels' home.

Connor guided the old Chevy two thirds of the way around the drive so it was aimed back down toward the road, just in case he had to make a run for it. Then he turned off the engine and sat for a moment, wondering if Charlene Marks and the rest of the Babic clan had moved on, or maybe someone was lining him up in a scope right now, ready to take a shot. But that didn't seem to be the case, so he slowly opened the door and eased out, keeping his eyes and ears open for the slightest sign of movement or the thinnest of noises. Like the sound of a bullet being chambered in a gun.

Rather than hide the Glock in the waistband of his jeans or under his shirt, he carried it openly in his right hand, displaying it for all eyes to see. If there were any eyes, and he was growing increasingly confident there weren't. He mounted the fifteen steps to the front porch, where just two days ago he had encountered Kenny the Gunman, then edged close to the glass beside the front door and peered inside to the entry hall. He detected no movement inside so he leaned on the buzzer and heard the deep chime of carillon bells playing the first bars of "Dixie" through the bowels of the house. No one came to the door so he did it again, then knocked loudly, as if the sound of someone pounding on the door would bring different results.

Nothing.

He tried the knob, and naturally found it was locked. He peered through the glass again, then glanced over his shoulder at the driveway. Still no activity: no cars pulling up through the trees, no signs of armed guards or cops or hired hands anywhere. Not even the faint sound of someone playing the piano in an upstairs room, as he had detected the last time he was here.

So, he aimed the gun at the lock and shot it out.

The first thing he noticed was that the air conditioning had been turned off. On his first visit the interior of the house had been chilled until it almost felt like a walk-in freezer, but now it was hot and stuffy.

No breeze, no noise from a compressor—just thick, stale air that seemed to be draped over the furniture and the floor. The second thing he noticed, and this was much more unsettling than the first, was the distinct hum of flies buzzing not too far away. He recognized that noise from the door-to-door reconnaissance he and his squad had done in small villages in Iraq, knew that it usually meant death and decay was somewhere nearby.

It was the stench of decomposition that led him to the bodies. There were two of them stuffed in the half bath—what Connor figured might be called a powder room—right off the entry hall, and from the appearance of flies and grubs it appeared they had been there for at least a day. He recognized the two men as the guards who had patted him down on his last visit, and both of them had since been relieved of their automatic weapons. Connor knelt down, looked for signs of entry or exit wounds, but found none that were visible, which suggested blunt force trauma might be involved. He wasn't about to touch them to find out, so he slowly stood up, momentarily considering the whereabouts of Kenny, whose brother Jimmy had been killed by a car bomb in Iraq.

Connor left the two bodies where they were, thinking this scenario seemed eerily similar to the visit he paid to Bodean Barr, found him shot-gunned just inside his front door. Except in that case Barr's body had been left where it had fallen, whereas these two guards obviously had been moved into the power room and placed with their backs against the wall.

Again, he thought, *where's Kenny?* Which then led him to think, *and Charlene?*

He spent the next twenty minutes looking for answers to both questions, but came up empty-handed. Malcolm Nickels' house turned out to be bigger than it already looked, and Connor went through each of the six bedrooms and five full baths. One of the bedrooms on the third floor had been converted to a music room, with a baby grand piano that he figured must have been brought up in the elevator that ran through the core of the house. This was where Charlene had been playing the last time he had been here, so he took his time going through drawers, closets, and a large armoire that stood against one wall. Since this was Nickels' home, each was stuffed with clothes and other belongings that may or may not have belonged to Charlene, or whoever else had been staying here with her. Possibly one or more members of the Babic clan, or maybe she was just here with a few guards, hiding out. Still, there were no signs of her or anyone else squatting in any of the bedrooms.

The guest house out back was a different story.

This obviously was where the three guards had been holed up. Connor could tell the moment he pushed his way through the unlocked door and found two bedrolls, half-emptied duffel bags, clothes strewn about the floor and furniture and bathroom. Obviously, the belongings of the dead guards in the powder room. The antique oak double bed in the bedroom had been slept in and not made, signs of a pecking order that suggested this was where Kenny had stayed. There was a duffel bag in there, too, again with clothes scattered about the floor, leading Connor to suspect that Kenny was not far away, either. He didn't like what that implied, whether the guy was dead or alive.

He went through the two dead guards' duffels first, checking trouser pockets and balled-up socks and even underwear for any sign of who they were or where they were from. Their wallets were missing—probably lifted off them by whoever had killed them—but Connor did find assorted pieces of mail, some addressed to a Jeffrey Woods in Gulfport, Mississippi, and a Delta boarding pass for a Frank Gilmore, who had flown from Mobile to Atlanta. Connor knew enough about U.S. geography to know both Gulf cities were not far from Biloxi, home of the Babic family.

From the date on the boarding pass it was clear that Gilmore had flown to Atlanta three days ago, and a separate boarding pass Connor found in a copy of *Guns and Ammo* revealed that Gilmore had then flown on to Charleston that same day, after a five-hour layover. And, Connor assumed, after calling the ten-digit Atlanta phone number that had been scribbled in black ink on the back of the boarding pass.

He pulled out his phone and began to punch the number into it, see who or what answered, but before he was finished he realized it already was stored in his contacts. The name the phone's memory associated with it was Andrew Corliss, DEA.

For just a second Connor thought about letting the call ring through. After all, what would one of Babic's gunmen possibly have to say to a DEA agent who was trying to lock down a drug trafficking ring that probably had ties all throughout the Babic clan. But Connor didn't want to ask Corliss any questions that he didn't already have some semblance of an answer to, nor did he want to bug the guy any more than he already had. So, he hit the "end" button and slipped the phone back into his pocket.

Connor slowly walked back to his car, thinking as soon as he was out of here he'd give the local cops a call to tip them to the carnage he'd just found. But not from a local gas station with a surveillance camera; he'd learned his lesson the first time. He slid into the driver's seat and drummed his fingers on the steering wheel while he assembled all the mental parts of this scenario, fitting tab "A" into slot "B." After about thirty seconds' hesitation he eased his foot to the gas pedal and started to pull through the circular driveway. The windsock in the field to his left was starting to fill in the slight morning breeze, and a flurry of birds rose into the pale blue sky.

That's when it hit him: an *a-ha* moment that almost caused him to pop the heel of his hand into his forehead, just like the V-8 commercials on television. He shifted into reverse and slowly edged the car back around the drive to the side of the house. Connor knew it wouldn't be easy to hide a bright orange Camaro with a scooped hood, but just about anyone he wanted to hide it from was lying dead either in the main building or somewhere nearby. He backed it as far as he could into a small copse of trees at the rear of the Nickels compound, where he spotted a narrow path clogged on both sides by the thick trunks of old live oaks. In fact, if someone hadn't been looking for it the pathway would have gone unnoticed.

He popped the trunk and checked both guns. He decided Richard Simmons' Glock would afford him more movement and better aim than Jacob Wheeler's pump-action shotgun, then edged his way down the path, keeping his body stooped over in the foolish assumption that lowering his stature would keep him from getting shot.

Five minutes later the trees gave way to the field. In the fall it would be full of corn but at this time of year only bright green seedlings were protruding from the dark, rich soil. About fifty yards to his left was a metal storage building, and beyond that was a paved landing strip that stretched several thousand feet to the west. Connor dropped into a crouch, took a deep breath, and slowly took in the scene from this new vantage point. The shed itself held little interest for him, but parked next to it was an airplane, a large engine with twin engines, one affixed to each wing. There was no doubt in his mind: this was the missing Beechcraft King.

Connor hung there a minute or two, eyeing both the plane and the windsock in the distance. Nothing seemed to be happening—no movement, no sounds, not even the smell of a cigarette—and for a couple of seconds he wondered if he'd misjudged this whole thing. Then he realized the aircraft's door was open, the stairs folded down and almost touching the tarmac. No one would leave it that way unless someone was nearby.

Connor was tired of waiting. When he was in Kirkuk, waiting had been someone else's job, someone who usually was lying prone on a rooftop with a sniper's rifle, waiting to take a shot. He had been a front-line recon grunt, which usually meant moving from one dark doorway to the next, checking for bad guys and occasionally getting shot at. More dangerous, sure, but more going on, as well. His mindset was not one that could remain inert for long, and that's what came over him now as he watched plenty of nothing happening.

So, he edged out of where he had been hiding in the brush at the edge of the path and scurried in a low run toward the garage. The soles of Connor's running shoes were muffled by a thick carpet of weeds, and when he reached the metal wall he lowered himself to the ground, then quickly glanced around. He had targeted a door that was set into the back of the building and now he tried opening it, but it was locked. He also realized that if someone suddenly came through it he'd be totally exposed, but it was too late to do anything about that.

Connor inched along the edge of the storage building, taking care not to make a hint of noise. When he got to the corner he leaned back, his spine against the wall, then ventured a peek around at where the airplane was parked.

Any second now he expected someone to come around from the front of the structure and maybe climb up inside, maybe load luggage or boxes into the cargo compartment. His gaze was momentarily drawn to a large tire that appeared to have been tossed aside, and now that he really focused on it he could see that the side of the tire had been shredded. Probably got that way when the plane landed at this airstrip, which looked as if it had not been resurfaced for quite a long time.

That's what he was thinking when he took the hot round in his leg. The crack of the subsonic rifle followed almost instantly, barely muffled by the sound Connor made when he pitched forward onto the ground.

Chapter 30

Connor's thigh hurt like there was no tomorrow, and his eyes burned from the face full of dirt he'd taken when he went down. He spat out a mouthful of it as he found purchase with his hands and lifted his head, sensed more than saw movement cross between him and the early morning sun. Whoever had shot him was approaching him from about a hundred yards beyond the path that led from Nickels' house. Connor had exposed himself as he darted across the open grass to the back of the storage building, giving himself up to a pretty damned easy shot.

He pushed himself upward and glanced at the dark, wet bloom that was forming on his jeans. He grabbed the Glock from his waistband and skittered around the corner of the building.

"You either have the biggest balls or the smallest brain of anyone I know," a voice called out from behind him.

It was not the voice he had expected, but he wasn't surprised by it, either. His leg was burning as if a hot spike had been driven into it, and he really wasn't sure that what he'd just heard was real or simply the byproduct of pain. He'd felt it this intense only once before, when he'd suddenly been launched into the air by the same roadside bomb that had torn through Eddie James, except that incident hadn't been caused by what they call "friendly fire." The only thing Connor was surprised at, in fact, was that DEA Agent Andrew Corliss hadn't already planted a second round in him, this time in the back of his skull.

"Like I warned you, you should have stayed away from this," Corliss continued as he approached the back of the storage building, a jeering edge to his voice. "You had no idea what you were dealing with, and now look where it's got you."

Connor didn't say anything, just pulled himself up into a low crouch and half-limped along the side of the metal building. He'd scored pretty well with firearms when he was in the Army, usually able to form a tight five-inch group at twenty-five yards, and a couple of times opening up just a single hole in the target. But the last time he'd fired a gun was when he was still up at Fort Drum, and he hadn't been wounded in the leg at the time.

He could hear Corliss' footsteps now as he approached the rear of the storage building. Connor knew he'd been shot with some sort of long-range rifle, probably whatever DEA types were issued these days, but he figured Corliss also was carrying a handgun. Mostly likely the one he'd had with him the other night when he showed up at Connor's house without invitation. Whatever it was, he was outgunned, and his chances didn't look good.

But then his mind played a trick on him, and rather than being hunched over at the corner of a steel shed in the middle of a Carolina field, he allowed himself to be carried back to Iraq. Aside from the hole in his leg, which was seeping but not pouring blood, he'd found himself in similar situations at least a half dozen times. He'd had good back-up then, platoon buddies looking out for him and vice versa, as well as his M4 rifle. Once or twice a handgun, too. But a Glock was a damned good weapon, and today that's what he had in his hand.

"I am not a man you screw with," Corliss called out to him. Maybe fifteen yards away now, taking his time as he approached.

"Big brave G-man," Connor yelled before he scooted around to the front of the building, where he found two rolling metal doors. "You gonna kill me along with all the others?" "What others?" Corliss snapped back.

"I saw that mess you left up at the house—"

"Loose ends," the federal agent said. "Just like you."

Connor took advantage of Corliss' snippy reply to move closer to the rolling doors. Both of them were in the down position, but the one closest to him seemed to have caught on something in the steel tracks and was wedged open about five inches from the concrete floor. Connor dragged himself to the center of the door and pulled himself into a crouch, then used both hands to try to push the door upwards.

It was heavy, but still it moved. Just a few inches at first, then a foot, and another foot, creating a large enough gap for Connor to roll underneath. As he scrambled inside he released his grip and the door crashed back down, smacking onto the stone patio paver that had held it open. He hit his head on something hard and cursed under his breath, but then he pushed himself up into a sitting position and glanced around.

Or at least he tried to. It took a few seconds for his eyes to adjust to the darkness, and when he did he realized he was in the middle of a mechanic's shop, with winches, a lift equipped with heavy-duty chains, a tire-changing machine, drills attached to pneumatic hoses, and several air compressors. A large metal stack-type tool chest was pushed in one corner, and a bad-ass Triumph motorcycle had been pushed into the other garage bay. A workbench, scattered engine parts, a piece of cowling from an airplane and about a dozen large batteries completed the picture.

"Don't be stupid, Connor," Corliss said, his voice reverberating through the metal wall. "Let's finish this thing now."

Like most men who grew up on the blue-collar side of town, Connor had acquired a harsh education about conflict and struggle and power, one that had helped him to form a valuable yet sometimes cynical approach to the world. Whether it was cowardly bullying or protection scams or extortion schemes or just pathetic losers getting their kicks from knocking other people around, the streets of Lansing—like many American towns—were rife with sociopathic trash looking for an angle or an edge. Their own perception of a world they saw as both wretched and vile perpetuated a particular brand of violence that reflected the worst of human nature. It was as if there was some sort of dedicated survivor gene that was insistent on spreading itself like a virus throughout the species. This gene was the root cause of all wars, and entire nations had been built and destroyed because of it.

Of course, Iraq presented the worst of the worst, both in himself and in others, no matter what side of the gun they were standing on. In the end it came down to men and women killing other men and women, all in the name of God or country. Or oil. Young boys barely past puberty agreeing to have a bomb strapped to their bodies, or football captains signing up for a noble cause and being shipped over to a desert country just to kill some rag-heads. Connor had seen bodies without heads and heads without bodies. He had seen the craters where bombs had exploded, and bloody body parts that would never again be properly matched to a human life. He saw soldiers urinating on the burned bodies of the people they had killed, and he had seen enemy combatants on leashes forced to crawl on their hands and knees and bark on command. He would be awakened at night by the lasting images of cowardly rebels wearing black hoods removing the heads of American infidels while they were still alive, and—like most Americans—he would never forget the news footage of the planes flying into the twin towers. These were the images that told him how far a human being could sink into the abyss of depravity, and that's what Dr. Pinch at the V.A. was helping him deal with to this day.

Connor didn't know Andrew Corliss' back story, nor did he care to fall into whatever pit of vipers from which the man had crawled. But he assumed that the ease with which the DEA agent seemed prepared to take an innocent life for his own gain originated in a horribly dark place in the brain. And because Corliss was employed by the U.S. government he had one distinct advantage: he knew how the system worked, and he knew the people he worked with would back his play, whatever it was. Corliss' account of the truth would always trump any other version because it was the easiest to believe.

In other words, Connor was screwed. But then, he already knew this because of the throbbing hole in his leg and the blood that he had left on the ground outside and now here in the dark garage. And all of this was causing his brain to wander off to places where it should not be going, when what he really needed to do was focus on the here and now.

Connor grabbed the edge of a work table and slowly pulled himself to his feet. Then he limped over to the tool chest in the corner, which stood close to six feet high. He slipped in behind it, a small gap between the stacked metal boxes giving him a clear view of the front of the building.

"You're starting to really piss me off, you know?" Corliss barked at him from outside the shed.

Connor remained silent and still.

"Don't make me come in after you—"

Stupid to say, because that was exactly what Connor wanted.

Corliss must have been thinking this through because he didn't say anything for a long while. Then Connor saw a shadow move toward the center of the door that he had recently slipped under, and then it started to roll up. As it did more and more light flowed inside, giving him a better look at where he was, and what he was up against.

"Give it up," Corliss said, his voice actually sounding bored. "You're not leaving here alive."

Connor had checked the bullets in the magazine just yesterday, knew there were eight of them. He'd already fed one into the chamber, and now he was watching Corliss as he took a tentative step into the garage, moving toward the opposite wall. As he expected, Corliss was carrying a rifle that looked like a Remington bolt-action with a scope fixed to the barrel, and he also had a semi-automatic in a leather shoulder holster.

"C'mon, Connor. I know you're behind the tool chest—"

"You can kill me, but you can't make me go away," Connor finally said.

"The soil is loose out there in the field," Corliss told him. "Easy to dig a hole this time of year."

"That's not what I meant," Connor said, wincing as something in his leg seized up. "This gig's coming apart, and you're going down."

"Funny thing to say, since you're the one trapped there in the corner."

"You going to tell me why?" Connor asked. "All of this, I mean?"

"Waste of breath." Corliss took another step further inside the garage, but not any closer to the tool chest. "You'll be dead soon enough."

"Then I'll tell you," Connor said. "How you got mixed up in all this, I mean."

"Save your words," Corliss snapped. "I know you got a nasty hole in your leg."

"It's just a flesh wound," Connor replied, thinking it was an odd time for an old Monty Python bit to run through his head. "It's all about the money, isn't it?"

"Despite what they say, it buys a shitload of happiness." The DEA agent was now squarely inside the garage, and strangely was making no move to keep himself covered. "Don'tcha think?"

"What I think is when the Wheeler brothers got nabbed with that truck you saw an opportunity, and you ran with it. Engineered this whole thing—drugs, guns, Hilborn and Nickels. Jacob and Leland, too."

"You're sounding tired ..."

"Way I see it, a DEA agent probably doesn't make that much." Connor watched as Corliss set the rifle down and pulled the pistol out of his holster. "Especially compared to all the truckloads of cash rolling out of the Port of Charleston. And Biloxi and Mobile."

"You're right about that," Corliss said. "Compared to what those shit-for-brains were getting from one job, it wasn't a tough choice for me to make."

"You killed Jacob Wheeler," Connor grunted. "Shot him in the head and fried him like a pork rind."

"Got what he had coming," Corliss said, as if that justified everything. "Him and his brother. If it wasn't me, someone else would have gotten 'em, sooner or later."

"Vigilante justice?"

"For a guy's about to die you sure can talk."

Connor ignored him. "Your snitches were gonna rat you out. Like Bodean Barr. He really had your number, didn't he?"

"You're still not seeing it, Connor."

Connor heard him rack the slide of his gun, moving a bullet into the chamber. "I'm seeing it plenty good. He stole Hilborn's money, left him high and dry."

"Hilborn was getting nervous," Corliss snarled. "Scared-like. Wanted out."

"And that would have really screwed the pooch."

"Whatever." Corliss leveled his gun, squeezed off three shots, each of them smacking into the hard steel casing of the stacked tool chest. Then he said, "You still there, Connor?"

Connor replied by extending the Glock around the edge of the tool chest and taking two shots in Corliss' general direction. Both rounds went wide, but not by much.

"Damn … you got a gun!" Corliss snapped. "Shit on a stick!"

"That's you, in a minute." Connor took a deep breath, then said, "Hilborn killed Nickels. Made it look like he jumped. Then he took whatever cash he'd been able to scrounge up and split."

"That was my money he took," Corliss said. Connor watched as he waved his gun in the general direction of the Beechcraft. "Soon as Hilborn shows up—and he's going to—he's dog food."

Connor felt a film of dizziness wash over him then, feeling as if he'd just finished off a couple martinis and a total eclipse of the brain was in the works. He glanced down, saw that he'd lost more blood than he'd figured, sitting here having this discussion with Corliss. He knew that if he was going to make it out of here in one piece he'd have to move fast, and with finality.

"So, was it you who killed Bodean Barr, or was that Hilborn?"

"No more talking, dick-head. Say good-bye to Hollywood." Corliss raised his gun and aimed it toward Connor again, then hesitated as he heard the sound of tires on gravel outside.

Connor heard it, too. He drew his gun around the corner of the tool chest and when Corliss turned to see what was going on outside, he fired off two shots. One of the slugs pinged off the barrel of the rifle Corliss had set on a workbench, and the other went wide. Corliss instantly recoiled and the next instant Connor felt a burning pain in his shoulder, where the DEA agent had grazed him.

Connor winced at the pain, gave a quick glance at his upper arm and saw blood oozing from what appeared to be just a nick in the skin. He transferred the gun to his left hand and took another shot at Corliss, figuring this was bullet number six. Corliss was waiting for him to do this and squeezed off another round. It pinged off the corner of the tool chest, about six inches from Connor's head.

Connor took a deep breath, bit down on the pain that now was pulsing through his arm as well as his leg. Then he raised himself up a few inches and peered through the gap between two of the stacked tool boxes. Corliss had edged closer to the open garage door and now was peering out from the shadows, his hand tightening on the gun's grip. He shot a quick look back in Connor's direction, dropped to his haunches, then snapped his gaze back to whatever vehicle had pulled up outside.

Connor saw his opening. He raised the Glock in his left hand, knowing he had just two more rounds left, then squeezed the trigger and watched as Corliss spun in a helpless dance as he fell to the floor.

Chapter 31

Five seconds later Charlene Marks came charging into the garage, yet another semiautomatic in her hand. She hesitated in the doorway, called out, "Hold your fire, Connor," then moved over to where Agent Corliss was bleeding out on the warm concrete.

Connor held his fire. He had no interest in shooting Charlene or, for that matter, being shot by her. A fleeting question raced through his head—*how did she know I was in here*—but he decided not to press the point right now. Outside he heard a plane engine starting—a low rumble at first, then a steady roar as all the pistons began firing in rhythm. A moment later the second engine roared to life.

"Nice aim ... looks like you got him in the lung," Charlene said. Then she kicked Corliss in the head, hard, and Connor heard a muffled grunt. The DEA agent looked up at her and Connor could see a pained and very confused look in his eyes. She gave him a long, dark look and then, without even hesitating, she pointed her gun and squeezed off a round.

"Damn," Connor called out to her. "That was brutal."

"No, that was the full Babic experience."

"You're risking a lot, hanging around here," he said. "I woulda figured you'd be long gone by now."

"Plane had a flat tire. Not easy to fix on your own."

"So, how'd you know I was in here?"

"Orange doesn't hide well," she said. He watched as she checked Corliss' pulse, using his wrist because there was blood all over his head and neck. "You hurt?"

"I'm shot, but I'll live. Unless you finish me off."

She picked up the agent's handgun, then collected the hunting rifle from the workbench. "I'll call 9-1-1 soon as we're in the air."

"We?"

"That's what I said. And you're not going to find him. Us."

"You can't run forever," Connor replied.

"Lots of countries don't do the extradition thing with the U.S.," Charlene said. "Just so you know."

"Not my business to run after you," he assured her. "Take my word for it."

Charlene was facing the stacked tool chest, trying to get a look at him through the gaps in the individual boxes. But she was holding the gun low, angled down near her waist. Not much of a threat. "Is your word good?"

"I've got no interest in messing with you or the Babics," Connor told her. "He's your old man, isn't he? Hilborn."

"Sorry, Connor. No time for family history."

"Come on, Charlene. A simple yes or no."

"Let it go," she said. "Now, if you don't mind, I've got a plane to catch."

"You'll never get all those guns past security."

"Funny guy."

"Yeah, that's me," Connor said. Damn, his leg was hurting, and bleeding. "I just want to know one thing: Your old man spent a lot of time along the Mississippi coast in the late eighties, knew the casinos were coming. Got to know the Babics pretty well. And then along came you."

"You're smarter than you look," she said. "So, what's this all about, anyway? What are you doing here?"

"Bleeding."

"A real comedian—"

"Your old man owes my boss a painting."

There was a brief silence, then Charlene said, "Jesus! You've got to be shittin' me."

"It's my job." Connor leaned back against the wall, exhaustion starting to overtake him, the throbbing in his arm and leg beginning to take its toll.

"Work is overrated," she said.

"Your father pushed Malcolm Nickels off that balcony, didn't he?" Connor pressed her. "After he bashed the guy's face in so no one would notice the victim wasn't really him. Caused all that blood, but he probably figured he had no choice. And as soon as Nickels was dead he raced down to his brother's place in Hilton Head, waiting for the call from the police. But he had a problem. Bodean Barr had stolen all the cash your daddy meant to take with him, so he paid him a visit along the way."

But Charlene didn't respond, and when Connor cautiously peeked around the corner of the tool chest he saw she was already gone. Five seconds after that he sensed a change in the plane's twin engines, then heard the pilot throttle back as the Beechcraft King started taxiing toward the runway.

Connor stayed where he was for a good ten seconds, just in case this was a trap and Charlene hadn't actually gotten on the plane. He tried to pull himself to his feet, but the pain in his leg forced him to crawl out of his hiding place and toward the open garage door. By the time he got there and looked out he spotted the plane nearing the far end of the tarmac, starting to turn around in preparation for its long race down the runway. In the distance he heard the engines rev, watched as the Beechcraft started to move forward, building speed as it hurtled down the airstrip faster and faster until it lifted up and eased into the sky. Very much like the lowcountry angels he had seen rising over the marsh just a few hours ago. Except this time the wings weren't flapping.

He struggled out into the bright morning sun, watched the plane climb higher and higher into the cerulean sky. Eventually it disappeared altogether, generally heading south to wherever Jon Hilborn and his daughter figured they could disappear into a haven of expatriated murderers, smugglers, and thieves.

That's when he saw the cardboard mailing tube lying on the pavement where the airplane had been parked.

Chapter 32

It was late afternoon when Connor opened his eyes and found an I.V. rack towering over him, a bag hanging there and tubes and a bunch of wires connected to him. Light was streaming through the blinds of the window to his right, but the slats had been adjusted so he couldn't see anything except the sky. He was lying in a bed that had guardrails and an electronic control of some kind, and there was a digital monitor on yet another rack that he knew from watching enough television indicated that his heart rate was stable. One of his legs was throbbing from where he now remembered he had been shot, and his shoulder also seemed to be pounding with a dull pain.

He heard a rhythmic beeping sound that made him think of Bob Marley and the Jamaican Jerks and Jimmy's Buffet, but those thoughts faded away as quickly as they had come to him. A clock over the door told him it was a little after three, which meant that a good six hours had passed since he'd been shot. The fact that he could perform the simple math told him that he was still alive, and likely would stay that way. He edged upward in the bed to take some of the pressure off his leg, and that's when a nurse appeared in the doorway and looked in on him.

"You're awake," she said brightly as she stepped into the room and came up to the foot of the bed. She was young, late twenties, with blonde hair cropped at her shoulders and steel blue eyes. A plastic tag pinned to her white lab coat said her name was Diana Pearson, RN. Intense, dark eyes, and pretty in an athletic way that suggested she might have been into kite boarding and surfing. "You lost a good deal of blood."

"Not my plan when I woke up this morning," Connor told her. "Where am I?"

"The medical university," she told him. "By the time you got here your blood pressure was awfully low, but the docs sewed you up and gave you a couple pints."

"Blood or beer?"

Nurse Pearson grinned at him. "You have a lot of very interesting tattoos."

"You've been peeking?"

"You may not realize it because of the painkillers, but we threaded you with a catheter," she told him. "Ouch!" he winced in response.

"It's just a precaution, but you're definitely not going anywhere without help." She entered his vital signs into a tablet device and seemed pleased with his stats. "Oh, and by the way—there's a detective waiting outside to talk to you."

"About what?"

"Probably those bullet holes in you and the dead man they found near you," she said. "But I'm only guessing."

Nurse Pearson was right about the detective, who turned out to be Bryan Hallam from SLED. After she relayed the message to him that he, Connor, was awake, Hallam strolled into the room and came up to the side of the bed. He stood there a minute, staring down at this patient who had two tubes stuck in him, one feeding fluids into his system, the other one draining fluid out.

Hallam shook his head for a moment, then said, "You sure do know how to piss people off."

"Nice to see you, too," Connor said with a weak grin. Or was it a grimace?

"You know something? You can be one royal pain in the ass."

"Mr. Hemorrhoid … that's me. You here to ask me how I ended up getting shot and how Agent Corliss ended up dead?"

"You're on drugs," Hallam said. "Whatever you tell me, any lawyer's going to try to throw out as inadmissible."

"What lawyer? You can't possibly try to pin this one on me—" "Down, boy," Hallam told him. "Don't get your catheter in a knot. No, we know Corliss shot you and someone else shot him. What we don't know is why."

Connor lifted his shoulder in a light shrug and said, "It's because he thought I knew more than I did. And he was right."

There was no reason for Connor to withhold what he'd learned about Corliss' role in the drug ring or the subsequent bust, so he explained that the DEA agent essentially had confessed to being the lynchpin behind the operation.

Hallam sighed and massaged his temples with his fingertips. "So, what were you doing in the middle of all this? The last I knew, you'd called in a murder scene out in Walterboro. I assume it's all connected—"

Of course, it was, but the painkillers coursing through Connor's system were making things a little fuzzy. At least it made for a good excuse. "I wouldn't be here if it wasn't."

"So, what can you tell me about whoever shot Corliss out there at the air strip?"

Connor had known this question was coming, and he had already decided he had no reason to protect Charlene Marks or her father. Truth was, he'd found what he'd been looking for, and just because he'd waited until the Beechcraft King was in the air didn't negate the fact the plane was carrying a cold-blooded killer and his daughter, who was an accessory to his crimes. "I'd lost a lot of blood," he said. "I was pretty light in the head."

"What do you mean 'was'?" Hallam said with a grin. "There were two holes in him—two different kinds of holes. That means two guns. We didn't find either of them."

That was a good thing. After the twin engine plane had lifted off into the sky Connor had hurled Richard Simmons' Glock as far as he could into the tangled brush. It was a left-handed pitch, but a good one. Until or unless someone came out with a metal detector, it would stay put.

"It's a long story," he finally said to Hallam.

"I've got all the time in the world."

"But I don't. You were right about the drugs, and I've got about five minutes before my brain hits the snooze button."

The SLED investigator rolled his eyes, then said, "So talk fast."

Connor managed to go about seven minutes. It was more than enough time to give Hallam a rough thumbnail of Jon Hilborn and the fake suicide, Malcolm Nickels' murder, and the stolen airplane, which now had touched down somewhere in the Caribbean basin. If Connor had to guess he'd figure they'd headed to Venezuela, maybe Belize, but there were a lot of banana republics where a couple of Americans with a pile of cash could easily disappear. The last thing he remembered Hallam asking was why the hell he hadn't mentioned the plane six hours ago when the EMTs were rolling him into the back of the ambulance.

"I'd just been shot," Connor explained, his eyelids beginning to grow heavy. "My mind was a bit slow at the time."

"You're about as much help as a tub full of piss," the detective observed.

"There's a bag of it hanging at the foot of my bed," Connor said. "Go ahead—help yourself."

At two minutes after five Jordan James appeared in the doorway carrying a sturdy brown leather bag with a hand-stitched handle. He glanced up and down the corridor, a twinkle of conspiracy in his eyes, then he eased the door closed and came over to Connor's bedside table. Without saying a word, he opened the bag and pulled out a bottle of Hendricks gin, two crystal martini glasses, a stainless-steel shaker, and a Tupperware container of ice. Plus, a small bottle of vermouth and a small jar of olives stuffed with blue cheese.

Connor couldn't remember if he'd ever seen Mr. James fix his own martini—a waiter or household employee had always brought them to him—but the man went about it now with a practiced ease that suggested he'd done this many times before. When he was finished shaking his concoction he poured the icy mixture into the two glasses, then speared two sets of olives with plastic toothpicks to finish off the presentation. When he was finished he handed one of the glasses to Connor and raised the other in a toast.

"Here's to maximizing all the gifts of life and staring death straight in the eyes," he said. "And to helping my son. He hasn't stopped talking about that little unauthorized drive you took him on the other day."

"Act first, ask permission later," Connor replied.

"I remember those days," Jordan James said in a wistful voice.

"Cheers!"

Connor touched his glass to that of Jordan James' and took a tentative sip, knowing hospitals had rules for a reason. One of them most likely was that alcohol didn't mix well with whatever other substances they were dripping into his veins. Of course, if anything catastrophic suddenly happened to him, he was in a good place.

"You came close to losing the game this morning, son," James observed after he had taken a healthy swallow of gin.

"Not something I was expecting," Connor admitted.

"I heard the shooter was a federal agent of some sort—"

"DEA," Connor said, and then launched into the brief confession Agent Corliss had made just before he'd gone down.

"And this ties in with Jon Hilborn how?" Jordan James wanted to know.

"Hilborn got himself in deep with certain members of the wrong family," Connor explained. "Way too deep, it turns out. When the bottom dropped out of the real estate market and financing dried up, he had to cover his action."

"He lost everything."

"Totally tapped out. He even had to siphon the principal from his foundation to cover what he and his partners owed."

"Should've just declared bankruptcy," James observed as he casually took another sip of his martini.

"I don't think the Babics would have liked that."

Jordan James shot Connor a sharp glance and said, "Did you say Babic?"

Connor gave him a slow nod, then eyed the clear liquid in his glass. "Seems Hilborn fell in with them a long time ago when he was putting together financing for some Mississippi casinos. He even fathered a child at some point, a girl. Fast-forward twenty-five years and he's into them so deep he's forced to fly money to the islands for them."

"And that's where the dead DEA agent comes in," James said.

"Right. He figured out what was going on and wanted a piece of the action."

"So Hilborn paid these Babic thugs the half million bucks I gave him." James sighed. "And eventually he saw the only way out was to jump off that balcony."

"Not exactly," Connor told him. "The thing is, Hilborn's still alive."

Jordan James had just taken a healthy sip of gin, and almost spat it out. "You're shittin' me—"

"He staged the whole thing. The blood, the slit wrists, everything."

"Pretty elaborate scheme, wouldn't you say?"

"It was a cover for the mess he knew he'd make when he bashed in the head of his stooge, a guy named Malcolm Nickels."

"I know that name—" James said. "One of the Babics' people."

"Yeah, and he was in way over his head, too," Connor replied. "I figure Hilborn got him drunk or drugged-up, knocked him stupid with a cinder block so it would be consistent with going face-first into a sidewalk. That way no one but a close family member could I.D. him. Then he slit his wrists and wrote a note to housekeeping to explain all the blood. The cops bought the story, too."

"But his brother identified him," James pointed out. "Don't you think he would have recognized Jon, no matter how mangled he was?"

"Jon waited until his brother was on a boat in the middle of the Atlantic, no phone," Connor said. "After staging the whole thing Jon went down to his brother's place in Hilton Head, just in case the police dropped by."

James just stood there shaking his head. "He identified his own body—"

"And then he disappeared. Looks like he stole a plane in Georgia, a Beechcraft King. Has a range of two thousand miles, so he could get himself pretty well lost if he wanted to. Took your cash and whatever else he'd managed to scrounge up."

"Well, I guess that's it, then," James said as he tossed back the last of his martini. "I knew it was a long shot, really, but I figured you'd have a good a chance as anyone at getting my money back. You did a great job … damn, you even got yourself shot. But in the end, I guess I'm just shit out of luck."

James picked up the martini shaker, swirled it moment, then poured the diluted remnants into his and Connor's glasses. Good to the last drop. He lifted his glass to his lips and poured it all down his throat in one single gulp.

Connor gave a look at his own glass, left it where it was. His brain was already foggy from the first sip, and he'd experienced enough mischief for one day. His eyes momentarily lost their focus and traveled beyond James and the shaker and the gin bottle and came to rest on something that was leaning against the wall in the corner of the room.

"Maybe not. See that cardboard tube in the corner, there?"

"Someone give you a get-well poster?"

Connor didn't answer the question, just said, "Don't suppose you can get it for me?"

Jordan James set his empty glass down, then fetched the mailing tube and handed it to Connor.

"You check it out. My arm's all bandaged up."

James turned the tube in his hands, then pulled a white plastic cap off the end. He tentatively reached in and gently slid out a stiff canvas that was inside. He started to unroll it, quickly realized what he was looking at.

"Holy shit, Connor!" he gasped, the look on his face bordering on shock. "You found it!"

"You might say it found me," Connor corrected him. "Hope you have a safe, private place to hang it."

James cast a suspicious glance at Connor, then focused his attention back on the painting. He lightly rubbed his index finger and thumb on the canvas, then studied the signature in the corner. "How did you … oh, never mind. I'm probably better off not knowing the details."

"Plausible deniability," Connor said.

James shook his head in disbelief as slipped the still-rolled painting back in the tube. It was at that moment Nurse Pearson pushed the door open and came into the room. She spotted the two martini glasses on the rolling bedside table, and snapped, "Alcoholic beverages are strictly forbidden in this hospital. We are not running a honky-tonk—"

"Just finishing up here, ma'am," Jordan James said, flashing her the most gentlemanly smile he could muster. "We were toasting the life of my friend—"

"I don't care if you were toasting a bag full of marshmallows—I want those glasses, that bottle, and all that other shit out of here. Right now. Before I call security."

"Party pooper," James muttered as he began stuffing everything back in the leather case from which it had come. But Connor could tell from the look in the man's eyes that he was secretly pleased to have caused a scene, no matter how small. "We'll continue this later. There's a little matter of your job future. And your finder's fee."

"Something you can talk to him about tomorrow," the nurse interrupted him. "Right now, Mr. Connor needs his rest."

The parade of visitors continued about twenty minutes later when a young woman, thin with close-cropped stringy hair and a doll's button eyes and nose, poked her head through the doorway. Connor had been watching the local weather report on a flat screen TV that was hung over the bed, but caught the motion out of the corner of his eye.

"May I help you?" he asked her.

"Tat Man? I heard you'd been shot, but I couldn't get away from work all day."

A smile formed on Connor's lips and he said, "Caitlin?"

"It's my name," she told him in that high-pitched squeak of hers as she stepped into the room, her hands clasped behind her back. "That DEA agent did this to you?"

"Could've been worse."

"Oh, listen to the valiant soldier, playing it all brave."

"That's me. The brave man of Tat."

She grinned at that, then handed him a vase filled with daisies and carnations and other flowers he didn't recognize. "I thought these might add some color to you room, but they're no match for all that ink on your arms."

"They're beautiful," he said. "You can put them right there on that table."

She did, then stepped back and gave him a long look. "They say you came that close to dying."

"Whoever *they* are, they were exaggerating."

"Still, that really would have sucked. We'd never even met."

"Good thing they were wrong."

She nodded but didn't say anything for a minute. Then: "What I don't get about all this is the connection between Hilborn and the guy who fried in the trailer."

"Jacob Wheeler. Actually, it's pretty simple. The way I figure it, when his brother Leland met up with Bodean Barr at the prison in Bennettsville, they started scheming. Bo Barr was already into Hilborn for a lot of money, and he always had a line on a new business deal."

"Wait," Caitlin said. "This Bodean Barr … what's the link between him and Hilborn?"

A sudden spasm stiffened Connor's leg and a jolt of pain shot through the calf muscle. He winced, then shifted his position in the bed.

"With Hilborn it was always business," he eventually said. "Bad loan, high interest. A gentleman's loan shark."

"Barr doesn't exactly strike me as a gentleman—"

Connor flashed back to the day he'd found Barr crumpled against the door of his shack out in Walterboro, minus his head. "You got that right," he said. "Anyway, when Leland and Jacob got nabbed with a truck full of shit Agent Corliss had them by the balls. Pardon me. They agreed to be his eyes inside the drug ring, and Hilborn was already in way deep with a certain Southern crime family. He figured he could earn his way out of his problems, and when the Wheelers started cooperating with the government they figured they were home free. Jacob rented the trailer in the woods north of Myrtle Beach, but Leland didn't even move, the two dumbasses thinking they were untouchable because they had federal heat behind them."

"They had no idea that Corliss was playing both sides," Caitlin observed.

"Truth. Way I see it, Corliss was keeping his eye on Charlene Marks and followed her out to the trailer, where he saw her talk to Jacob. Saw me out there, too, which made him all worried that maybe I was about to blow this whole gig for him. So that night after I left he came back and killed the guy, then went looking for Leland."

She fell silent for a bit, and Connor could almost see her mind at work. Then she said, "So who killed David Hilborn?"

"Who do you think?"

Caitlin thought about this a moment, then said, "Jon Hilborn's not dead, is he?"

"Fooled everyone, at least long enough for him to disappear. "

"You think he's out of the country?"

"That's my guess. Someplace that won't send him back if he gets found."

"And what are you going to do about that?"

276

"Me? Nothing. That's what the FBI is for. And when they find him—and they will—I'll raise a big double martini and toast the long arm of the law."

The Laws of Physics

The last person Connor expected to see was Danielle. He had kissed her goodbye just that morning as she drove off in her sister's silver Acura, just before he had driven down to Malcolm Nickels' place outside Beaufort.

Ninety minutes later he was hiding in a dark corner of a metal garage at a secluded airstrip, blood oozing from both his arm and his leg. By that time Danielle would have been on the other side of the Savannah River, probably listening to something by Adele or maybe Coldplay on the radio, totally oblivious to what was unfolding up in South Carolina. She would have had no way of knowing what had happened, not until Connor managed to call her and fill her in.

In fact, that's what he had tried to do earlier when he'd awakened, but he didn't have his cell phone with him, and without that he didn't have her number. He thought about calling information in Orlando and asking for a number for Richard and Danielle Simmons, but he didn't want to go there. So, he just lay there in his bed and stared at the ceiling, the walls, the flowers Caitlin had brought him, and the plastic olive spear that was left over from his martini with Jordan James.

And now his eyes were fixed on Danielle as she stood there in the doorway, which made him think that maybe the Percocet or whatever it was had kicked in again and he was just dreaming this.

"I leave you alone for just a few minutes and look what happens to you," she scolded him, her hands placed firmly on her hips as she shook her head.

"What the—?" He had been watching *Jeopardy* on the overhead TV but now was staring at her staring at him. He gave a quick glance at a wristwatch that wasn't there, then said, "You should be down in Orlando."

"No ... you should be in Orlando!" Danielle edged into the room and came over to the bed, where she planted a long kiss on his lips.

"That's how we'd left it, until you went and got yourself shot." "Not something I planned," Connor assured her.

"I should hope not." She studied the chrome bedrail, clicked a latch and pushed it down so she could sit directly on the mattress. "And I won't ask what happened, because I'm sure you've tired of telling *that* story."

"You're a very perceptive woman."

On the TV screen Alex Trebek was reading a *Jeopardy* answer that went, "The name of this Mary Shelley scientist is often confused with his ghastly creation."

"Who is Frankenstein!" Danielle said without pausing a moment to think.

"Who is Frankenstein," one of the contestants on the game show responded.

"We used to watch *Jeopardy* all the time when I was growing up," Danielle said by way of an apology. "Once it gets in your blood it stays there."

"I'm pretty familiar with the properties of blood," Connor agreed. "So, what I want to know is what you're doing here. Last I saw you this morning, you were pulling out of my driveway for a long drive home."

"I actually got just south of Jacksonville when I saw it on TV," Danielle explained. "I stopped for coffee at a truck stop and the news was on. It said something about how an Iraq war veteran in South Carolina had been shot, 'allegedly,' by a DEA agent who also had been shot and killed. I knew you still had Richard's gun—"

"So, you thought I'd killed him? The DEA agent?"

"I didn't know what to think. I called the radio and TV stations here in Charleston, got an unverified report that the last name was Connor, but no one knew anything else except the victim was lifted to M.U.S.C. So, I turned around and here I am."

Up on the TV Alex Trebek was saying, "On October 20, 1803, the U.S. Senate ratified the treaty for this land acquisition."

"What is the Louisiana Purchase?" Danielle answered. Or, rather, asked. Then she shot Connor another sheepish look and added, "Sorry."

"Don't worry—I'll get the next one," he told her. "So, you just left your new wildebeests high and dry?"

"It's called priorities." She leaned down and gave him another kiss, this one much longer than the first.

"I'm glad you turned around," he said when they finished. "In fact, my leg feels so good I think I can walk right out of here."

"Are you forgetting about that bag that's hanging at the foot of the bed? I saw it when I came in."

"Oh, yeah," he said, a touch of embarrassment creeping into his face. "That could complicate things a little."

"All great things come to those who wait."

"Whoever said that never lay in a hospital bed with a shot-up leg and the most beautiful woman in the world sitting next to him."

Up on the TV the camera was fixed on a mid-shot of Alex Trebek, who was saying, "Physics for one thousand it is. The answer: The acceleration rate at which anybody falls under the pull of gravity."

Danielle stared at the TV, then looked back at Connor. "I got nothing," she said.

"What is thirty-two feet per second per second?" he said, making sure he phrased his response in the form of a question.

None of the contestants on the show responded properly, and up on the screen Alex Trebek eventually said, "What is thirty-two feet per second per second?"

"Damn …!" she said. "How'd you know that one—?"

"There's a lot about me you don't know," he said, a cunning grin filling his face. Using his good arm, he picked up the remote control and clicked off the TV set, then put it aside as he leaned up and pulled Danielle close.

"Jack Connor … just what do you think you're doing?"

"Confirming another law of physics," he said as he gently eased her toward him.

"And what law would that be?" she asked, doubtfully.

Connor pictured Ms. Benson standing up there at the chalkboard, looking out over her classroom full of rapt young males, and recited from memory: "The acceleration produced by a particular force acting on a body is directly proportional to the magnitude of that force." "Meaning what, exactly?"

"Meaning that once a body is put in motion it tends to stay in motion," he told her as his lips met hers. "And now seems as good a time as any to put it to the test."

End

Acknowledgments

It is impossible to write a book without the creative input and valued advice from a great number of people, and I'd like to recognize a few individuals who were of great assistance in helping me bring *Carolina Heat* to life. Many thanks to:

Bill Flynn and the entire crew at Complete Scene Intervention in Florence, SC for their continued assistance in helping me grasp the details of cleaning up crime scenes. Anything I got right in these pages was because of them, and whatever I got wrong is all on me.

Bob, Judy, Barbara, and Rebecca at Ingalls Publishing Group, for their faith in this book and their belief in the continued adventures of Jack Connor. I thank you for your unwavering commitment and dedication to seeing this book through to the printed (and digital) page.

My friend and former colleague Anne Snook, private investigator extraordinaire and owner of ESS Services, Inc. in Florida for her help in explaining the details of running skip traces and background checks, and the process of tracking down missing persons.

My great friend, colleague, and soul brother Al Bell, for granting his permission to partially cite the lyrics from his classic recording "I'll Take You There," and for providing me an understanding of the song's genesis and depth.

The real "Jon Hilborn," an old friend whose suspicious passing many years ago fueled the ongoing speculation that prompted me to write this book.

My daughter, Jennifer Leigh, for her meticulous editorial scrutiny of the final manuscript, and for all her spiritual input along the way.

And, of course, my wonderful wife Diana, for her continued inspiration, encouragement, love, and support. Thank you so much for understanding this lifelong writing addiction, and—as I've said before—for sharing this bold and dashing adventure with me!

About the author

Reed Bunzel is a mystery writer, biographer, "media anthropologist," and president of Bunzel Creative Services, LLC.

The former President/CEO of an online music company (TheRadio.com), Bunzel also served as Executive V.P. of Al Bell Presents LLC. Previously, he was editor-in-chief for United News and Media's San Francisco publishing operations; earlier in his career he was editor-in-chief of Streamline Publishing's *Radio Ink* and *Streaming* magazines, as well as an editor at Radio & Records and Broadcasting magazine. Additionally, he served in an executive capacity at both the National Association of Broadcasters and the Radio Advertising Bureau.

A graduate of Bowdoin College in Brunswick, Maine, Bunzel holds a Bachelor of Science degree in Anthropology, *cum laude*. A native of the San Francisco Bay Area, he currently resides with his wife Diana in Charleston, South Carolina.